PRET ...NGS ON ыHELVES

A SECOND CHANCE ROMANCE

MAGGIE GATES

LANDON GATES

ISBN: 9798864467534

Editing and Cover Design by Jordan Loft.

Stock images licensed and used with permission from Adobe Stock.

To the ones who kissed dating goodbye.

FORWARD FROM THE AUTHORS

P*retty Things on Shelves* is the fictional story of Blair and Caleb Dalton, a divorced couple who grew up together, married, and eventually left a high-control group. This book does have a swoony happily ever after!

We have intentionally kept the details and identity of their community vague. It does not describe any specific religion, denomination, or sect. We respect the many readers with positive associations with organized religion and religious beliefs just as we respect those with negative associations with them.

In this book, we have chosen to use the term "high control group" rather than "cult" to better identify the goals of Blair and Caleb's community, rather than attaching them to the high-profile stories that you see on the news or in middle of the night Wikipedia deep-dives.

This book details religious deconstruction as well as childhood and parental trauma, child endangerment, and familial estrangement.

Please treat yourself with care while reading.

. . .

- MAGGIE & Landon Gates

1

BLAIR

High society is a circle-jerk pyramid scheme. The thought made me smile as I walked away from the mayor and surveyed the crowded room, searching for my next target.

The Drake Hotel buzzed with the melodies of a jazz band and the scent of haughty indifference. I had to give it to the Chicago Arts Preservation Society; they knew how to throw an incredible party.

I was scanning the room, making note of attendees, when I spotted Meredith Thompson heading toward me.

Oh, great.

Meredith, the event chair, had a supermodel physique and the personality of a corpse. She floated through the room like she owned the place rather than simply being a member of the planning committee.

I spun around, hoping to find someone else to talk to, but everyone seemed engrossed in their own conversations.

"Blair Dalton, is that you?" she called out with feigned surprise. "I was so thrilled to get your RSVP."

I forced a smile. After all, I was here to make connections.

Even if I'd give my left kidney to be in pajamas, eating takeout, and watching a new-to-me movie right about now.

The glittering boulder sitting pretty on her ring finger glinted in the light. It was obnoxiously big, but not big enough to distract from the fact that she was using it as one of her two talking points as she strutted from guest to guest.

"It's me," I said with as much excitement as I could muster. These heels were killing my feet, the gown that Sophia had promised would help me blend in was squeezing the air out of my ribcage, and I was all-too aware of the breeze across the tops of my boobs.

Meredith's grin was unnervingly flawless. Like a manufactured doll, created to look human but was completely lifeless. "You're really making a splash this event season," she remarked with a lilt of disbelief in her voice. "I've heard your name come up more than almost any newcomer to the scene. Have you been able to make some good connections this evening?"

And there it was: the subtle dig that was dipped in a compliment glaze and dusted with a sugary question for some extra pizazz.

"I have. Thank you for extending the invitation to join the festivities this evening. I'm impressed with the amount of work the Preservation Society has done this year."

"And with *such* a tight budget," Meredith clamored in dismay.

Was she about to cry?

"We rely on these events to bolster our budget so we can continue to—"

I tuned her out as a man in a bespoke suit caught my attention from across the room. Blond hair was pushed back in a proper comb-over that screamed *old money*. He stood at the bar and sipped something amber from a short glass.

He had a half-sickled smile as his eyes locked on me. Amusement was painted on his face.

Meredith hadn't stopped talking about the next fancy dinner she had in the works, where she hoped to raise even more money than tonight's event did.

Probably so she could use that money to plan yet another dinner. And another. And another.

It confirmed my pyramid scheme theory.

I laughed in my head as I tried to think of how I could work that notion into a podcast episode without royally angering the snooty one-percenters who had invited me to their dinner with the hopes of a little positive chat about their "work" on my show.

"Pardon me, Ms. Thompson," tall, blond, and handsome said as he sided up to Meredith. The rocks glass dangled from the tips of his fingers. A Rolex caught the light, glinting in a wink of confident wealth.

Meredith arched an eyebrow, but the rest of her lab-perfected face didn't budge. "Collin Cromwell," she said by way of a greeting. "Did I see you chatting with the Vulkon executives?"

I shifted awkwardly in my stilettos.

Collin's eyes never left me. His gaze wasn't lewd or entirely unwelcome, but it still made my skin crawl.

I resisted the urge to adjust my dress for more coverage. It was no more revealing than any other dress in the room, but I still felt naked.

"I was," he said, lifting the glass to his lips. "But then I saw you talking to this stunning woman, and I was hoping if I came over that you'd make an introduction, so I didn't come off as desperate."

Meredith's face pinched in a hostess smile. "I'd be delighted to." She nodded at me. "Blair, this is Collin

Cromwell. He's a VP for Allegiant Holding Group." She looked up at Collin. "This is Blair Dalton. She's the voice behind the *One Small Act of Rebellion* podcast and has made quite the splash since entering Chicago's social scene."

I laughed politely. "Ms. Thompson is overselling me." I offered my hand. "Pleasure to meet you, Mr. Cromwell."

"I don't think she's overselling you at all, and I assure you —" he said as he gently took my hand, his thumb stroking over the top of my hand "—the pleasure is all mine." Blue eyes glimmered, and the slight twitch of his mouth made my heart flutter. "And please. Just call me Collin."

The handshake lingered just long enough for me to become distinctly aware that Meredith was still standing there while Collin didn't pay her any mind. Her practiced smile slowly melted into a frown. Still, Collin didn't let go of my hand.

"Well," Meredith said, fastening her smile back on. "I believe dinner is about to be served. Excuse me."

Collin didn't even give her a second glance. As soon as she sashayed out of earshot, he was retracting his hand.

"Thank you for the very timely intervention," I said as I brushed nonexistent strands of hair away from my face.

He plucked a champagne flute from the tray of a passing waiter and deftly slipped it into my hand. "You looked like a deer in headlights."

I looked over my shoulder to see if Meredith had circled back, then looked down at the bubbles effervescing in brilliant strobes and quickly debated whether or not I had to drink it. I didn't want to be rude, but I really didn't like champagne.

I lifted the flute and let the bubbles touch my lips just long enough to make it look like I had taken a sip. "Ms. Thompson caught me off guard is all."

"No date?"

I shook my head. "Flying solo."

His eyes crinkled in the corners. "Likewise. At least now we can save each other from the ice queen."

I hid my laughter behind the champagne flute. "She has quite an intimidating presence."

"Her prowess is wasted on overpriced dinners. She should be scaring the shit out of people in boardroom negotiations."

"Thank you again."

"It was the least I could do." Collin's attractive confidence suddenly turned a little sheepish. "And maybe I was hoping my good deed would earn me a minute of your time." His chuckle faded as he turned ever so slightly to stand beside me and take stock of the room. "Between you and me, she must have a pair of brass ones under that dress to have the nerve to invite her ex to this thing."

I scanned the crowded room. "Who's her ex?"

Collin pointed to a man with dark hair who wore a tailored suit. "Vaughan Thompson. He's in finance. The company I work for is being courted by the company he works for. It's a hostile flirtation."

A shorter woman in a black dress was on Vaughan Thompson's arm. Her hair was the color of ink, and her natural tan and muscle tone suggested that it was earned honestly.

If Meredith was the ice queen, the new woman in her ex-husband's life was an obsidian dagger—a beautifully lethal edge. Her cool, collected façade was a coping mechanism.

My stomach soured because it was the same look I was wearing.

"Something you should know, Miss Dalton," he said as he turned back to face me. "If this was a slightly less stuffy event, I would have already asked you to dance."

"This is a charity dinner. Not a ball. And if you're going by

Collin, then please call me Blair. I hate being called Miss Dalton these days."

"My point exactly." His smile became endearingly boyish. "So, please don't be surprised when I find you at the end of the night and steal that dance even if there's no music."

My face flushed with heat. It blasted across my cheeks in a wave before waltzing down my spine. I relented and took a sip of the champagne to break the awkward silence.

Ugh, it was awful. Dry and fancy.

"That's quite forward for a man who asked the ice queen to make an introduction rather than doing it himself."

Collin laughed. "That's where you're wrong, Blair." His palm slid down my arm, fingers gently circling my wrist. "I already knew your name. I think I've seen your face nearly every day for the last year. All I needed was a chance to look like your knight in shining armor, and Meredith cornering you gave me a golden opportunity."

I tapped my lips. "I can't tell if you're about to turn me into a skin suit or if you're flirting with me."

Collin chuckled as he lifted his hands in a gesture of peace. "There's an advertisement with your face on it at LaSalle and West Monroe. I pass it every morning on my way to the office."

The flush on my cheeks moved to my neck. "You probably think I'm some vain socialite."

"On the contrary," Collin said as Meredith stood front and center and invited everyone to take their seats for dinner. He took the liberty of placing his hand on my lower back and guiding me across the room to the tables. "I think you're fascinating. And I'm wondering if it's too forward to ask for your number."

Butterflies flurried inside of me. I felt like a kid riding a bike; wobbling and unsteady.

I could do this. I was doing it. I am doing it.

Please don't crash.

"Do you have a business card?"

He chuckled as he reached inside of his suit jacket and produced a slim card with his name and contact information listed under an Allegiant Holding Group logo. "You're old school like me. I like it."

"Which table are you at?" I asked as I slipped the card into my clutch, hoping that he'd be somewhat close. I could wolf down my dinner and find him again before I got cornered into some mind-numbing conversation or, worse, isolated.

"Table two."

I forced a tight smile. "Bummer. I'm at fifteen."

But Collin was unbothered. "There's always *after*." He winked. "I'm counting on that dance, Blair."

Nerves simmered low in my gut. I was so bad at this. Make conversation for an hour with a guest on my podcast? Absolutely. Flirt with an attractive man? Absolutely not.

I lifted my mostly untouched champagne in a polite toast. "Then here's to hoping that our dinner has ridiculously small portions that are quick to eat."

Collin and I went our separate ways. I took my seat between a scowling quarry executive and another blasé sixty-something in a suit who looked like he was about to fall asleep before the first course was served.

Meredith's ex-husband, Vaughan, was seated at my table and struck up polite conversation while his girlfriend observed the players at the table.

"I love your dress," I said, craning my head around and offering her a smile.

"Thanks," she said with the kind of fake confidence I respected.

We were all playing a game here. I wasn't actually alone, I

was just working my half of the room while Tina, the Chief Revenue Officer of EarTreat Studios, worked the other half.

Make connections. Find episode guests. Find investors with deep wallets.

Two of those jobs were mine. The investor bit was all on her. Since we had vastly different goals for this charity dinner, there was no need to be tied to each other.

"I'm Blair Dalton," I said as our emptied salad plates were whisked away.

"Jo—er—Joelle," she stammered. "But just call me Jo."

"Love the name. It's very *Little Women*."

She snorted. "Nah. I was named after Jo Dee Messina. The country singer."

I matched her laugh with one of my own, like I was in on the joke. "What do you do?"

Jo let out a sigh of relief when her picked-over salad was taken away. "I'm an ag pilot. I take care of crops. Dropping seed. Fertilizing. Sometimes watering."

"Badass!" I said with excitement. *Hello, potential podcast guest.* "How did you get into that?"

My question was cut off by Chastity Bergstrom—an insufferable old bat—butting in and sneering at Jo.

I recoiled in my seat. Attending these events alone was the worst part of attending them at all. Luckily, I wasn't stuck shooting polite smiles across the table for long. Servers flooded the room, carrying massive dinner plates.

Good. I was starving.

I peered around and found Collin Cromwell in the thick of a riveting conversation at his table.

I'm counting on that dance, Blair.

I could flirt. Flirting was just making conversation with some eyelash batting.

I could bat my eyelashes.

I could laugh at jokes.

Looking at Collin certainly wasn't a hardship.

From across the room, he caught my eye and winked.

Hello, heart eyes. Long time, no see.

A plate was placed in front of me at the same time Collin was served his dinner. We exchanged sheepish smiles as we turned back to our respective tables.

My chicken was pristinely plated. The aroma of butter, lemon, and capers was enticing. Everyone else at the table seemed to have opted for the seafood option with the exception of Jo, who had pasta in a red sauce.

The first bite was extraordinary. Every flavor and texture melded in perfect harmony.

I cleared my throat to rid it of an irritating itch. "Jo," I said as I reached for my water. "You were telling me about how you're an ag pilot. That's fascinating."

Jo smiled. "It's fun." She looked up at Vaughan. "Drives him batshit crazy, but that just makes it even *more* fun."

Vaughan raised an amused eyebrow at her antics.

I took another sip of water. When that didn't do the trick, I swallowed another bite of chicken to scratch the itch.

"How—" I cleared my throat again. "How did you get into that?"

Jo prattled on about her work as a crop duster, but I couldn't focus.

I reached for my water again and took a deep breath, but a wheeze was all that escaped.

"Blair?" Jo dabbed her lips with the napkin. "Are you okay?"

I blinked. Vaughan Thompson looked at me with concern, as did everyone else at the table.

They were all staring.

I looked down. Red splotches bloomed on my arms as my throat tightened.

Oh no.

The plate next to me caught my eye. Were those...

"What are you eating?" I wheezed.

"Scallops," Chastity Bergstrom huffed.

Scallops. *Shellfish. Not just seafood.*

I had denoted an allergy on my RSVP, but someone handling the scallops must have touched my plate.

"Blair?" A warm hand landed on my shoulder.

I tipped my chin up and found Collin standing over me. Worry filled the deep crevice that dipped between his brows.

"Okay," he said with a hint of hesitant awkwardness as he knelt beside my chair. "Very obvious that something's wrong. Can I call someone for you?"

I nodded, my breath threadbare and waning. "911."

———

THE METHODICAL *BEEP, beep, beep* of a monitor was the first thing I noticed. I was freezing and lying down.

Did I pass out on the floor of the Drake Hotel?

"Mrs. Dalton?"

I peeled one eye open at the sound of the woman's voice.

Bright fluorescent lights pierced my eyes, and I shrank back. *Not the Drake Hotel.*

"Mrs. Dalton, do you know where you are?"

I licked my lips. It was a little easier to breathe now, but it still felt like an elephant was sitting on my chest. "Drake... Hotel. Arts Society... Dinner."

"Do you remember what happened?"

A shadow loomed over me, and I opened my eyes again. A

woman in blue scrubs towered over me as she fiddled with something hanging over my head.

"I was eating dinner."

"Do you have a shellfish allergy?" she asked.

I nodded, then chanced a look around. "Am I in the hospital?"

She nodded. "You had an allergic reaction and went into anaphylaxis. Do you carry an EpiPen?"

"Most of the time."

She grunted. "It should be *all* the time. You were lucky the ambulance got to you when they did."

"Ambulance?"

She nodded. "Paramedics brought you in. The gentleman at the hotel who called them made sure they got your phone and your clutch." She pointed to the bedside table where my things were stashed in a clear patient belongings bag.

Collin. What a godsend.

"We called the emergency contact on your phone. He's on his way."

I blamed my poor memory on the lack of oxygen. "Who?"

The nurse fiddled with the controls on the hospital bed until the back was lifting to help me sit up. Her face was perfectly pleasant as she dropped the atomic bomb. "Your husband."

2

CALEB

The sterile scent of antiseptic filled my nose as I stepped off the elevator into the hospital corridor. Dim fluorescent lighting and the rhythmic beep of machinery made my heavy eyes even heavier. I yawned.

Damn, it was late.

Running a hand through my hair, I tried to ignore the hollow pit forming in my stomach.

Why the hell did I answer my phone?

"You called *who?*" Blair's shrill panic carried from her room into the hallway as I rounded a corner.

Hearing her voice after all this time was bizarre and familiar at once. It hit me like a splash of freezing water to the face. Suddenly, I was awake and all too aware of the reasons I shouldn't have been anywhere near Northwestern Memorial Hospital or this entire friggin' city.

I paused outside her room and listened.

"Your husband, uh, Caleb Dalton. He's listed as the emergency contact on your digital medical ID."

Blair unleashed a clumsy string of profanities. The sudden

outburst nearly forced a smile onto my face. She rarely cursed, but it was always adorable when she tried.

"Is there a problem, Mrs. Dalton?" the nurse asked.

"Caleb is my *ex*-husband."

I winced. The ink on our divorce papers had been dry for two years, but the label still hurt.

"Ah," the nurse responded awkwardly. "I apologize for any misunderstanding. We simply followed protocol. Is there someone else you'd like to call?"

Might as well get this over with.

I sucked in a nervous breath, knocked twice, then pushed the door open.

The room fell silent.

Blair greeted me with a look of horror from where she lay in bed. A loose hospital gown covered her, along with a thin white sheet over her lap.

I crossed my arms. "Sorry to crash the party."

The nurse spun on her heels to face me. "Not a problem," she said with a forced smile, then turned back to Blair. "If you'll excuse me, I'm gonna make sure everything is squared away for you to go home."

Without another word, she made a beeline for the door. It clicked shut behind her as she disappeared, leaving me alone in a room with my ex-wife for the first time in two years.

I cleared my throat. "So."

Blair sat up and stared at her lap, fidgeting with the sheet. Her blonde waves were more platinum than honey now. That was new. Makeup was smeared around her eyes, and a shredded ball gown lay in the corner.

"Caleb, I am *really* sorry about all of this," she said. "I had no idea you were still listed as my emergency contact. I was unconscious and I had no idea they called you."

"Yeah, I gathered that from all the swearing."

Her face turned bright red. "Shit."

I cracked a smile, but quickly hid it behind my fist. "Wanna tell me what we're doing here?"

"Apparently, the EMTs went through my phone—"

"Yeah, I got that part." I huffed and rubbed my temples. My morning alarms would be going off in a few hours and I'd have to be back at work. *So much for driving home and going back to bed. No way was I going to be able to sleep after this.* "Why are you in a hospital in the first place?"

"If you must know," she said, arching an eyebrow, "I was at an event and my food was cross-contaminated with shellfish."

I arched an eyebrow of my own. "Uh-huh."

"Excuse me?"

"Oh, nothing. I'm just waiting to hear why you were completely unconscious in the hospital after you used your EpiPen."

Blair pursed her lips. "Complications arose."

I pinched the bridge of my nose. "So help me God, if you tell me I drove all the way to Chicago to pick you up from the hospital because you forgot to carry your EpiPen, I will throw you out the window."

She glanced over at the windows. "The windows don't open."

"Through the glass, then."

"I didn't *forget* to carry my EpiPen." She looked down at her lap. "My dress didn't have pockets, and my clutch was full."

"So you *chose* to not carry your EpiPen," I said, dumbfounded. "I take it back, I'm gonna jump through the glass myself."

"Well, pick a different room to go all Kool-Aid Man. It's cold outside, and I don't want a draft."

I crossed my arms and glared.

She closed her eyes and let a soft sigh escape from her lips. "I'm sorry, Caleb. Go home. I'll figure this out and send you money for the gas tomorrow."

I let my hardened expression slip. "I'm not worried about that, I'm just disappointed. Thought I was coming to identify a body or something."

Blair cracked her first genuine smile since I'd arrived. "At least I would have stolen the joy you would've gotten from murdering me yourself."

I suppressed a chuckle. "Come on, psycho. Let's get you home."

"I can't," she said, gesturing to the ripped dress that was draped over the chair. "Apparently they cut my dress off in the ambulance. I don't have any clothes. Or a bra. Or a jacket. I'm basically wearing a paper towel. It's thirty-two degrees outside."

"You're great at this whole, 'complications arose,' thing," I said with a sigh. "Alright, give me the keys to your place and I'll go get you some clothes."

Blair burst out laughing. "Um, no. No way. There's got to be a rule against giving your ex-husband a key to your apartment."

"Yeah, it's right next to the rule about not calling your ex-husband to pick you up from a hospital after midnight. Besides, it's either this or walk home naked."

Blair eyed me for several moments before giving in with a groan.

"Fine. You win." She pulled the keys from her clutch and tossed them to me. "I'll text you the address. Call me when you get there. Don't be a weirdo."

———

I STARED at the gilded numeral placard for Apartment 1205 and regretted all of my life choices. How the hell did I end up on the twelfth floor of a Chicago high-rise in the middle of the night? Part of me wanted to just get back in my truck, drive home, and forget this weird-ass night ever happened. But I knew that'd make me an asshole.

Besides, I wouldn't be able to snoop if I bailed.

My phone buzzed in my pocket for the umpteenth time since I pulled into the parking garage. I dug it out and rolled my eyes at the litany of messages.

BLAIR

Call me when you get there.

BLAIR

Are you there yet? Please don't ransack my place.

BLAIR

If you want to smash something, just don't break the cat statue on the coffee table. It was an apartment-warming gift from my neighbor, and I adore her. She's the sweetest.

BLAIR

Please don't break the cat.

BLAIR

How are you not already there?

BLAIR

Caleb...

BLAIR

...

I tapped the call button and Blair answered by the time I put the phone to my ear.

"Do you ever check your phone?" she asked in a panicked tone that I'm sure she hoped sounded angry.

"At this time of night—or morning? Not usually."

"Touché."

I fished the key from my pocket and opened the door. "Alright, I'm inside."

Static burst over the line, muffling her voice. It sounded like she was sitting up in the hospital bed. "First door on your right, there's a closet with some luggage. Look on the top shelf and grab the weekend bag."

I slid the closet door open and scanned the shelves. Everything was organized in bins with color-coded labels. "Good Lord, how many labels does one closet need?"

"It's a closet," she hissed. "It's for storage. Ergo, I need to be able to find things quickly when I'm looking for them."

I chuckled. "I guess some things never change, even for Blair 2.0."

"Would you focus? Duffle bag. Top shelf."

I grabbed the powder-pink bag from the top and slid the closet door shut. "Yeah, yeah, I got it. Where to next?"

"*Without touching anything—*"

"I know. Don't touch the cat." I eyed the hideous figurine.

She let out a petulant little huff. "Look to the left. The door closest to the Ficus is my bedroom. I need a bra, some pants, a shirt, coat, and shoes. Preferably something that matches. And can you get it without the running commentary?"

"Hang up and let me wander your apartment in peace if you don't wanna hear my commentary."

"Over my dead body."

"Honestly, not a deal breaker for me." I crossed the room toward Blair's bedroom door. "Also, who plants a Ficus in a high-rise apartment? What the fuck even is a Ficus?"

"It's a perennial that does really well indoors, but it can be moved outside. For instance, if I need to plant it over a fresh grave to hide a body."

"Good luck. I'm bigger than you." I opened the bedroom door and flipped a light on. "Holy crap. I take it back. The closet labels were a smokescreen. Blair 2.0 is disgusting."

Dirty laundry, pizza boxes, and a multitude of other fun sights and smells littered what I imagined was once human living quarters.

"Don't touch my nest. I have everything the way I like it. My favorite bra is on the chair by the bed."

I spotted the hint of a chair-shaped object beneath an avalanche of clothes, accessories, shoes, and ... *half a peanut butter sandwich?* Amid the chaos was a faded gray piece of fabric that could generously be referred to as a bra.

"Yeah, I'm not touching that thing. I'm not up to date on my tetanus shot."

I heard a growl and wondered if it came from Blair or the bra.

"Whatever. Just look in the top drawer of my dresser. There should be a sports bra in there or something. Can you hurry? I want this nightmare to be over with."

"I have peanut butter residue on my fingers from sifting for your favorite bra. You *are* the nightmare." I pulled open the top dresser drawer and cautiously picked through the options until I found *my* favorite bra of hers. I tossed the unlined lace thing into the bag. My hand tingled, faintly recalling the tactile memory of what it felt like to slide my palm over her chest and claim those perfect tits with my grip.

"You're being quiet. Why are you quiet?" There was a pause, then a groan. "You're not doing something weird in my bedroom, right?"

"Pretty sure cleaning is the only thing that would qualify as *weird* in this pit." I closed the top drawer and pushed the memory of her body from my mind. "A bra has been rescued. What else am I getting?"

"Bottom drawer. There's sweatpants. I need a pair. Socks are in a basket at the foot of the bed. There's a hoodie under the covers. Shoes are by the door."

"Be honest with me, Blair," I said as I rummaged through the debris field and threw everything into the bag. "Is anything gonna bite me when I pull the covers back to get that hoodie? Pretty sure I heard something growl a minute ago."

Her voice was sarcastically sweet. "The dust bunnies have been getting a little unruly lately. They require a human sacrifice from time to time. This was my plan all along. Marry you, divorce you, lure you back to my apartment, and have you eaten alive by bed critters. Till death do us part, darling."

I could picture it now. Blair sitting in that hospital bed with a smug little smirk on her face.

"Pretty elaborate scheme for someone who forgot her EpiPen."

"Will you shut up about the fu—*freaking*—EpiPen? Grab my shoes, and get out of my apartment."

"Just looking out for you. In sickness and in health, *darling*." I tossed her sneakers into the bag, made my way back to the front of the apartment, and opened the door. "I think I've got everything. I'm walking out the do—"

Whack!

Something hard came out of nowhere and slammed into my face. My vision went black and my ears rang.

"What the fuck!" I yelped. My phone dropped to the ground as I grabbed my nose to stop a stream of blood from gushing out.

There was something to be said about a good curse word. No matter what language it was said in, the intent was always clear.

The one aimed at me just happened to be in Russian and had the cadence of "fucking bastard."

My vision returned, revealing a tiny elderly woman dressed in a nightgown. Her hair was up in curlers and she was holding a broom upside down. "What is your name, thief?"

"Thief? What are you talking about?" My head slowly stopped spinning but still throbbed with pain. "Did you hit me with a broom?"

"*Name!*" the geriatric lunatic shouted, lifting the broom as if she were cocking a gun. "Speak, thief. Or I'll hit you again."

"*Caleb?!*" Blair's muffled voice carried from the speaker of my phone.

I scanned the ground quickly and picked it up. "You warned me about the carnivorous dust bunnies, but you didn't tell me you had an attack grandma."

The broom came down on my head again, cracking against my temple. "Geez, woman! Blair gave me a key!"

"Show me!" she snapped. "Where's Miss Dalton's key? What did you do with Miss Dalton?"

I fumbled around in my pockets and pulled it out.

The lady snatched it out of my hand. "You're bad at this. If you're going to be a criminal, at least be a good one."

"I'm not a criminal!"

She reared back with the broom again. Before she could get another swing in, I snatched up the duffle and stomped down the hallway.

All those worries I'd had about Blair's safety when we separated...

The pounding headache pushed those latent memories out of my mind as I hoisted the bag over my shoulder and headed back to the hospital.

I STOOD outside Blair's hospital room with my arms crossed, listening to her grumble and complain at a not-so-subtle decibel as she pawed through the bag I had so kindly put together for her.

It almost made the head trauma worth it.

Friggin' attack, grandma...

Finally, the door whipped open.

Blair, wearing sweatpants and a sweatshirt with a stain on it, scowled at me.

"You just *had to* grab that bra, didn't you?" she snapped as she shoved the discharge paperwork in the bag.

I grabbed the floor-length ball gown that had been cut in half by EMS and threw it over my shoulder. "Anything else?"

"No," she groused, listing to the left as she lost her balance.

"Whoa—" the dress fell to the floor as I caught her.

Blair reacted to being touched like a moose running through an elementary school. She flailed and flung herself the other way.

"Fucking hell, Breezy," I snapped as I yanked her back and forced her into my side.

"Let me go," she argued.

"It's either this or you go out in a wheelchair. Your choice."

Blair huffed. "Give me a shrimp to lick and take me to the morgue." After a moment, she grumbled, "I'd rather just take an Uber home."

I rolled my eyes. "And I'd rather not be suspect number one when you get chopped into a million pieces because you got in a car with a stranger in the middle of the night."

I dropped her into a wheelchair and maneuvered her to the lobby without much fuss. She waited like a good girl while I brought my truck around and all but shoved her inside.

The ride back and the walk up to her apartment was made in silence. Not that I expected her to say much.

For someone who talked for a living, Blair had the art of silence down to a T.

"Need anything else?" I clipped as Blair lumbered into her apartment, sidestepping the blood stain in the hallway.

"I'm fine," she clipped defensively. Her posture softened. "Sorry." She rubbed her eyes. "Long night and I never got to eat dinner. I'll send you gas money in the morning."

"Don't worry about it," I said, curling my hand into a fist around my keys to keep from reaching for her.

Blair chewed on her lips. "Thanks for... Just... Thanks."

I nodded.

She hesitated to close the door. "You look good... by the way. I hope things are good."

They weren't. I was miserable, but I wasn't about to tell my ex-wife that. I'd rather she not see the gaping wound that still bled for her.

I could pretend.

But what was I supposed to say?

See you later? Not a chance.

See you around? I didn't live here anymore.

Have a nice life? Honestly, a sick part of me wanted her to hurt as much as I still hurt two years later.

But I'd never say that to her. And deep down, I knew I didn't mean it.

So, I settled for, "I hope you're happy."

Because I meant it.

3

BLAIR

The dissolution of marriage feels like a terminal illness.

First, there's the diagnosis.

We're not the same people who made those vows.

Then a treatment plan is made.

Therapy is helping.

Maybe it's not helping.

Then the day comes where you sit down and say the words no one ever imagines saying on their wedding day.

I can't do this anymore.

Thus begins the slow fade of depression to acceptance.

Separation.

Tear-filled nights of packing.

New leases being signed ... alone.

Breaking the news to those around us.

Finally, after nearly a year of agonizing, ink flows across the papers and the time of death is called.

Divorced.

But instead of sleeping peacefully in my grave, someone

saw it fit to unearth me, brush the dirt off, and throw that terminal illness right back in my face.

I groaned as I hunched down into the collar of my heavy winter coat like a turtle, and picked up my pace.

So this is what it felt like to be a zombie.

The sky held the gray promise of snow, but the sharp slices of frigid wind were bare.

"Morning, Miss Dalton." Tony, the security guard for the Hannover Building, offered a tip of his chin as he stood by the outdoor heater.

I shook off the post-anaphylactic fog and handed over the cup of coffee that had been keeping my hands warm for the three-block trek to the studio.

Tony's silver mustache curled up at the ends in a whisper of a smile. "Much appreciated, Miss Dalton." His eyes lowered to the white waxed bakery bag in my other hand.

I held out for another second, enjoying the twinkle in his eye. "Have you had breakfast yet?"

His mustache twitched again. "I'll take a break in ten minutes."

Finally, I dramatically relented and handed over the bag with the Kelch's bakery logo stamped on the side.

Tony took a peek inside, then looked up with a bashful smile. "You know me too well."

Bienenstich—Bee Sting cake—was his favorite. The bakery next to my apartment made it every Monday, but Tony reported for work before they opened and it was usually the first thing to sell out.

"Make sure you take that break and stay warm," I said as I strolled to the door.

Tony chuckled. "Stay warm? This is ice cream and baseball weather. I'd be in shorts if the boss wasn't a stickler about the uniform." Using the hand still holding the bakery bag, he smoothed down the tweed coat that hid his suit jacket.

"Maybe for you," I said with a laugh. "But I'm going to get inside before I turn into a popsicle."

Tony elbowed the door open for me. "Have a good day, Miss Dalton."

"You too," I called over my shoulder.

Waves of warmth from the lobby surrounded me like a blanket. *What I wouldn't give to go back to bed right now.*

After a measly three hours of sleep, I wasn't on top of anything, much less my game.

Could I get away with a nap under my desk between the production meeting and recording the episode?

I poked the elevator button with an icicle finger and danced between my feet to warm up while I waited for the doors to open.

Something hard bumped against my hand when I shoved them in my coat pockets. *EpiPen. Right.*

We wouldn't be replaying that fiasco.

I groaned as a movie montage of last night's debacle played through like a horror film.

I kept hoping it was all some sort of oxygen-deprived dream and, at any moment, I'd wake up on the floor of the Drake Hotel with Collin hovering over me.

But no. That hellish nightmare was, in fact, the last twelve hours of my life.

My ex-husband riffled through my underwear drawer in the middle of the night because I couldn't be bothered to find a bigger clutch that fit my EpiPen.

Great. Just great, Blair. Way to freaking go. Two years without so much as a smoke signal from him and that's how you have the first contact after blowing up your life.

"You're late," Sophia sing-songed as she shoved a mug into my hand as soon as I made it up to the fifteenth floor.

I fished my phone out and looked at the time. "Two minutes late. Not bad considering I was in the hospital eight hours ago."

Notifications filled the screen, but I glossed over them, looking for a text from—*no.*

It was the delirium. That had to be it. That was the only explanation as to why Caleb was still on my mind.

But he looked so good... That waffle-knit Henley he wore did stupid things to my brain.

Two years had aged him in the best way. He looked older. Stronger. More—

I stopped those thoughts right in their tracks. It was the oxygen deprivation. That had to be it.

"Hold on." Sophia came to a screeching halt as we neared the studio bullpen. "Did you say you were in the hospital?"

I took a long pull from the coffee, letting it burn all the way down. Maybe that would wake me up. "Long story that started with me flirting with a hot financier at the charity thing last night, and ended with me in the ER looking like a pufferfish while my ex-husband gave me a running commentary on my bras."

Sophia's jaw rolled across the floor. She snatched it up and ushered me in. "Um, okay. We have a lot to unpack there."

"Understatement," I said as I hustled in, crossing the bullpen to the corner I occupied. My office was little more than a closet tucked next door to the recording studio that housed my podcast.

Some days I still couldn't quite wrap my head around it.

I wasn't recording by myself in my bedroom closet using a thirty-dollar microphone from Best Buy anymore.

"Morning, Blair," Todd, a former math teacher who now

hosted a sports podcast, hollered from the bullpen. He and Mandy, one of the audio engineers, were in a riveting conversation about the Cubs.

I looked over at the kitchen and spotted a box of pastries. A rumble let loose from my gut, but I was still a little queasy.

"Do we have to record today?" I whispered to Sophia as she snagged a doughnut.

"Uh-huh," she mumbled around the glaze. "The first episode we prepped for the series on intuition."

I groaned. "*Great.* I'm going to fall asleep in the middle of talking to myself."

"You're the one who wanted to put that fancy psych degree to use." Sophia said as she mimed washing her hands of the situation. "I was more than happy to keep the 'my family is crazy and thank God I live in a different city now' train rolling."

I rolled my eyes, yanked open my office door, and shucked off my coat. I dropped it onto the back of my desk chair as Sophia gathered our presentation materials.

"Good morning, Miss Dalton," Eddie, the studio's program director, said as soon as I strolled into the conference room. He adjusted his tie and cuffed his sleeves. Eddie was the only one on the entire floor who wore a tie. He blamed it on his days of working for an airline out of O'Hare.

Tina, a sharp-dressed Asian woman rocking a pink pantsuit was next inside. "Good morning, Blair. How was the Preservation Society dinner last night? Were you able to make some good connections?"

I hadn't intentionally avoided her last night, but she and I were on different assignments.

Hopefully, she wasn't privy to the shellfish debacle. I still wasn't completely sure what had happened in the margin between passing out and waking up in the ER.

"I was able to chat with quite a few people, yes. It was a lovely event."

Tina hid a smile behind pursed lips. "You certainly had a memorable evening."

So she knew.

But memorable? She had no idea...

Genevieve Ewen, the VP of production and development, careened in, accidentally hip-checking me when her over-flowing tote bag smacked into the doorframe. "Oh!" she shrieked, yanking her glasses off the top of her head. The chain rattled against her chunky statement necklace.

If anyone knew how to make a statement, it was Genevieve. Her tie-dye dress was handmade and not at all appropriate for the looming Chicago winter. Stacks of beaded bracelets covered her wrists.

I looked down and wondered how her toes hadn't frozen off in her Birkenstocks.

Unbothered, she kicked the sandals off and padded across the carpet barefoot.

Eddie looked horrified.

"Oh good," Genevieve said, clapping her hands together. "Everyone's here. Let's gather 'round, family." She snatched a claw clip out of her bag and twisted her raucous red ringlets up and out of the way as everyone crowded in and took their seats.

Sophia slid in beside me and opened her laptop.

I needed toothpicks to keep my eyes open as Tina talked numbers and Genevieve waxed poetic about new concepts.

When Eddie took the floor, Sophia jabbed her pen into my thigh.

"Do you need an energy drink?" she whispered.

"Can you inject it directly into my veins?"

"Blair," Eddie said as he rotated back and forth in his chair.

"You're up. What's coming up on the next season of *One Small Act of Rebellion*?"

Sophia slid the outline of our twenty-episode haul over to me.

I sat up straight. Words blurred in a mirage on the page, and my stomach lurched.

"Blair?" Genevieve said with concern lacing her voice. "You alright?"

I blinked, trying to make sense of the episode breakdown.

"I—uh, I'm so sorry. I just need a moment," I stammered apologetically. "I was in the ER last night and I'm a bit out of it this morning."

Murmurs of concern lifted in the room.

"Nothing serious," I lied with a smile on my face. "Just an allergic reaction. I'm still feeling a little woozy."

Sophia's pen stabbed me again to get me to shut up.

I took a sip from my cup and cleared my throat. "This season on *One Small Act of Rebellion*, we're moving away from deconstruction and moving into a series on using and trusting your intuition. I think a lot of my listeners struggle with trusting themselves and their instincts. Not just people who left high-control groups like I did. We're targeting individuals who just got out of relationships. People working toxic jobs. People who are gaslit by friends or family and don't know how to trust themselves."

Genevieve's bright eyes narrowed. She was a free-spirited creative, but that didn't detract from her command over the content each podcast created. She tapped her finger on the side of the cup that held her oat milk latte. "And you don't think generalizing your content will turn off your audience? The numbers don't lie. Niche podcasts do better than general lifestyle programs."

My stomach sank.

Sophia jabbed her pen into my leg again. *I was going to have a bruise by the time this meeting was over.*

"The show is called *One Small Act of Rebellion*," Eddie chimed in. "How does that tie into the intuition series? What are the things you're encouraging your listeners to rebel against? The show has been successful because each episode is like a challenge. You give your listeners homework. Generalizing things..." He cringed. "It might be a step too far."

Genevieve nodded in agreement. "Overkill is bad, but familiarity is good. Find a way to pivot enough to keep things fresh without making it uncomfortable for your listeners." She turned her attention to the Watson sisters who hosted a true-crime podcast. "Moving on. Ladies, tell us what's on the docket for *The Slay Sisters?*"

———

Sophia and I retreated to our recording studio with matching tails between our legs. I dropped down into my second home—the pink chair behind my desk—while Sophia took the couch.

"Great." She tossed the series outline into the garbage can.

I groaned, slumping in my chair as I rubbed the tension headache that had settled between my brows.

"Not that I was crazy about the season, but I didn't think we were 'generalizing.'"

Sophia huffed. "I don't want to say they're right, but..."

"Then don't say it."

"We still have to record an episode today."

I whined. "For a season we haven't planned."

She cracked open the mini fridge we kept stocked with water bottles and iced coffee for guests, pulled out one of the last remaining energy drinks, and tossed it to me.

"This means I have to find a whole new roster of guests," I said as I caught the can and cracked it open. "I had field experts, psychiatric colleagues, keynote speakers—"

"Which is great," Sophia soothed. "But they're right. There's no flash. We need some sparkle on it."

I guzzled half of the can and set the rest on my desk.

"So are we ever going to get around to talking about what the hell happened to you last night? And why it was so bad you would call—"

"He who shall not be named," I clipped.

"It's 'he who *must* not be named,'" she corrected.

"Close enough, considering I've never read those books or watched the movies."

"Spill," Sophia clipped.

I toed off my shoes and kicked my feet up on my desk. "They served scallops at the charity dinner last night. Some must have touched my plate. I had an allergic reaction and didn't have my EpiPen with me. The paramedics—or nurses— or whoever went through my phone and called my emergency contact."

Sophia's eyes widened, and I saw her move for the mics. We hadn't sound checked or prepped notes. It was raw and old school—the way I used to record.

The neon sign with the podcast logo flashed to life. *RECORDING.*

"It was the worst night ever," I said with a laugh as I tugged my microphone closer. "I got cock-blocked by shellfish and my neighbor beat my ex-husband with a broom."

Sophia cackles. "No! Tell me everything!"

We talked through the rundown, starting with my meet-cute with Collin and moving on to my anaphylactic nightmare.

"So the nurse walks in and tells you that your husband is on his way."

"*Ex*-husband," I clarified. "I panicked. I thought I was going to have a heart attack or a stroke or an aneurysm or something."

"What went through your mind?"

I laughed. "*Oh shit! They called my ex.* I don't know if I was more surprised that he showed up, or that he answered the phone at all."

"How long has it been since you've seen him?"

"Two years. The day we signed the papers."

"Oh shit," she snickered.

"All I had was a ballgown that had been cut off my body and a thong. So, he offered to go back to my place and pick up some clothes for me."

Sophia's eyes bugged out. "And you let him?"

"I had two options: walk home in paper scrubs and freeze my tail off, or let my ex-husband go through my underwear drawer."

"Ooh, spicy. What'd he pick?"

"He made fun of my favorite bra."

Sophia gasped. "No one slanders the favorite bra! My favorite bra has been with me longer than my last four relationships."

"He brought me this little scrap of lace that barely covers a nipple!"

"Oddly specific. Why do I have a feeling he has memories with that bra?" She waggled her eyebrows.

"Once upon a time it was definitely his favorite and I definitely haven't worn it since then."

"But you wore it to leave the hospital."

"I should have gone with the paper scrubs," I groused. "But he was bleeding, and—"

"Hold up, why was he bleeding? Did *you* make him bleed?"

"My neighbor thought he was breaking into my apartment to steal my underwear, so she whacked him with a broom when he went to leave. When he came back to the hospital, it looked like he had gotten in a bar fight."

"Did he watch you get dressed?" she asked like this was the juiciest Whitney West book.

"Absolutely not. I yelled at him about the bra, and then he threatened to make me walk home naked. So I made him stand outside while I changed."

"Is he dating someone?"

Bile hung in my throat. "I have no idea. It's not my concern anymore."

I had the words, but I didn't have the music. Seeing Caleb last night was a reckoning.

Calling him my ex-husband was easier than saying his name. *Caleb, the boy I had grown up with and trusted more than anyone*.

"He drove me home," I offered up. "We fought about it, of course. I just wanted to take an Uber, and he didn't want to be suspect number one if I was kidnapped and chopped into a million little pieces."

"Okay, he has a point there."

"He walked me up to my apartment and it was the most awkward goodbye ever. There's no handbook on what to do when your ex-husband walks you to your door."

"Kisses and hugs are definitely out of the question," Sophia said with the resolve of a general.

"I waved him off," I admitted.

Sophia groaned. "You did not."

"What was I supposed to do? Fist bump him? We were married for *years*. I've known him since I was born."

"He's your *ex*-husband. Who cares if he did one thing that any decent human being would do? You were in the hospital."

"I broke him."

"No, your neighbor did that."

Inspiration struck like a bolt of lightning, and I smiled into the microphone. "So, here's the question, little rebels. What do you do when you see an ex again?"

"Make sure you have a bigger, better, scarier boyfriend on your arm," Sophia said.

I laughed.

Her smile was nefarious. "You haven't dated—and I mean *really* dated—since your divorce."

"You're right," I admitted. "If I'm being honest, I don't know how to date. I got married at eighteen. For lack of a better word, he and I were betrothed when we were kids."

"So maybe this is your sign to jump into the dating pool."

"Okay rebels," I said, addressing my listeners. "Usually I have homework for you—something for you to do to rebel against the expectations that are put on you. But this time you're going to help me. On the *One Small Act of Rebellion* website, Soph will post a series of polls you can vote on to help me build my dating profile."

She gave me a thumbs up.

"If the assumption is that life after divorce sucks, I'm going to rebel against it. Who says starting over has to suck?"

Sophia hit the button to stop recording. "You know what?"

My heart was racing. "What?"

She grinned. "I think we just recorded the season opener."

4

CALEB

The sharp rap of knuckles against glass jolted me from somewhere between a dream and reality. My eyes snapped open, momentarily disoriented. I gripped the steering wheel. Through the dusty driver-side window, Dominic came into focus.

"You alright in there, boss man?" he asked, his voice muffled by the glass. Mild concern etched his face.

My pulse thumped in my ears. I blinked a few times, regaining my bearings, then rolled the window down an inch. Cold morning air invaded the cab of my truck and burned against my face. "Yeah, I'm good. What's up?"

"Oh, shit!" His eyes went wide and he tried not to laugh. "What happened to your face?"

My hand instinctively lifted to the cuts on my nose. "Just bumped into something last night," I said, wincing at the memory.

He raised a suspicious brow. "What the hell'd you bump into? A rabid dog?"

I cut my eyes at him. "What do you need, Dom?

"Gary wants to talk to you," he said, turning to walk away. "He's in the garage."

My Uncle Gary had a bad habit of sending people to drop the ominous *we need to talk* bomb on me without further explanation. I'd worked as his foreman for nearly ten years and it still made me nervous.

I cut the engine off and hopped out of the truck, pulling on my gloves as I took in the job site. A patchwork of newly laid foundations and skeletal wooden frames of soon-to-be homes stretched out along a residential road. A chorus of hammers and saws filled the air, punctuated by the occasional shout or laugh from the workers.

I stifled a yawn and squinted to block the sun. Early mornings never bothered me, but my bizarre Chicago fever dream had left me with barely enough time to make it back home and change clothes, much less sleep.

The crew and I had given a lot of blood, sweat, and time to this construction project over the last several months. A company our size building a dozen homes at once was no small feat. But today?

I would've burned it all to the ground if it meant thirty minutes in my bed.

Through a maze of building materials and equipment, I made my way across the dirt lot.

"Enjoy your nap time?" Gary asked sarcastically, looking up briefly as I entered the unfinished garage. He turned his eyes back to the blueprints in his hands. "I was worried about you. Thought you might've inhaled too many fumes and died."

I snorted. "And you just left me there?"

"No, I sent Dom to check on you after an hour or two."

"I think you're confusing hours with minutes."

"You say tomato, I say potato."

I shook my head. "Not how that goes, you old fart. What'd you wanna talk to me about?"

"Oh, right," he said as he set the plans down and turned to me. "I need you to meet with a potential client tomorrow and take a look at their property."

Interacting with clients wasn't my favorite thing in the world, but hey, I welcomed a break from the usual grind. "What kind of property is it?"

"Big retail space in Chicago. They're lookin' to remodel."

"Seriously?" I asked incredulously. *Why did the world suddenly insist on sending me to that damn city?* "Since when do we look for projects that far away from Lily Lake?"

"It's only an hour away. Last time I checked, people in Chicago use the same currency as us. Could be a nice chunk of change if we land this thing." He handed me a business card with the client's information. "They're expecting you there at 9 a.m."

Gary tilted his head to the side and gave me a scrutinizing glare. "Why's your face look like you made out with a shovel?"

"Um, first of all, rude," I clipped. "Second, it was a broom handle, not a shovel."

Gary just blinked. "Please explain how you got your ass handed to you by a broom?"

"Blair ended up in the emergency room last night and the hospital called me to take her home. Long story short, a belligerent old lady beat me with a broom handle."

His eyebrows shot up. "Now it makes even less sense, but we'll circle back to the broom. You saw Blair last night?"

I crossed my arms and looked at my boots. "Yeah. Probably a stupid choice. I don't know why I answered the call in the first place."

"It's an unconventional approach to divorce, I'll give you that," he said with a chuckle. "Don't let your mind punish you for being a good man, Caleb. It's honestly the least stupid thing about you." His phone went off and he glanced. "Ahh, shit. I've gotta take this."

Gary shuffled off to his truck and left me to my work. I looked at my watch and groaned. It wasn't even seven in the morning yet and I already wanted to collapse. *Fuck.*

The rest of the day passed like a kidney stone—slow and painful.

I spent the morning checking in with the crews at each house to make sure everyone had what they needed for the day. Everything that happened after that was a blur. I don't know what was more distracting—being gripped by exhaustion or being inundated with the memories of my ex-wife that I had worked so hard to suppress.

The scent of her perfume still clung to my senses. It was the same one she wore on our honeymoon.

I could still feel the lace of her lingerie on my fingertips—the same pattern I'd traced when I first felt her body on our wedding night.

The sound of her voice echoed in my mind. I'd spent two years imagining what I'd say if I ever found myself in a room with her again. Countless nights running through a monologue of grievances and vicious truths I wanted to unleash on her. Of course, when the moment finally arrived, we traded light-hearted jabs to lighten the tension.

I wanted to believe my uncle—that I simply answered the call for help because I'm a good man. That it had nothing to do with her and everything to do with me.

With thoughts of her swirling in my mind, it was hard to tell the difference between being good and weak.

———

EVERY MUSCLE in my body ached for reprieve, and my sleepless mind, swirling with remnants of the last twenty-four hours, longed for a moment of silence. By the time I made it to my front door, it took every ounce of energy I could muster to push it open. The familiar scent of home enveloped me as I trudged to the living room and collapsed face first onto the couch.

I breathed a deep sigh of sheer, unadulterated relief.

The hum of appliances and the HVAC soothed my mind and my eyelids grew heavy. My thoughts slowly calmed from a maelstrom to a trickle.

Finally, some peace.

I shut my eyes and could practically feel the warmth of sleep lingering just ahead of me.

A faint buzz stirred in my pocket and my eyes snapped open. I fished my phone out, heart racing, and glanced at the screen, hoping to see Blair's name only to find … nothing.

You've gotta be kidding me…

It had been a phantom vibration.

Why was that so disappointing? Did I really *want* to hear from her again?

I tossed my phone on the end table next to the couch and buried my head in a throw pillow. My stomach growled for dinner and I groaned. *Why can't I have more than five seconds of rest?*

Reluctantly, I lifted myself off the couch and wandered to the kitchen. I rummaged through the fridge and pulled out a few slices of leftover pizza to reheat in the microwave before plopping down at the kitchen table and mindlessly downing a few bites. My fingers traced the grooves of the table's wooden surface as I chewed, flooding my mind with a burst of nostalgia.

I'd built that table when Blair and I were newly married.

Gazing at the empty chair opposite me, I could almost see her sitting there. Fragments of happy memories played through my mind, but were quickly replaced by visions of our last conversation. There'd been no laughing or joking that night. I remembered searching her eyes for the familiar warmth they once held for me, only to find cold, distant sadness and resolution.

The room seemed to fold in on itself, the air thinning as I struggled to breathe. My throat constricted and a torrent of memories rushed in: our first date, our wedding day, the countless nights we'd whispered to each other beneath the covers...

...and the countless nights since our divorce that I'd slept on the couch to avoid lying next to her side of the bed and hearing nothing at all.

My nostrils flared as I thought back to my unexpected trip to Chicago the night before. Two years of moving on and rebuilding myself from the ground up unraveled in the blink of an eye.

Sadness gave way to resentment as I stared out the window at the setting sun. I clenched my jaw and balled my fists as if I were strangling the knot in my throat, determined to force my emotions into submission.

I stood up from the table and stumbled back to the couch. Stretching out on my back, I fixated on the spinning ceiling fan to distract myself from the raging war behind my eyes.

A battle between hope and dread screamed inside me at the thought of returning to Chicago in the morning. Being in such close proximity after all this time created a sliver of hope that she might reenter my life in some way. That sliver of hope filled me with dread because I knew it was a false one. Being in the same city as her felt like visiting the grave of a lost loved one. Sure, it brought me closer to her, but it only served as a reminder that our marriage was dead and buried.

I closed my eyes and breathed deep and slow, welcoming the grip of exhaustion as it smothered my thoughts and feelings into silence. Slowly, the warm embrace of sleep wrapped itself around me and I surrendered to it.

Ding-dong!

The piercing ring of the doorbell jerked me awake. An instant surge of irritation coursed through me. Once again, I'd been right on the edge of rest only to have someone snatch it away from me.

The doorbell rang again; its sound shrill and insistent.

I released a growl and slammed my fist into the couch cushion. Every fiber of my being protested as I sat up. My neck was stiff from the awkward angle of my nap. The idea of answering the door seemed like an insurmountable task.

The doorbell rang a third time, more impatient than before.

"Alright, alright!" I shouted, rubbing the sleep from my eyes as I shuffled toward the door. "I'm coming!"

As I reached for the doorknob, I took a deep breath and tried to push away the lingering tendrils of sleep and irritation. It took a moment to regain my composure, but I was reasonably confident I wouldn't murder whoever was waiting outside.

With a heavy sigh, I opened the door to find a woman waiting on my porch.

I tilted my head to the side in confusion. "Priscilla?"

"Hello, Caleb," she said, lifting her gaze to meet mine. Her airy, almost childlike voice contradicted the appearance of a woman who was about my age. Her sickeningly sweet tone made the hair on the back of my neck stand up.

Priscilla was dressed as if she'd stepped out of another era.

She wore a muted-gray dress that grazed her ankles and buttoned up to a high, protective collar. The sleeves reached her wrists, concealing every inch of skin. Her face was bare, devoid of makeup, and she wore no jewelry except for a locket necklace. A tight bun held her sandy-brown hair in place. The sight of her would have been surreal had we not grown up in the same community.

"I hope I'm not intruding on your evening," she said with a soft giggle. "We were on this side of the lake and I just wanted to stop by to say hi."

"Oh, um, that's—we?" I stuttered.

Priscilla looked over her shoulder at two bicycles that were propped up against my mailbox. A woman, maybe a few years younger than Priscilla, lingered there, watching us like a hawk.

"Lydia had to come along, of course," she said in the sickeningly sweet whisper all the women around here spoke in.

I rubbed the back of my neck to ease the growing tension between my shoulders. "Right..."

Priscilla giggled again. "It's really nice to see you. We've missed having you around The Fellowship."

"Yeah, it's been a while, hasn't it?" I mustered the bare minimum of a polite smile. A chill ran down my spine when I noticed the wrapped loaf of homemade bread in her arms. *Dear God, no.* "So, why are you, uh—what can I do for you?"

She looked at me through her lashes, batting them like she was a movie princess or some shit.

Aw, hell.

The hem of her dress swished as she swayed back and forth like a little girl, not the grown woman she was. "Well—you see —when you moved back to town, I was so sorry to hear about everything you had gone through in the city with that—" Her infantile voice slipped just for a second, but she recovered. "My apologies for my outburst." She looked at her feet, contrite and demure ... like a kicked puppy. "I've been waiting for Father to give me permission to bring you bread." She lifted the still-steaming loaf, offering it to me with a hopeful smile on her face.

Women are to speak softly and have a bright countenance. I could still hear the words of Reverend Reinard as he stood behind the century-old pulpit.

I cleared my throat and my mind raced to think of a way out of this conversation as quickly as possible. "That's really thoughtful, Priscilla, but I, um—"

"I hope you'll receive it as a token of my affection." She unwrapped the top half of the bread and gave a coy smile. "It's cinnamon raisin."

Did she just ... come on to me? With sweet bread? Damn... she was really shooting her shot. I panicked and blurted out, "I'm allergic to raisins. Deathly."

"Oh goodness," she said, her face turning beet red as she pulled the loaf away from me. "I'm so sorry, Caleb, I had no idea. I'm so embarrassed."

"No worries," I said as I reached for the door.

Her dress floated across the threshold. "Please accept my deepest regrets for my wrongdoing and my sincerest apologies."

Oh, for fuck's sake. "Uh... Okay. No need to apologize, but it's alright. I appreciate the gesture. It was thoughtful."

She brightened immediately, like flipping a switch.

Fuck me. I forgot how the women were around here. For the majority of the two years I had been back, I was—for lack of a better word—shunned.

It was nice. Peaceful.

Her cheery smile stretched from ear to ear. "I'll be sure that no raisins even come near the next loaf!"

"Next loaf?" I asked nervously. "Oh, that's not necess—you don't have to do that, Priscilla."

An awestruck breath escaped her lips. "Baking you a loaf of bread would be my greatest honor, Caleb Dalton."

Great. Now she was looking at me the way Blair used to look at Ryan Reynolds.

"Well." I clapped my hands together. "I've got an early day tomorrow, so I should probably get some sleep."

She nodded sternly. "Of course. Lydia and I should be on our way. Father doesn't approve of us being out after dark, you know."

"Yeah, I know," I said with a nod. "You ladies be safe."

"Goodnight, Cale—"

I slammed the door shut and breathed a sigh of relief. Suddenly, a day trip to Chicago sounded like a fantastic idea. No one to tap on my window, knock on my door, or offer me ... *courtship bread.*

I staggered back to the couch and flopped onto my side with a grunt.

Fucking Blair... I should have gone back to my bed. I was too old to be sleeping on the couch.

Maybe walking into her apartment had put a curse on me. Like the Cubs and the guy with the goat.

One mistaken phone call and the two-year-old wound that had finally scabbed over had been ripped back open.

5

BLAIR

"Blair, can I see you before you leave for the day?" Eddie said when he popped his head into our recording studio.

Sophia gave me a panicked, wide-eyed look as Eddie sauntered off. "What do you think that's about?"

After recording advertising snippets that would get placed into episodes, we had spent the afternoon plotting the new season concept.

I hated flying by the seat of my pants, but a successful show was better than a comfortably planned show.

I gathered the remnants of my takeout dinner and tossed it in the trash. "Your guess is as good as mine."

She grabbed her last pierogi and wolfed it down. "It's like being called to the principal's office."

I stared at the grid of sticky notes plastered across the windowed wall. Each one was a different episode.

The Rebel's Guide to Dating after Divorce.

I wasn't crazy about the title, but it worked for now.

I didn't feel much like a rebel today.

When I looked in the mirror, I didn't see thirty-year-old

me in jeans, thigh-high boots, and a crimson lip. I still saw twelve-year-old me in a prairie dress, covered from neck to wrists to ankles.

Only whores wear red, Blair. A righteous woman should not bring attention to her appearance.

Trousers are for men. You are to dress like a lady.

Don't be an eye trap and cause your brothers in the fellowship to stumble by drawing attention to your body.

Never mind that I was a child. Men shouldn't have been looking at my body to begin with.

Maybe that's why, all these years later, I left the studio when Sophia left the studio.

Eddie was a great boss. We had an easy rapport and a working relationship that was built on professionalism and respect. But I never sat in meetings alone with him or any other man, for that matter.

Blair, your sister said she saw you speaking to Caleb Dalton after Sunday fellowship. You know the courtship rules. Where was your chaperone? What would the congregation think if they believed you to be in sin? Go to the closet and don't come out until you've repented.

If only they could see me now.

Thirty years old, divorced—*the horror*—and wearing red lipstick.

Maybe that girl who blew up her life and took it back one small act of rebellion at a time was still in there after all.

"Do you want me to sit in the meeting with you and take notes?" Sophia asked as she cleaned up the Post-its and pens we had been using to storyboard our season.

Just do it. Do one small act of rebellion.

"No, you go ahead and cut out for the day. I've got it."

She arched an eyebrow. "You're not bailing on your date

tonight, right? If you bail on this date, we don't have a podcast season."

"I'm not bailing," I reassured her. "Does it make me an awful person to be using a date to have something to talk on here about so that we have ad space for advertisers?"

"You're not using him," she countered. "Sure, the listeners voted on how to build your dating profile, but you matched with this guy all on your own. You do actually want to date, right?"

In the days leading up to the divorce being final, I thought I wanted to date. I thought I was ready. I even mustered up the courage to make the first of many online dating profiles that I would never put to use.

I managed to go on two dates—one with a man, and one with a woman, both set up by Sophia and her fiancé—before realizing I really wasn't ready.

It wasn't just that I didn't know how to date after a failed marriage.

I didn't know how to date at all.

"It's not even dinner," Sophia said. "It's just drinks. It's a good baby step for you. Like dating with training wheels."

I laughed. "Episode one: Dating with Training Wheels. I like it."

"Is that what you're wearing?" she asked, pointing a nail at my jeans, tall suede boots, and chunky sweater.

I looked down. "I was planning on it. You said something casual but still sexy, right? I figured the sweater was casual and the pants and boots were sexy."

"No, it's great. You'll knock his socks off." She smirked. "And maybe his pants, too."

I snorted. "I'm definitely not ready for *that*."

"Sex, Blair. S-E-X. You talk about it all the time on the show."

"Yeah, I talk about sex all the time, but not *my* sex life." *Nonexistent as it may be.*

She softened. "It's been two years, and your marriage was over long before there were lawyers involved. You're ready for this. Don't let one freak encounter with your ex throw off your mojo." Sophia braced her hands on my shoulders and looked me dead in the eye. "Put on your lipstick, shake your tits, and get out there."

———

I AM AN INDEPENDENT WOMAN. I can vote. I renew the tags on my car by the time they expire … sometimes. I have a retirement account that I invest in … occasionally. I can record a conversation with a stranger for an hour and then have millions of people listen to it.

I can go on one date, have a drink, and make conversation for forty-five minutes.

How hard could it possibly be?

Cameron Jenkins was seated at a high-top table in the corner of the Rohan Tavern. True to the promise he made to wear the same thing that was in his dating profile picture, he was dressed in a navy suit, crisp white shirt, and red tie. His blond hair was in a neat comb-over, and he was cleanly shaven.

When he spotted me slipping through the crowd, he eased off of his chair and buttoned his suit jacket.

"Hi!" I said as I hustled through the crowded bar. "I'm so sorry I'm late. My boss needed to chat before I left for the day."

I immediately stiffened when he gave me a quick hug. But, as soon as it happened, it was over.

Cameron pulled out my chair for me.

Okay. Gentleman move. Not too bad.

"Not a problem at all." He flashed a smile. "I'm just glad we both had time in our schedules to meet up. Let me tell you—I don't always have time in my day like this."

He didn't always have ... dinner time?

"I told you I work for the mayor, right?" he continued.

I stowed my purse on the hook beneath the tall table and sat. "You mentioned it."

In your dating profile, and in every subsequent message we exchanged.

He flashed a shiny grin. "The mayor's a busy guy, which means that his team is even busier."

"I have no doubt," I said with a nervous laugh.

Mark, the only full-time bartender at the tavern, dropped a rounded martini glass full of amber liquor in front of Cameron. "Your Manhattan."

Instead of a 'thank you,' Cameron took a sip, then winced. "It'll do. Not as good as the one I had at the 27th Ward Alderman's house." He winked. "But not bad for a grass-root constituent hangout like this."

Mark barely concealed an eye roll before turning to me, surprised. "Blair."

"Hey."

Mark eyed my date suspiciously. "Out for drinks?"

I pursed my lips. "Mhmm."

He shifted so Cameron couldn't see his face. "What can I get for you tonight?"

Cameron had ordered something classy, so I should probably match that.

"Martini with a twist, please."

Mark cut his eyes at Cameron. "The usual way?"

I let out a sigh of relief and smiled. "Yes."

This was the exact reason I had made the Rohan Tavern

my go-to when I moved into my apartment. Bartenders were excellent secret keepers.

Mark headed back behind the bar to make my drink, and I turned my attention back to Cameron.

"So, working for the mayor's office. I'm sure that keeps you on your toes."

He drummed his fingers on the table. "You have no idea. He's up for re-election too, which means *I* have to find funding for the campaign."

Okay, I could work with that. I dealt with advertising deals all the time. I could do this. It was just like an interview for the show.

Sure, there wasn't a stomach butterfly in sight, but the first date didn't have to be perfect. I just had to get this one over with.

"I'm sure getting donors can be quite a task. Advertisers can be the same way. Everything is a negotiation. They're pinching pennies and I'm counting the seconds on a commercial break."

He sneered politely as Mark dropped a martini glass in front of me with a curled lemon peel on the edge.

I took a sip of crisp, refreshing lemon water and smiled at the fact that Cameron was none the wiser.

It's not that I had a problem with getting drinks, it's just that I didn't like the taste of alcohol, and I *really* didn't like feeling out of control.

Especially in situations like this.

Growing up believing that men were inherently wicked and couldn't control themselves didn't turn me into a meek, modest housewife. It turned me into a terrified, hyper-vigilant woman.

But, if growing up in the Fellowship had taught me anything, it was how to fake it to fit in.

"Right," he said over a sip of his Manhattan. "You do that —uh—livestream thing."

"Podcast," I corrected.

"Such a shame that journalists these days are resorting to flashy social media schemes rather than hard-hitting news. I miss the days when they put in the work."

"I'm not a journalist," I clipped. "I actually got my psych degree here at the University of Chicago. I worked as a Psychosocial Rehabilitation Specialist before the podcast took off. I gained so much insight from that job and met some really fascinating people."

"Speaking of fascinating people, I was at an event catching up with Senator Bell when he said he was looking for a new aid in his D.C. office." Cameron leaned back in his chair all smug and self-satisfied. "I don't want to put the cart before the horse, but I think he was eyeing me for the position. Washington would be huge. Think of the connections. The opportunities. Congress has always been the dream, but I could see myself in the White House." Instead of pausing for a natural break and giving me the opportunity to say something, he leaned forward. "I would make a great president. I'm educated, well spoken, tenacious—"

So help me. If he described himself as a jackhammer alpha male, I'd actually laugh.

Cameron was over six feet tall, but he was giving off some serious short guy energy.

"I think good leaders are made from good listeners," I countered.

He scoffed. "Maybe for psychiatrists, Belle."

"It's Blair," I corrected. "And as I was saying, my bachelor's was in psychology. I'm not a psychiatrist."

"You know what I think?"

I didn't want to know what he thought, but I had the distinct feeling that he was going to tell me anyway.

"I think people are too soft these days. What happened to

the era of men who ran into battle and women who held down the homefront?"

I took a sip from my martini glass full of water, wishing for once that it was liquor. Mark knew I didn't like to drink and had a secret menu of mocktails and look-alikes so no one but us would know I wasn't actually partaking. I could fit in socially without being vulnerable.

I smiled over the rim of my glass. "The men came back from war to a generation of women who realized that they had skills, knowledge, and talents that were valued outside of the home."

His lip curled in contempt.

Ooophf—derisive wasn't a good look on him.

I arched an eyebrow and took another sip. Sophia and I were going to have to figure out a creative way to recap this date before we recorded the episode tomorrow, because it definitely wasn't the salacious tale I thought it was going to be.

Maybe there was something in Chicago tap water, but I was feeling feisty. "Back to what you were saying about men running into battle. Were you in the military?"

He chuckled, regaining his composure. "No. I believe we need good men making policies, not just on the front lines."

"Absolutely," I said all too enthusiastically. "But let's say you're making those policies one day. First-hand experience outshines second-hand knowledge every time, right?"

"Are you saying you wouldn't vote for me?"

A slow smile spread across my face. "I don't usually talk politics on a first date."

Or any date, for that matter. But he didn't need to know that.

"You know, we could be a real power couple." He downed the rest of his drink. "You're gorgeous. You'd make a splash on my arm."

"Who's to say you wouldn't be my arm candy?" I countered

with a smug smile. "I had a lovely chat with the mayor at the Chicago Arts Preservation society dinner last week."

And there it was. My wild card.

Cameron paled.

"He didn't mention you, though. I met the deputy mayor, the city manager, quite a few aldermen, and a few of his high-ranking staffers." I propped my elbow up on the table and rested my chin in my hand. "Were you there? I don't remember seeing you."

He stammered. "You were at the Preservation Society dinner?"

"Yes."

"How did you get in?"

Instead of cutting down his obviously fragile manhood, I simply tapped into my inner Elle Woods. *Thank you, Soph, for making me watch movies.* "Is it hard to get in or something?"

He was about to grind his teeth into sand. "Excuse me," he said, fishing his phone out of his pocket. "I need to take this. It could be important."

His phone wasn't even ringing.

I slumped in my chair as Cameron made his way out, and let a heavy breath release from my lungs.

"You look like you need something strong," Mark said as he came by to clear our glasses.

"Did he at least pay for his drink?" I asked.

Mark chuckled. "I know his type. I made him put a card on file and charged it as soon as his ass left his seat."

I snorted. "Smart."

"Word of advice," he said. "The rich ones work too much to get drinks after work, the ones who pretend to be rich talk about how important they are, and the ones who are *really* rich don't talk about it at all."

"Wise man," I said as I rubbed my temples. "At least that nightmare is over."

He disappeared for a minute, then returned with a glass of bubbling pop. "I poured you something strong."

"You know I don't like—"

"It's a Cuba Libre. Virgin."

I took a hesitant sip and then laughed. "Is that—"

"Rum and Coke with a little lime juice." He smiled sheepishly. "And no rum."

I stirred some of the bubbles out with the thin black straw. "Thanks, Mark. I'll be out of your hair in a minute."

He spun his ball cap backwards and nodded. "Take your time."

Could this day get any worse? So help me, if I had to scrap one more season concept I was going to scream. Not only did I not have a good dating story to tell on the episode tomorrow, I had wasted a first date on that walking identity crisis.

Was dating this awful?

Cameron seemed like a perfectly normal, well-spoken guy.

I took a sip, letting the bubbles dance on my tongue.

The bells over the door chimed, and I looked over my shoulder to make sure it wasn't Cameron coming back.

No.

It was much worse.

Caleb strolled in, turned, and looked right at me.

6

CALEB

The cold night air bit at every inch of my skin, forcing me to pull the collar of my jacket a bit closer. My lungs burned, and every breath produced a visible plume of mist. Up ahead, a neon sign that read *Rohan Tavern* promised warmth and a shield from the bitter wind.

The ambient noise of the city dimmed as I neared the door. Just as I reached out to grasp the cold metal handle, the door swung open abruptly.

A well-dressed man stormed out and brushed past me. He was clearly flustered, his face red from the cold or anger—or both.

"Mouthy bitch," he hissed, followed by a torrent of colorful profanities. His polished shoes tapped hastily against the pavement as he fled.

I couldn't help but chuckle, imagining how bad a date must be to make a grown man bolt like that.

Must be in Blair's neighborhood.

Shaking my head, I pulled the door open and stepped inside the Rohan Tavern.

Cozy warm air surrounded me immediately, driving the

chill from my bones. The dim atmosphere and wooden accents gave the place a welcoming feel, and the low murmur of conversations and clinking glasses contrasted with the bustling noise outside.

I unzipped my coat and scanned the room for a place to sit. My eyes landed on a beautiful woman seated alone at a high-top table in the corner of the room. My breath caught.

You've got to be kidding me.

Blair stared back at me like a deer in the headlights.

Shit. I conjured her.

I ran my hand through my hair and steeled my expression the best I could. This had to be a conspiracy. Attempting to appear unfazed when her gaze fell on me, I nodded and strolled over to her table.

Blair stiffened and took a long sip from the drink in her hand. As I neared, she set the glass down and rolled her eyes. "This night just keeps getting better and better."

"Ah, so you must be the reason that guy ran out of here like his tail was on fire."

"He didn't run out of—" She cut herself off and looked down at her drink. "I don't know what you're talking about."

"Uh-huh," I said, then shrugged. "My bad. He was probably referring to another—how did he put it—'mouthy bitch.'"

For a split second, she flashed a self-satisfied smirk, before quickly changing her expression. "What are you doing here, Caleb?"

I eyed the glass in front of her and smiled to myself. "Same as you," I said, innocent as a newborn lamb. "Getting a drink before I head home for the night." I nodded at hers. "What'cha got there? Looks pretty strong," I teased.

She rolled her eyes. "Real funny."

"Let me guess," I said, crossing my arms over my chest. "Fake cocktail so you could fit in with the human Ken doll."

She pushed the glass away, sending the pop sloshing up to the rim. "You know what? I don't need this tonight."

Before she could stand all the way up, I put my hands up in surrender. "I'm sorry."

Blair sighed deeply, her shoulders slumping as she sat back down. "It's just been a long day. I don't need anyone else to push my buttons."

I studied her for a moment. Her eyes were tired; not the usual firebrand I was used to. The thought of that sleazy douchebag sitting across from her did something funny in my chest. "Hey, I'm—"

"Welcome to Rohan Tavern," the bartender said as he approached Blair's table. "Can I get you something to drink?"

I glanced between the bartender and Blair. "I'll be over to the bar to order in a—"

"Sit," Blair said, gesturing to the stool opposite her.

I eyed her hesitantly. "You sure?"

She softened her expression. "You're already here, and to be honest, I don't want that chair to be empty if Cameron comes back."

I sank down onto the stool and turned to the bartender. "I'll have what she's having." There was a ninety-nine percent chance it was just whatever cola they had behind the bar.

He nodded and shuffled away, hiding whatever judgmental thoughts he had behind a professional smile.

"We're both terrible at bars," Blair said with a snort.

God, I loved hearing her laugh.

I cracked a smile. "Hey, I've gotta drive back to Lily Lake tonight. What's your excuse?"

She shrugged. "I'm a wimp."

"Yeah, me too," I said with a wink.

The bartender set my pop on the table before making his rounds to other customers.

"So." Blair poured half of my glass into hers to refill it. "Why *are* you in Chicago?"

"Work," I said, taking a sip. "Met with a potential client this morning."

She looked at her watch. "It's after dark. That's one long freaking meeting."

"Well, not exactly. The meeting only took a few hours. I've just been hanging out since then."

"Sounds like you're avoiding going back."

"That is an outrageous accusation," I said with an exaggerated scowl. "Accurate, but outrageous."

She shook her head and cracked a smile. "Uh-huh, that's what I thought."

"Fine, but you'd avoid going home too if you risked being ambushed with Courtship Bread."

Blair burst out laughing. "Someone baked you *courtship bread*? Surprising. I thought you'd be getting the silent treatment. Or is it just me who's exiled?"

I groaned. "Not just anyone. It's—"

"Wait, let me guess ... oh my God, my mind is blanking. All I remember is I hated her."

I chuckled. "It'll come to you. Just wait."

She thought for a moment longer, then her eyes went wide. "No!"

I nodded. "Yep."

"Priscilla the Chinchilla?! The *mouse*?!"

I dropped my face into my hands.

She threw her head back and cackled. "Does she still talk like a child ghost in a haunted house?"

"Worse, actually. And it's extra weird now that she looks like an adult pilgrim."

"Is today our divorce-a-versary or something? She's probably been counting down the days until she could bake you a loaf of bread." Blair took a sip, then pointed a finger at me. "You know what really sucks? How freaking good that bread is. And now I can't even make it without hating myself."

"She didn't bake me the normal stuff. It was sweet bread with cinnamon and raisins in it."

"Excuse me?" Her gasp was dramatic. "She baked *my* ex-husband a loaf of courtship bread with *sugar* in it?! That *hussy!*"

Hearing her refer to me as *hers* sent a warm tingle down my spine, even if it was only as *her* ex. "It's true. I panicked and told her I was allergic to raisins."

She snickered. "You did not."

I hung my head. "I thought it would get her to go away, but it just made it worse. She's gonna bake something else. Now I can never go home again."

"You should have told her you were allergic to gluten. Raisins are too easy to get around. The women are expert bread bakers, but tell them to use something other than wheat flour and..." Her voice trailed off, and she quickly looked away from me. Something sad, almost haunted, crossed her face.

But just as quickly as it came, it was gone.

Blair looked down at her glass. "Good luck with that one. She's nothing if not persistent, and she always wanted you."

And I always wanted Blair.

I didn't know what I expected from this. From her.

If I was being honest, I never thought I'd see her again. The hospital was a freak coincidence, but coincidences don't happen twice.

Still, something inside of me was always drawn to her. I felt it now.

Or maybe that was just indigestion.

"You never made me courtship bread."

Her smile was sad. "I never had to."

"Yeah, that's true," I said, taking a sip. "Our parents kind of did the courting for us."

"Yeah, but that's how it goes, I guess," Blair said with a shrug. Her smile faded.

Seeing the light in her eyes dim brought me back to some of our last conversations, stoking a fear in me I hadn't felt in years. A fear that told me she was slipping away from me.

It was a silly thing to be afraid of considering I'd already lost her.

But it made me realize how desperately I wanted the conversation to continue. I didn't know why, though.

"I would've still taken the bread, though," I said with a half smile and nudged her with my elbow. "If I had known what a hot commodity I was, I might've made you try a little harder."

"I guess I could have done worse than you." Somehow that admission eked a smile out of her, even if it was directed at her glass. "But I haven't baked bread in a long time."

I looked down at my glass, thinking about what she said. *I had always been hers.*

The bartender swung by and topped off our glasses. A prolonged silence hung between us, but not an awkward one. It was the type of heavy silence that said a lot of things neither of us had the courage to put into words.

I cleared my throat. "So. You never explained what happened with that guy earlier."

Blair snorted. *God, I missed that sound.* "My sad attempt at not being alone for the rest of my life. But he was awful, and I'm kind of glad he bailed." She smirked. "I'd hate for him to be stuck having drinks with a—what did you tell me he said— a *mouthy bitch?*"

I laughed. "Yeah, I'm taking a real bullet for him here."

"First you save me from walking home in a shredded ball gown, and then you save him from having his ego decimated." She gave me a slow clap. "Caleb Dalton—contractor by day, Superman by night."

I squinted and stared at her shirt.

"What are you doing?" she asked, glancing down at her shirt. "Do I have something on me?"

"Oh, sorry," I said, shaking my head in disappointment. "Just seeing if that whole X-ray vision thing works."

She swatted my arm, lithe little fingers bouncing off my bicep like raindrops on a roof. "And here we were, having such an amicable conversation."

I hung my head in shame. "I know, I know. Once a woman throws her sugar bread at you, it's hard not to get a big head."

She rolled her eyes at my sarcasm.

"So." I hitched my thumb toward the window, in the general direction the attitude-in-a-suit had gone. "I'll take a guess and say that he won't be getting a second date?"

"He's lucky I don't make a complaint to the mayor's office."

I snickered. "Blair 2.0 with her high-society beaus."

She laughed. "High society is just as much of a cult as the fellowship. Same rungs, different ladder."

She had a point there; not that I'd know much about high society.

"What about you?" she prodded. "Seeing anyone? Or are you playing hard to get so you never have to buy bread again?"

"Nothing too serious," I said with a shrug. "I've been on a few dates over the years."

She hummed. "Vague. Okay. I respect that."

"Well, I mean, recently I had a girl call me in the middle of the night asking me to take her home."

A look of pure, unadulterated jealousy flashed across her face before she realized I was talking about her.

"Very funny," she deadpanned. "Thank you, though. I..." she let out a reluctant sigh. "I'm glad you picked up the phone."

"Me too." I chuckled. "It was nice to see I could actually get a woman to take her clothes off."

"You grabbed that lace bra even though it hasn't seen the light of day for years."

The two of us laughed, but she had a point. Sex between us ... there had always been a lot left to be desired.

And man, did I desire it.

She propped her chin in her palm and studied me. Wheels were turning in her mind, but I couldn't be bothered to wonder what she was thinking about. It was the sharp edge of her jaw that caught my eye first. The graceful line of her throat. The way she would roll her lips together to wet them when she was nervous and didn't know what to say.

She had been doing that a lot.

It was the way that, even after all these years, she still wore the same perfume.

I loved that perfume.

Her hair was styled in loose waves and I wanted nothing more than to tangle my hands in it.

"I forgot how itchy it was, but I wore it, thanks to you."

I snapped out of the haze. "That you did. Good girl."

Her eyes went wide.

"Then again," I said, quickly recovering, "you didn't have much choice."

She regained her composure, but the deep rise and fall of her chest told me her mind was racing. "Well, if picking me up from the hospital is your most memorable date in two years, it sounds like we've both had an equally fun time playing the field."

I grinned. "That bad, huh?"

"I'm surprised I'm not rotting in a garbage bag or at the bottom of the river. No one told me how *hard* dating is. Why are people so weird? Sophia and her fiancé set me up on the first date I went on after the divorce. The guy asked the server to bring him a tray of ice so he could select which cubes he wanted in his drink. Who does that?"

I grimaced. "The kind of guy that turns people into skin suits, that's who."

She shuddered. "Maybe you were on to something when you moved out of the city."

"Yeah, I'm not interested in sharing my skin suit with anyone."

Blair laughed mid-sip, snorting her drink into her nose. "Yikes. *Anyway.* How's life in Lily Lake?"

"Life's good. Just working a lot. Evading chinchillas. You know. The usual stuff. How's city life? How, uh... How's the podcast?"

She took a long pull from her cup. "Oh, just great."

And there was her signature sarcasm.

I arched an eyebrow, but waited her out in silence.

She folded. "The program director—"

"Eddie?"

Blair looked surprised. "You remember him?"

"Of course I remember him. You told me about him."
Granted, it was right before we separated, but I still remembered.

I remembered everything.

She sighed. "Eddie scrapped my season and told Soph and I to come up with something flashier. My date tonight was supposed to be the start of me exploring 'dating after divorce' so I have something to talk about for an hour every week. But considering I'm catching up over Coke with my ex-husband instead of flirting with a dating app match, I'd say I'm not off to a stellar start. No offense."

"First of all, offense taken," I said, feigning outrage. "I haven't analyzed my ice cubes or anything, but I'm sure you'll find something to talk about. You're a mouthy bitch, after all." I winked.

"You know," she said with an amused twinkle in her eye. "That name's growing on me. I'm sure everyone back home would agree." She paused, trepidation radiating from her shoulders. "How is home? Your family, I mean. How is everyone?"

"Same old, same old, I guess," I said with an apathetic shrug. "I try to stay busy and engage as little as possible these days."

She fiddled with the thin straw poking out of her glass.

"Have you..."

Blair shook her head with pursed lips. "No." Much like her, it was definitive.

Blair was many things. Beautiful. Intelligent. Quick-witted. But she was also stubborn as a mule and impossible to reason with.

I threw her a bone. "Your sisters are well."

She blinked and stared out the window. "That's nice." It was a whisper full of resolve. She wasn't saying it to me. She was trying to convince herself.

"You know, I—"

"I should get going," Blair said as she frantically looked around for the bartender. "You know, to head home and salvage what's left of the content I have planned ... for work."

"Oh." I suppressed a pang of disappointment in my chest. I pushed back from the table and stood. "Yeah, I should probably get on the road. I've probably waited long enough to avoid another love loaf from Priscilla."

Her smile was tight.

"Tell me something, Breezy." I fished out my wallet to

square up for my drink. "If I happened to be back in the city for a job, how likely am I to run into you here?"

She jolted at the nickname I hadn't uttered in years, then trained her face to be just that. *Easy, breezy, and unbothered.*

Blair rolled it over in her mind. "I'd give you seventy-thirty odds." She stood and smoothed down the skin-tight jeans wrapped around her legs.

Holy shit.

"Why?" she prodded. "Are you trying to avoid me? I thought we were doing pretty well at this whole post-divorce getting drinks thing."

"We are," I countered as we strolled to the front of the bar, paid up, and headed for the door. "Which is why I don't want to push my luck." I grinned, tipping my head to my truck. "My tires are expensive. I don't want you going all Carrie Underwood on them."

She laughed as I held the door for her. "A truce, then. The bar is neutral territory."

I stuck my hand out and offered a handshake. "Deal."

Neutral. We could do that.

But the touch of her skin against mine was anything but neutral.

7

PODCAST TRANSCRIPT

One Small Act of Rebellion
Season 2
Episode 17
"Shot Glass in a Tea Party"
Aired Two Years Prior

"**B**e feminine, but don't tempt men by existing in a woman's body. You're supposed to believe the body that was divinely created for you is a holy thing, but you're also supposed to hate having breasts. Having hips. Having legs. You're supposed to be ashamed of them. You're supposed to hide them. 'Be a girl' is what they mean; even when you're a woman. Even when you're simply existing in the form that was created to protect your soul. But no—they want you to be a child. Look like a child. Be quiet and meek like a child. Children are easier to control."

"But you weren't little girls," Sophia chimed in.

"No. We were women. It's ironic, really. Innocence and naïvety are touted as holiness, and everyone wonders why there's such perversion in religious communities when it comes to children. You *see, all my life I was taught that there was safety under the umbrella of authority. Of course, that authority was always my father or our reverend. I got married the day after I turned eighteen and that authority was transferred to my husband. Who, under the community's beliefs, still had to answer to my father."*

Sophia hummed in understanding. "You never had autonomy."

"When you're born, you're put into this hierarchical ladder. As you grow up, more and more rungs are added to the top of the ladder. Teachers. Elders. Other men and the occasional woman in the community. And then you get married. You're not living with your family anymore. You're taking care of a home, managing finances, and raising children, but you're never treated as an equal. Every decision is made by someone in the umbrella above you, or above them."

"Do you think that had anything to do with the downfall of your marriage?"

"Yes and no."

"I mean, you got married at eighteen. You were basically a child."

"I was ready for the wedding. I was prepared to get married, but I wasn't prepared for the marriage."

"What do you mean?"

"We were paper dolls, easily made and easily damaged. My father used to call my sisters and me his 'teacups'—fragile, delicate things that were to be treated with care and kept safe. Something brittle and breakable that was supposedly treasured and admired but rarely brought to the table. Silent, pretty things on shelves that were to be seen and not heard."

"But you're not a tea cup."

"No. I was a shot glass in a tea party."

Sophia laughed.

"There was a reason that our wedding invitations started with

both sets of parents cordially inviting you to the marriage of their children. It wasn't about my ex-husband and I. It was about them. I got married because it's what was righteous. I got divorced because it was right. We were both miserable. I respect Caleb, but I also grew to respect myself. That's why it ended. Because I wasn't ashamed to exist anymore."

"What was it like to date him?" Sophia asked. "Were you allowed to go out alone?"

"Oh, absolutely not! For lack of a better word, we were betrothed from the day I was born. Our families were close, and he and I were two years apart. We grew up knowing we'd be married one day. We were almost resigned to it. We were formally engaged for a month before our wedding. Just long enough to go through the premarital counseling that the reverend required everyone to do. Every conversation, every face-to-face visit always had a chaperone. We didn't kiss until we were pronounced man and wife. Leading up to that, the only time he touched my hand was to put a ring on it."

"You're smiling."

"I'm not smiling!"

"You're smiling. Spill, Blair!"

"Growing up, I lived on one side of the lake and he lived on the other. One of my small acts of rebellion was sneaking down to the lake in the middle of the night after everyone was asleep. It wasn't easy, either. I shared a room with three of my younger sisters and they were light sleepers."

Sophia gasped. "You hussy!" she said with a laugh.

"We would meet under this big oak tree and just sit and talk."

"And no touching? Not even shoulder-to-shoulder."

"Nope!"

"What did you talk about?"

There was a long sigh. "I think we were fourteen or fifteen when we started meeting up under the tree. He was my best friend. My confidante. I trusted him with my secrets."

"What kind of secrets?"

"I think the first secret I told him was that I wanted to go to college."

"Did he rat you out?"

"No. If I'm being honest, I was a little surprised."

"Why is that?"

"He could have turned me in. I mean, it's not like I would have gone to jail or something, but I definitely would have spent some time in the prayer closet until my heart was right."

"Or until you lied and pretended like you had a change of heart," Sophia filled in.

"Exactly. He knew he would have been praised for ratting me out. My father would have seen it as a sign that Caleb would make a good marital leader. A strong umbrella of authority to keep my weak, wicked heart in line."

"So why didn't he do it?"

"He promised."

"That's it?" Sophia asked.

"He kept my secret when I said I wanted to go to college. There were smaller secrets after that, and then a big one. Even though it was forbidden, we used a condom on our wedding night. When we left for our honeymoon, he drove me two counties over to go to a doctor's appointment so I could get on birth control without anyone knowing. I wasn't ready to get pregnant at eighteen. I had spent most of my childhood raising my sisters and being a homemaking daughter. I had been a parent already. He had listened to me talk about it and understood where I was coming from. We were thick as thieves. In a community where I was supposed to trust men to be my authority, but also fear and be solely responsible for the way they thought about or reacted to my body, I had found one who didn't look at me *like a porcelain doll. He saw and honored my humanity. I think that's the weird thing about our divorce. When I look back, there were no knock-down drag-out fights. There was a lot of silence; a lot of resentment that grew out of that silence. And that's what hit me the hardest when we separated. I lost the one person I trusted the most."*

"Alright, Little Rebels. We'll be right back with Blair's challenge for you after this message from our sponsors."

8

CALEB

"That's good for today, Dom. You can head out," I said as I strolled through the maze of construction mess.

"You heading home, boss?" Ricky as he sided up to Dominic and recorded his time for the day.

I stuffed my hands in the pockets of my coat as I shook off the cold. It chilled me to the bone.

"Not for a few more hours." I gave the job site a nod of approval. "I gotta go into the city and pick up the brick for the entryway arch."

"That backordered shit finally come in?" Dominic hollered.

I chuckled. "Yeah. Took long enough, but the buyers insisted they wanted to wait it out. They wanted that fancy brick from Colorado. I tried to tell them that they were paying out the nose for something that was going to be a pain to maintain, but they had their minds made up."

"Brick mason coming on Monday?" Dominic asked.

"Yeah. I got up with him earlier. I'll probably give him Danny if he needs an extra set of hands."

Danny was our eighteen-year-old gopher. He was still green and, frankly, all we could trust him with was getting lunch and moving supplies from one place to another. Maybe he'd move up to holding a tool next month.

Dominic snickered. "Good luck with that."

I waved them off for the weekend and the guys cleared out in a mass to get back to their lives. I didn't blame them. I wanted to get back to my truck and crank the heat as high as it would go.

I waited until the site was clear before hopping behind the wheel and peeling out.

Rural roads gave way to the highway by the time the cab of my truck warmed to a habitable temperature. My phone rang as I turned onto Highway 88. Dread filled my gut when "Mom" popped up on the screen.

I groaned. It was never a good sign when she called in the middle of the day... Or ever.

"Caleb," her soothingly sweet voice filled the cab the moment I answered on speakerphone. "How are things?"

"Fine. Just working," I groused, trying to suppress the mix of irritation and apprehension bubbling up in my voice. "What's up?"

"Just wanted to check on you, dear," she said in an overly sweet tone that told me she was displeased with me. "I just received a very concerning phone call."

Knowing her, that could mean pretty much anything. "From who?"

"Priscilla's mother. She was calling to ask about you."

Shit. I scrubbed my hand down my jaw. "What about me?"

Please don't say bread. Please don't say bread. Please don't say bread.

"She told me that you didn't accept the loaf of bread her daughter brought to your door. I had no idea you were allergic to raisins. Is that something you found out while you were away?"

I rolled my eyes.

"Away" is what she called the nine years I had been married to Blair. Eight of those years we had been living in Chicago, blissfully *away* from everyone who shared our DNA.

Well, most of it was blissful.

Some of it was blissful.

Being married to Blair was... complicated. I shook the thought out of my head.

"Uh, yeah." The white lie rolled off my tongue easily.

"Any other allergies I should know about? Mrs. Aldridge said Priscilla was hoping to bring you another loaf."

You've gotta be fucking kidding me.

"I don't want her bread." It was a ridiculous thing to say in this day and age, but some traditions never died ... no matter how much I wanted them to. "I have no intentions of courting her or anyone else for that matter, so whatever rumors you're spreading around about me, just cut it out."

Her gasp over the line nearly changed the pressure in my ears. "Gossip? I would never. You know that gossip is a—"

"A sin," I finished for her. "Just like women initiating a romantic pursuit is apparently a sin, too. And yet every generation has found some loophole around it. Baking bread is just baking bread, right? It's *definitely* not how women tell a man she wants him to ask for her hand in marriage. Sharing someone else's business in a prayer circle *definitely* isn't gossip. You're just being a devout member of the fellowship."

Fucking archaic. But I didn't swear... at least not to my mother. I had some semblance of civility after all. I sighed. And she was my mother... For better or for worse. I loved her whether I wanted to or not.

She put on her "kicked puppy voice" and went for the kill.

"That horrid woman did so much damage to your heart," she whimpered, sniffing fake tears away.

Blair was many things.

Opinionated.

A work horse.

Stubborn.

Impossible.

But she wasn't horrid. At least not the way I remembered her.

Then again, she was my ex-wife for a reason. Maybe it was the two chance encounters that had rose-colored glasses dropping over my eyes.

Blair was all those things and more. Wickedly sharp. Quick-witted. Belligerently sassy and mouthy as hell, but God, I loved it.

Still, she was beautiful as ever.

"Keep her name out of your mouth," I clipped before hanging up the phone.

Each bump of the asphalt under my tires only served to ramp up my adrenaline.

I made the choice to move back to Lily Lake. I could have stayed in the city when Blair and I split. Reconciliation and finding middle ground with my family was a thread of hope, but two years ago it was the only thread I was still hanging by.

Fuck it.

I shifted my hands on the wheel and reached for my phone, scrolling through a streaming app until I found Blair's podcast. Before I could think better of it, I tapped the latest episode and sat back in the driver's seat as I cruised down the highway.

Admittedly, it had been a while since I punished myself with her voice, but damn if I wasn't a glutton.

"What's up, little rebels? It's your hostess Blair, and do I have

some tea for you. Get comfy now, because after this episode, I've got an uncomfortable challenge for you—" she paused as the music reached a crescendo "—welcome to One Small Act of Rebellion.*"*

The sound of Blair and Sophia laughing like the listener was walking into a party faded in as the music died down.

"You're joking," Sophia gasped.

"I wish I was!" Blair said with a laugh. "Alright, rebels. I know, I know—you're tuning in to the episode today because you want to know how my date with—"

"Mr. President," Sophia said, jumping in. "I think we should do the guy a solid and just call him "Mr. President" to protect his identity ... and very fragile ego."

I snorted, thinking back to the twerp who had bolted out of the bar where I had found Blair.

"Okay," Blair said. "We'll protect his delicate masculinity and keep him anonymous. Not even a first name. All you internet sleuths out there would find him in a heartbeat."

"So, you matched with Mr. President using the profile that the listeners voted on," Sophia said, getting the conversation back on track. "And we had planned for today's episode to be a recap of your date."

"The idea of dating after divorce is scary. I mean, hell—divorce is scary. It's like standing on a landmine. Either you're perpetually living precariously on something extremely volatile or you step away and let it explode."

"And dating afterward is like bringing someone else into the blast zone to see the wreckage."

Something uncomfortable churned in my gut. For the last two years, I had actively avoided listening to the podcast. As curious as I was, I had already gotten Blair's side of things in couple's therapy. I didn't need to listen to the replay and review of our marriage being broadcast to weirdos on the internet.

But here I was. Glutton, party of one, craving the buffet of punishment.

"So get this," Blair said like she was cozying up to a circle of girlfriends. *"I sit down with Mr. President and it's not bad at first. I was really nervous because it was my first one-on-one date in a long time, but I showed up and I was proud of myself for that."*

"As you should be."

"We get our drinks and start talking. He was well spoken, and arguably attractive, but the man talked over me."

Sophia gagged.

"I swear—I talk for a living and I couldn't get a word in edgewise. This guy was a steamroller looking for arm candy."

"Please tell me you threw a drink in his face," Sophia begged.

I chuckled to myself. That would have been a sight to see.

Blair snickered. "I scared him off when I called him on his BS. He was trying to act all big and bad and I may or may not have knocked him down a peg ... or ten."

"Savage woman."

"I prefer to not use my light to illuminate his ego, and he preferred a quiet date who fawned over him."

That's my girl.

I scrubbed my palm over my mouth in an attempt to get rid of the smile that crept up my face, but it didn't work.

"So he made an excuse and bolted." Blair gave space for a *dramatic pause. "And just when I thought I was home free, guess who walks in."*

"Who?"

Sophia would have already known, but I respected the schtick.

"My ex-husband."

I was honestly surprised that Sophia didn't fade into the *Jaws* theme song before cutting to the first message from their advertisers. I could practically hear a *dun-dun-duhhhhh.*

"So your ex-husband crashes your date," Sophia said when they came back on.

I mean, technically I didn't crash the date. The date was already over. And crashing a date implies that the crasher had knowledge of the event that they crashed. My appearance was just a happy accident.

Maybe I liked seeing that waste of space running out with his tail between his legs.

Not everyone could handle my—

Nope. No. She wasn't my anything anymore. Just someone I used to know.

I listened to Blair's objective recap of our interaction. Her word choice made it sound more salacious than it was, but I guess that's what kept people listening.

"It was odd..." Blair's voice trailed off. *"After the hospital incident, I never expected to see him again. But there he was, standing there cracking jokes about me scaring Mr. President off."*

"Have you heard from him since?"

"No," Blair said. *"Honestly, I think he was just as thrown off as I was. Caleb is so hard to get a read on. He's like a brick wall sometimes."*

"You're talking about him in the present," Sophia noted.

Huh. That roiling in my stomach hadn't gone away, but it shifted to something warmer. More familiar.

Blair groaned. "Oh God."

"Okay, B. Spill. Are you gonna see him again?"

"This was supposed to be dating after divorce! Not revisiting the ghost of marriage past."

I smirked as I peeled my eyes off of the road and swiped to my contacts. Before I could think better of it, I tapped on the number that I had been staring at for days and typed out a text.

———

FRIGID AIR HIT me like a Mack truck as the door to the Rohan Tavern swung wide open.

Frosty tendrils of platinum hair danced on the gust. Ice blue eyes sliced through the air, cutting through the lingering scent of beer and bar food.

Blair's phone was in one hand, the edge of it tapping on her open palm as she assessed me from a distance, not even caring that I was sizing her up too.

This was weird. I could admit that.

I didn't want to think about the hundreds of times I wished I could take that text message I sent back, but she viewed it with lightning fast speed.

Of course, her only response when I asked her to meet up for a drink was a "70."

Because, of course, she'd do that. Blair and that Machiavellian mind of hers...

I bet she wanted me to overthink that response while I was waiting for fancy bricks to be loaded into the bed of my truck.

I could picture her and Sophia, hunched over Blair's desk, pouring over the text, deciding what kind of a response would keep her cards as close to the vest as possible.

Divorce was either a bar brawl or a cold war.

She and I had always been the latter; frigid silence, gritted teeth, and rubber bullets.

Kind of like now.

Satisfied with her assessment, Blair decided she'd join me on the battlefield. She cut through the crowd, unbuttoning her fur-lined parka and revealing a thick sweater in crimson red. It matched the scarlet lip that curved up like a sickle as she draped her coat on the back of the tall chair opposite me.

She lifted her phone, flashing the illuminated screen at me

before reading off the text I'd sent her. "Question, Breezy. Is tonight a seventy percent night or a thirty percent night?" She punctuated my call-back to our previous run-in with an arched eyebrow.

I pushed the glass of bubbling cola toward her. "You said seventy, so I took my chances."

She let a prissy *humph* slip, deeming me worthy of an hour of her time. "How long have you been waiting?"

"Half an hour."

"And how long would you have waited?" she asked, sliding on to the chair and lacing her fingers together on top of the table. "Can't say I'd give up an hour of sacred after-work time to sit in a crappy bar drinking overpriced pop."

"Thanks for getting me a drink, Caleb," I retorted in a girlish falsetto. "I really appreciate it."

Those shrewd eyes narrowed on me as ruby lips split in a smile. "I'm still trying to figure out what the heck I'm doing here, and if you're trying to poison me or something."

I chuckled. "If I wanted to kill you, I would have done it before you took half in the divorce."

"Fair," she said, stirring the bubbles out of the soda.

She was in shades of black and red like a black widow spider; beautiful and deadly. But it was the flash of pale blue flames in her eyes every time her lashes raised that had my chest tightening.

We sat in tense silence for the longest thirty seconds of my life before she finally cracked.

"Why did you text me?"

I clasped my hands together, mimicking her posture. "I was in the city."

"There are a million other bars in the city—" her gaze floated down to the drink in front of me that matched hers "—and you don't even drink."

"I drink sometimes."

She raised that sassy eyebrow again.

I folded. "I wanted to see you."

She blinked—once, twice, then let out a weighted breath. "Yeah," she said, looking over her shoulder for the bartender. "I need liquor tonight."

9

BLAIR

"It looks radioactive," Caleb said as he judged the neon green drink that Mark dropped in front of me ten seconds prior.

I took a sip and gave it a smile of approval. "It tastes like sour apple Jolly Ranchers." I nodded toward his rocks glass. "So. Caleb 2.0 is a whiskey man?" I said, teasing him with a spin-off of the moniker he had given me right before we separated.

Blair 2.0. New job. New friends. New opinions. New attitude. New clothes.

It's not like I was going to apologize for it.

Not all of us had to be stuck making amends with the past.

He took a sip of Jack Daniels and winced. "You know, I thought I was. Turns out I don't like the taste of burnt trees and regret."

I snorted and took pity on him, pushing my glass over to his side of the table.

He eyed the drink suspiciously. "What is it?"

"An appletini." I crossed my arms. "Either you can try it or you can enjoy your wood water."

He flicked the festive umbrella out of the glass, sending it skittering across the table.

"Hey!" I said, snatching it up. "The umbrella is what makes it fun."

Caleb pushed the straw aside and sipped from the rim. He paused, letting it sit on his tongue before giving it a look of reluctant approval and going for another gulp.

"Okay, okay, that's enough. My drink. You want one, you order it yourself."

He scowled and looked longingly at my drink as I pulled it back.

"Ordering something that tastes good doesn't make you any less of a man," I teased.

He rolled his eyes and flagged down Mark, hand-gesturing to order a second glass of what I had from across the room.

Curious, I plucked his whiskey from his side and gave it a sniff.

It wasn't atrocious. It was woodsy and warm with a note of sweetness like aged honey. I brought it to my lips and took a sip.

"Oh God, no." I grimaced and pushed it back toward him. "Smells better than it tastes."

His smirk was victorious. "What's the matter, Breezy? Not man enough for it?"

And just because he said that, I grabbed the glass, lifted it in a sarcastic toast, and downed it.

Never again. That was atrocious.

Victory burned like a lightning storm down my throat, but the surprise on his face was the cherry on top.

Ice cubes clinked and rattled as I dropped the glass back in front of him.

"Looky there," I said with a saccharine smile. "I have a big dick too."

Mark appeared with another appletini and pointed at the empty whiskey glass. "Do I need to cut you off, Miss Dalton?"

Caleb stiffened.

"I just had—" I hiccuped "—one."

He grabbed the empty glass and pointed the rim at me. "You usually have none. Take it easy. I don't want to have to stuff you in a cab tonight."

Another hiccup escaped.

I lifted two fingers in a solemn salute. "Scout's honor."

Mark shook his head. "Nice try, but it's three fingers."

Caleb pulled the umbrella out of the fresh drink. I watched as he wrapped his bear paw of a hand around it to hide the majority of the liquor that looked more like a vat of acid that cartoon characters would fall into than a beverage.

Those hands...

I loved his hands. They were always, *always* dirty. I couldn't even count the number of times I had scrubbed dirt and grease stains off of our furniture or walls because he'd be filthy after work.

His palms and fingertips were always rough and calloused.

I wondered if they still were...

Need more alcohol.

I went back to slowly sipping my original drink, thankful that it didn't taste like the rotten remnants of a cheap cigarette. "You still have some explaining to do."

"About what?"

"Us. Why we're here. Pretty sure you got your truck in the divorce and I got the city."

He chuckled. "We might have to negotiate shared custody of the city. We're gonna start a job up here soon."

My stomach roiled, and I blamed the whiskey.

"Is that why you're here?" I asked as I listlessly swirled the thin black straw in my drink.

He shook his head. "Had to pick up some brick to take it back to a job site."

I nodded in understanding, waiting a long beat before piping up. "How's... business?"

Caleb laughed, reclining in the chair like he didn't have a care in the world. "Is that really what you want to ask me?"

No. But if I asked what I really wanted to, I'd have to let my guard down.

When I didn't say anything, he took a shot in the dark. "Seeing each other in the hospital was an accident. Running into you here was happenstance."

"Neither of which explains why you texted me."

He scraped his thumb over his lip, drawing my gaze to his mouth.

His stubble was somewhere between a five o' clock shadow and a beard. And honestly? It was a good look on him.

He had always been clean-shaven when we were married. I didn't want to admit it, but I was attracted to the rough edge that age had brought out in him.

"I wanted to see you."

Honesty. Huh.

I didn't expect that, and I didn't know what to do with it.

"Why?"

He shrugged and took another swig of the Chernobyl juice. "Why not? I was in the neighborhood."

"Where'd you have to get the brick from?"

"Morrison's Building Supply."

I racked my brain. "That place in Burbank that you used to get stuff from?"

He tipped his chin.

I did the math. "So, you drove an hour from Lily Lake to Burbank, and then just so happened to teleport to my neighborhood, forty-five minutes away?"

He looked just the slightest bit guilty, but didn't deny it.

"Teleportation devices have come a long way. You barely even feel your atoms being ripped apart now."

I giggled and helped myself to the remnants of candy apple goodness. You could barely taste the alcohol and I wasn't mad at it. I wasn't drunk; just buzzed enough to have the courage to sit through whatever this was.

Caleb flashed a smile.

"What?"

He shook his head. "Nothing."

"That was something. Why did you smile at me?"

"Who said I was smiling at you?"

"Your eyeballs and your teeth."

"I haven't heard that laugh in a long time."

I could feel my shields being raised. "What do you mean?"

He flattened the paper umbrella and fiddled with the edge, peeling it away from the stick. "You have your fake 'I'm laughing to set the right mood in a podcast episode' laugh, and then you have your real laugh." He tore the umbrella a little more forcefully than he probably intended to. "I dunno..." His throat constricted as he swallowed.

I was mesmerized by the way the cords and tendons flexed.

Was it hot in here? I had already taken off my coat. I couldn't strip any more. I shifted in my seat, clenching my thighs together to get rid of that annoying craving between my legs.

Screw him for reminding me just how long it had been since I'd felt anything remotely akin to sexual desire.

"You stopped giving me your real laugh—" he paused in thought "—a year before you moved out?" The umbrella ripped again. The unintentional tear of flimsy paper seemed like it was louder than the growing noise in the tavern.

I never had anything to laugh about back then.

But I didn't say that.

His eyes lowered from my face to the dip in my sweater that ended at the top of my cleavage.

Unaired grievances hung heavy like a growing storm cloud between us.

After downing the entirety of his cocktail, he said it.

Three words that flayed me open.

"I missed it."

I replaced the acid in my throat with vitriol. "Don't."

"Breezy—"

The nickname stung. As much as he wanted to think I was easy, breezy, and unbothered, I wasn't.

I never had been.

I wasn't bulletproof. I had just learned to hide the pain every time a shot ripped out a piece of me.

"Blair," I clipped.

His nostrils flared, and he clenched those hands I used to love around his glass.

Why had he really sent that text and why did I respond to it? I should have deleted it the moment it came up on my screen.

He abandoned the glass and ran his hands through his hair. "I wasn't lying. I wanted to see you."

Liquid courage made me say it.

"Why? I'm happy. You're happy. We've moved on. What... what are you looking for? Closure?"

"I'm not looking for anything!" he countered in frustration. "I just wanted to have a fucking conversation. I thought we'd grab a drink and catch up." He pointed to the door. "But you marched in here with a battle plan just like you did every time we sat down for mediation."

"Right," I said on an exasperated breath. "Because this is all *my* fault."

"I didn't say that."

"You didn't have to." My head swam and my pulse raced. Anger and attraction battled inside of me.

I wanted to hate him. I really did.

I wanted to have the kind of ex-husband that would make a good target for darts, but I didn't.

I always imagined what it would be like to see him again. I wanted to be dressed to the nines with an upgrade on my arm that would make him jealous. I wanted to have moved so far on that he and I were on different planets.

Yet here we were, going tit for verbal tat over neon drinks and glowing beer signs.

Until now, I had been guarded but polite during our run-ins. I blamed the liquor for the fact that I was willing to call him on his crap.

"You wanted to catch up," I retorted. "Sure, maybe it's because we ran into each other twice. Or maybe it's because a ghost from our past brought you a damn loaf of bread. Or maybe you saw me attempting to go on a date with someone who wasn't you?"

Bingo. His reaction said it all.

The widening of his eyes and the way his mouth opened to say no, but his head nodded yes was a dead giveaway.

I just want you to be happy.

Everything he had said to me in teary-eyed conversations when we both sat down and admitted it wasn't working had been a lie.

Happiness would have been letting me move on, but here we were.

But could I blame him?

I didn't have the good grace to tell him that I wanted him to be happier without me.

Back then I wanted to be happy with him, but we weren't.

The idea of being numb alone was preferable to being miserable together.

Tears stung the back of my eyes, and the momentary regret turned to anger.

I was not going to cry in front of him.

I'd cry on the inside and let it out later.

"Excuse me," I snapped. The words hissed from between my teeth as I brushed past him on my way to the bathroom.

"Breez—"

Caleb's sharp, bellowing voice was an echo at my back as I quickened my pace. The dominating rumble made shivers race down my spine.

I slipped into the narrow hallway illuminated by a single light and turned the corner to the recessed alcove that housed the bathroom door.

"Hey—" A strong hand shot out and wrapped around my wrist, pulling me back.

I yanked free. "I'm going to the bathroom," I snapped.

Caleb called my bluff. "No, you're not."

I spun on him and jabbed my finger in his face. "You don't want me, but you don't want me with anyone else. Is that it? You can't stand the fact that you saw me on a date with another man."

He stammered, but didn't retreat.

My back bit into the concrete wall of the alcove as he took a step forward. Warm eyes pierced mine. "I forgot how much I liked it when you mouthed off to me." He pressed in further, his wide chest completely shrouding me from the view of the hallway.

Caleb steadied himself by planting his hands on either side of my head.

I was about to tell him off when his knee pressed between my legs. The contact was incidental, but that didn't stop a zing of electricity from racing down my spine.

A gasp of delight escaped my lips at the pressure. My head swam with whiskey and lust.

His eyes darkened as they locked on my mouth.

I blamed the drinks for the way he looked at me.

Caleb looked like he'd devour me in one bite if he could. The big, bad wolf, about to chow down on a snack.

He shifted his feet, closing the last of the space between us. I was pinned against the wall, seated with his thigh between my legs.

Every repressed feeling I had ignored for the last two years ached to be released in a flood.

"You always did look good in red," Caleb said in a low rumble as he trailed the tip of his finger down the V-neck edge of my sweater.

Goosebumps cropped up in the wake of his touch. I gasped when he rocked his knee again, teasing the apex of my thighs through layers of denim.

I couldn't control the way I still craved sex, but I needed to hold on to something; to some kind of power. "I used to wear red because I wasn't supposed to. Now I wear red so you don't see how much you made me bleed."

I thought saying it would make him back down, even though I didn't want him to.

It was true, after all.

The old Caleb would have stepped back. But I didn't quite recognize the man in front of me because he didn't back down. No. He pressed into me, sliding his hands down my arms before jumping over to my hips. He anchored me to his knee, levering up to tease me.

The back of my head hit the wall behind me with a thud as my teeth sank into my lip.

"Or maybe," he countered, "You wear red because victors carry the blood of the fallen."

His grip was firm, keeping me steady as my hips moved of their own volition.

"Fuck you," I whispered. I had the words, but I didn't have the music. My body was a lightning rod and he was the storm.

Heat brewed and bubbled low in my stomach, driving me to chase ecstasy.

Caleb's cheek pressed against my temple and I could feel his smile. "You wish you could."

Before I could come up with some snarky retort, one hand left my hip and shackled my throat, squeezing just hard enough to keep me pinned to the wall. I could feel my pulse race against his touch. Those familiar callouses scraped my skin in the most delicious way.

I wanted to be consumed by him.

Caleb's whisper was thick with lust. "Go ahead, Breezy. Take what you want. It'll be our little secret."

"I told you not to call me—"

He squeezed my throat and rolled his hips, sliding his thigh up against my pussy.

I let out an involuntary moan.

"That's what I thought."

I stopped fighting it and, for once, chased happiness.

"There you go," he soothed in the most condescending way possible.

I didn't even care. I just wanted an orgasm.

"You dirty girl," he growled. "Getting yourself off by humping my thigh." His hand left my throat. I sucked in a breath, but it escaped when he fisted the back of my hair and yanked my head back.

Just... a little... more...

"Please," I whimpered.

His grin was malefic. "Say my name. Beg me to let you come."

I shook my head, mewling in desperation as the orgasm grew closer and closer.

Pinpricks of heat lanced at my scalp as he pulled at the root of my hair and kept my head in place. "Beg. Me." He nipped at my ear. "Or I turn around and go back to the table like nothing ever happened and leave you here, horny and desperate."

Who the hell was this man? He certainly wasn't the one I was married to for nearly a decade.

I rolled my hips across the muscular width of his thigh, brows furrowing as I focused on reaching—

"No!" I whimpered when he backed away.

He kept his hands planted on the wall, bracketing my body. "If I'm the one getting you off, then you're going to be saying my name. You're going to be thinking about me. Praising me. Begging me. Thanking me. Not whoever else you've been with. Me, Blair. Do you understand?"

I grabbed the front of his shirt and pulled him back. "Make me come."

He shook his head with a derisive click of his tongue, but returned his thigh to its place between my legs. "What's the magic word?"

"*Please... Caleb.*"

In a rush, he grabbed my ass and lifted me off the ground, guiding my body back and forth against his leg.

My back arched and I left the chain reaction. "*Caleb.*"

Everything combusted, igniting me in the explosion.

The universe around me went glittery. I was floating in a haze as every atom in me electrified.

"There's been no one else," I admitted, uninhibited by the buzz of endorphins and liquor. "Not like this... Not since you."

If he was dynamite, then my statement was the match that lit the fuse.

The heel of his boot careened into the bathroom door, kicking it open as he hoisted me up, wrapping my legs around his waist.

"Hold on," he grunted like a neanderthal before pitching me onto the counter that held the bathroom sink and kicking the door closed.

In one second he was flipping the lock and the next his mouth was on mine.

He tasted like apples and spite, and God—I loved it.

Caleb pushed his tongue into my mouth as he fumbled with the zipper on my jeans.

I hopped off the counter and shoved them down before going for his belt.

As soon as his fly was down, he spun me away from him, bent me over the sink, and kicked my ankles apart.

"Yes or no, Breezy." His hand smoothed down the curve of my butt—close, but not touching where I wanted him most.

"Yes," I gasped.

He didn't need to be told twice.

Two thick fingers slid inside of me, slowly stroking my still-throbbing inner muscles. He groaned in approval and satisfaction. "That's my girl. Still wet for me." I felt the blunt head of his length as he lined up. "You better hold on," he warned.

I grappled at the sink, but it wasn't fast enough.

Caleb thrust into me in one motion, sheathing himself deep inside of me.

My muscles stretched to accommodate his size, but the fit stole my breath.

He didn't waste any time. Each thrust hit its mark with precision, bringing me closer and closer to a second orgasm.

Yeah. This definitely wasn't my ex-husband. Married Caleb didn't do double orgasms. This was some impostor in his body, and honestly? I wasn't mad at it.

"More," was all I could choke out. I was soaring through the air and knew I was going to crash-land, but the high was worth it.

Fingers reached around and found my clit, teasing it in just the right rhythm to have me teetering on the edge.

"You'd better come," he growled.

"I'm—oh!" I gasped as I shattered. "Oh, God—"

10

CALEB

"Oh-oh God." Blair's strained, muffled voice fractured the silence and jolted me awake. Her words wafted in from another room, garbled by an eruption of vomit and profanity.

My eyes snapped open and I sat up—a decision I immediately lived to regret as my vision swirled. A storm of nausea churned inside me. I hunched over and covered my face until I wrestled my gag reflex into submission.

The candy-apple scented reminder on my breath hit my nose and filled my mind with fragmented memories of the previous night.

The bar. Drinks. Blair. My name on her lips as she begged me to finish her.

More drinks.

My dick hardened at the thought of her bent over that sink last night...

Oh, right. Blair.

"Breezy?" I called out.

A second guttural hurl was her only response.

I tossed the covers to the side and hobbled out of bed,

stumbling over Blair's nest of obstacles littering the floor. Gently, I tapped on the bathroom door. "You okay in there?"

"I'm fine," she croaked before dry heaving. "Just need a minute."

I cracked the door open and poked my head inside. Blair was on her knees with her back toward me. She was sprawled over the toilet in nothing but her underwear. Her hair cascaded over her shoulders and around her face as she clutched the bowl for dear life.

"Those appletinis betrayed us, huh?"

Blair groaned before hurling again. "How is stuff still coming out?"

Instinctively, I reached out and pulled her hair back from her face. She leaned into the touch slightly and sighed. For a moment, it was as if nothing had ever changed. Like the last two years without her had been a fever dream.

I shook my head and tried to push away the sense of longing that threatened to undo me.

Several more waves of vomit passed before the retching finally stopped.

"Fuck appletinis and your big dick," Blair rasped, leaning back.

I chuckled and helped her to her feet.

She brushed her teeth and stared blankly into the sink. Tears and sweat had left her with raccoon eyes and streaks of mascara down her cheeks. She washed her mouth out and looked at me in the mirror.

"What the heck are you wearing?" she asked, her eyes narrowing. "Are those my leggings?"

"Huh?" I looked past her and saw my reflection for the first time. It took my brain a few seconds to comprehend the freak show staring back at me.

Black spandex stretched down my legs to just below the

knee like baseball pants made of panty hose. I had apparently gotten cold in the middle of the night and pulled on one of Blair's baggy old sweatshirts.

Well, baggy on her. I glanced down at my exposed belly button. The thing was a crop top on me.

"Well, damn," I said, turning to the side to get a better look in the mirror. "At least they make my ass look good."

Blair burst out laughing. "Oh, I'm looking."

"This isn't doing it for you?" I turned to give the full view.

"The pants *do* make your ass look good." She flashed a playful smile, then feigned a serious expression. "But exposing your midriff like that?" She clicked her tongue in sarcastic disappointment. "What will the ladies at The Fellowship think?"

"What can I say? I'm kind of a hussy."

Blair cackled. "Scan-da-lous. Go cover up all that sinful flesh. I need to shower."

"Are you sure you don't need help?" I asked, moving a little closer as my eyes dropped to the graceful lines of her collarbone. "We could get a little more shameful before you wash it all away."

"How are you horny? My face was literally *just* in a toilet bowl."

I shrugged. "The rest of your body wasn't in the toilet, though."

She placed her hands on my chest and peered into my eyes. "I'm about half a second away from covering you in whatever 'shame' is left inside me."

"Fine," I said, playfully throwing my hands up as I turned to the door. "I'll take my midriff and go."

I heard her laughing as the door clicked behind me and the shower turned on.

My stomach lurched and growled in harmony with my

throbbing head. Food sounded absolutely disgusting, but I had to find something or I wouldn't get through the day. More importantly, *Blair* needed to eat something.

I'd never seen her hungover and hangry at the same time, but I imagined it wouldn't be safe for anyone.

I plodded over to the small kitchen that connected to her living room. She had to have something that could tide us over. I rifled through the cabinets for something bland, but couldn't find a crumb. Empty shelf after empty shelf. Absolutely nothing but a couple of sad-looking spices and a box of baking soda.

Not even a can of soup.

The fridge was my last hope. Eggs were good for a hangover. That's what the guys at work always ate. I pulled the door open but found another dead end. Just an empty milk jug, butter, and—

"How..."

Bewildered, I pulled my jeans from the refrigerator shelf. *What the hell goes in an appletini? Jolly Ranchers and cocaine?*

Whatever. That was a blackhole in my memory I didn't care to dive into. Not without some breakfast, at least.

Mobile ordering it is.

I closed the door and fished my phone from the pocket of my frosty jeans. With a few swipes, I found a few of the least offensive things I thought we could stomach and scheduled them for delivery. My phone buzzed with a confirmation text that a guy named Todd would be at the door within thirty minutes.

I loved Todd.

On that hopeful note, I trudged back to the bedroom and swapped Blair's pants for mine. I pulled the tiny sweater over my head and tossed it on a chair, scanning the room for my shirt. Nowhere to be found.

I sighed and flopped onto the bed, burying my face in the pillow.

The shower cut off, followed by the sound of curtains sliding open. A few minutes later, the bathroom door popped open.

"Oh God," Blair groaned.

"You keep repeating that," I said, lifting my head. "Please tell me it's an orgasm this time. I don't know if your plumbing can handle more vomit."

"My apartment. How did this happen?"

"How did *what* happen?" I shuffled off her mattress and outside the room to where Blair stood in the bathroom doorway, gawking at the space around us.

I hadn't noticed before, but the place was a wreck.

Remnants of her ficus lay scattered on the carpet, surrounded by soil spilling out of its broken pot. Couch cushions, picture frames, pillows, and the contents of her neatly organized closet covered the floors.

"It was so clean." Blair looked at the chaos in forlorned resignation, then gasped. "The cat! Where's the cat?"

Seeing the empty spot on the coffee table triggered a moment of clarity. Moments of our lust-fueled rampage through the apartment floated through my mind in a drunken montage. Almost instinctively, I paced back to the kitchen and opened the oven.

The horrifying cat figurine stared at me in judgment, glowing in the hellish warmth of the oven light.

That thing was creepy.

"Tell me again why you have that ceramic demon?"

"Sabina gave it to me when I moved in. She said it would keep me company."

"In your nightmares," I mumbled.

She shot me a silencing look.

Blair gave the mess another assessment as she pinched the bridge of her nose. "How the hell did this happen?"

"If memory serves—"

"—unreliably," she clarified.

"We—uh—hooked up at the bar, did some shots, and then—"

"—walked back here and went at it like animals?"

I rubbed the back of my neck, feeling a pang of stress lingering there. *Had I used a condom?*

Protection hadn't exactly been on the forefront of my mind when all I could think about was *her.*

"Blair—"

"I'm fine," she said in that fake voice she used when she wanted to feel in control. "Safe, sane, and consensual." Denim blue eyes met mine. "I didn't exactly push you away. Actually, I'm pretty sure I begged you to fuck me harder."

"Two out of three," I said awkwardly. "I... don't think I used a condom."

"I'm still on birth control and it's the safe part of my cycle," she countered.

"Right."

The two of us lingered in tense silence, knowing everything that lived behind that weighty statement.

The ring of the doorbell shattered the moment.

"Crap," Blair muttered, quickly fixing her damp hair for spontaneous company.

"I've got it." I moved through the sexcapade wreckage and opened the door, only to find Todd the delivery driver being accosted by Sabina and her broom.

Her wrinkle-lined eyes turned to me and narrowed.

I snatched up the grease-soaked bags. She forgot Todd and raised the broom handle at me. I sent up a feeble prayer for his safe escape.

"Thanks, man," I clipped as I slammed the door and dead-bolted it for good measure.

Blair had an expectant look on her face. "Wanna tell me what that was all about?"

"Well, you're never going to get delivery service here again if you don't put a leash on your attack grandma."

Blair grabbed the bag out of my hand and opened it. She turned a little green, but maintained her air of superiority. "Sabina would never. She's a saint."

"Do saints assault people with brooms?"

"You probably provoked her."

I took the bag back, found the breakfast sandwich I'd ordered for her, and tossed it her way. "Eat," I said as the familiarity of bantering with her sent heat wrapping around my neck. I couldn't have that. "You're more agreeable when your mouth is full."

"It'll make me throw up again."

"You drank as much as I did last night. You need food."

"I need to get my apartment back in order. You know—since you decided to act like a caveman last night and destroyed my living arrangements while you fucked me."

There was something oddly satisfying about hearing her say, "while you fucked me."

It was so improper.

I loved it.

Never in my wildest dreams had I imagined that the freckle-faced girl who was taught to be demure, soft-spoken, and submissive would be talking to me like that.

To my knowledge, I had only heard her say the F-word once when we were married, and it was close to the end.

But instead of eating like I told her to, Blair set the paper-wrapped sandwich on the askew coffee table and started picking up the throw pillows that had been—well—thrown.

There was the stubborn woman I knew and lov....

No. She was just the woman I used to know.

"Eat," I demanded. "I'll pick everything up." Muttering, I added, "It's probably my fault anyway."

She nudged the couch back into place with her knee before planting the pillows back on the cushions with precision. "My apartment. My mess. My upturned ficus."

I found her vacuum in the closet and decided to tackle the potting soil that was sprayed everywhere.

My stomach disagreed with the delay of sustenance, but it was tempered by the satisfaction of Blair's shrewd gaze as she watched my every move.

"So," she said after a few minutes of silent cleaning. "Are we going to talk about this?"

I laughed wryly as I shoved the vacuum back into the closet. "Do you want to talk about this?"

"I had raunchy bar bathroom sex with my ex-husband. My therapist is going to have a field day with this."

I snorted. "You mean talking to yourself in the mirror?"

She rolled her eyes. "Very funny."

"Let me guess," I said as I reluctantly grabbed the cat figurine out of the oven and dropped it back onto the coffee table. "You sit in an office every other week and talk about me like I'm the boogeyman."

She giggled. "Oh, no. I come armed with PowerPoint presentations. You know—so I can more effectively talk about everyone. There are photo montages and diagrams. But you'll be disappointed to know that it's rarely you that I rant about."

"Your mom still pissing you off a decade later?" I gandered.

She paused and looked at me curiously like I had just read her mind. "How did you—"

"I know you, Blair." I stacked stray Whitney West novels and placed them back on the bookcase.

Yeah... That's right. I had fucked her against the bookshelf, too. Every time I thought she had enough, she just kept begging for more.

Blair had been insatiable last night. That sex drive contradicted everything I thought I knew about her.

Outside, police sirens blared and horns honked as the Saturday traffic began to build. Being in a high-rise, hovering above it all didn't matter. It was annoyingly loud.

"I will never understand why you like living here..."

Satisfied with the half-assed cleaning job—or maybe she was just sick of me—Blair grabbed her breakfast sandwich and stomped into a pair of furry boots.

"I need some air." When I didn't immediately follow her, she looked over her shoulder, annoyed, and said, "You coming?"

After rifling through the hazardous materials known as her bedroom, I found the rest of my clothes and coat, and followed her up a winding staircase to the roof.

Frigid air sobered me up faster than the realization that I'd had sex with my ex-wife.

Great sex, though most of it was a blur.

We sat on the roof, side-by-side, as the sun broke through the gray fog. In the distance, the water of Lake Michigan sparkled on the horizon.

"This is why," she said simply before taking a hesitant nibble of a croissant dripping in bacon grease. Deciding that accepting my offering was better than starving, she took a bit of egg and cheese. "Growing up, I always felt like a goldfish. Stagnant water, small bowl, tired of being watched all the time." She pulled her knees up and rested her arms on top of them. "Remember when I started college and we lived in the married residence hall?"

I nodded. It felt like another lifetime ago.

"We went from being two fish in a glass jar to swimming in a bigger pond. No one really cared what we were doing. They didn't care if we went and saw a movie in a theater. They didn't care if I wore a skirt that was above my knees. Or hell—if I wore pants. They didn't care if I wore makeup or the color red. People minded their own business. I liked the hustle and bustle because it gave me room to figure out who I wanted to be, not who I was scared into being."

"Have you figured it out?" I asked after a stretch of silent chewing.

She tore the edge of the paper wrapping. "I thought I had."

"What do you mean?"

"Some people call it 'going through deconstruction'; but is it really deconstructing faith and religion if everything you peel back and grapple with doesn't even touch faith? It's just all the bullshit fallible people tout as faith. They pretend like they're okay with you questioning everything, but really they're only okay with you questioning what you believe if you come to the conclusion that everything you believed before remains true."

"I get it."

Growing up under the authority of the Fellowship meant every breath you took was done under a microscope. The pressures and expectations for men and women were different, but equally suffocating.

Shame is a terrible motivator. High-control groups like the Fellowship didn't raise obedient servants. They created excellent liars.

"I thought the bridges I burned would light the way, but all I ended up with was scorched earth." Blair let out a quiet laugh as she balled up the sandwich paper. "You know what's ironic?"

"Hm?" I asked around a bite of bacon, egg, and cheese.

"The first time I had unmarried sex was with my ex-husband." She rested her chin on her knees and closed her eyes. "How pathetic is that."

Sober as a judge, I wrapped my arm around her shoulders and pulled her into my side. "Not to brag, but it could have been way worse."

11

BLAIR

"Happy Monday. You look like shit."

I shuffled into the bullpen of the studio and beelined for the coffee maker. "Not you too," I groaned. "Tony said the same thing when I got to the door."

Sophia's eyebrows lifted. "Really?"

I plucked an "If at first you don't succeed, it's only attempted murder" mug out of the cabinets and gave myself a generous pour from the pot. "Not in those words, but he asked if I was feeling sick."

"You look like the petrified leftovers in the back of my fridge that I keep forgetting to throw away."

"I'd blame the hangover, but at this point I think it's just regret."

Her eyebrows winged up in surprise. "Well, that's a loaded statement if I ever heard one. Is this NSFW or can we use it for the session today?"

"I wish it wasn't safe for the podcast," I grumbled as I trudged into my office with Sophia on my tail.

She dropped onto the couch while I dumped my things

onto the desk and drowned myself in black coffee, hoping the bitterness and caffeine would make me human.

"Oooh," she said with a devilish grin. "That means it's juicy. Do I get a recap before we record or do you want to jump right into it?"

As much as I didn't want to rehash this particularly embarrassing moment of appletini-fueled weakness with millions of strangers, I was nothing if not honest. Authenticity outshines being calculated every single time. For better or for worse, it's what got *One Small Act of Rebellion* to the top of the charts.

"I'd like to minimize my abject humiliation."

Her smile was cheshire. "Then let's get right to it."

Even though the alcohol had completely left my system and I had forced myself to eat balanced meals and over-hydrate after Caleb left my apartment, my stomach still roiled at the thought of rehashing everything.

We got the all-clear from the on-duty sound engineer and settled into our seats before queueing up the perfunctory intro that was accompanied by the snappy show music.

Soph and I made our usual small talk, recapping things that had happened on the show's social media pages over the last week before cutting to the first advertising spot.

"Alright, Little Rebels," I said, situating myself in front of my microphone. "Last week's small act of rebellion was to prove to yourself that dating after divorce—or a breakup—doesn't have to be awful."

"Jenny H. from Brooklyn sent us a message and told us about how she got dressed up and went out for drinks with a hot neighbor and it ended with plans for a second date next weekend. Way to go, Jen!" Sophia said. "Speaking of weekend plans, Blair's behind her desk looking like the cat that ate the canary."

"No birds were eaten in the production of this podcast," I sassed.

Sophia laughed. "Wanna share with our listeners what *you* were up to this weekend?"

"Do we have a title for this episode yet?"

"Not yet," Sophia said.

I snickered. "Then you're going to love this. How about we call today's episode 'The one where I got drunk with my ex-husband and had an orgasm in a bar bathroom.'"

Sophia spit out her water.

"Hey! Not on the mics! Those are expensive!" I said with a laugh, trying to play up the bit.

"I'm going to need *every* detail. Spill!"

"So get this—" I cozied up to the mic "—I was in my office on Friday and my phone goes off. Guess who it is?"

"I'll take a whack and say it wasn't the guy you scared off by being a—how did he put it?"

I laughed. "Mouthy bitch."

"I want that on a t-shirt. I'd wear it with pride," Sophia said.

"Same. But you would be right. It wasn't Mr. President. It was my *ex-husband*. So, we've run into each other twice."

"When you had your meet cute in the ER and then when he crashed your date."

"Gold star for you."

"Please tell me it wasn't a dick pic."

I laughed. "It definitely wasn't a dick pic, but we'll get to the dicking around in a minute. So, he says that he's in the city and wants to meet up for drinks."

"Verbatim or are you paraphrasing?"

"Paraphrasing," I clarified before pausing thoughtfully. "He... He actually made a little joke, recalling a conversation we had about running into each other again."

"Wow. A man who listens and remembers things. Do you have to have an exotic pet license to marry one of those?" Sophia quipped.

I laughed. "Listening was never his issue. He was actually a great listener. There were a million things I could blame on the downfall of our marriage, but what it really boiled down to was passion... or a lack thereof. Toward the end, we were just roommates. Going different directions, living different lives."

"You just grew apart. Ten years is a long time, and who you are at eighteen isn't who you are at twenty-eight."

"I wish it was that simple. But when it came down to it, I was lonely. He was always so quiet. Sex was boring and unfulfilling at best. It was my least favorite chore rather than something I craved. Which is really ironic since it was something that, growing up, we were taught was supposedly irresistible."

"Which brings us back to the episode title," Sophia said. "An orgasm in a bar bathroom? Details, please."

"I don't know why I said yes, but I showed up and met him for drinks. Things were a little weird in the beginning. The first two run-ins were just that. Accidents. But this was intentional and I didn't know how to process that. We haven't seen each other in two years and then all of a sudden we're having weekly rendezvous? Anyway, we were having drinks and muddling through polite conversation."

"Why do I feel like there's a but coming?"

"Because we did get divorced for a reason. He and I might disagree on those reasons, but they exist."

"So what happened?"

"He made a backhanded comment about me being calculated around him, and I nearly lost my cool. After all, he was the one who invited me to meet up. I may or may not have downed more alcohol than I had ever consumed in my entire life and stomped off to the bathroom so he wouldn't see me cry."

"When—"

"When he comes up behind me, pins me to the wall, and goes from Jekyll to Hyde. A very, very sexy Hyde."

"Ooooh."

"It was not my greatest moment, and I blame the liquor and two years of being single."

"Just get it off your chest. You'll feel so much better."

I groaned. "I dry-humped his leg like a horny puppy while he whispered all these phenomenally dirty things in my ear. And then he picks me up, yanks me into the bathroom, and we bang it out right then and there. Which was fantastic and awful. Okay, it was awesome. But now I can't ever go back to my favorite bar. It's officially a no-trespassing zone."

"And then what? You two just went your separate ways?"

"I wish! But no, we had more drinks then somehow made it back to my place and went full wrecking ball across my furniture. He woke up wearing my leggings and I woke up spooning the toilet. But that's not even the worst of it."

"I'm starting to think it can't get worse, but please prove me wrong."

"The worst part of it all was how awesome the sex was the night it happened and how freaking sweet he was the morning after. I mean, where was *that guy* when we were married? The guy who ordered breakfast and helped no matter how much I told him I didn't want it. The guy who knew I was feeling vulnerable and put his arm around me."

"That's the thing about ending a relationship," Sophia said. "Someone else always gets the better version. The upgrade. You just happened to beta test the new-and-improved him."

"It makes me jealous of some fictitious woman."

"Are you going to see him again?"

"Honestly? I have no idea. Seeing him like this—all confident and brash and secure—it makes me angry that I never got that from him. I wanted the passion. I wanted the heat, and all I ever got was silence and distance. We were married, but I had never felt more lonely." I worked it over in my mind for as long as I could without slowing down the episode. "Sex aside, the last forty-eight hours have been completely unsettling. He was completely unsettling."

Sophia left me to muse on that final note while she ran through a segment of submission forms from our listeners on all the ways they had been rebelling against things that were expected of them, but dragging them down.

I looked at the wall decor that read *Do one thing every day that scares you* and wondered if forging a new path really was better than reverting to the safety of how I was brought up.

That musing never lasted long. I'd think about all the times I dreamed of being right where I was now, and find myself grateful for the journey—painful as it was—that brought me here.

————

"HOW ARE YOU REALLY?" Sophia asked as we wrapped up two hours' worth of recording advertisements.

I slumped in my chair and stared at the remnants of my lunch. "I have no flipping clue." I picked at the corner of a sticky note, curling it up with the pad of my finger. "It all happened so fast and I've tried to work it out in my head, but I can't. Why now? Why us? I was moving on and he came in like a wrecking ball."

"Who says you have to stop moving on?" she asked as she stretched her arms.

"I can't move on if I'm stuck in the past."

"Or maybe this is closure. Maybe it's a good thing."

"How can a spontaneous hookup with Caleb be a good thing?"

"Good dick and no future. You already know you hate the man. What's the worst that could happen?" She laughed. "You get divorced? Been there, married that."

But I didn't hate him. Not completely, anyway. At the end of the day, I was more hurt than anything else.

Caleb meant something to me. Or at least he used to.

This version of him—the new him. It was exactly what I had called it when we were recording the podcast.

Unsettling.

I did the math, and when I was subtracted from the equation, it changed the outcome.

He was so much better after me, which meant that I had always been the problem.

Admitting it felt like a knife to the heart.

"I'm just saying," she said as she pitched a water bottle into the trash can. "It could have been way worse."

Caleb's words on the roof echoed in my mind.

It could have been worse.

12

CALEB

Maybe The Fellowship was right.

Blair was, in fact, a witch. Or a demon. *Demoness?*

Whatever being she was beneath the surface of bright, blonde, and bold had possessed me, and it was really fucking inconvenient.

"You okay over there, boss?" Danny, the incompetent lackey I'd saddled the brick mason with, called out.

I looked up from the mess of wiring I'd been trying to unfuck without ripping into the drywall. "What's that?"

Danny dropped his scrawny shoulders. "You look like you're having a stroke or something. Isn't that what people do? They freeze up and then get all droopy?"

I pointed back to the spot where he was supposed to be shuffling fancy, overpriced bricks. "Get going. I need that archway done before the temperature drops."

I blamed the bout of spitting rain and frozen air that had delayed that damned archway all week. I wanted this project wrapped up sooner rather than later. Later meant we'd be finishing the house in the midst of winter snow storms.

If we could get this nightmare of a house wrapped up, this group of guys could enjoy a few months of indoor renovations in the city. The daily commute would suck, but it would beat freezing their balls off every day.

Chicago.

I hadn't stopped thinking about it. Thinking about *her.*

Those soft little moans she made when she was right on the edge. The way her fingers curled into my arm as she clung to me for dear life. The way her body fit against mine like a missing puzzle piece.

She felt like coming home after a long trip.

For the last two years, I had done nothing but actively shove every memory of Blair out of my mind. But after one night with her, it was all rushing back like a flood.

I couldn't control the fact that I was thinking of her at every waking moment. Every time I closed my eyes, she was my first and only dream.

Always had been.

Always, Madly. It's what we had said to each other when we were first married. *I'll always love you madly.* Eventually, we shortened it, but the intent was still there. Always, madly.

If we were both honest, we let the mad love disappear first. And behind it went the 'always.'

But one taste of her and I was slipping further and further down the rabbit hole, going mad once again.

I found the problem with the wiring and went to work, stripping the coating and fixing the jumble until the currents were connected.

My fingers were icicles by the time I was done. I shoved my hands in the pockets of my coat, feeling the warm vibration of my phone. I pulled it out and looked at the notification.

New Episode: One Small Act of Rebellion - Oh Sh*t! I F*cked My Ex-Husband. Listen now!

I would definitely be listening to that.

After two years of Blair sobriety, I had doubled down, listening to every podcast episode she had recorded during our separation and divorce, all the way up until today.

Some nights I sat in front of the fireplace and stared at the flickering flames as I took in her side of things. Some nights I fell asleep listening to the sound of her voice.

I slept better than I had in years.

I wasn't sure what tonight was going to be like. All I knew was that hearing her voice each night as I caught up on blocks of episodes at a time wasn't enough.

I craved her.

Every part of her.

Her mouth. Her wit. Her snark and sass. The weird way she was so peculiarly tidy about her apartment, but her bedroom—the inner sanctum—was a dump. The way she was actually an excellent cook, but relied mostly on takeout these days. *Her barren cabinets were proof of that.* The way she was so insistent on being self-reliant, proving that she didn't need me anymore, but still trusted me enough to show her soft side.

It was that slim swatch of trust that had me turning on the episode as soon as my phone connected to the speakers in my truck. I kept the volume low as the site cleared out for the day.

I hopped on the road and did drive-through errands, swinging into the bank and doing my business on the ATM before heading to the supermarket to have my grocery order loaded into the back of my truck.

"Someone else always gets the better version. The upgrade. You just happened to beta test the new-and-improved him," Sophia, Blair's long-time friend noted.

The thought that I hadn't given Blair my best made my stomach churn.

Then again, hindsight was 20/20, and she wasn't completely innocent in this either.

"It makes me jealous of some fictitious woman," Blair admitted.

Huh. If I was honest, I kind of liked the thought of her being jealous. Jealousy was far better than indifference.

Indifference is a slippery slope. When you stop caring, it's all downhill from there.

"Are you going to see him again?"

"Honestly? I have no idea. Seeing him like this—all confident and brash and secure—it makes me angry that I never got that from him. I wanted the passion. I wanted the heat, and all I ever got was silence and distance. We were married, but I had never felt more lonely. Sex aside, the last forty-eight hours have been completely unsettling. He was completely unsettling."

Unsettling? I was unsettling?

She hadn't seemed unsettled when we shared quiet conversations over hangover food on the roof of her building. Then again, she was a damn good actress.

I rolled the word over in my mind as I unloaded the groceries, haphazardly shoving them in the pantry and refrigerator.

Had Blair remembered to get groceries this week?

"So, what's the challenge for our listeners this week?" Sophia asked from the speaker of my phone as I shoved a half gallon of milk into the fridge.

Blair's voice was crisp and calm. The exact opposite of unsettled. *"Alright, Little Rebels. If you're like me and feeling unsettled, this is your challenge to take charge. Have the awkward conversation. Sort it all out. Be brave enough to put yourself in a temporarily uncomfortable position if it will give you long-term peace. You deserve clarity."*

My heart rammed inside my ribcage as I eyed my truck keys. Blair's words rolled around in my head.

"And what about you?" Sophia asked Blair as the end credit music began to fade in. *"Are you going to have the awkward conversation? Get in that uncomfortable position?"*

Blair laughed. *"I guess you'll just have to tune in next week to see what happens! Thanks for listening!"*

I was already out the door.

———

"Thief!"

I blew past Sabina's open door on a warpath to Blair's. I ignored the swish of the broom fibers as she, no doubt, reached for her weapon of choice.

The heavy thump of my work boots was replaced by the pounding of my fist on Apartment 1205.

"Someone had better be dead or dying," Blair called from inside.

I hadn't bothered giving her a heads up that I was on my way. If she had company, they could fucking leave.

I knocked again, harder this time.

Blair cracked the door open as Sabina's broom handle whacked my ass. I flipped off the old lady and pushed my way inside.

Blair was in silk pajama pants and a matching button-up top. Her hair was piled on top of her head in a nest, giving me easy access to her throat.

"Caleb—what the—"

"Unsettling, huh?" I kicked the door closed. "You think I'm unsettling?"

Her cheeks turned cherry red. Rosy lips parted to speak, but nothing came out.

"Tell me to leave," I said in a low rumble as everything else faded away.

The noise from the busy street outside disappeared. The screech of her feral next door neighbor quieted. The TV in the background was just white nose.

It was just her and I.

And she didn't tell me to leave.

Blinking, she started to come out of her senses. "It's—what time is it?" She looked around. "Did you drive all the way out here from—"

I spun and had her pinned against the door before she could finish rambling. "Tell me to leave, or I'll show you 'unsettling.'"

"Why are you here?" she whispered. Her breath was fresh with the scent of mint toothpaste. A dot of it still lingered at the corner of her mouth.

I closed the space between us, pressing my hips to hers. Sliding my hand up her neck, I fisted her hair at the nape and tugged her head back, forcing her to look up at me. "Maybe I just wanted to give you a little bit of clarity." I trailed the tip of my nose along her temple, breathing in the scent of her shampoo. My lips lingered over hers, brushing with every breath. "And maybe I just couldn't stop thinking about you."

Her eyelids lowered until they were locked on my mouth. "I think I want that clarity."

We crashed together like waves, giving and taking as our lips became one. I kept her pinned to the door. Breaching the seal of her mouth, I pushed my tongue against hers, sharing long, languid strokes. I swallowed down every little whimper. Every quiet moan.

I had never kissed her like this. She had me feeling like a cannibal. I wanted to devour her. Consume her.

Blair had been mine once, but I let her go. Now, I was ready to reclaim what was mine.

Her back arched into me, soft silk sliding in my palms as she pressed closer, trying to work herself against me the way she had at the bar.

But that's not how this was going to go.

I slid my hand beneath the drawstring tie of her flowing pajama pants, cupping her sex and stalling her advances. "Not tonight."

Her eyes popped open in a flash of blue. "Then what the —"

"Tonight," I said with a cocky grin. "You're not going to be taking orgasms without asking."

Her lips turned to a frown, obviously annoyed, but her body told a different story. She rolled her hips, pushing her pussy into my hand to steal a little more pressure.

"Ah-ah-ah—" I pulled back before giving her tender sex a light slap. "Use your manners."

She was breathless and desperate already.

Good. That's how I had felt without her for the last two years. Slowly suffocating.

"Please," she whispered.

I grinned triumphantly and rewarded her by sliding my fingers through her wetness and circling her clit. "That's a good start."

Her knees buckled and she fell into me.

A groan of satisfaction reverberated from my chest as I hoisted her up and over my shoulder. I locked the front door and flipped the deadbolt for good measure before marching her soon-to-be-sorry ass into her lair.

The bedroom was just as much of a nightmare as it was the night fate saw fit to throw us together again, but that didn't matter to me. I tossed her on the bed, grabbed the ends of her silk pants, and yanked them off.

"Hey!"

I laughed as I tossed them onto the laundry heap in the corner. "Are you really worried about one more piece of clothing being on the floor?"

She rolled her eyes.

So that's how this was going to go. I flipped her over. Grabbing her hips, I yanked her ass up, pulled her thighs apart, and spanked her.

Blair tossed her head back like a mare, blonde hair spilling down her spine. Her breath caught in her throat and she went silent.

I palmed her ass, firmly squeezing the spot where my handprint marked her perfect skin.

"I told you to use your manners," I warned.

A devilish smile crossed her face. "What gets me an orgasm faster? Being good or being bad?"

I couldn't help but laugh. "I missed that smart mouth." Sliding two fingers inside of her pussy, I curled them up and stroked her slowly, reveling in the way she went slack.

"Oh my gosh," she whispered.

"As much as you want to test me, I think you'd rather be my good girl." I thumbed her clit until her legs were shaking.

"Caleb—" she gasped on the precipice of release.

I gave her a patronizing smile as I pulled my fingers out, dripping in her arousal, and flipped her onto her back.

Her reverence turned to annoyance. "Caleb!"

I liked seeing her desperate for me. It was night and day compared to the indifference I remembered.

I clicked my tongue. "I know, baby," I soothed with just a hair of good-natured teasing. "I know."

Her breath was thready and wanton. I couldn't remember hearing a more beautiful sound.

"Now, spread your legs for me."

Blair whispered something that sounded a lot like "who the hell are you" as she parted her thighs an inch.

I shook my head and ignored the throbbing in my cock. "That's not what I said," I growled as I grabbed her knees and opened them wide. "All the way. You don't get to hide from me."

Her pussy was wet and bare. Absolutely perfect in every way. I was salivating at the sight.

Blair moved her hands to cover herself, but I didn't give her the chance. Keeping my hands on her thighs, I dove between her legs and met her with one long lap of my tongue up her sex.

This is what had been missing from our drunken hookup.

I wanted to take my time with her. Remember every line and curve. Appreciate every sound. Every breath. Every plea. I wanted her writhing and screaming my name.

I sealed my mouth around her clit, slid two fingers back into her pussy, and listened.

She gasped as I crooked them, slowly working up and down her inner walls until I felt the rough tissue of her G-Spot. I lingered there, teasing it gently as I lathed her clit with my tongue.

Her fingers curled in the sheets, fisting the fabric as she squirmed under my hold.

A sharp cry of delight and desperation ripped from her throat.

"That's it, beautiful. Let it out."

The high-pitched whine that slipped from her clenched teeth nearly made me come in my jeans. As soon as I felt those tale-tell flutters inside of her, I let go of her thigh and pressed firmly on her lower stomach.

The pressure made her detonate like a bomb.

Blair's back arched off the bed, hair fluttering behind her as she gasped and went silent.

Her eyes were clenched shut as she rode out wave after wave of pleasure.

With supersonic speed, I pushed off of her, yanked my jeans down and my shirt off, and was back on the bed.

"This has to go," I said as I fumbled the buttons on her pajama top.

Blair had melted into the mattress, dazed from the orgasm. "I feel all tingly. Don't ruin it."

I chuckled. "Breeze, if you think we're done, you're sorely mistaken." *Fuck the buttons.* I grabbed either side of her collar and yanked down the middle, sending buttons flying across the room. "I didn't drive all this way to get you off once."

Her eyes met mine and I saw it—the vulnerability she hid so well.

"Why did you come?" she said in a small, meek voice.

I settled on top of her, my knees sinking into the mattress as I cupped her cheek. "For you."

13

BLAIR

"I couldn't get you out of my head," Caleb admitted as he lined up our hips, teasing my entrance with the head of his cock. "I had to see you again."

"And kick my door in?" I asked with a nervous laugh.

Caleb buried his nose in the crook of my neck, breathing deeply. I felt his unfairly thick lashes brush against my skin as he closed his eyes. His touch was tender.

His voice was husky as he said, "I wanted you."

Maybe once upon a time.

"I've always wanted you."

"Are you a mind reader?" I whispered as I ran my fingers down his back, feeling each taut muscle. His body was new and familiar all at once.

Caleb's chuckle was warm and comforting. "No. But I know you. Or did you forget that?"

I tipped my head to the side, looking away from him before he saw the glimmering sheen of tears in my eyes. "I didn't forget."

"Look at me," he said as he gripped my chin and turned

my head back. "You keep your eyes on me when I'm inside of you."

And there it was again. The stranger.

How was he both the boy I remembered and a man I was wholly unfamiliar with?

Slowly, I trailed my eyes up his muscled chest, lingering on the tattoo that I hadn't gotten to study during our drunken reverie.

"Eyes on mine," he demanded. "You can look your fill after I've fucked you so hard you can't feel anything but the ghost of me inside of you."

There wasn't a hint of deception in his warm brown eyes. He meant every word.

Caleb notched his dick at my entrance, slowly stretching me wide, inch by inch.

I was captivated by his eyes, but he wasn't looking at mine. He was watching me be filled.

"Fucking beautiful," he murmured. "Seeing you like this." His breath caught, and he paused. "I always wanted you this way," he confessed. "And there's something you should know."

I couldn't handle the adoration in his voice. I needed the beast to come back.

"What's that?" I asked as I dug my fingers into his hips and urged him on.

"I haven't stopped wanting you. Not one day has passed where I haven't craved you."

And with that, he slid home.

"Caleb," I begged as I held on to him for dear life.

Each thrust hit its mark, steady and true. He pleasured me the way I had only ever read about in books. Even in our good years it had never been like this.

"You have the most beautiful breasts I've ever seen," he

said reverently, palming my heavy swell as he leaned forward and pulled my nipple into his mouth.

I bit my lip to keep from going completely feral when he sucked the tight bud between his teeth.

The mellow crash from the first orgasm he gave me was quickly building again. Slow and steady, he rolled his hips, grinding against my clit until I was trembling again. Warm hands, strong and wide, massaged my breasts and toyed with my nipples. Every part of me was electric.

I scraped my nails down his chest, savoring the animalistic groan that escaped from his mouth.

I circled the base of his shaft as he teased me with slower, gentler thrusts.

"You keep doing that and I'm going to fill your tight little pussy to the brim."

Maybe I wanted to hold on to a little control, or maybe I just wanted him to make good on his promise. I reached lower and let my fingertips graze his balls.

Caleb swore at the ceiling and grabbed my hips. "I warned you."

My only response was to wrap my legs around him and hook my ankles together, drawing him impossibly closer.

Sweat shone on his tanned skin in the dim light, making him glow. We were ethereal.

"I'm gonna come," he warned as his tone became slightly unhinged.

"Then do it," I clipped.

"Not unless you're coming with me."

"Caleb, I—"

"If you say you can't, I'm going to take you into the bathroom and fuck you over the sink until you do. You seem to do well in bathrooms."

My cheeks glowed with embarrassment and shame. But there was something else too. The thrill of it all.

Pride.

Rebellion.

He lowered his lips to my ear and smiled. "Come on, Breezy. Be a good girl and come for me."

It was his hand on my clit that did it. I shattered as he collapsed on top of me, grunting as his release spilled inside of me.

His chest pressed against mine and, in this moment, it was like we were back to the way we used to be.

I looked down when he started to ease off of me, only for Caleb to pause and brush his thumb over my entrance, pushing his release back inside off me.

Goosebumps raced down my arms at the satisfied look on his face. The way he puffed his chest out.

"That's my girl," he said before pecking the corner of my mouth.

When I went for a full kiss, he replaced his mouth with his thumb, pushing it between my lips and cupping my cheek as I sucked and teased it like I would if he had put me on my knees. I tasted both of our orgasms on my tongue.

His eyes were midnight black as he watched the slow swallow as I cleaned it off with my mouth.

Gently, he removed his hand and kissed me. "Just lay still. I've got it," Caleb whispered as he eased off of me and headed for the bathroom.

The temporary high was replaced by that unsettling ache in my stomach again.

Was it the guilt from having sex outside of marriage?

As much as I had worked through the way I had been conditioned to be terrified of the consequences, taking that step was still terrifying. Shame was a terrible motivator, but it was definitely a good leash.

Was it because it had been with Caleb? There was safety in him being the one I had sex with, but it felt like I had ripped my heart wide open.

I felt exposed. Unsteady. Vulnerable.

Or was the unsettling churning in my gut from the simple fact that I had liked it?

"You've got that look on your face," Caleb said as he lumbered out of the bathroom with a washcloth in his hand.

"What look?"

"The look you have when you're talking to yourself in your head rather than talking to me."

Reason #102 that you shouldn't hook up with your ex-husband.

He can read you like a book.

I rolled my eyes. "I'm not."

"Liar," he countered.

Reason #103 that you shouldn't hook up with your ex-husband.

He has no problem calling you on your crap.

The bed sank as he stepped over a pile of mostly clean clothes and climbed back on. "Open your legs, baby."

I groaned. "I can't go again. I'm gonna be so sore tomorrow as it is."

"Good," he said with a satisfied smirk. "But that's not what I meant." Caleb nudged my knees apart and pressed the warm washcloth to the apex of my thighs, tenderly cleaning up the mess he had made.

I peered through one eye and watched him.

Unsettling.

That word rang in my head again.

"Caleb?"

"Hmm?"

"How did you..." I sighed. "What you said at my door... About being..."

"Unsettling?" he guessed.

I nodded.

"How many listeners does the—uh—the show have now?"

I racked my brain, but he had fucked all of the demographic statistics out of my brain. "A few million?"

His eyes met mine with honest contrition. "Well, as of about a week ago, you have a few million and one."

The unsettling acid in my stomach turned to stone, sinking deep. "Oh." I worked it over in my mind. "So you've heard me talk about..."

"All of it."

I closed my eyes, wishing I could dissolve into thin air.

I had tried to air my grievances with Caleb years ago, but everything fell on deaf ears. So, I stopped. What was the point?

But the man in front of me wasn't the one I had married. *Or the one I had divorced.*

And that was the most unsettling thing of all.

"So you heard me talk about the night at the bar where we..."

He grinned. "I liked your version of it. You made me sound way manlier than 'I got drunk on sugary cocktails and had my ex-wife dry hump my leg.'"

I dropped my palms onto my face as he tossed the washcloth through the open bathroom door, managing to hit the sink.

"Not my finest moment," I groaned.

His hands lingered on the inside of my thighs. Caleb leaned forward and pressed an open-mouthed kiss to my pussy. "Yeah, well, I think we made up for it."

He blazed a path up my body, kissing my navel, my sternum, my throat, and finally, my lips. "What can I get for you?"

My brows furrowed.

"Water? A snack? A bulldozer for your room?"

I swatted his arm. "I'm fine."

"I'll be right back. I'm just gonna grab some water."

"I told you I'm—"

Caleb poked his head back in. "I know you're lying." He pointed at me. "Sit."

"I'm not a dog," I snapped back at him, staring at his bare ass as he strutted through my apartment. Screw him and his perfectly shaped butt cheeks.

I wondered if he still wore those painted-on white washed jeans to work... The ones that hugged his lower half in an obscene way.

One of the many things the Fellowship got completely wrong was their take on modesty. It wasn't about covering up. Caleb could be in a long-sleeved Henley and those faded Levi's, and I'd be salivating.

He returned with a glass of water, cock swaying as he strode through my bedroom door. "Here you go," he said under his breath as he slid it onto the bedside table.

I watched him cautiously as he moved around my space, completely comfortable, and I hated that.

I wanted Caleb to feel as uneasy as I felt.

He fished around for his jeans and pulled his phone out, checking his messages before tossing it back on the floor and climbing onto the bed with me.

"Whoa—" I said, putting my hands out. "What are you doing?"

He looked left and right. "Uh... I was gonna lay beside you. You used to like that."

"No," I clipped as the unsettling acid inside curdled the sweetness he was giving me. "What are you doing here?"

"I thought I made my intentions pretty clear." He sat up against my headboard and brushed my hair out of my face. Sighing, he showed his cards. "I haven't been able to stop thinking about you since the other week at the bar." Scrubbing his palm down his cheek, he amended the statement. "I haven't been able to stop thinking about you since the minute I got the call that you were in the hospital... And for a long time before."

I rolled away from him and wiggled under the covers. "Willingly signing divorce papers is a weird way to show it, but okay."

"Pot, meet kettle," he countered.

Maybe he had the slightest point.

Irreconcilable differences. That's what the papers had said.

Yeah. Things were pretty irreconcilable when he was always choosing everyone else over me. Over us.

I didn't know how to reconcile that resentment with the new version of him that was in front of me now.

Silence hung between us.

"Just tell me what's on your mind," he said as wide hands met my hips. Caleb stretched out behind me, wrapping his arms around my waist.

My spine met his chest, and I tensed. Closing my eyes to hold back the urge to cry, I let out a trembling breath. "Where was *this guy* when we were married?" I pressed my fingers to the corner of my eyes. "I mean, we never had sex like *that.* Seriously? Where the heck did that come from? And the washcloth? And the water? Who are you?"

He didn't laugh. He didn't even let out the loud breaths he used to when he was biting his tongue. Instead, he tightened his arms around me. "My world was destroyed the day you told me you couldn't do this anymore." He buried his nose in the top of my hair and inhaled deeply. "I hated you until I realized you were right. It wasn't working anymore because we stopped working at it."

A lump hung in my throat. "It was over before I told you I couldn't do it anymore."

"I know," he admitted.

Sophia was right, I realized. Someone would get the better version of him, and it wasn't going to be me.

"You were the last person I wanted to fail," he admitted, and it was a knife to the heart. "I have a lot of regrets."

I could say the same, but I didn't. It was easier than getting hurt again.

"And as far as the sex..." He kissed my shoulder. "I've had some time to uh, reevaluate my skills." He nipped at my ear. "Continuing education and all that, right?"

The sheer thought of someone else having sex with my husb—with Caleb—made me sick.

"Blair..."

"Wow," I choked out. "You really showed me, huh?" I ripped the covers back and went for my pajamas, but he kept me anchored against his stomach. "Moving on and coming back just to rub it in my face."

"It wasn't like that," he clipped.

I pushed away from him, harder this time. "Then what was it like?"

"I tried moving on," he said, raising his voice just a hair. It made me shrink back, halting in his arms. "I really fucking tried, Breeze."

"Don't call—"

"Let me finish," he clipped. "I need you to hear me. I tried. And yeah—maybe I learned some things. I learned that you deserved better. It wasn't my fault for not knowing, but it was my fault for not trying to learn. Or are you forgetting that I was raised the same way you were?" He found my hand and laced our fingers together, pressing our clasped hands against my heart.

I was silent as it sank in.

"But for all intents and purposes, you made it sound like you had moved so far past 'on' that I wasn't even in your rearview mirror anymore; talking about sex and dating on your show. I was trying to be the good guy. I was trying to let you live the life you wanted."

"I wanted my best friend."

"We both signed those papers."

"Then what are we doing here?"

His hand slid up my thigh, smoothing over my hip. "I don't know," he said with a sigh. "But it feels good, doesn't it?"

I shook my head. "That's not a good enough answer for me."

"What do you mean?"

I sat up and yanked the sheet around me to cover myself. "If the paramedics hadn't gone through my phone, we wouldn't be here."

"So?"

"So it's convenient for you! You can't come in here and fuck me senseless and then talk about not being over us and regretting our divorce when I haven't heard from you in two years. Two years, Caleb!"

His phone chimed, startling me.

Caleb groaned.

"What's that?" I asked as I pawed around for a shirt to sleep in since he had gone all 'caveman,' busting the buttons off of my pajamas.

"I gotta drive back to Lily Lake. I need some sleep before work tomorrow."

I let out a dry laugh. "So you really did just drive all this way to fuck me."

He muttered under his breath as he grabbed his boxers and jeans. "I came all this way because I wanted to see you."

I couldn't deal with this. Not now. Not like this. All that head knowledge about coping skills, conflict resolution, and healthy and effective communication that I'd learned in college went out the window when it was my heart on the line.

He toed on his shoes as he straightened his shirt. "When can I see you again?"

I knew what I wanted my answer to be, and I knew I couldn't give it to him. "I don't want to be your safety just because you're afraid to move on and get hurt again."

Caleb's eyes were sharp when he turned them on me. "That's not why I want to see you. I know how much you can hurt me. I've experienced the full range of the pain threshold, and I know I can survive it. But that's not what this is. Maybe I'm not over you. But we were both in that marriage, Blair. I deserve closure."

I let out a sarcastic laugh. "If this is closure to you, then you need to see a therapist."

"Blair—"

I turned to him. "Don't come back here."

The hurt in his eyes was palpable.

"Not without knowing exactly what you want from me. If I hear from you again, you better have a good reason for it. You better know what you want."

"Yeah?" He pocketed his phone and found his keys. "And what are you going to be doing?"

"Figuring out what I want." I reached for the light switch and turned it off. "Goodnight, Caleb. Lock the door on your way out."

He stood there, looming over the bed for a moment before turning and walking out. "This isn't over, Breezy. Not by a long shot."

14

CALEB

I t had been ten days since I'd seen Blair. Ten days since I'd touched Blair. Ten days since I felt her writhing beneath me.

Ten days of having her invade my every waking thought. And that didn't even begin to cover my dreams.

She consumed me.

"What's up your ass?" Gary snapped as he caught up with me on the second floor of the build site.

I snapped out of Blair-induced haze. "Huh?"

"You've been loping around here like a zombie. You keep it up and you're gonna be walking straight through drywall like the Kool-Aid man."

It took a minute for his statement to register. "I'm fine," I clipped as we surveyed the progress the crew had made.

Gary and I had spent most of the afternoon arguing with a bored cop who had nothing better to do than pester us about where the dumpster was positioned on the curb.

He chuckled like he didn't believe me. "You going to your folks' place for dinner tonight?"

I kicked at a stray nail and watched it skitter across the dust-covered floor. "Haven't decided."

He checked his watch. "You're down to an hour."

I swore under my breath.

I really didn't want to go across the lake for a family dinner with fifty people. *And that was just the immediate family*. But the expectation was that I'd take my seat at the table, make polite small talk, not choke anyone, and beg for forgiveness.

At least the food was good, and it meant I wouldn't have to cook for myself.

If I kept my mouth full the whole time, I wouldn't have to talk. I'd bounce my eye contact from group to group, never lingering on one conversation too long, and nod occasionally before looking back down at my plate.

I sighed. "I'll probably end up going."

Gary laughed like he knew I was walking into my own execution.

This would be my twenty-third family dinner since the divorce. I had avoided them for a little while as I licked my wounds and recused myself from the ongoing commentary about my personal life.

My brothers and their wives and kids would mostly ignore the neon elephant in the room. Unfortunately, I'd still have to suffer through snide remarks about Blair from my mom, and disappointment in me from my dad.

"I'm rolling out," Gary said. "We got the green light for the retail space in the city. I'll need you there tomorrow for demo."

I nodded and waved him off.

Honestly, smashing shit might take the edge off. The drive sucked, but I was almost looking forward to heading back to Chicago.

It would have been even better if I could figure out an excuse to see Blair.

The notion reminded me of the hurt in her eyes when she had told me not to come back.

But it wasn't just hurt. It was a menagerie of things.

Fear. Trepidation. Anger. Resentment.

But there was also lust. Longing.

Phantom vibrations from my phone danced down my leg. It was as if my brain was trying to will a message from her into existence.

Something. Anything.

I reached for my phone. *Shit.*

Blair didn't mince her words. If she said not to come back unless I knew what I wanted, she meant it. If I didn't have a good answer for her, she'd slam the door in my face.

Was I actually considering...

I shook the thought out of my head and jogged down to the ground floor, stepping over boxes of tile that had just been delivered. Even though I wanted to be at my parents' house for as little time as possible, being late would be worse than a few extra minutes.

As I made the drive home, I kept eyeing the turn I would take to head out of Lily Lake to get to Chicago.

Don't do it, man. Don't do it.

But I didn't, no matter how strong the temptation was.

Dread sat heavily in my gut as I went through the motions of showering, changing my clothes, and heading around the lake to the house I grew up in.

The single-story ranch had a large footprint. The house was modest, but three thousand square feet felt like a tin can when it was shared by ten young boys, two adults, and four cats.

I fucking hated cats.

I avoided parking in the pile-up in the driveway and, instead, opted to park on the street. I didn't want to get trapped in and be at the mercy of whoever parked behind me to either move their vehicle or leave before me. And, if I was a betting man, I'd put money on me being the first to leave.

Voices echoed from inside the house. A cacophony of kids and babies tested the fortitude of the lightbulbs. I was sure that one of my nieces or nephews was about to shatter every lamp in the house, given how loud they were screeching.

Blair never wanted kids. In fact, she was actively opposed to even discussing the matter. I didn't exactly blame her. Coming from a big family like this, the older kids became nannies as soon as they were old enough to change a diaper and fix a bottle. Especially the girls.

But growing up in a brood of ten mangy boys, things were slightly different than her house of girls.

We were raised as laborers. Nevermind childhood and normal adolescent things like playing sports, hanging out with friends, or—heaven forbid—dating. We were put to work. School was simply a hobby.

Going into construction at fifteen wasn't even a second thought. It's just what I had always done.

"Caleb," my mom said as soon as I stepped through the screen door and into the kitchen. "You made it." She was wearing her favorite apron, embroidered with flowers, as she stirred a pot on the stove.

My stomach rumbled in anticipation.

"Hey," I said as I toed off my boots and added them to the pile at the door. "Smells good."

She beamed proudly. "I've got chili, tater tot casserole, macaroni salad, and gooey butter cake for dessert."

We were interrupted by a train of my nephews bolting through the house. They nearly flattened two of my nieces, who were overseeing the army of little girls putting out the long line of place settings down the row of folding tables.

"You know," I said. "At some point you're going to have to let me put on an addition."

She waved off the suggestion. "We're just fine in here."

I shrugged. "It's either add more space, cancel your monthly dinners, or sell off some children. The family's not going to fit in here much longer."

She snickered. "Well, you'll have to take that up with your brothers. They're blessing us one little bundle of joy after the next."

That was evident by the sheer number of high chairs stuffed along the wall.

I felt bad about it, but I had already lost count of how many nieces and nephews I had. I couldn't remember all of their names.

If I really put my mind to it, I could recite them by birth order, but it would take me twenty minutes and a few tries to get it right.

I was just the weird uncle with no family of his own that everyone pitied.

"Mrs. Dalton, I've gotten all the water glasses out and the kids' cups at their places. What else can I do to help—*oh*!"

I blinked, wondering if I was hallucinating.

The version of Blair I had grown up with stared back at me, wide-eyed. Her dress was long and dotted with tiny flowers. Blonde hair was pulled back with some of it still spilling down her shoulders. Ice blue eyes looked at me, partly in horror and partially in curiosity."

"Greta, do you remember our oldest son, Caleb?" my mother said in the sweet, reedy tone all the women of the Fellowship were taught to speak in.

Well, all the women except for Blair. She was loud, opinionated, and laughed like a foghorn.

But it wasn't Blair, and I wasn't hallucinating.

It was her younger sister, Greta.

I sang the ABCs in my head to remember which younger sister she was.

Anna, Blair, Carrie, Danielle, Emeline, Faith, Greta. Number seven of sixteen.

That made her—what—seventeen? Maybe eighteen years old? If memory served, she was twelve or thirteen years younger than Blair, which means she had probably been around seven or eight years old the last time Blair saw her.

Greta smiled softly and nodded politely. "Yes, ma'am. Of course." Her soft-spoken timber matched my mom's.

I was just about to ask what she was doing here until I spotted my brother, Cade, child number eight of ten, eyeing her from across the room.

Mom wiped her hands on a dish towel and placed them on Greta's shoulders. "Cade and lovely Greta have officially begun their courtship. Isn't that wonderful?"

It wasn't wonderful. She was a child. Seventeen and dating —sorry—*being courted by* my twenty-one-year-old brother.

"Greta's been over here spending lots of time with me. It's been so wonderful to have a daughter—" she paused to fake a childish giggle "—*future* daughter who wants to learn about keeping a proper home so she can honor her husband."

And there it was. The subtle dig at Blair.

Greta looked at her feet, and I couldn't quite read the expression on her face. "I've loved learning how you maintain such a peaceful home."

Ha. Peaceful home my ass.

According to my mother, a peaceful home was one where her husband—my father—had no worries. She cooked for him. Cleaned for him. Washed his clothes, folded them, and put them away for him. She'd pull out his clothes for the next day, iron his underwear, and make sure everything was just so, even though he was a grown man who could grab his own shirt and pants.

She'd serve him his plate before getting her own. She'd clear his dishes away and serve him dessert so he didn't have to lift a finger.

Never mind that she had ten boys to wrangle, too.

But she did it all because that's what her mother did for her father. People always assume that cult leaders hold all the power, but that's not it at all. It's the followers who purport it to the next generation.

When I really thought back on it, it was never the men telling the women they were supposed to do these things. It was the women teaching the girls.

Peaceful... It was honestly hard for me not to laugh.

Was it peaceful for her to cry in the pantry when she thought no one was around because she was overwhelmed?

But she never complained, because 'righteous women didn't complain.' They were supposed to be grateful to have a husband at all.

But if a 'good' husband simply meant he wasn't a physically abusive human being, then the bar was on the floor.

Maybe that explained why Blair had gone on a date with a woman after our divorce. That podcast episode still rolled around in my head.

At least I always picked out my clothes and manned the dishwasher.

Blair was the "cram everything in and pack it tight" type. I was the dishwasher architect, only loading what fit in the clearly defined spaces.

I had a theory that one type always married the opposite.

Greta didn't make eye contact with me. Not that I expected her to. I almost opened my mouth to tell her that I had seen Blair and that she was well, the way I used to update Blair after I ran into someone from her family.

Blair had gone no-contact with them shortly after we were married and moved to Chicago, but I knew deep down that she still cared. *Even if she didn't know how to show it.*

I was shooed into the open-concept space that served as the den and dining room. A few years ago, my mom finally conceded and let me knock out a non-load-bearing wall so we didn't have to split the family in two different rooms. I blamed Blair for making me more acutely aware of it, but it always tended to fall where the men and boys sat around the large farm table that me and Cameron—my next younger brother—had built. The women were always left to wrangle the younger children and babies and get them fed in the den.

Maybe it didn't fix the unequal burdens, but taking down that wall had been a silent middle finger to it all. It didn't fix anything, but at least my brothers had to hear the noise and see the chaos.

It was my one small act of rebellion.

Blair would have been proud.

I took a seat next to my fourth brother, Cody. At twenty-three, he already had three kids with his wife, Janey.

As the brood of Daltons filled in around the table, I was acutely aware that the seat next to mine remained empty.

"Just in time," my mom said, beaming as a shadow appeared behind me.

No.

No... No. No. No.

Cody choked back a laugh.

Priscilla craned over the back of the chair parked beside me and put an oversized basket of dinner rolls in the middle of the table. "My apologies. With the nip in the air, the dough took a little longer to rise than usual."

I didn't miss the pleased nod of approval my mom gave Priscilla when she took the seat beside me.

Thankfully, I didn't have to come up with something to say to her. My father stood, the cue for everyone to bow their heads for him to say grace. But as soon as he said 'amen,' she pounced.

"Oh, don't you worry about a thing," Priscilla cooed as she snatched my plate from in front of me. "I'd be honored to fill your plate tonight."

I managed to keep one hand on it before she could make a beeline for the buffet set up in the kitchen. "That's not necessary."

A rough cough caught my attention. I looked up only to find my father raising a silver eyebrow. "Let the young lady fill your plate, Son. Someone oughta do it. At least she was raised right and knows her place as a helpmeet. Not like that no-good, worldy—"

Someone elbowed him and shut him up before he said her name.

I looked across the table and spotted Greta's eyes bouncing to me before quickly darting away as she picked up Cade's plate and hurried into the kitchen.

My father harrumphed. "I'm thankful for my six boys who head their families the way a man's supposed to. And I'm thankful for the three boys below them who are following in the older ones' footsteps." His disappointed gaze slid to me. "The prodigal son may have been a disgraced failure in need of repentance, but at least he came home. I suppose I should be grateful for that first step."

My mother reappeared with his plate piled high, and a lifeless smile on her face. "At the very least we should be so grateful that your quiver is still empty and that you still have some time to fill it with good, strong arrows."

Because that's all us boys were to them.

Arrows.

It was something the reverend often called children. *Arrows*. And parents with a quiver full of arrows were blessed.

But the thing about arrows is that they're supposed to be fired. Launched. Sent out.

That was never their end game, though.

Their quiver was full, but collecting dust. They put us on a shelf. Never to be used, only replicated and treated like a trophy.

My stomach soured as Priscilla placed a dinner plate in front of me. "I hope I got everything you like." She eyed me up and down with a look of what could only be described as sin, and smiled bashfully as she picked up her plate to get back in line. "You work so hard. You must need a lot to fill up."

My stomach stirred again. I wanted to blame it on acid reflux, but that wasn't anywhere close to the culprit.

It was the memory of sitting here with Blair beside me during our courtship, the way Greta and Cade were sitting.

Not touching, barely speaking, trying to learn to communicate with silent looks as not to break the rules.

I'm scared to get married, Blair first said to me in a stolen moment when I was fifteen and she was fourteen.

I had just shrugged it off and told her that our marriage would be blessed if we just followed all the rules. If we didn't step out of the umbrella of safety our reverend upheld, nothing could go wrong.

Right?

I was naïve then, just like I was naïve now, thinking that I could sit here, make small talk, and keep Blair out of my memory.

She was a ghost. But instead of haunting a room or even a house, she haunted me.

Priscilla reached for the bread she had brought. "Would you like a roll? No raisins this time."

My stomach turned again.

"You know," I said, spearing a green bean out of the tater tot casserole. "I'm trying to go low-carb. Turning thirty last year hit me like a ton of bricks."

My dad nodded in agreement.

My mom facepalmed.

My brothers and their wives snickered at the dodge.

Priscilla's eyebrows drew in with determination. "Low-carb bread with no raisins for next time. Got it."

Fuck me.

———

"How's that development coming along?" Carter, brother number three, asked as we sat around the living room, talking over the clink and slosh of dishes being washed in the kitchen.

"Good." I drained the rest of the coffee in my mug. "We're finishing up the last property for this portion of the development, and Gary's got a retail renovation lined up next."

Cade nodded. "Probably good to be inside for the winter."

"You can say that again."

Before I could set my mug down, Priscilla had the coffee pot in hand and was about to refill it.

"I shouldn't," I said, putting my hand on top of the mug. "It'll keep me up all night."

Her smile was cloying. "Of course." She scurried off to the kitchen, tittering amongst my mother, Blair's sister, and my sisters-in-law.

"Nice girl," my father said, tipping his head toward Priscilla.

Nice girl who can't take a hint.

I grunted and wished I had taken the refill just so I'd have something to aid in circumventing the awkward comments.

"She'll make a good wife for the right man, I suppose," he continued.

Cade cut his eyes to me.

I cut my eyes back before turning them down into the empty mug. *Yeah. I know he's egging me on.*

"But even the most righteous of wives still need a strong leader to keep order and peace in the house." He shook his head in dismay. "Nothing worse than a quarrelsome wife." His eyes narrowed at me. "And nothing worse than a man who can't be *a man.*"

I scoffed, earning myself a sneer from his direction.

"I never thought my oldest son—my namesake—would be such a disappointment. Letting the wife we picked for you wear pants in that failure of a marriage."

"It's 'wear *the* pants,' Dad," Cade chimed in.

He just grunted. "Works both ways in his case." He pointed a finger at the open kitchen door. "And now there's a pretty lady willing to be courted—something you should be grateful for at your age—and you're looking down at her like she's chopped liver."

How did we get from talking about construction jobs to this?

I glanced at the time on my phone and willed a text or call to save me from the inquisition.

Nothing.

Not even one of those stupid videos of mic'd up football players that Gary sends me.

The footrest to his recliner snapped back into place, and he sat up. "Reverend Reinard's agreed to see you for counseling," he said rather definitively. "Since you're *divorced*—" he uttered the word like it was coated in poison "—should you pursue one of the available girls in the Fellowship for courtship, you'll need to rejoin the congregation and go through the necessary steps to make amends for your transgressions."

I stifled an eyeroll and a snide comment.

Mend my relationship with my family. That's why I was here, I reminded myself. And if it meant I had to sit through three hours of judgment, so be it.

"Now, before the Reverend will grant permission for you to initiate a courtship, he wants to see that you can provide financially for your wife and family so you don't lead her astray by letting her have a worldly job. That was your first mistake last time. There's no need for your wife to go to college and rack up all those bills just to be a mother and homemaker. Not like that good-for-nothing whore you couldn't keep on the straight and narrow would have ever given you children and served you the way a woman should. Worldly institutions like universities only serve to infiltrate their minds." He snorted. "Women are the weaker sex, after all."

My blood boiled and I nearly crushed the ceramic mug in the palm of my hand.

"It wasn't like that," I grunted. "*She* wasn't like that."

Cade's eyebrows lifted in surprise, but he didn't speak up.

Me defending my ex-wife two years after we cut ties definitely wasn't on their family dinner bingo cards.

But stranger things had happened.

Memories of Blair crying in the bathroom after we told our families we were moving to Chicago so she could go to college were burned in my memory. We had only been married for eight months.

I thought the conversation had gone well. I never understood what she was so upset about. It was her choice and she knew how cataclysmic the fallout of going against The Fellow-ship would be.

I looked my father dead in the eye. "Did you ever say that to her?"

He played dumb. "What?"

I set the mug on the carpet. "Did you ever tell Blair she was the weaker sex? A good-for-nothing whore who should serve her husband."

He scoffed, then hemmed and hawed.

That was my answer.

I pulled my phone out of my pocket, firing off a text I should have sent ten days—or two years—or twelve years ago, then stormed out the door.

15

BLAIR

ut we were both in that marriage, Blair.

Eight words had been echoing in my mind for the last ten days. In a pragmatic sense, I knew he was right.

Caleb and I had been married to each other for nine years.

But in an idealistic sense, we weren't two people sharing one life. We were each doing our own things. Chasing our own goals. Living our own lives.

Not that couples have to be tied to each other in a joint-Facebook account kind of way, but shouldn't a marriage have unity? A common direction?

We never had that.

The more I pulled away from our upbringing in Lily Lake, the more he resented me for it.

The more he tried to maintain a connection with our past, the more bitter I became.

Until one day, it all fell down.

Our schedules were opposite. He would wake up early in the morning to drive to whatever job site he had to be at that day, while I started my day later and worked until midnight. We saw each other in passing during dinner time, but I was always in the middle of something and Caleb was too tired to care.

I didn't want to spend our only waking hours together fighting.

So I stayed silent.

Silence turned to loneliness.

And loneliness turned to leaving.

"It's a crime, really," a warm baritone said, startling me out of my thoughts.

The buzz of Chicago's People of the Year awards swirled around me, but a familiar cologne was what snapped me out of my daydreaming.

I looked over my shoulder and spotted tall, blond, and handsome grinning at me like the two of us shared a secret.

"Collin Cromwell," I said by way of a greeting. I hadn't even thought about the man since we flirted at the Preservation Society dinner. Granted, I had been a little busy suffocating to death and dealing with my ex-husband.

Now, with a glass of something amber in one hand, he stood in front of me looking sinful like the devil. "Miss Dalton," he said with a step forward.

Instinctively, I fiddled with the place my wedding band used to sit.

It had been modest; a thin silver band with one small diamond.

Caleb promised me that, when we could afford it, he'd get me—in his words—a better ring.

A teenager could only afford so much.

But I loved that ring... I had never wanted a bigger one.

I just wanted Caleb.

Nostalgia made way for outrage.

How dare he invade my thoughts right now?

When I looked Caleb dead in the eye after we'd finished fucking like rabbits, I had meant every word.

Don't come back here. If I hear from you again, you'd better have a good reason for it. You better know what you want.

And then there was what I had said when he asked what I was going to be doing in the meantime.

Figuring out what I want.

Growing up, I never had many choices to make. They were always made for me; whether it was my parents, our reverend, or the beliefs of The Fellowship.

What I wore. What I ate. How I spoke. Who I talked to. How loud I got to be. What my opinions were. Who I was going to marry. Where we would live. What every day of my life would look like until I died.

Going to college had been a culture shock in more ways than one. It wasn't just that I was out in the world. I got to make my own choices.

And if figuring out what I wanted meant that I got to flirt with a handsome man without feeling guilty, then dammit, I was going to.

Caleb could kiss my ass for making me think about him when I owed him nothing.

"I'm glad to see you're well," he said with an air of concern lacing his voice.

I laughed nervously. "Going to the ER the first time we met definitely wasn't my finest hour."

His smile was kind. "But we're here now. I think that counts for something."

My stomach churned, but it wasn't that light flip-flop that happened whenever Caleb was near.

I blamed it on the champagne in my hand. It was the first time I had been near alcohol after the appletini debacle, and just the smell was making me queasy.

At least I knew I wasn't pregnant, thanks to shark week tearing me to bits the day after Caleb—well—tore me to bits.

Flirt, Blair. You can do this.

I looked around the room. "Are you here with someone?"

"A few colleagues, yes," he said. "But if your question is if I'm here with a date, then the answer is no."

I smiled as I brushed my hair off of my shoulder. "Tell me you're not sitting ten tables away tonight."

He smiled with his lip trapped between his teeth; a bashful sort of look. "Tell me you didn't throw away my card."

It was probably still in my clutch from the charity dinner.

"I still have it," I said. *I think.*

He looked genuinely surprised. "And here I was, thinking you had asked for it just to throw it away when the night was over to let me down easy."

I laughed. "That was my master plan, but I got derailed by some shellfish."

"Then, as sorry as I am for your near-death experience, I'm glad you never got the chance."

I opened my mouth to retort when my phone buzzed. I fished it out of the pocket of my dress just to make sure it wasn't anything life-or-death.

CALEB

What are you up to?

Definitely not life-or-death. He could kiss my ass for all I cared. I was Blair motherfreaking Dalton. Sure—I still had his last name because, frankly, changing it the first time was a pain. I didn't want to do it again, and I hated the people who shared my maiden name even more.

But that was neither here nor there.

He had no hold over me tonight.

"Tell me," I said as Collin's palm found the small of my back, leading me across the event hall in the Chicago History Museum. "If the Preservation Society dinner hadn't ended in me being whisked away by paramedics, where would we have gone after the event ended?"

Collin said polite hellos to acquaintances as we wove through clumps of the Windy City's elite. "You really want to know?"

"I want to know how tonight might end if you don't steal my breath like you did last time."

Nice line, Blair. You can totally flirt!

Screw you, ex-husband with a monster dick.

He paused by a museum display and slid his hand just a little lower, caressing the curve of my ass. "I would have found the closest drive-thru and ordered the biggest cheeseburger they had."

I let out a long laugh. "Good answer."

He snickered. "Don't get me wrong, I like a nice dinner at an upper-crust event every now and then, but I'm always starving afterward."

My phone buzzed twice.

Collin lifted an eyebrow. "Emergency in podcast-land?"

I ignored my phone and danced around the topic of my ex-husband blowing up my phone. "Nothing urgent."

My heart raced as his eyes locked on a darkened corridor.

His smile was adorably boyish and panty dropping at the same time. "Let's explore."

I picked up the hem of my floor-length gown and chased after him as he tugged on my hand. When a server passed by with a tray of discarded drinks, Collin took the liberty of relieving us of our glasses.

My phone kept vibrating.

"I bet you say that to all the girls you pick up at fancy dinners."

We hid behind a large bust of some notable person from three hundred years ago. Collin shrouded me with his body. "Only you, Cinderella." He cupped my cheek. "You ran away without leaving me so much as a glass slipper last time."

I met Collin's eyes, but his were locked on my mouth.

"Maybe I'll leave you more than a shoe."

His hand slid up my waist, slowly memorizing every curve. "Oh really?"

Our lips brushed. I tasted bourbon as his breath danced along my mouth. I tipped my chin up just as he—

"Your phone is vibrating again," he whispered.

I closed my eyes. "It's nothing. Where were we?"

But the buzzing never stopped. Collin rested his forehead on mine. "See what it is and then we can—" he stepped in, closing the gap between our bodies "—pick back up where we started. I won't let you turn into a pumpkin at midnight."

"It's really not—"

Motherfucker. The damn thing started going off again.

I was about to throw it in the closest trashcan. Did I actually need a phone?

"Blair, I can see you're thinking about whatever it is." That easy smile turned playboy. "And I don't want you distracted for the foreseeable future. Check your phone. Make sure it's not your mom or your neighbor or your landlord saying your place flooded and caught fire."

"Fine." I relented, quickly fishing my phone out. As I typed in my passcode, something warm pressed to my neck.

Goosebumps danced up my spine as he kissed my skin.

Caleb. Four texts, three missed calls. Two voicemails.

I swiped and opened the texts.

CALEB

I need to see you tonight.

CALEB

Answer your fucking phone.

CALEB

Fuck it. I'm driving to your place. Be there in however long it takes me to blow the speed limit signs and get into the city.

CALEB

I know what I want, B.

"Everything okay?" Collin asked as he nipped at my earlobe, then scraped his teeth along my neck.

My 'uh-huh' was warbled.

"No floods or fires?"

Incoming call: Caleb Dalton

The name on the screen caught Collin's attention, and his face fell. "Why do I have a feeling that's not your brother?"

I swallowed. "Well, I don't have brothers, but I'm guessing if I did they wouldn't call me over and over again."

He ran his tongue over his lips while he waited me out.

"My ex," I admitted.

Collin stiffened. "Is he harassing you? I'll take you to the police station if he's—"

"No, no—" I shook my head. "He's my ex-husband, but he's not like that. He's... We're..." I looked up at him with regret filling my eyes. "I don't know what's going on right now."

"Well," he said. "I don't like being a consolation prize, but if you figure it out and find yourself remembering that you have my card, call the number on it." Before I could make sense of what was happening, Collin placed the softest kiss to my lips.

And there it was. The first time I had been kissed by someone other than Caleb Dalton.

It tasted like poison.

There were no sparks. No butterflies. Just a churning hatred in my gut.

And I knew exactly who I was going to take it out on.

———

"*You*," I hissed as I stormed down the hallway in front of my apartment.

Caleb stood at my door, pounding on it like a ghost was going to answer. His head snapped to the left, eyes narrowing on me as he watched the hem of my dress swish along the floor. "Why do you look so pissed? I told you I was on my way."

I stabbed a finger at him. "You motherfucking cock-blocker!"

He actually looked surprised. "What the hell are you talking about?"

I planted my hands on his chest and shoved. *Hard.* "I was this close—" I held up pinched fingers "—this *freaking close* to finally—"

My back slammed into the door as his mouth latched on mine. I let out a squeak of surprise, but it was muffled by a swipe of his tongue along my lips.

"Get that fucking dress off," he rasped.

I reared back and swung. The clap of my palm against his cheek would have felt so good if he hadn't caught my wrist and pinned it to the door.

"I told you not to come back here," I panted as he pressed his entire body against mine.

"Unless I knew what I wanted," he countered.

"Don't play games with me," I snapped, shoving again, but he didn't budge.

"I'm not fucking playing, Breeze."

Now I really wanted to smack him.

Caleb threaded his hands up my neck, tangling in my hair. He yanked, tipping my chin up. "I want you. I haven't stopped wanting you. I don't fucking care if you're trying to move on. I'm not going to let you."

"We got divorced."

"Yeah, because of other people."

I scoffed. "Is that what you think? Or did you sleep through the therapy sessions we went through to try to revive something that was already dead?"

His eyes darkened. "I don't care what my reasons were or what your reasons were. They weren't fucking good enough for me to walk away from my best friend."

There was conviction in his voice as he trailed his hand down my waist, fisting the satin. "I hate myself for losing you."

Desire was the fuel and anger was the spark. "Then you'd better prove to me that you're not the guy I married, or the guy I divorced."

Before I could make a move to unlock the door, his hand shackled my throat, pinning me to the door. With a velvet touch, the pad of his thumb grazed my neck. "You smell like someone else's cologne," he growled. "And there's a mark on your neck."

I didn't cower. "I told you I was figuring out what I wanted."

His smile was slow and sinister. "Then I guess I'll have to

kiss this body until the only marks on it are mine, and fuck you like the dirty girl you are until all you smell like is me."

I smirked. "Put up or shut up."

Caleb yanked my keys out of my hand and unlocked the door. "Just to make one thing perfectly clear."

"What's that?" I asked, breathless as we stumbled in.

"I'm not going to fuck you like I did when we were married."

16

CALEB

F abric tore as I gripped the back of her gown and pulled it apart. I didn't have time for thirty tiny buttons.

"You're going to do exactly as I say," I ordered as I stomped on the hem of her dress and made it drop to the floor.

The silhouette of her spine made my dick thicken as fabric pooled at her feet.

Microscopic strings of satin forming a "T" dipped between her ass cheeks and wrapped around her hips. She wasn't wearing a bra under that dress and, fuck me, I loved it.

"Are you going to be my good girl?" I whispered as I trailed my knuckle down her spine.

"Probably not," she sassed.

I chuckled. "Yeah, you will." I skimmed my palms over her shoulders and down her arms. "You want to obey me." I pulled her thong aside and trailed my finger through her sex. "You're wet just thinking about it."

Her knees wobbled. "I'm n-not."

I pushed one finger inside of her and slowly curled it against her inner muscles. "Yeah, you are. All those years of following the rules and it not being enough—I'll make it enough. I'll make you feel better than you ever have. Do exactly as I say and I'll tell you what a good girl you are."

She whimpered with need, and it was music to my fucking ears. "Caleb—"

"But I don't appreciate you lying to me, so we're going to have to do something about that first."

I grabbed the back of her thong and yanked, forcing the thin line of fabric to pinch her sensitive pussy.

She squealed in shock and delight. Before she could say anything else, I grabbed both sides and ripped them apart.

The whip of my belt sliding through the loops made her gasp. "Kneel."

Her knees dropped immediately.

I doubled my belt over. "Over the coffee table."

She reached out to push off the couch and stand when I gave her a firm swat across her ass.

"You'll crawl. I like watching the curve of your back. Show it off to me, baby."

Blair was hesitant at first, shuffling across the floor before she fell into a feline strut, swaying her hips back and forth.

I hung back, watching her as she laid her torso on the coffee table and arched her back, presenting her ass nicely.

"Such a pretty little body," I said as I toed off my shoes. "You want me to wreck this body, don't you?"

Her cheek was pressed to the glass, but I caught her nod.

"Knees wider," I said as I trailed the loop of the belt up her inner thigh.

She wiggled, shuffling until her legs were further apart.

Her pussy peeked out at me, pink and glistening.

"That's my good girl."

Her smile was punctuated by a cry when I cracked the belt across her ass. I knelt behind her and squeezed, dampening the sting with my palm. "How'd that feel?" I said quietly, checking in with her.

I had a feeling I knew what she was craving after a near-decade of blasé, under-the-covers, lights-off, missionary sex. I wanted to throw her into the deep end.

"Good," she panted, chest heaving on the table.

I hunched over her body, covering it with my own, and cupped her pussy with my hand. The pressure was enough to make her cry out again. "That's good, baby. God, I love hearing you make that sound. Do it again."

A smile winked at the corner of her mouth. "Then give me a reason too."

I grinned. "That's what I want to hear, beautiful. Give me that mouthy girl I fell for. I've missed her."

Before she could retort, I whipped her pussy.

Again.

Again.

Again.

Her cries of pleasure were music to my ears.

"You're dripping," I rasped as I knelt behind her and lapped at her pussy.

She squealed, bucking back at me as I flicked her clit. "Caleb!"

"Keep my name on your lips."

I straightened up, but kept two fingers at her entrance, spreading them in a 'V' to hold her open.

She tried to close her legs, but I trapped them open with my knees.

"Is this pussy tired of being empty?"

Blair clawed at the glass top for purchase. "Yes."

I opened her wider and flicked her clit. "What would make it feel better?"

"You—*Please*."

"I don't think you want my cock bad enough." I spanked her pussy with my open palm. "I don't think this pussy is wet enough."

"It—it is—" she gasped.

I stroked her clit, making her legs shake. "There you go. That's better."

I teased between her legs until she was a trembling mess. When I started to hear her promised chants, pleading for an orgasm, I wrapped my arms around her waist and threw her over my shoulder.

"Caleb!"

I marched toward the kitchen, undeterred.

She squirmed. "Bedroom is the other way."

"I'm not fucking you in a goddamn bed, Blair." I cleared the table with one swipe of my arm, sending plates shattering across the floor, and laid her out on her back. "You're not hiding under the sheets, and the lights are going to be fucking on so I can see every little piece of you. You don't get to hide from me anymore."

I dropped my jeans, hooked my hands behind her knees, and pulled her ass to the edge of the table. If we broke it, I would build her a new one.

She opened her mouth to speak as I notched my dick in her entrance, but I cut her off with one sharp thrust.

"Shit," she hissed, eyes screwing shut.

I gripped her thighs, holding on in a feeble effort to restrain myself. "Relax."

"I can't."

"Fucking *relax*, Blair," I gritted out. "I'm not in yet."

"Too big," she whimpered.

"You took me before."

"I was drunk the first time."

"You were sober the last time. You're scared." I cupped her cheek. "I'm not going to hurt you, baby."

"You might," she whispered.

We both knew she wasn't talking about sex.

I bent over her rigid body and kissed her, soft and slow like a waltz. It was familiar yet invigorating, like a cup of hot coffee on the first cool morning of the season.

"Relax for me," I whispered on her lips. "It's safe to let go."

The promise was enough for her to let a breath slip from her perfect lips. I realigned my hips and pushed forward.

"There you go," I said as sheathed myself in her warmth. "So good. You feel fucking amazing, Blair."

I smiled as her eyes opened. Blair swallowed, then exhaled.

"That's better. Keep breathing."

I steadied my pace, watching the bounce of her breasts with each thrust.

Blair raised her arms to cover her chest, but I grabbed her wrists and pinned them to her sides.

"Wrap your legs around me."

She locked her ankles together behind my back while she fought against my grip.

"Caleb," she said softly, closing her eyes to hide from the light hanging overhead. "I need a blanket or something."

I shook my head and drove in harder, grinding against her clit. "You don't need to hide. Let me show you how perfect this body is. How much it deserves to feel good."

I pulled out, but instead of pushing in hard and fast, I sank in slowly, savoring the feel of her. "You're so beautiful." I let go of her wrist and cupped her breast. She writhed in delight when I squeezed her nipple. "So goddamn beautiful. I love seeing you laid out in the light." I leaned over her and kissed her sternum. "So beautiful. I will burn every sheet and blanket in this apartment so you're never able to hide from me again."

I released her other wrist and massaged her clit. Blair's back went rigid.

"There you go," I whispered as I felt my own release creeping in on me.

Her toes curled. Nails clawed at the table. Blonde hair was splayed out in a mess behind her head.

I pushed my cock deep inside of her and memorized the fluttering pulses of her impending orgasm.

"Just like that," I soothed as I played her like an instrument.

Her breath hitched, and then she detonated.

I thrust into her as she jolted on the table before grabbing her hips, slamming into her, and spilling my release inside of her.

I dropped forward, resting my forearms on either side of her head. Her lips were parted as she caught her breath.

"You did so good," I said as I brushed loose strands of hair out of her face. "So fucking good. You're incredible, you know that?"

Blair hit me with a lazy smile as she squeezed her thighs together, keeping my cock deep inside of her as it softened. "Don't move. I feel all glittery and if you do it'll go away."

I chuckled. "I won't." I pecked her cheek. "I'm not going anywhere."

———

THE SHOWER CUT OFF, and I listened as Blair rummaged around with the jars of face goop and hair goop she had lined up on the bathroom counter like soldiers.

Finally, the door cracked open and she slipped out. A

fluffy white towel was wrapped around her body, tucked in between her breasts.

I eased out of her bed and caught her by the waist before she could start pawing through the pile of clothes on the chair in the corner like she was a first responder digging for landslide survivors.

"C'mere," I murmured into the top of her hair.

"I need to get dres—"

"You got somewhere to be?"

I knew what she was doing. Blair was reverting to the dynamic we shared when our toothbrushes lived side by side.

But that's not how this was going to work.

Not this time.

"No," she said weakly.

"Good. Me either." I untucked the towel and let it fall away. "Get in bed."

"But I have to—"

"Get in the fucking bed, Blair," I clipped. "Don't be difficult."

She opened her mouth to retort when I picked her up by the waist and threw her on the mattress.

"You cleaned in here," I noted as I crawled across the sheets. "Mostly." The chair of no return was full of clothes, but at least I could see the floor.

"Rage cleaned," she clarified. "After the last time you were in here."

I knew she meant it as a dig, but I didn't care. "You can put your claws in," I said, shuffling she sheets over us. "Fighting won't make me do anything except hold you closer."

She was stiff as a board as I settled on the pillow with her head tucked her in the crook of my arm. Blair's nose gently bumped my chest.

I pressed my mouth to her forehead. "What's on your mind?"

Blair just shook her head. "Nothing," she whispered.

Liar.

Her fingertips came up and dabbed at her eyes.

"Hey–" I wrapped her up in my arms, holding her against my heart. Her head fit so perfectly in my chest. For the first time in years, I felt like a completed puzzle. "Talk to me. You like talking." When she didn't, I pried. "Are you hurting? Sore?"

"I'm fine."

I tucked a strand of damp hair behind her ear. "I'm asking you to tell me what's going through your head because I want to know."

She was silent but I could see her working it over in her mind, forming her argument, deconstructing it, and putting it back together again.

Still, I waited.

"I shouldn't like that," she said quietly.

"Like what?"

"Sex... Like that."

I smoothed my hand down her hip and over her ass, gently caressing it. "Why?"

She sniffed and curled in closer. "I shouldn't want to be pinned down and—"

"Fucked," I supplied.

A pretty blush painted her cheeks.

Blair closed her eyes, hiding those baby blues from me. "I shouldn't want—need—to be called a good girl. I've worked so hard to get past that. I shouldn't want to—"

"You're allowed to want whatever you want, baby." With long, smooth strokes I rubbed her back. "It's okay to crave the affirmation you never got before. It's okay to want to cede control for once in your life. It's okay to reclaim a part of yourself that was defined by others and find pleasure in it." I tucked her head under my chin as she softened into me. "It's okay to trust me. Even if it's just for the next ten minutes, I'll take it."

17

BLAIR

*N*othing you can do will ever be good enough.
  If you feel accomplished because you think you did something well, that's pride. Is committing one of the seven deadly sins worth feeling like you're good?

I could still hear the Reverend's voice between my ears. But it wasn't just his voice. It was my mother's. My grandmother's. My father's. The deacons. My sisters.

Everyone.

You are not good. At your core, you're a dreadful wretched person.

Maybe that's why I hadn't stopped pushing myself—well —ever.

Caleb's heartbeat was the only thing that grounded me.

I was about to combust. I wanted to scream, throw up, run a marathon, have a good cry, and have another ride on his dick, all at once.

Unfortunately for me, the crying won.

Caleb had settled in my bed, taking his old spot and pulling me into his chest the way he used to.

It was all too familiar and completely strange at the same time. Like being trapped in the twilight zone.

It made me remember the early days when we tried.

It made me remember the slow fade where we went from best friends to strangers.

I blinked through the tears and traced the tattoo on his chest. I'd never gotten a chance to ask him about it, but there were more pressing things on my mind at the moment.

"Why did you pick up the phone when the hospital called in the middle of the night?"

Caleb wasn't shocked. He didn't even flinch. "Because I've been waiting for you to call for the last seven hundred days."

My heart clenched. "Why didn't you call me?" Closing my eyes was easier than constantly wiping away the tears.

Caleb caught one on his thumb and brushed it away. "Because all I ever wanted was for you to be happy and to have the life you dreamed of." He sighed. "I tried to work hard enough to make it happen for you. But you being happy meant that I didn't get to be a part of it. So I stepped aside." He tilted my chin up and placed the softest kiss on my lips. "Because you have always been the most important thing to me. Always."

He had the words, but he didn't have the music.

Something had always come before me.

His family.

The community we left behind.

His job.

It's why I had started working later and later into the evenings when the podcast took off. I preferred to sleep alone than beside a stranger.

"Keep your eyes closed," he murmured into my hair as he pulled the blankets over our tangled bodies. "Remember sitting under the tree by the lake when we were kids?"

I nodded.

"Picture that in your mind. Just you and me. It's dark. The world's asleep." He paused, breathing with me as calm rushed over us in a flashback. "You used to tell me everything under that tree."

"It was..." I stopped myself and thought it over. "*You* were my safe place. When I lost that, I lost everything that was important to me."

Caleb grunted in disagreement. "You had your degree. The podcast was taking off. You had the lifestyle. You had all these other people telling you what a good job you were doing. You didn't need to hear it from me. You didn't need me anymore."

"You were the only person I wanted to hear it from!" I cried, pushing him away and rolling onto my side. "I wanted *you* to be proud of me."

But instead of rolling to his side and giving me his back the way I had, he pulled me backward into his chest. "I didn't want you to do those things for me. I wanted you to be proud of yourself." There was a long break in the conversation before he spoke up again. "Why did you end it?"

I shook my head. "That's a dead horse and we've beaten it in couple's therapy."

"Tell me," he said. "If all you cared about was me, then tell me why you ended it."

"Because I was alone," I blurted out.

"We were married."

"Yeah, we were. And as I started to grow up from the eighteen-year-old you kissed at an altar, I felt invisible. I was there, but you didn't really see me. I was just half of the chores. Half of the rent or mortgage. And half of a bed." I wiped my eyes. "I wanted so desperately for you to see me. What hurt the most is when I left, you only saw the empty pillow. You didn't see how empty I was inside because I was missing you."

His frustrated exhale danced down my spine, and I stiffened. But I kept going.

"After we moved to the city, it's like you looked for any chance to go back to the life I wanted to leave in the past. Driving back to Lily Lake every day for work, then to your family's house on the weekends... We never had a life here."

His grip tightened. "I was doing it all for you."

"What do you—"

"Remember the first secret you told me under that tree?"

I nodded. "That I wanted to go to college."

He kissed the back of my head. "I started saving up the next day. Every time I got paid, I would put a little of it away so I could help you with the application fee and books and whatever else tuition aid didn't cover. You wanted that degree, and I wanted that for you. So it meant I had to be away. I picked up every job I could so we could make ends meet. So, yeah. I was working every day Gary could put me on a job. And when something came up on the weekends where I could make a little side cash, I jumped on it. You got those scholarships, but they didn't cover everything and they were dependent on your grades. I busted my ass so you didn't have to work full time and you could study more."

Something dawned on me that a psych degree and months of couple's therapy had never unearthed.

All the things he did to make me happy ended our marriage. But having everything I wanted didn't mean anything if I didn't have him.

As elementary as it sounded, it took me losing him to realize that.

"Hey—" Caleb rolled me back to face him. "Look at me."

I didn't. If I did, I'd start crying again.

He cupped my chin. "Look at me, Breezy."

"I know why you started calling me that," I said with a swallow. "But it's not true."

His thumb stroked my cheek. "Easy breezy. Able to cut people out of her life without flinching."

I let out a derisive scoff. "Are you calling me a serial relationship killer?"

He smirked. "If the skin-suit fits."

I dropped my forehead onto his chest and couldn't help but snicker.

"You put up a good front," he said. "I'll give you that. But I know you care. You just don't want to show how much you got hurt in the process."

He had me dead to rights.

"I saw Greta tonight," he hedged cautiously. And because he knew I wasn't going to let my poker face slip, he kept going. "Cade is courting her. I'm a little surprised about that. She was at the house for family dinner. She looks well." He snorted. "I mean... about as well as someone who hangs out with my mom can look."

That did it. I cracked a smile.

"There she is," he said with a victorious grin. "The girl under the tree." He rose up on one thick forearm. "That irreverent, smart-mouthed—" he hovered, straddling me "—little rebel."

His lips were warm and soothing, but only for a moment. Caleb's body pressed against mine and everything went white-hot once again.

His mile-wide hand opened between my legs. At this point, I was starting to care less and less about who he had learned all these tricks from and was starting to seriously consider whether or not a muffin basket or one of those overpriced charcuterie boxes was a better "thank you" gift.

His mouth latched onto my neck, sucking and biting at the spot where, not five hours ago, someone else had been.

"Mine," he said in a rasp before biting down again.

Sparks danced up and down my spine.

"Always. Madly. *Mine*."

It was too much. Too much too fast.

"Caleb—" I pressed against his heavy pectorals. "Stop."

He froze.

"What are we doing?" I said with a sigh. "I mean..." I swallowed.

"Say it, Blair."

I stayed silent.

Caleb shook his head and sat up, but stayed straddling my hips and pinned me down. "You know, for someone who talks for a living, you really suck at communicating."

"It's because it's you!" I exclaimed as I tried to wiggle out from under him. "I can't think straight when I'm near you."

He caught my wrists and pinned them above my head. The sheets had fallen away and I was acutely aware of the air dancing across my bare breasts. I jerked my elbows down to try and cover myself, but Caleb didn't budge.

"Let me look at you," he said gently.

"Caleb..."

"Let. Me. Look. Blair." There was pain in his eyes. Caleb shook his head, exasperated. "You never let me see you before. It was always changing behind a closed door or sex in the dark. I want to see you. I've thought of nothing more than seeing you since well before I should have ever been thinking about it."

I knew in the depths of my heart that I could trust him. That I was safe. That he wouldn't hurt me. That he wasn't judging me or condemning me.

But I still couldn't shake the shame I felt about the body I had been given.

There was nothing exceptional about it. Not that I had seen many naked people, but I assumed I looked about the same as the average woman. But that wasn't the point.

In The Fellowship, a woman's purity was the most important thing about her. It was currency. It made you valuable. Desired.

But heaven forbid a man lust after you. Then it was definitely your fault. Lust was a sin, and you were the one guiding him to it. And if he acted on it, consensually or not, that was your fault too.

You're either someone's guide to heaven or a one-way ticket to hell," the reverend used to say.

Perpetually being responsible for everyone else's choices—even the silent, secret ones—was a crushing weight to bear.

And then one day you stand up in the front of the sanctuary, say some vows, and you're allowed to have sex.

But the fear never goes away.

The shame never goes away.

The resentment toward something that's supposed to be so natural never goes away.

Being scared of being seen as a woman never goes away.

I could talk a good game on the podcast. Early in our marriage I could fake orgasms the way I could fake being interested in a conversation with a boring guest.

But the girl inside was still scared, and I didn't know if that was something I'd ever get over.

"Close your eyes," he said as he widened his knees. I could feel his cock pressing between my legs. "Go back to the lake. Blair and Caleb sitting under a tree…"

"K-I-S-S-I-N-G?" I quipped.

Caleb kissed me before letting go of my wrists and sliding

his open palms down my chest. "We've got some things to work on, but I promise you, I won't hurt you. You've always been sacred to me." He bent down and kissed one nipple before pulling it between his teeth. "All those things you want to try—because I know you have a list in that dirty mind of yours, whether you want to admit it or not." He switched, sucking on my other nipple. "You can try them with me."

I liked to think I would have gone through with hooking up with Collin Cromwell. Maybe even just to stick it to Caleb. He had sex with someone else, so why shouldn't I? We were divorced after all.

But I knew myself. I wouldn't have gone all the way.

"What are we even doing?" I said, exasperated as he eased off of me and sat up against the headboard, pulling me to sit between his thighs.

A girl could really get used to being manhandled all the time.

"I mean, are we hooking up? Are we dating? Are we divorcees with benefits?"

"Spend the weekend with me."

I peered over my shoulder, confused.

"At my house," Caleb clarified.

I raised my eyebrows. "You want me to come to Lily Lake."

"I want you to come spend forty-eight consecutive hours in my bed. We can figure out our Facebook relationship status later."

"I think I would immediately get struck by lightning when I get near the town limits."

"Come on, Breezy." Caleb yawned. "I have to work in the morning. Come to the house this weekend."

"So it's just like when we were married. You leaving me alone in Chicago to go back to Lily Lake. Us and our separate lives."

He shook his head. "I'll be in the city. I have to work here tomorrow. Retail space reno. I'll be a few blocks away from the studio. Might even stop at the Tavern for a drink afterward. It worked out pretty well last time." Caleb kissed my neck. "Meet me halfway. I fully plan on going back down to my truck to grab the overnight bag I packed in a hurry, so I can sleep right here. I'll spend time on your loud, obnoxious, traffic-filled turf, if you promise to come to mine."

I reclined against his chest and closed my eyes, letting the weight of assorted emotions and mixed feelings pin me to him. "What if we see my family? Or your family?"

Caleb's chest rumbled beneath me as he chuckled. "They'll probably be grateful. A pillar of salt the size of you will last them at least a year."

18

PODCAST TRANSCRIPT

One Small Act of Rebellion
Season One
Episode 20
"I Couldn't Kiss Dating Goodbye Because Kissing Is Sinful."
Aired Three Years Prior

"**Y**ou're created specifically for your betrothed. Every time you date someone who is not your betrothed, you give them a piece of your heart. The more pieces you give away, the less you have to give to the person that has been divinely chosen for you."

Sophia pretended to gag.

"Sometimes the analogy was flowers. The more crushes you have, the more petals fall. Sometimes it was a piece of paper—the more people who 'handle' you, the dirtier and more damaged you are. At the end of the day, it demonized choice and elevated obedience. Trust your parents. Trust the reverend. Don't trust yourself. Shame was the primary weapon in a war of submission. You don't want to give your husband a withered stem when he could have had a beautiful rose."

"It seems like a fast-track to abusive relationships," Sophia said.

"Oh, it absolutely was. Courtship was elevated over dating because it skipped dating entirely and went to this weird middle ground where you're not dating, but you're not formally engaged yet. It was basically a series of job interviews. And you know who knows how to give all the right answers?"

"Abusers," Sophia said. "Sociopaths."

"Everyone in the Fellowship learns from the earliest age how to play the game. Some people genuinely believe what the reverend says to do and say. Some people just do it to avoid confrontation. The reverend always said that 'pretending and playing the game when your heart isn't in it is bad,' but he also said to be obedient whether you feel like it or not."

"Fake it or fake it. There's no making it," Sophia mused.

"It's a recipe for disaster. The older generation in the Fellowship like to point to their own relationships as proof that courtship works. It's this weird mix of confirmation and survivorship bias."

Sophia chimed in. "It's the perfect example of a straw man argument. Dating can have negative results, so the supposed answer is to not do it."

"Rather than teaching healthy boundaries, consent, self-respect and respect for others, they decided to take away dating all together. They touted courtship as this flawless system. It was this belief that if you just followed all the rules, you would be blessed with a happy marriage. And guess what happened when a marriage didn't work or when a spouse was abusive? You blamed yourself. You kept it to yourself because you didn't want the rest of the community thinking you were sinning in secret, and that the hardships in your relationship were a result of that. Of course, that just keeps the cycle going because no one says anything. I was lucky—Caleb was never abusive. He was the farthest thing from it. But there were so many women who weren't as lucky as I was."

"Why do you feel lucky?"

"The Kings and Daltons have been close since before I was born. I'm the second-oldest daughter in my family. Caleb was the oldest son in his. In the eyes of the Fellowship, we were the right age and we came from good families who got along, so it was agreed upon that we would court when I was of age. Who you are as a child is not who you are as an adult. Think about how many times an adult does something horrific and the response is always, "but he was such a sweet boy.""

"How old were you the first time you remembered hearing that you were to marry Caleb?"

"Four or five maybe? Probably earlier than that, but I didn't know what it meant. Could you imagine telling a child exactly who they were going to marry and not be joking?"

Sophia sighed. "Honestly, it's disturbing when you think about it."

"Courtship was supposed to be this flawless system for purity. If you were never alone with a boy, you couldn't be promiscuous. If you didn't date casually, you couldn't be sexually active. But what it did is set the bar impossibly high—with expectations that you should have a happy, fulfilling marriage without ever getting to know the person you're going to marry. You never got to exist as a couple without the pressure of divorcing before the marriage ever happened. It puts so much pressure on people whose prefrontal cortex hasn't fully developed yet."

Sophia laughed. "Sex isn't a good enough reason to get married."

"Tell that to the group of people who claim that 'the world' puts too much emphasis on sex, but they were the ones talking about sex since I was a child."

"What would you go back and tell your younger self?" Sophia asked. "To the girl who believed she had to go from zero to marriage in the blink of an eye."

"I would tell her that you don't have to dive into the deep end without having ever dipped a toe in the water. That it's okay to fall *in love and have your heart broken. It'll heal. That she's not a flower. She's not a piece of paper. She's not something dirty, torn, and used if something doesn't work. That you can learn a lot about yourself in different relationship dynamics. That you're not giving your soulmate less of you. That hurt is a part of life and there's no way around it. The biggest problem that all of this boils down to is that you're never allowed to love yourself. How you feel about yourself is always dependent on someone else. More than anything, I wish I could tell my younger self to learn to love herself first. Set the standard for how others should love you. Don't rely on them set the standard for how you love yourself."*

19

BLAIR

I watched for out-of-season lightning strikes as I passed into Kane County. Luckily, the only weather around me was a pre-Thanksgiving flurry.

While it was technically a village, Lily Lake was the small town where I had spent the first eighteen years of my life.

The next twelve years were spent undoing the damage the first eighteen did.

A text from Caleb popped up on my phone, obscuring the GPS map that I didn't actually need. I just liked to think I didn't remember the way back to what had, at one time, been home.

CALEB

> Don't bail. I bought groceries you like and if
> you don't come, the kale will rot or I'll have to
> eat it myself. I really don't want to do that.

I snickered and looked back at the road. The morning after Caleb had nearly beaten down my door still messed with my mind.

Waking up beside him was sweet for the first fifteen seconds. Then it turned into a bucket of cold water on my head.

He snuck out just before six without so much as a good-bye. I had rolled over, snuggling my pillow and trying not to cry until I heard the door opening again.

He came back.

Caleb had gone out and picked up breakfast so we could eat together before he had to go to work.

It stole my breath and hurt my heart all at once.

He really was trying this time...

"*But for how long*?" the devil on my shoulder whispered.

I had never gotten this side of him before, and I was a little more than skeptical.

Caleb and I didn't have an arranged marriage the way some people did; not knowing their future spouse until they were engaged. From my earliest memories, it had just always been assumed that we would get married.

Our mothers talked about it constantly. People made incessant comments about what our babies would look like. Old men would make lewd remarks about what Caleb would have to look forward to when I "blossomed and became a woman." Of course, that was done under the guise of encouraging him to remain pure.

We courted, which really just meant we got to sit beside each other in church and go to each other's houses for dinner sometimes.

Always chaperoned.

Never touching.

We were forced together and simultaneously observed under a microscope. Every member of The Fellowship waited for us to slip up.

Caleb and I never got the chance to experience falling in love. We were just told that we loved each other.

Unease gnawed at me. Instead of feeling giddy that I had a sexy man wooing me, I wanted to hide. It didn't make me excited. It made me wary. It made me not trust him.

It was incredible how the things said to you at a young age could latch into your psyche like a tick and feed on you without consequence for a long time. Until the day you realize that something's wrong, and you don't know how to fix it.

Unlearning is far more difficult than learning.

My phone rang, and Caleb's name appeared on the screen.

"Hey," I said as I fed the call through the speaker system in my car.

"Why are you on your phone while you're driving?"

I rolled my eyes. "Really? That's the tone you're taking with me?"

"You could be fleeing to Mexico by now for all I know. I'll believe you're really coming when you're at my front door."

"I'm coming through Elburn. I'll be there in ten minutes."

He grunted something almost sounded like a concession. "Drive safe."

I made a left at the single stoplight by the gas station and circled the lake.

Women in boots and long, muted dresses trudged through the frost-covered grass.

Thank goodness my windows were tinted. I didn't want word to get out that Jezebel was back in town.

It was like driving through a ghost town, except I was the ghost.

The whole thing was eerie and unsettling. Lily Lake was exactly how I had left it, but I was completely different.

A pretty two-story Craftsman house with white siding and

dark blue shutters came into view. Barren trees lined the walk. Their branches were covered in ice, twinkling in the afternoon light.

I had cut out early from the studio to make the hour drive before nightfall, promising Sophia that I'd listen through the episode that the sound engineer had mastered before it went live next week.

Since my efforts at dating after divorce had died a painful death, we had rebranded the season's episode run to be called "The Ex-Capades."

It was fitting.

Especially with the escapade—*sexcapade?*—I was about to embark on as soon as I cut the engine.

The front door opened and Caleb filled the frame. His hands were braced on the top, leaning casually.

Great. There was no turning around after seeing that. My lady bits immediately fired up.

How many belts did he own and could I try them all out?

Before I could blink, he was opening my door. "Stop over-thinking and get inside before you freeze to death."

"Hello to you too," I grumbled. "Way to make a guest feel welcome."

He snorted, his breath clouding in the air. "Go on in. I'll get your bags."

"I'll get it," I said as my boots hit the gravel drive.

He was already making a move for the trunk. "I know you *can*. But I'm going to do it. Inside. Now."

I lifted an eyebrow. "Someone's grouchy today. I can leave if your invitation is too much of an imposition."

My overflowing weekend bag hit the ground with a heavy thump, and I was pinned to the icy body of my sedan.

Caleb's lips were cool as he kissed me hard. Hands grappled at any piece of my body he could find. "I haven't thought about anything but you for the last few days. So, you'd better get inside before I take you right here and you end up freezing around my dick like that time you stuck your tongue to a lamp pole in January."

My lips turned up in amusement. "And there you were, standing three feet away with a thermos of water that could have unstuck me, but you left me there just long enough for me to start squirming and freaking out."

He crossed one thick arm over the other. "You waste any more time out here arguing with me and I'll make you squirm in a different way."

And just because I could, I stuck my tongue out at him.

Caleb smacked my butt, nudging me inside while he helped himself to the trunk of my car.

I took advantage of him pack-muling my things inside and looked around. The house was warm and cozy. Small accents in reds and blues complimented the dark wood beams that stretched across the ceiling. A roaring fire crackled in the stone fireplace. It was all very *Caleb Dalton.*

I smoothed my palm over the wooden farm table that was far too big for his dining room. The ridged planks were delightfully imperfect. A tree of mugs was perched beside the coffee maker, ready to be filled at a moment's notice. A lit candle flickered from the stovetop, making the whole house smell like a Christmas tree.

And beside that was the ugliest porcelain cat figurine I'd ever seen.

"Snooping already?" he said with a chuckle as he lugged three bags and my purse inside.

"You snooped around my place weeks ago," I countered.

"Fair. You won't find as many pairs of sexy underwear in my drawers, I'm afraid."

I clicked my tongue. "Disappointing." I picked up the cat

figurine and held it up for his inspection. "Do you have a belligerent attack grandma too?"

He smirked. "I went to the thrift store and paid an exorbitant amount of money for the ugliest tchotchke they had."

I swear the painted-on eyes moved to stare at me. "And why—pray tell—did you buy a demon cat for your countertop?"

He pecked the red-tinted tip of my nose. "To make you feel more at home."

I let out a sarcastic, "Ha-ha."

"C'mere," Caleb said as he unceremoniously dropped my bags on the floor and pulled me into his arms. His mouth met mine in the gentlest kiss. Calloused fingers teased my skin as he cupped my jaw and threaded his fingers up into my hair. "I missed you."

"It's been forty-eight hours," I countered. "We once went two years without speaking. And now you miss me after two days?"

He shook his head and went in for another kiss. "I never said I didn't miss you."

A soft smile painted my cheeks as I wrapped my arms around his neck. "What's the plan for this weekend?"

With two wide steps, he had me pinned against the kitchen island. One dip of those powerful thighs and he was lifting me up to sit on the edge. "Well," he said as unzipped my marshmallow coat. "My plan tonight is to feed you."

"I like that."

"And then get you naked."

"Uh-huh," I whispered as he kissed up my neck.

"Take a break. Rehydrate. Get a snack."

"And then more sex?" I guessed.

He smiled against my skin. "You always were the smart one."

I ran my fingers through his hair, admiring the flecks of gray that streaked through his all-American boy brown. "We have two years to make up for."

Caleb shook his head. "No. We have twelve years to make up for."

I sat on the island. While Caleb went through the motions of making a respectable spaghetti dinner, I filled him in on what Sophia and I had in the works with the podcast. He countered by telling me he already knew all of it because he was caught up on listening to me talk about him, before pivoting to telling me about the retail space renovation that they'd be starting soon.

Caleb stood at my back, hands on my hips as we finished dividing and conquering the kitchen cleanup. He hooked his thumbs around the hem of my shirt and slid his palms around my waist. "How about I give you the rest of the tour?"

I smirked as I wiped my hands on a dishtowel. "Is that code for your bedroom where you have a bed with no headboard, a single set of navy or gray sheets, and you Febrezed everything rather than cleaning?"

"No, babe. That would be *your* bedroom," he said with a laugh as he took my hand. "Come on."

Caleb led the way down the hall, socked feet padding down hardwood floors that had been stained to be the color of espresso.

He stalled at the last door on the left and flipped on the light before stepping back to let me take a look.

The room was warm and cozy. A king-sized bed with a handcrafted headboard took up the majority of the floor space. Two end tables were situated on either side with sconces mounted on the wall above. A drafting table with a complementary iron and leather seated stool had been pushed up against a window. My guess was that was where the light was best.

Caleb liked building furniture in his spare time and always sketched out the pieces beforehand.

A heavy dresser, matching the end tables and headboard, was on the opposite wall.

The room was simple and neat. It could have been plucked right out of a furniture ad. *Have your bachelor bedroom delivered with two-day shipping*—or something like that. But I had never felt more at home.

At peace.

"What do you think?" he asked; his baritone rumbling behind me.

I trailed my fingertips along the footboard. "You made all of it, didn't you?"

He shrugged sheepishly. "I had some time on my hands."

"Question..." I said as I gave the bed a testing squish.

He lifted his eyebrows.

"Has anyone else ever slept in this bed with you?"

Caleb smirked. "If I didn't know any better, I'd say you were jealous." He trapped my chin between two fingers and tipped it up. "Maybe even a little possessive."

I huffed. "Just answer please."

His smile was kind. "No. I've never brought anyone back here."

I lowered my eyes to the floor. "Oh. Right. Okay."

"Blair—"

"It's fine. We were—are—divorced. Not like you were doing anything wrong. It's—"

"If you say fine—"

"It is."

He raised an eyebrow like he didn't believe me, then sat on the edge of the bed. "What do you want to know?"

I chewed on my lip, rolling it around in my mind. "Who... No, don't tell me that." I thought about it again. "What was it like?"

"You really want me to talk about having sex with someone else?"

I shrugged. "Kind of."

"I've been with two other women," he said, testing the waters. "One was a one-night-stand a few weeks after the divorce was final. I was angry and it was the best revenge I could think of."

The corner of my mouth trembled, but I sucked it in.

"After a few months of nothing to do but sit in an empty house, I started picking up odd jobs on the weekends. The other woman I was with was a homeowner I did a bonus room renovation for. She always hung around while I was working and we started talking. One thing led to another and..."

"You can spare me the details," I clipped. "Let me guess— she wanted you to bang her like a hammer?"

Caleb laughed. "More like she took pity on me after the first time we hooked up."

"What do you mean?"

He looked at his feet, his voice more serious now. "I know I never satisfied you. Sex between you and me was always..."

"Clinical?" I provided.

He shrugged. "This woman... She was probably ten years older than me. Figured I had grown up in the Fellowship and offered to help me..." He rubbed the back of his neck. "Learn."

My eyebrows darted up. "She taught you how to have sex."

"Before you give me those judgmental eyebrows, think about the orgasms you've had," he leveraged.

He may have had a teeny tiny point.

"Who ended your..."

Situationship? Relationship? Hookup? Sex lessons?

"I did," Caleb said. "Because as much as I appreciated the distraction, I'd go home alone and feel like absolute shit." He took my hands, linking our fingers together. "I'd come back here, lay in bed alone, and think about you."

20

CALEB

"I didn't know people still used DVDs," Blair commented as she perused the collection I had lined up in a row under the TV.

I stole a moment to admire the curve of her spine while her back was to me.

This is how Saturday mornings are supposed to be, I thought to myself. *Blair walking around the house in nothing but those cheeky underwear she likes and a sweatshirt she stole out of my closet.*

We woke in a tangle of limbs, completely spent after I woke her up in the middle of the night for round two. We scrapped the breakfast spread I had planned for the morning, and opted for cold cereal after round three.

Snow had fallen overnight, giving us absolutely no reason to leave the house.

"Find something you wanna watch?" I asked.

She sat criss-cross applesauce and studied two plastic cases. "I don't know. It's a tough choice between generic action movie number one and generic action movie: the sequel."

"Smart ass," I said with a laugh as I grabbed a pair of work gloves from the metal bucket by the fireplace hearth. "Look in the closet. There's more in there."

I let myself out the back door, trudging through a thin sheet of white powder, and loaded up my arms with split logs. Central heating and air was great, but if there was one thing I knew for sure hadn't changed about Blair, it was how much she hated being cold.

After two trips of hauling kindling and logs inside, we had enough to keep the fireplace toasty all weekend.

I dropped the gloves back in the bucket and looked around. "Blair?" I peered down the hall and heard a creak by the open closet door.

Her back was to me, blonde hair spilling down her shoulders as she held a box in her hands.

But it wasn't the DVDs.

I swore under my breath, but it was too late. Pointing to the shelf above, I said, "They're up there."

She didn't say a word, just stared at the pink envelope in her hands. It matched the other seven I kept tucked away in the shoebox.

Her name was scrawled across the back of each one. *No way I could pretend like they were anything other than what they were...*

Fuck me.

"What is this?" Her hands were shaking as she slid the envelope she was holding back into the box and thumbed through the others.

They matched—each one in a pink envelope, sealed, with her name on it.

"Birthday cards," I mumbled. "Mostly."

She looked up at me curiously.

I shrugged. "Anniversary cards... Valentine's day."

"I..." She stopped and touched her lips in disbelief. "I don't understand. Why would you—"

Instead of letting her spiral like I knew she would, I took the box from her, tucked it under my arm, and led her back to the kitchen. Blair stood at the island, still as a statue, as I set the box down and rummaged through the junk drawer.

Her eyebrows lifted when she saw me pull out a pink envelope. "Your birthday was the week before you got taken to the hospital." I patted the card on my open palm. "And we just kept finding our way back to each other, so I never got around to writing anything in this one." I opened the white card with gold lettering that read *Happy Birthday*, and showed her the blank inside.

"But..." She looked from the card I was holding to the box. "You never sent them."

I tossed the blank card in the box before handing it over to her. "Unsaid words can't hurt."

She trailed a red-painted nail over the edge of one envelope. "But they also can't fix anything..."

"Then take it home."

She looked up with wide eyes. "What?"

I shrugged. "I want to fix things."

"Why now?" Her voice was a little stronger. "Why not when we were in couples therapy for years? Why not when we were separated?" She was making herself mad. I could see it in the way her eyes darted left and right.

Whenever Blair raised her voice or expressed anything other than sweet submission, she became a flight risk.

I kept still, not moving toward her. Even after all those years of fighting against the demeanor that had been ingrained in her since she was just a baby on a blanket, she still struggled to let herself be angry.

I wanted her to be angry.

I wanted her to fight with me.

I wanted her to yell and shout and scream.

I didn't want her to go back into courteous silence.

"Because I didn't realize how broken we were until it was over."

Her fingers twitched, curling in and out as she rolled it over and over in her head.

"Why didn't you move on?" I asked out of the blue.

"I tried," she countered.

I shook my head. "Two years divorced and only after we saw each other. You weren't trying very hard."

She shrugged. "I tried at the beginning. I went on two dates."

"And?"

Sad eyes met mine. "And all I wanted to do was talk to you."

———

"You look beautiful," I said, coming up behind Blair and smoothing my hands all over her waist. I buried my nose in the crook of her neck and nibbled on the bare skin peeking out.

"I'm nervous," she admitted with a coy smile as she leaned closer to the mirror and fastened an earring.

I laughed. "Why?"

"Because I'm going on a date with my ex-husband."

"It could be worse." I smacked her ass. "You could be going out with the twerp who thinks he belongs in the White House."

Blair groaned. "Don't remind me. He made me want to exfoliate my eyeballs with razor blades."

"Are you almost ready to go?"

"I just need to touch up my makeup."

"How long?"

"Give me ten minutes."

I dropped to my knees and shoved the hem of her dress up. "I only need three."

She shrieked and dropped her mascara when I pulled her thong to the side and licked up and down her pussy. Blair's knees buckled, and I caught her ass in my hands.

"Better hurry," I murmured around her sweet sex.

Elbows thumped on the vanity, as heavy pants escaped her mouth. "Caleb," she whispered.

"Right here, love."

She shuddered as I sucked on her clit. Her hips bucked, desperate for more.

But she wasn't getting more.

Not now.

"Babe, I'm—I'm—"

Right before she reached orgasm, I leaned back and pulled her panties back in place.

"No!" she begged. "I was so close!"

I stood and cupped her pussy.

Her breath hitched.

"Behave yourself at dinner and I'll let you come later."

Fury flashed in her eyes like pale blue flames. "That's not fair."

I smiled against her lips. "All's fair in love and war."

Blair fixed her makeup and her dress, then threw on some fleece-lined leggings and boots before we made a hurried attempt to leave on time. We ended up being ten minutes late for our dinner reservation at a steakhouse two towns over after a steamy make-out session by my front door.

Blair fixed her lipstick in the front seat of my truck, and I made an attempt at smoothing out my clothes.

By the time we were walking into the restaurant, the

hostess was giving me a mean side eye. It looked like she was about to auction off our table.

I racked my brain as I sliced through bite after bite of my perfectly cooked medium-rare New York strip.

When was the last time I had taken Blair on a date? An intentional date where we got dressed up and she wore something from her closet that had been waiting to see the light of day. Not the kind of date where it was just the two of us being too tired to make dinner.

We didn't date as teenagers. There were no nervous trips to the movie theater. *Because movie theaters were the portal to hell, according to The Fellowship.* There were no coy smiles over milkshakes at the drugstore. In the beginning of our marriage, we didn't go out because we were two broke kids. We lived off of pancake mix and peanut butter. But as things got a little more stable, we never went on dates either.

Seeing Blair through the candlelight of a dim restaurant made me appreciate how fucking pretty she was. It gave me time to admire the way her eyes crinkled at corners when she smiled. I smiled at the way she'd start talking faster and faster when she was telling me about something she was excited about.

Is this what they mean by 'stop and smell the roses'?

The check came, but neither of us made a move to hurry out and get back to the grind.

We lingered. My hand was draped over hers, fingers tracing the veins on her forearm.

When we finally vacated the table, it wasn't a rush to get back to my place. We cruised back to Lily Lake, taking the meandering route.

The gas tank flashed a warning that I was close to empty, so I pulled off at the one gas station in town and hopped out.

"I'm going to run inside and get a drink," Blair said as she slid out of the passenger side. "I think I'm going to need some electrolytes around two AM."

I smirked as I fiddled with the pump. "I can go in and get it for you when I'm done filling up the tank."

I didn't know why I bothered arguing with her. Blair grabbed her purse and scurried inside.

My fingers froze around the pump as I stood outside the truck, watching the numbers tick through on the screen.

I heard the jingle of bells as Blair yanked the gas station door open.

The pump handle jolted as the tank reached its max.

See cashier for receipt.

I groaned as I read the message over the pin pad, returned the pump to the cradle, and trudged inside.

Blair was standing in front of the line of coolers, debating between a red or blue sports drink that had legendary football player TJ Bryant Jr.'s face on the label. I had been hoping he'd get traded to Chicago, but it looked like he would be riding out the rest of his career in Rhode Island.

She turned, opting for the red one, just as the bells on the door jingled. A gust of frosty air swept through the small store.

Blair spotted me, mouth parting to say something before morphing into a shocked 'O.'

Her face went ghostly white.

I looked over my shoulder as the cashier handed me my receipt and immediately understood.

Anna, Blair's oldest sister, walked inside, holding the hands of two of her children. Greta, their seventh sister and my future sister-in-law, walked in, carting in three more of Anna's children.

The entourage stopped, staring at Blair like she was public enemy number one.

Because in their minds, she was.

Anna's cold gaze turned to me, and her countenance changed. "Caleb," she said sweetly before elbowing Greta.

But Greta was forlorn as she looked at Blair. "Hi, Caleb."

I nodded. "Ladies."

Blair hadn't moved from her spot.

Anna barely restrained a sneer of contempt as she looked Blair up and down, taking in her painted-on dress that peeked through the open sides of her winter coat. The thigh-high boots made her a femme fatale. It was a complete contradiction to their long, shapeless dresses. The makeup she had on, tasteful and pretty, was a stark contrast to Anna and Greta's bare faces. Blair was savage in red and black while her sisters melted together in shades of beige.

The door whipped open as a burly trucker bustled in and beelined for the coffee maker. No one else so much as blinked.

Deciding it was up to me, I wove around baskets of impulse-buy snacks and took the drink out of Blair's hand. "Want anything else?"

"No." It was barely a whisper. Her eyes never left her sisters.

I took her hand in mine, internally reveling in Anna and Greta's shock when we walked toward the register together.

I squared up with the cashier, never letting go of Blair.

Anna was clutching her children close as we dodged them and aimed for the door. "Have a good evening, ladies," I said, tipping my chin to Anna and Greta as I led Blair outside.

She was silent on the ride back to the lake.

"You okay?" I said as I reached across the cab of the truck and twined our fingers together.

She mulled it over. "Fine."

"Blair—"

Shrugging, she said, "I didn't think coming back here

would feel like going to a funeral for someone who died a long time ago."

"You mean seeing your sisters?"

She shook her head, the corner of her mouth trembling. "I mean me."

21

BLAIR

"How'd you sleep?" Caleb murmured as he wrapped those thick arms of his around my waist and pulled me into his chest.

I hadn't, but I didn't say that.

"Fine," I said, nuzzling into the pillow that smelled like him. "You?"

I felt him smile as he peppered my bare shoulder with kisses. "I would have slept better if you had slept."

Dang it.

His lips were warm against my neck. "You tossed and turned all night."

"I'm sorry I kept you up," I murmured, careful not to attack him with rancid morning breath.

Caleb's breathing steadied as he settled again. "Why couldn't you sleep?"

"Just too wired, I guess."

"I know you're lying."

"It was weird seeing them yesterday." Swallowing, I added, "I didn't know Anna had more kids. I mean ... it tracks, but still. And Greta... She's an adult now."

I had always been labeled the 'rebel' in my family. It was my scarlet letter. It was a label of shame until I redeemed it and made it my own.

Not speaking in an insufferable childlike voice. Not having children. Wearing makeup. Buying pants.

That was just the start of it.

Going to college had been the last straw. To my family it had been the ultimate betrayal. *Women weren't to have a higher education than their husbands.*

High-control groups functioned off of shame and fear.

I distinctly remembered the moment I realized I wasn't afraid to lose them. I didn't have their love to begin with.

That was the moment I stopped crying over their judgment.

That was the moment I stopped getting angry when they wouldn't let me see my sisters.

That was the moment I stopped minding the silent treatment.

That was the moment I stopped caring.

Or as Caleb called it, the day I became easy-breezy.

But old wounds still stung. Sometimes it was the phantom pain of going through a birthday with nothing but silence.

Seeing Anna and Greta in the flesh… It was hard to wrestle with how long it had been.

"Cade's a good guy," Caleb said as he ran his hand up and down my thigh. "He'll take care of Greta."

When I didn't respond, Caleb trailed his fingertips up and down my arm. "Want me to talk to him? See how things are for your sisters?"

I swallowed. "No."

"Breezy…"

I gritted my teeth.

"Blair," he said a little more softly. "I'm going to take a chance on saying something that's going to piss you off."

I shrugged. "Might as well. What am I gonna do? Divorce you?"

Caleb laughed under his breath. "You can't blame your sisters for not talking to you. At least not the little ones."

It was strange to hear him say that. I'd always called half of my sisters, "the little ones." It was the vernacular I had adopted because it's what my mother had called them. Anna, the oldest, was her right arm. I was the left.

By the time the first set of twins, Emeline and Danielle, were born, numbers five and six of sixteen, I was big enough to change diapers, use a stepstool to get them out of the crib, and rock them when they wouldn't get quiet for anyone else.

When I was twelve years old, Greta was born. She had been mine to take care of from her first day home, and had been mine ever since.

Leaving her was the hardest.

Noel was a newborn when Caleb and I got married, and I had never met my youngest sister, Poppy.

What did they think about me?

"You can blame Anna," Caleb conceded. "She's a clone of your mother. I'll even let you blame Carrie, Danielle, Emeline, and Faith. They were old enough to speak up, not that they would have. But not Greta."

"I don't like it when you play devil's advocate," I clipped.

"Hey—" Caleb had me pinned beneath him in the blink of an eye. The mattress sunk beneath his weight as he bracketed my hips with his knees. "I'm not playing devil's advocate. I'm telling you it's not her fault. You left. We left. We moved." He cupped my cheek. "They're blindfolded in a pit with their hands tied behind their backs. They don't have anyone left to show them where the ladder out of the pit is. Changing people for the better means putting yourself in the proximity of people who don't think or act like you. You walked away. And that left them without anyone to counter the beliefs and ideas they were being spoon-fed."

I looked away from him and blinked. "Are you telling me I should have stayed?"

"No. I'm saying you should have raised hell to see them. To show them the way out. You're really good at—how did that guy put it? Being a mouthy bitch?"

"I didn't sleep, so my verbal sparring is going to be sub-par."

"Then don't fight with me."

"I don't know why we're talking about this. It's not like I care." My voice betrayed me, warbling on the last note.

"It's okay to care," Caleb said as he pressed a kiss to my forehead. "Your secret is safe with me."

"I don't."

He found my wrist and wrapped his hand around it, bringing my fingers to his lips and kissing each one. "Don't lie to me." He kissed the center of my palm. "Like you said earlier. What do you have to lose? We're already divorced."

That annoying pressure behind my eyes threatened to spill over. "I don't care."

He pushed the sheet away and peppered light kisses across my breasts. "You do."

Everything went glassy. My vision warped as tears flooded my eyes. "No."

Caleb shuffled down the bed, pushing the covers away. "You do. Now stop pretending like I don't know every part of you and open your legs."

He didn't give me a chance to act. Wide hands captured the inside of my thighs and pushed them up and out.

Cool air danced across my sex, and I shivered at the draft.

"Keep your knees nice and wide for me, sweetheart."

My brain was slow at anticipating what he was doing. Before I realized what he was talking about, Caleb cupped my ass in his palms and lifted me up to meet his mouth. I squealed as his tongue swept across my pussy and circled my clit.

Caleb's laugh was warm and did funny things to me inside. "Stay still. You're gonna kick me in the face."

"Warn a girl."

He bit down on my clit and sucked. "You're in my bed. That's warning enough. I told you—I don't want you hiding from me ever again." Thick fingers slid inside of me, scissoring open and stretching me. "I didn't do right by you before, but that won't be happening again. Every time you're in this bed, I want you naked and ready for me. I want you to know that anytime you need a little stress relief, you can find me right here, between these pretty legs."

Caleb twisted his fingers, curving them up as he withdrew.

I gasped as every part of my body went electric.

"You like that?"

I whimpered, nodding as the feeling faded away.

Caleb pushed his fingers back inside of me and pressed the heel of his palm to my clit. He held there, curling his fingers and slowly stroking the inside of my pussy. The pressure against my clit was exquisite.

"Caleb," I whispered as my eyebrows knitted together in concentration.

"Tell me what you need."

"More. That. You. Please."

I didn't know exactly what I was begging for. My entire vocabulary was the equivalent of mental mashed potatoes.

All I knew was that I needed him. Wholly and completely.

"You're going to come for me."

I nodded a desperate agreement.

"And then you're going to ride my cock and come again."

"I just..." All I wanted in this moment was to finish.

I was floating, riding an incomparable high. My lungs burned as my body focused every ounce of energy on reaching completion.

"Breathe, baby," he urged. "Breathe for me."

My mind's eye was too focused on the pooling pleasure filling me from the inside out.

"Blair," he scolded as he trailed his free hand lower, pressing his thumb to—

"Caleb!" I shrieked.

"I told you to breathe, and you didn't. Now fucking breathe or it'll hurt."

I gasped, fisting the sheets as he worked his finger against the tight ring of muscle between my cheeks.

The two fingers stroking my pussy never let up. He shifted his hand and teased my clit.

My legs shook as the orgasm ramped up faster and faster. I chanted his name as every muscle in my body seized and shook with indescribable pleasure.

Caleb cupped my throbbing sex as I crashed. "Deep breaths for me."

I could barely think. Every part of me fizzled like a live wire dancing on asphalt.

I melted into the bed, delightfully languid. "I'm gonna go back to bed now," I said with a lazy smile.

Caleb pulled his hands free and shook his head, dipping down again to lap at my soaked entrance. "Nope." He groaned in delight as he devoured me.

I was too sated, resigned to simply lying there and enjoying it.

He shucked off his boxers and rolled, making me airborne

as we switched places. Caleb manhandled me over his hips, the blunt head of his cock nudging my pussy.

Limply, I said, "I can't ... not again."

His smile was kind, like a devil pitying you before he announces your damnation. Fingers dug into my thighs as he lifted me, lining up his cock, and slowly lowering me down. "There you go, baby. Just like that."

I whimpered as he stretched me. The first orgasm left my inner muscles relaxed and positively dripping. Still, I ached as he pushed inside.

"Come here," Caleb said, pushing his hips up and tipping me forward.

I collapsed on his chest, tucking my head in the crook of his neck.

"Now you can go to sleep," he said as he levered his hips down, then quickly thrust inside me again. "I'll wake you up when I'm done filling this pussy with my cum."

I lingered in the blissful medium between slumber and consciousness as he stroked my back and fucked me to his heart's content.

His measured breathing and soft grunts lulled me into a trance. Everything was so *right.*

So why wasn't it right before?

Caleb didn't even warn me when he came. His hands tightened around my hips, holding me down as he filled me. Jerky thrusts as he finished shook me out of the sex stupor.

"Shh," he said, brushing my hair away and urging me to lay back down on him. "You need to take more. Now, be a good girl and lay still while I come inside you again. I want this pussy to be dripping for days. That way when you're back in the city, lying in your bed all alone, you still have a reminder of who you belong to between your legs."

I whimpered as he pushed inside of me again, hard as a

damn rock. I could feel the mess we were making, but Caleb didn't seem to care. I held on to him, trusting him to take care of me.

The realization hit me like a runaway train.

It was something I hadn't done before.

I had trusted him with my secrets. With my dreams. With the good parts of me. The parts that I thought were lovable.

But I never trusted him with the part of me that was scared that I wasn't good enough. The part of me that still believed that I was exactly what had been branded on my heart at an early age.

Rebellious.

Unworthy.

Wretched.

Wicked.

Inherently evil.

The day we said our vows, I gave Caleb half of me; unwilling to believe that he would want my darkness.

The part of me that never really got over the first eighteen years of my life.

I fled this place with a broken heart and wounded mind. But instead of rebuilding who I wanted to be with him, I went at it alone.

In hindsight, I think I was hoping to wake up one day and be whole again. Good enough. The woman he deserved.

Caleb didn't leave The Fellowship unscathed either. Maybe he had done the same.

Two people rebuilding themselves alone rather than helping each other.

Caleb tightened his arms around me as he jolted, spilling inside of me again.

"I need you to know something, Blair."

I turned my head and kissed his neck in acknowl-edgement.

"I never stopped loving you. Even when I was angry. I never stopped. No matter how we got here, I've always been madly in love with you. It'll always be you." He tipped my chip up and pressed a soft kiss to my lips. "But I need you to do something for me."

"What's that?" I whispered through choked tears.

Caleb laid a reverent kiss on my forehead. "I need you to read the letters."

22

BLAIR

"Y ou sure you have everything?" Caleb asked as we lingered in the foyer; hands slowly roaming over each other as we waited out the inevitable.

I looked down at the packed bags at my feet. "I think so."

His mouth slanted over mine as he leaned me back against the wall. "Is it bad that I'm tempted to unzip your bags and unpack so you don't leave?"

I smiled against his lips. "Then you'll have to put up with Sophia being here so we can record together."

His fingers snuck under my thick sweater. "You're not making a good argument. I can build you a recording studio."

"This was a good weekend," I admitted.

I still felt cautious about where Caleb and I stood with each other, but the last forty-eight hours had been pivotal for us.

Maybe we were crazy, but if anything in life was worth being crazy for, it was love.

Caleb took my hand and walked me out the door, pausing at the bottom of the steps to make sure I had support as I navigated the slick ice. He lugged my things to my car and loaded them in while I cranked up and immediately blasted the heat.

"Call me when you get back," he said, hunching down to steal one last kiss.

"I will."

"And call me if you get tired. I don't want you falling asleep at the wheel."

I laid my hand on his cheek. "I'll be fine."

"That won't stop me from worrying." He cracked a lopsided grin. "You sure you don't want me to drive you back?"

"As much as I want to say yes, you have a life and a job and commitments and so do I."

"Fuck it all, Breezy." He pecked my lips before softening his tone to an intimate plea. "Fuck. It. All."

We spent our last few minutes obscenely making out in his driveway without recourse before I left him and the ghosts of Lily Lake in my rearview mirror.

———

THE METAL BENCH scraper smoothed over the countertop as it swept up tiny tendrils of dough that had worn off the bottom of the boulle I had shaped. The loaf was proofing in its banneton, which meant I had at least an hour to summon the courage to open Pandora's box.

Well... more like Pandora's shoebox.

Seven pink envelopes stared at me from the coffee table.

I had done my laundry, folded my socks, and made bread.

Two of the three I hadn't done in years, which made me acutely aware of the fact that I was putting off the inevitable.

I need you to read the letters.

Setting the shoebox on the coffee table had been the first thing I did before stepping back and deciding I'd get settled first. A random string of texts back and forth with Caleb had kept me company while I unpacked, put my clothes in the washing machine, and avoided doing what he had asked.

With the wash and dry cycle done, the bread proofing, and a quick goodnight back-and-forth with Caleb over text—it was time.

I wasn't much of a drinker, but I felt the occasion called for a glass of something strong.

Maybe something to help me sleep after I learned whatever it was that he insisted I know.

I curled up in the corner of the couch with the box on my lap and a glass of red wine in my hand. I took a healthy sip, set it on the table, and opened the first card.

~~Happy Birthday.~~

It had been scratched out at least four times.

There was a difference in penmanship between the "I" in the first sentence and the rest of the message; almost like he had started to say what he really wanted to say, then waited and thought about it for a long time before writing again.

I don't even know why I'm putting words in here. I got the card by accident. Birthdays and anniversaries were a big deal to you since we never really got to celebrate them growing up. I guess it was just habit this time of year to pick up two cards so I wouldn't forget.

So, happy birthday, Breezy.

I hope it's everything you wanted.

-Caleb

I stared at his neat handwriting. The last line hung in my memory. *I hope it's everything you wanted.*

A date had been noted on the bottom corner of the white and gold card. It had been the first birthday I'd had after the divorce was finalized.

Everything I wanted...

What he didn't know was that I had spent it crying in bed.

The wine was bitter on my tongue as I downed the glass and prepared to dive into a world of hurt.

I ripped into the next pink envelope and barely registered the date. Our first divorced wedding anniversary.

So, I guess this is going to be a thing now.

No one thinks about getting divorced when they're standing at the altar saying wedding vows. No one thinks about all the fights that are going to happen. All the miscommunications. All the sleepless nights.

All the times you fail the one person you never wanted to hurt.

I wish I had thought about those things on our wedding day, but it wouldn't have changed a thing. I still would have married you, even if I knew how it was going to end. Because at least for one moment in time, you were mine.

Happy Anniversary, B. I fucking hate this.

-Caleb

Tears streamed down my cheeks as I tore into envelope after envelope. Each message was longer than the last. It was a time capsule of the last two and a half years.

It's been over a year since I've seen you. I can't remember ever having gone this long without you. It'll probably piss you off to know that I moved back home. Well, at least what used to be home. It doesn't feel like it without you.

You'd be happy to know I knocked out that wall in my parents' house that separates the den from the dining room. When I was ripping the drywall out, all I could think about were all the times you'd roll your eyes when we couldn't sit beside each other at dinner because you had to sit with the women and kids, and I had to sit with the men.

Taking a sledgehammer to it felt pretty good.

I'm sorry you didn't get to do it yourself.

Happy Birthday, Blair. I hope you're happier now than you've ever been.

-Caleb

I SNIFFED and ripped into the next.

TODAY'S OUR ANNIVERSARY, so I guess I get to punish myself with this damn card. Not that it'll ever do anything but sit in a box.

I started seeing a therapist and then I fired him. He was a quack —talking about me having stalled in the stages of grief over the divorce and that I'm conflict-averse. I'm fine. There's nothing wrong with not wanting to fight and yell about stuff, and I don't need to pay some guy with your college degree to tell me shit you told me for years.

Dammit...

Well. Not like you're ever going to see this.

So maybe you were right about one ... or two things.

But you and me—we did everything right. We did everything we were supposed to do to have a blessed, holy marriage. We didn't have premarital sex. We didn't even fucking touch. We didn't cuss or drink or go against the umbrellas of authority in The Fellowship. We did all the counseling. We did it all, Breezy. Every fucking thing.

But maybe that's where we went wrong.

We did all those things to get to the wedding. To qualify for it like it was some kind of test.

Because when you take away the white dress, the pressed suits, the flowers, the invitations, and the cake, we were just kids.

I guess when I think about it that way, I don't resent you quite as much.

I guess I don't resent them quite as much either (which would piss you off if you ever read this).

I gave you one day of vows and disregarded the three thousand days I should have been fulfilling them after that.

Whether or not the Fellowship would admit it, a wedding was not what was required of us. It goes much deeper than that.

It should have been nine years of us putting each other first. Nine years of me putting you before all else and you doing the same.

But, just like our divorce, we did everything fifty-fifty.

I hope you get the 100% you deserve. I hope I do too.

-Caleb

The kitchen timer rang, signaling that it was time to tip the bread out of the bannaton.

Just because I hadn't made bread in over a decade didn't mean I couldn't kick Priscilla's drab granny-panty ass.

I used my sleeve to wipe my tears and hurried into the kitchen. The motions of gently unmolding the dough onto a sheet of parchment were soothing. I used a small spray bottle to spritz the boulle with water before giving it a light dusting of flour. My hands were steady and calm as I used the edge of a razor blade to knick and slash the loaf, scoring it with a wheat pattern.

My phone rang as I was washing my hands, and Caleb's name appeared.

That was weird. He had already gone to bed.

"Hello?" I said, wondering if it was some kind of REM cycle butt-dial.

His voice was groggy. "Hey, baby. Did I wake you up?"

"No, no." I wiped my damp eyes with my sleeve. "I was just surprised. I thought you went to sleep."

"I did," he said.

That's when I heard soft voices in the background.

"The doorbell camera made an alert go off on my phone."

Something akin to fear pricked at the back of my neck. The Fellowship had never resorted to violence, but I could remember a time or two when my dad and a few other men had gone out to—as they said—put the fear of God in someone when they were straying from the path of right-eousness.

"A-Are you okay?"

"Yeah. Yeah, I'm good. Everything's fine." There was a pause, almost like he was waiting for someone to speak up. "Someone found our tree."

"You mean…"

"Cade and Greta," he said. "They were sneaking by the house to meet up and the doorbell camera caught them."

I didn't understand what he was getting at. It's not like we owned the tree…

"Blair," he said gently. And that's when I knew whatever he was calling about was big. "Do you have a few minutes? Greta wants to talk to you."

She must have been standing right there for him to phrase it that way.

He was giving me an excuse. I could say I didn't have the time. Greta didn't know a damn thing about my life. For all she was aware of, I worked at night.

Footsteps echoed as Caleb moved for more privacy. "She doesn't have much time before she has to get home."

I knew that feeling all too well.

"Okay," I croaked. "I'll talk to her."

"Greta," Caleb said, beckoning her to take his phone. "Sit by the fire, sweetheart. It'll warm you up."

"Thank you," she said sheepishly. "Opening the closet to get my coat would have woken everyone up."

I cupped my hand over my mouth, knees buckling as I slid to the floor. My back pressed to the lower cabinets as tears flooded my eyes.

She sounded so grown up.

Caleb's voice carried over the line. It was almost fatherly as he managed the situation unfolding at his house. "Cade and I will step into the study to give you some privacy."

Her 'thank you' was soft, and I waited until all was quiet.

"Blair?" Greta's voice was meek and small.

"Hi," I said, unsteady and unsettled.

She sniffed. Whether it was from tears like me, or the cold nipping at her nose, I didn't know.

"I don't have much time," she began. "You know how early everyone wakes up."

"Yeah," I rasped. "Are... Are you okay? What's going on?"

"I'm okay," she said quickly. "At least... I think I am."

"Caleb told me you and Cade are..."

"Courting." I recognized the nerves in her voice all too well. It was the sound of a child realizing they were about to grow up all too fast.

"Caleb says he's a good man," I offered, though I knew it wouldn't mean much. Caleb was a good man, too, and we didn't work out.

"He is." She was hesitant, like she was looking around to make sure it was really okay to say the thoughts going through her head. "Cade is the one who suggested we meet up at the tree. We've been trying to see each other in secret—you know —so we can get to know each other a little. Please don't tell."

I laughed through the tears. "Who am I going to tell?" Softening, I composed myself. "But your secret is safe with me. And with Caleb. And if Cade is anything like his brother, you're safe with him too."

"I couldn't believe my eyes yesterday—when we saw you at the gas station. I thought I was hallucinating."

"Me too," I admitted. The warble was back in my voice. "You're all grown up."

"I miss you," Greta hedged, and it made my heart shatter

into a million tiny shards. "When you left… when Mom said it had been decided that we couldn't speak to you anymore… It felt like I lost my real mom and my best friend."

"I'm sorry," I whispered as my vision blurred completely. "I'm so sorry I had to leave."

"I know you and Caleb…"

She wouldn't say it. She wouldn't say that sinful word.

"Got divorced," I offered. "Yeah. We did. A few years ago."

"It was all anyone talked about in prayer groups after he moved back."

Because that's where all the good gossip was shared.

Greta paused a beat. "But you were with him yesterday. And he called you right away when Cade asked."

"We're…" I rolled it around in my brain, trying to figure out exactly what we were. "Figuring things out, I guess."

Masculine voices were muffled in the background. Cade was probably warning her that their time was up.

"Greta—" I blurted out, desperation taking over. "If you ever need anything, find Caleb. He'll help you. I'll make sure he gives my number to Cade. Call me anytime."

It would have been useless to give my number to Greta. She didn't have a phone. Women weren't allowed to have them, outside of household landlines. The Fellowship had caught up with the times some years ago and now allowed the men to have cell phones, but only after they had been in the community, sold out in their beliefs, for many years.

Phones had unlimited access to information, and information was dangerous. Information that would defraud every claim The Fellowship made.

You know what they say. The truth will set you free.

"Thank you," she said quietly.

"Be careful."

"I will."

I paused, a litany of pleas fighting to roll off my tongue. "Trust Caleb. And if Cade brought you to Caleb, then trust him."

"Okay."

"But Greta—" I chewed on my lip. "Trust yourself the most."

23

CALEB

"**B**oss," Dominic called from the first floor of the build site.

I was on the second floor, covered in joint compound, and silently cursing Gary for ever having hired Danny.

I was all about giving someone a chance, but the kid needed a map to find his own ass.

"Yeah?" I hollered back.

"You got visitors."

Visitors? Blair was the first possibility that popped in my mind, but there was no way it was her. She had a packed schedule of production and advertising meetings today. Besides, the only way I'd probably get her back to Lily Lake was kidnapping.

I didn't plan on becoming a felon today.

I wiped my hands on my jeans and got Danny's attention. "Finish up and have Dom or one of the boys look over it when you're done."

He grunted in acknowledgement and I left him to it, resigned to the fact that I'd have to fix whatever he did.

At least when we had started on the retail space in Chicago he put his talents of messing things up into the demolition.

I made myself as presentable as I could before jogging down the stairs, only to come to a screeching halt.

Seven of my brothers, just missing the youngest two who were still finishing their homeschooling years, stood in what was soon to become the kitchen.

Cameron, Carter, Cody, Clay, Charlie, Colby, and a very tired-looking Cade, lingered in a clump.

Great.

"Hey," I grunted as I looked between them. "What's going on?"

Cameron, the second oldest after me, looked to be leading the pack. He crossed his arms. "Jeremy Reinard said Anna saw you and that woman together this weekend. Is it true?"

There was so much holier-than-thou bullshit in that statement that I didn't even know where to start.

We all knew who Anna was. She used to be my sister-in-law. But Cameron made sure to name-drop her husband so I'd remember that she married the son of the reverend. It was the distancing language he used with Blair. He didn't say her name. He called her 'that woman.'

And his snarky "is it true?"

I quickly cut my eyes to Cade who looked stone-faced.

He knew damn well it was true. He and his soon-to-be bride had been in my living room at one in the morning so I could facilitate a phone call.

But I didn't blame him for not speaking up. He had a lot more to lose than I did.

I'd already lost it.

It took blowing up my life to realize that other people's

judgments meant absolutely nothing. But that understanding was easier to wrestle with in hindsight.

"Yes," I said, easy, breezy, and unbothered like Blair always pretended to be. "Blair spent the weekend with me."

Cameron's eyes flashed with rage. Knuckles clenched for a split second before he shoved them in the pockets of his coat. "Why would you bring that whore—"

Before I could blink I had Cameron pinned against the brand-new kitchen island. "You'd better be really fucking careful how you speak about my wife."

The shock of me dropping a well-placed F-bomb was enough to stall the rest of my brothers from piling me into the ground.

Though he was my younger brother, people assumed we were twins since we were so close in age. Cameron matched me in height and weight and used it, shoving back against me as he levered off the granite countertop. "She's nothing but a no-good—"

I decked him.

Knuckles cracked against his jaw in a swift punch. "What did I just tell you? Huh? Maybe it'll be easier for you to keep her name out of your mouth if your teeth are rattling around."

Cameron shook it off and lunged.

"Hey!" A weathered hand grabbed the back of Cameron's neck and yanked him away. "What the hell are you boys doing roughhousing like children on my job site?"

The rest of my brothers widened the circle as Gary, Dominic, and the rest of the crew gathered inside.

"Huh?" Gary looked around. "I know my nephews were raised better than that." He pinned Cameron with a sharp look. "Do you have anything to say for yourselves?"

Even though Gary was family, he had left the Fellowship long ago and lived mostly in spite of everything that had been taught for generations. Frankly, holidays where he and my aunt were present were entertaining because he would always stir the pot just for shits and giggles.

But it also meant my brothers didn't give him the same reverence they were supposed to give other men in their community.

Blood trickled from the corner of Cameron's mouth. He snarled as he used the back of his hand to wipe it away. "We have nothing to say to you." He cut his eyes to me. "Just looking out for our brother the way he should be looking out for us."

Cade had suddenly become fascinated with a stray nail on the ground, but I didn't call him out.

"If you have a problem with me, bring it up to me like a grown man. If you have a problem with Blair and I seeing each other again, keep it to your damn self."

Cameron opened his mouth, but Gary cut him off. "Anyone who doesn't work here, leave. Anyone left behind in the next thirty seconds will be considered an unpaid volunteer, and I've got shingles that need to go on the roof before the snow picks up."

That was enough to call them off.

One by one, my brothers backed off until only Cade remained. He stayed silent as they filed out.

Gary raised an eyebrow. "You got some spare time to freeze your fingers off on a roof?"

"No, sir," Cade said.

I looked at Gary and nodded for him to head to give us a minute. "He's fine."

Gary shuffled off, trudging through dust and debris.

"Sorry," Cade said.

I shrugged it off. "Don't worry about it. It was bound to happen sooner or later. Secrets don't stay secret here long." I looked left and right, making sure no one was close enough to hear us. "Did Greta get back okay the other night?"

"I think so," he said, looking over his shoulder. "Will you tell Blair I really appreciate her taking the call?"

I nodded, contemplating whether or not I should bring up what was weighing on my mind. I didn't want to volunteer Blair for anything, but if she was willing to stick her neck out for anyone, it was Greta. "Are you two trying to leave?"

He solemnly shook his head. "What do I have left if I let this all go?"

"A lot more than what you have now. You just have to be willing to stand on an empty lot and build your life from the ground up."

He scuffed the toe of his boot on the floor. "I gotta go."

"Hey—" I grabbed his shoulder before he could completely turn his back. "If you need anything, you can come to me. We're still brothers."

He hesitated, but nodded. "I'll try not to."

"Wanna tell me what that was all about?" Gary said as he lumbered back in.

"Eavesdrop much, old man?"

He pointed at the ground. "It's not eavesdropping on my own build site. You'll get that privilege when you're the head honcho one day."

I rested my ass against the newly installed kitchen island and flexed my fingers, trying to ignore the bruising pain. "Blair and I have been working things out and she spent the weekend here with me."

"Well, I figured that much. You've been in too good of a mood lately." He pointed out the gaping hole that was supposed to have a door. "What's going on with Cade?"

"Courting Blair's sister, Greta."

"Have they been sneaking around like you and Blair used to?"

I cracked a smile. "Seems like it. They showed up at my house in the middle of the night. Blair and I had run into Greta over the weekend, but they couldn't talk because Anna was there. So, I let her use my phone."

"They trying to leave the Fellowship before they have to get married?"

I shrugged. "I dunno. Cade was cagey about it."

"Don't push him too hard. It's a choice he's gotta make on his own just like you did. Just be there when he's ready to talk."

A moment of weighted silence hung between us. I knew firsthand that Gary's wisdom was good.

He's the one I went to when Blair and I wanted to leave.

That's the thing about the Fellowship. They don't live in a closed commune. They're not cut off from twenty-first century society. They have technology. There are no armed guards. No one to physically stop you from leaving.

There's the fear of the afterlife, but when it comes down to it, the fear of rejection is what keeps most people from leaving.

Of losing your family.

Of losing your job.

Of your children being alienated.

Of losing your roots.

But if the roots are diseased, it's only a matter of time before the tree is too.

My phone buzzed in my pocket, but I was too lost in thought to reach for it.

Gary pointed a finger at me. "I'd answer that if I were you."

My brows furrowed. "What for?"

He shrugged. "Just keeping the promise I made to you thirteen years ago."

Cryptic old fart...

I fished my phone out, but didn't recognize the number. "Hello?"

"Hey there, is this Caleb Dalton?"

"Speaking."

"Excellent. This is Allen Walker. I got your information from Gary Dalton. He's an old buddy of mine. Do you have time for a chat?"

By the time I was finished listening to Allen, my fingers were frozen around my phone and my nose was running, but I was too stunned to care.

I looked around for Gary, but he had already gone for the day.

That cryptic line was accurate.

He kept his promise.

One that, frankly, I had forgotten about.

My phone rang again and I fumbled to answer it. "Hey, gorgeous."

"Hey," Blair said. "Do you have time to talk or are you in the middle of something?"

"I'll always have time for you."

She laughed. "That would be a good line if we hadn't already done the marriage thing. I can cite my sources to disprove that statement if you'd like."

"Alright, smart ass," I chuckled. "I can talk. What's up?"

"So, you've been listening to the show this season..." There was mischief behind that sweet voice.

"Yeah?"

"And I've been talking about us..."

"Uh-huh."

"And listeners really like hearing about us... um... working things out..."

I shoved one hand in my pocket to keep it warm as I did a

walk-through of the house while Blair stammered over her words.

I liked it when she got nervous around me.

"It's really been a great topic for the season," she blurted out. I could practically see her bouncing on her toes as she worked her way around to her point. "I think people love an unexpected love story. Or an un-love story. Re-tying the knot? Fuck. I shouldn't have said it was a love story. I don't know why I said that."

Unraveling Blair was my favorite pastime.

"Breathe for me."

She paused, then let out a huff.

"Good girl. Ask me."

"It's just... It's been really positive and it's gotten a good response. And... You know... In a world where we hear 'in these unprecedented times' every single day, people like having something to root for. And apparently that's us."

"Blair," I said again, drawing out her name. "Whatever you want. Just ask me."

"Sophia thinks we should—"

"I don't give a shit about what Sophia thinks. What do you think? What do you want?"

She hesitated. "I..."

Fucking ask me already. This was our problem the first time; never talking to each other when we needed something.

But here we were, supposedly learning from our mistakes but not acting on it.

I stalled on the second floor landing and swiped across my screen, changing the call to a video chat.

Blair's face immediately popped up. Just like I had assumed, she was pacing in her office.

"There's my pretty girl." I leaned against the wall.

"Not that I'm opposed to seeing you looking rugged and

contractor-y, but I didn't mean to interrupt your day this much."

"I'm the only one here. And first, it's not interrupting my day. I'm glad you called. And second, it wouldn't be interrupting either of our days if you'd just tell me what you want rather than dancing around it for so long that I had to video call you just to look you in the eye so you'd tell me."

She sighed and flopped down in her chair. "I hate asking for things."

"I want you to ask for things, Breeze. It doesn't make you selfish or greedy. I want to give them to you. Let me."

She chewed on her lip before finally—*finally* speaking up. "Will you come on the podcast?"

That ... wasn't what I thought she was going to say.

"You mean—like—"

"Like as a guest. Sophia wants to do a question and answer episode where listeners can send in their questions and we..."

"Answer them?" I surmised.

"Yeah."

"Okay."

She looked at me curiously, eyes narrowing like a CIA profiler searching for any hint of deception. "Just like that?"

I nodded. "Just like that."

"You're serious?" she prodded. "You'll come on the podcast and answer wildly personal questions about getting back together."

I flipped it on her. "I like hearing you say we're back together."

She rolled her eyes. "Not the point."

"It's very much the point."

"Caleb," she growled, setting her phone on her desk and turning to her computer.

"Tell me you're mine."

Her fingers paused on her computer keys, and I could see those walls going up again. "What does that mean to you?"

I sat on the top step, rested my elbows on my knees, and stared straight at her. "It means we're gonna take it slow. It means we're starting from scratch as the people we are now, not the people we were when we said "I do" or when we said, "I can't anymore." It means we're going to communicate this time; so if there's something you want or you need, then you have to ask me."

Her lip trembled.

"I didn't know how much I had been missing you until I got you back. And now I'm not letting you go."

24

BLAIR

"I'm sorry, Miss Dalton. We just sold out."

Even the sweet aroma of bread and coffee inside Kelch's Bakery couldn't lift my disappointment. The barista gave me a pitying smile. "We have a really good strudel. Would you like to try it?"

"No thanks," I said rather glumly. "Just the coffee today." I fished out my debit card and handed it over as I checked the time.

Dang it. I was going to be late.

I grabbed the paper cup and hustled out the door.

Tony was waiting outside of the Hannover Building like usual. His mustache twitched when he spotted the lack of a bakery bag in my hand.

But his hands weren't empty.

I propped one hand on my hip and gave him some good-natured attitude. "Here I was, disappointed that the bakery sold out of Bee Sting cake before I could get you a piece, but you beat me to it."

He chuckled as a cloud of his breath fogged in the cold air. "Actually, someone else gave it to me."

I arched an eyebrow. "No one can buy your love except for me."

Tony winked as he opened the door. "Have a good day, Miss Dalton."

Cryptic, but okay.

I hurried in and out of the elevator, accidentally ramming into a giant body as I hopped off onto the studio's floor.

Before I could catch my breath, my body spun and my back hit the wall. Lips landed on mine in a breath-stealing kiss.

"I've been waiting for days to give you a good morning kiss," Caleb whispered against my lips. "I don't plan on waiting that long ever again."

I smiled. "So you maul me as soon as I walk into work?"

"Sophia was warned."

"There are security cameras."

"Like I care."

"I was planning to get here before you, meet you in the lobby, and show you up."

We backed off of each other when the elevator opened again and Genevieve waltzed in, smelling like patchouli and Chanel No. 5. She offered a knowing smile and a wink as she headed into the conference room.

Caleb tried to hide his cough. "Some things never change, huh?"

I snickered as I took his hand and walked through the bullpen, coming to a screeching halt in front of my office. "Why is there an obnoxiously large bouquet of flowers on my desk?"

Caleb stood behind me, his hands dropping to my hips. "Because I never bought you flowers before."

My heart skipped a beat as I touched one soft petal.

He produced a Kelch's bakery bag out of thin air and

dropped it in front of me. "And breakfast because you never remember to eat, and you cannot survive on coffee alone." He kissed my temple. "They were about to sell out of Bee Sting cake, so I got the last piece to take to Tony in case you didn't make it."

I spun on my heels and wrapped my arms around him. "How did you remember?"

His smile was soft and sad. "Because those were the only days you got up early enough for us to see each other before I went to work."

"I'm sorry," I whispered as I wrapped my arms around his middle.

Caleb dropped a kiss on top of my head as he rubbed my back. "It's in the past. We learn from it, but we don't linger on it."

"I'm glad you're here."

"There's something I've been waiting to tell you." Excitement danced in his eyes.

"Did you get Sabina arrested for assault?"

He chuckled. "As much as I would like that, no." Caleb took a deep breath. "I got a call yesterday. Gary gave my name to a development company based out of Austin. They're looking for a general contractor to oversee projects in the spring with the potential to be brought on as a partner."

My mind went completely blank. "You... You'd leave Gary?"

Caleb's smile was soft. "He doesn't want to be hanging drywall when he's retired, and he could have retired five years ago." He shrugged. "I think I'm the reason he stayed in business. Years ago he promised to use his contacts to get me a job when we were ready to leave for good."

Before I could think of a response, Sophia barged in.

"Alright, love birds!" she sing-songed. "Who's ready to spill their guts for posterity?"

Caleb bent, his lips grazing my ear. "How about we run away to Mexico instead?"

While Sophia and I went through our pre-recording run-down, Caleb fidgeted in the chair reserved for guests. He adjusted his headphones again and again, and stared at the mic positioned in front of his mouth like it was a snake about to strike.

"You ready?" I asked as we finished glossing over the questions that Sophia was going to ask as the Q-and-A moderator.

Caleb laid the page on the end table and picked up a branded podcast mug of coffee.

"Pace yourself," I warned. "Everyone drinks coffee or water to give their body something to do rather than focus on nerves, and then you get jittery and have to pee." I handed him a fidget spinner instead. "That'll help," I said a little more softly.

The three of us retreated to our corners and Sophia gave me the countdown.

Music filled my ears, and I recited the opening I knew by heart. "What's up, little rebels? It's your hostess Blair, and do I have a surprise for you. Get a drink and a blanket because today we've got a very special guest. But first—" I paused as the intro music hit its peak"—welcome to *One Small Act of Rebellion.*"

"Alright, Rebels," Sophia said. "This week we gave you the chance to submit the burning questions you wanted Blair to answer, and they were—"

"—Intrusive," I joked. "But it's okay, because we're all about being open and honest; which is something I've been doing a lot of lately."

Sophia held up two fingers to Caleb. "Any juicy updates on

your Ex-Capades? Finding love again with your ex-husband?" She held up one finger.

"Why don't we ask him?" I smiled at Caleb. "Rebels, I'd like you to meet sexy contractor, avid consumer of appletinis, and my ex-husband, Caleb Dalton."

"Caleb, welcome to the show," Sophia said as she pointed her one finger at him, signaling it was his turn to talk.

He cleared his throat and leaned in way too close to the microphone. "Thanks for having me."

Sophia and I silently swatted him away while trying not to laugh. The sound engineer could adjust it in post.

"It took a little convincing to get you here," I quipped.

"Mostly me trying to get you to actually ask me rather than hoping I miraculously become telepathic," he countered with a wink.

The listeners who watched the video livestream were going to eat him up.

"Don't mind me, I just need to get some popcorn so I can properly watch this circus," Sophia joked, and we all laughed.

"Caleb's right," I said, settling into the flow of conversation. "Asking for what I want is something I've had to—and still have to work on."

He nodded. "I think we both do. It goes back to growing up in an environment where asking for things, no matter how small or necessary, was considered greedy."

I swallowed. Hearing him talk about it was so different than doing it myself. When we were married, he would listen to me rant about the Fellowship, but rarely speak up about it himself.

I always took his silence as apathy, but maybe it was simply that his coping methods were different from mine.

"So much of how we innately react, our defense mechanisms, and our communication comes from what was shown to us in the early years of our lives. When all you're ever taught is that your needs matter less than an idea, you grow up believing you don't deserve to take up space. You make yourself small so you don't inconvenience others."

Caleb smiled as he listened to me speak.

"Caleb, our first question is for you from Jaqueline in Arizona," Sophia said. "What was it like seeing Blair for the first time when you showed up at the hospital?"

He smirked and turned his gaze to me. "I heard her before I saw her. Which is pretty on-brand for Blair. But when I did see her..." He paused, scraping his thumb across his lip. "I realized whatever was going to happen in the next ten minutes would matter more than everything that happened over the last ten years. You can't erase the past, but you can write a different future."

I melted, nearly missing Sophia asking me the next question.

"Blair, Andrea from Minnesota wants to know what made you take a chance on a second romance with your ex rather than leaving the past in the past?"

Caleb's eyes were soft as he waited for my answer.

"I kept asking myself why I hadn't moved from a marriage that had enough problems for us to end it." I looked at the flowers on my desk. "But it was more than just not finding someone else I was compatible with. I think you can be compatible with a lot of people. But I was missing my best friend. I was missing the person who always made me feel safe. Even when we sucked at communicating. Even when we put off having one bad night of fighting and settled for weeks of silent resentment. I always felt safe."

The corner of his mouth twitched in a coy smile.

"Let's talk about sex," Sophia said with a wicked grin. "Madison from Milwaukee—"

"Doesn't get to know a damn thing," Caleb said, shooting me a wink.

I laughed. "Things are excellent."

"Good girl," he said, slow and sultry.

Sophia fanned herself. "You keep going and we're going to have to put an explicit content label on this episode."

He chuckled.

"Sex was definitely something we had to talk about," I admitted. "And if I'm being honest—" I looked over at Caleb, looking for silent consent.

He nodded.

"—I think we still have some work to do there. It's so cliché, but it comes down to communication. Effective communication is hard when girls are taught to be subservient and submissive no matter what."

"And that's a big problem when you're raised in an environment that demonizes anything remotely related to sex, even outside of the bedroom," Caleb filled in.

I nodded. "Sex education. Sexual and reproductive health. Safety and consent, which yes, is still a big part of marriage. None of it is talked about," I said. "We were clueless and naïve when we got married. I was looking to Caleb for guidance because all my life I had been taught that if I obeyed what my husband said, then our marital life would be blessed. Which was code for having good sex."

Caleb took a sip from his cup. "The thing is, boys aren't taught anything about sex either. Like Blair said, it's just something that isn't talked about apart from telling you you'll go to hell if you do it. And then one day you stand in front of a preacher and your entire community, say some vows, and suddenly it's okay," he said. "I felt like a failure. I had this beautiful, precious woman who was the most important person in the world to me, and I was scared."

The admission hit me like a ton of bricks. I looked at him, absolutely floored. "You... you were?"

Sophia, the recording equipment, and the world faded away.

It was just him and I.

His eyes were soft and full of sadness. "Yeah. I didn't know what the hell I was doing, and I didn't want to hurt you. In the bedroom... In life... We were just kids who were put into situations we weren't ready for."

I swallowed, but my throat felt like sandpaper.

"I was afraid to make a mistake." Caleb leaned forward and rested his elbows on his knees. "And I guess, in my mind, doing nothing was better than letting you down."

Tears welled up in my eyes. Somehow, between three microphones and a desk, we had covered more ground than we ever had in a therapist's office.

Sophia caught my attention as she ran through the handoff to the ad space that would be cut into the episode in post. "I'll give you two a minute," she said after pausing the video feed and slipping out.

Caleb stood and flicked the blinds shut, shielding us from the windowed wall. "Come here."

I wobbled as I eased out of my chair and collapsed into his chest. He pressed a kiss into my hair as he rubbed my back in slow, soothing circles.

"I can deal with disappointment," I said as tears rolled down my cheeks. "I can deal with figuring things out together. I can deal with that." I clung to him. "But I can't deal with life without you."

Caleb tipped my chin up, his lips brushing against mine. "Make mistakes with me."

"I want you more than I want to do things right all the time."

We lingered in the glow of the neon recording sign, simply holding each other.

"Caleb?"

"Hmm?"

"Can I ask for a favor?"

He chuckled, swaying gently like we were slow dancing. "Just ask me. You don't have to give me a warning."

I smiled against his chest. "Will you come back to my place when you're done working in the city today?" I closed my eyes and breathed him in. "We can have a late dinner and—you know—talk. About everything."

"I'll bring dinner."

———

A KNOCK on my office door startled me. The studio floor had mostly cleared out, but I was still working. Caleb had gotten hung up at the retail space he was working at, and was running behind.

I paused the uncut edition of the episode we recorded today and pulled my headphones off. "Come in."

Genevieve popped her head in, bangles jingling as she offered a wave. "Do you have a minute?"

"Always a minute for you," I said with a smile.

Genevieve let herself in, bare feet padding across the floor. Instead of choosing one of the many chairs, she sat on top of my desk. "An opportunity has come up that I'd like for you to consider."

I nodded and gave her my full attention.

"EarTreat has begun the groundwork of opening a West Coast arm of the company based in Los Angeles. We've more than outgrown the space here, and rather than expanding in Chicago, the West Coast branch will support the studios we have here in Chicago, and our sister company in Texas."

"Are you looking for someone to do an exploratory trip to give notes on the space or to attract talent and programming?"

"An exploratory trip, yes. It would be right after Thanksgiving. So, quite the quick turnaround. But we're actually looking for a little more than that," she said.

I lifted my eyebrows.

Genevieve smiled like she was about to hand me a Publisher's Clearing House check. "*One Small Act of Rebellion* has so much potential. The Ex-Capades series has been smoking the rest of our line-up. We think, given the locale, more surprise guests would be at your fingertips, and you would have more networking and marketing opportunities. Los Angeles would be a better home for your show and we'd like you to anchor the West Coast branch."

My world tilted on its axis.

Genevieve hopped off my desk with a promise to give me some time to think it over and said her goodbyes.

The irony wasn't lost on me. Ever since I was a teenager, I had been trying to leave my past behind. I had been trying to break the mold of what I was supposed to become.

The opportunity to shed my past had been put in front of me on a silver platter.

But all I could think of was my past.

25

CALEB

"I'm starving," Blair said with a lazy laugh. The back of her head lolled across my stomach as she caught her breath.

Her skin sported the glistening sheen of sweat. The sheet was draped between her legs.

"Sorry," I murmured as I leaned over, cupping her jaw in one hand and kissing her. "To be fair, I did bring dinner."

Blair smirked as she arched her back and cracked it. "Uh-huh."

"Had to eat you first, though," I said, burying my face into the valley of her breasts.

"No arguments here."

We lay together, sprawled across her bed in a tangle of limbs. Hands wandered over bare skin as we simply lingered in the peace of familiarity. When lying together had my blood simmering again, I pushed the sheets away and braced myself over her, looking my fill.

I had never been so excited to get off of work. I sped the entire way back to her place just so I could throw her into bed and devour her to make up for lost time.

Blair moaned when I pinned her arms over her head and slid my tongue into her mouth. Her hips writhed and bucked against mine. Pert nipples scraped against my chest.

"That's my good fucking girl," I whispered against her neck as I pulled away and left a path of kisses from her collarbone to her ear.

I let go of one wrist and slid my hand down her stomach, keeping the heel of my palm pressing low on her pelvis as I curled my fingers and slid two of them inside her. "Are you going to come again for me?"

She let a little gasp slip, toes curling and back arching.

"Mmm." I stroked her G-spot and grinned when she let out a high-pitched whine. "Make that sound for me again."

It didn't take long. Blair's body did exactly what I demanded of it. She gave me every dirty, depraved cry I had been craving.

Her posture went rigid and her breath hitched. I teased her clit with the pad of my thumb as my hand brought her to a second orgasm.

She curled around me as pleasure fired in every nerve ending inside of her. I let go of her other wrist and caught her; one arm behind her back and the other hand between her legs, cupping her sex.

"There you go," I soothed.

Light blue irises barely peeked out of heavy eyelids. "How do you do that so well? I kind of hate you for it."

I laughed and pecked her lips. "There's more where that came from, but let's get you some food."

We dined on room-temperature takeout before sharing her postage-stamp shower to rinse off the day.

I caught her in my arms as she wrapped a towel around her torso. "Let me."

Her brows knitted together. "Why?" she hedged, pulling it tighter.

I tucked my towel around my hips. "Because I want to dry you off."

I dropped the toilet lid down and sat, beckoning her to stand between my knees. "Let me see you."

"You just saw me. I can dry myself off."

"Blair—" I slid my hands up her thighs "—enough of the back and forth. Enough of expecting us to go back to the way things were. I told you that's not happening and I need you to believe me."

I knew it wasn't going to be easy to erase our history. To heal the scars that we didn't even know we had. To forgive the people we were then, and fall for the people we are now.

"Let me see you, baby." Gently, I untucked the terry cloth that was wedged between her breasts. "There's no shame. No hiding. Let me show you how much I love this body. How beautiful I think it is."

Blair stood still while I took the towel from her and gently dried the droplets of water that clung to alabaster skin.

"Perfect," I whispered as I circled the heavy swell of her breast.

She closed her eyes, one hand gripping the towel bar and the other holding on to the edge of the sink.

"I'm sorry you were raised to believe you were less than." I pressed a kiss to her stomach. "I'm sorry if I ever aided in that." Shaking my head, I said, "Watching you today... Listening to you talk on the show today..." I sighed. "I'm sorry I never listened like that before."

Blair sniffed and dabbed at her eyes. "It's not your fault. You didn't know better. Neither did I."

"But I do now." I finished drying her off, then draped the towel around her shoulders like a cape so she wouldn't get cold. "I can't undo the past, but I can promise you that I've learned from it and I don't plan on making the same mistakes again." I stood, adjusted my towel, and pulled her into my chest. "I need you to meet me there."

"Okay," she whispered.

I rocked between my feet, squeezing her between my biceps. "Yeah?"

She looked up with a half-baked smile. "Yeah."

I grinned against her mouth. "I'm going to need something more enthusiastic than that or I'm going to put you over my knee and turn your ass bright red."

She smirked. "Don't threaten me with a good time."

We retreated to the bedroom for clothing. I looked over my shoulder as I rooted through the duffle I'd hastily packed before leaving the house this morning.

Blair, in a sexy little slip, was standing at the mirror, brushing her hair. Her eyes were lax, but her lips were pursed.

She was thinking about something.

"What's on your mind?" I asked as I found a pair of boxers and pulled them on.

"Huh?" was her response. Blair blinked. "Oh, nothing."

"Don't go breezy on me," I teased as I grabbed my sweat pants. "I told you about the Texas offer I got. Fair's fair." I came up behind her in the mirror and put my hands on her hips. "What's making that line between your eyebrows show up?"

The brush rattled on the vanity as she set it down. "I, um... I had a chat with Genevieve before I left the studio today."

"What about?"

Blair's eyes turned down. "Kind of the same thing as you."

"I don't understand."

Blair led me into the living room and started pacing. *That was never good.*

Instead of joining her as she walked a hole into the floor, I sat on the couch. "Tell me," I urged. "We can talk about it or I can listen while you talk it out."

She chewed on her thumbnail while staring at that god-awful cat figurine. "They want me to move to Los Angeles to be the anchor show for a new studio location."

Well. That was one way to rip the Band-Aid off.

Shit.

"Honestly," she said tentatively. "I'm thinking about saying yes. They want to fly me out there after Thanksgiving to look at the space and meet people."

Anger, regret, and resentment hung in my throat.

Just when things were getting good...

"Okay," I said through gritted teeth. "Why?"

"Why not?" she countered with a bite to her words. "It's the next step. It's what I've been working for."

I stretched and curled my fingers into the back of the couch to keep from saying anything rash.

"The show has been doing really well. They're expecting the Q-and-A episode to have record streams. This season has changed things for me."

Blood roared in my ears and before I could think, I was speaking. "This season has changed things for you?" I scoffed. "Why? Because you realized that this—" I pointed between the two of us "—was something worth saving, or because you used me to get people to tune in? Huh?"

As soon as I said it, I knew there would be no taking it back. But it fucking hurt.

"I didn't *use you*," Blair snapped. "In fact, I was trying very hard to move on from you once and for all! *That's* what this season was supposed to be about."

"Until you realized you could cash in a little more on our divorce. Rehash it for the masses. String me along, use me like a fucking step-stool, and then go on to fucking California like I never mattered. Easy fucking breezy."

"Get out," she hissed, hitting me with a searing glare.

"No," I clipped, coming off of the couch. "We're not *not* fighting about this. We didn't fight enough when we were married, so dammit we're gonna fight about it."

"Why!" she shouted. "It's not going to change anything! You're going to Texas and I'm going to California."

"Why do I want to fight with you?" I tipped my head back and laughed. "Because I care! Because I care about you enough to want to fight with you. Because I fucking love you and I'm not walking away this time."

I could see her shutting down. I could see it in the set of her jaw. The way her fingers twitched. The way her mouth turned down at the corners.

"What do you expect me to do, Caleb?" she ran her hand through her damp hair. "Turn it down? Walk away from the success I earned in spite of *them*? Let it all slip away just to go back to being the good wife?"

She was so infuriatingly wrong in every possible way.

I pinched the bridge of my nose. "I have fucking told you time and time again that where we came from is not where we're going. I don't know how you expect me to prove that, but I will. *I will.* Just tell me how."

"How is me wanting to take a promotion and move any different than you taking that job in Texas? Huh?"

"Because I'd be doing it for myself!" I crossed the room, bracketing her arms with my hands. "You're doing it because of *them*. You're still letting them control you. Living out of spite, doing the opposite of what you were taught just because isn't breaking free."

Blair was practically vibrating with rage, but she didn't lash out.

"Same fragile teacup, different shelf." I cupped her cheek. "Don't be a pretty thing that just changes owners. You're not a collectible."

"I want to go," she whispered.

It hurt. Because I knew that if California really was what she wanted for herself—not just to stick it to her family—I would let her go.

Blair's shoulders slumped and she wrapped her arms around me. "I do. It caught me off guard, and my head is still spinning."

I pressed a kiss to her forehead. "Then tell me about it."

I sat on the couch with Blair curled into my side, listening as she told me about the new branch in California and the pros and cons of her making the move.

The biggest pro was the fact that it was Los Angeles and not Chicago. She hated the cold. The biggest con was leaving behind everything she knew … again.

"I don't get it," she said with a yawn. "I was a firecracker at eighteen. I was ready to kick ass and take names and flip off anyone who dared get in my way. Now at thirty, I can't even be bothered to honk my horn when someone cuts me off in traffic. I'm just … tired. The idea of moving across the country…" She stuck out her tongue rather than finishing her sentence.

"You weren't just a firecracker. You were dynamite." I held her closer. "But you exploded, made your mark, and it's okay to admit that you're burnt out. Resting and reevaluating is work too."

She snorted. "Tell that to my schedule."

Unease still ate at me as I stroked her hair. "Sounds like you need to get away again."

If she wasn't flying out until after Thanksgiving, that meant I had time.

"Get away before I get away?"

"Something like that."

It was getting late, and I had to be back in Lily Lake at the crack of evil. I scooped her up and carried her back to bed. "You cleaned in here again," I teased as I laid her down, then checked to make sure everything was locked up. "No feral dust bunnies. No chair of no return. You actually have a floor. That was a surprise."

She snorted. "Admittedly, it had been a while since I've had to have a presentable bedroom for company."

I strode back in and shucked off my sweat pants. "I always knew there was a filthy girl under that squeaky clean exterior."

I turned out the lights and we snuggled together in silence before Blair spoke up. "My bedroom is the only place I let get messy, you know."

"Why's that?" I murmured.

She shrugged. "I guess it's because growing up, my job was to keep the house clean. Anna's job was to do everyone's laundry. Carrie cooked and did all the dishes. And then when there were more little ones than my mom could handle we each had two or three that we raised. But you know all that."

"You can still tell me," I said. "I like hearing you talk."

She sighed. "Cleaning a house with that many people living in it was exhausting. I got good at it. I had to be good at it. But I always told myself that when I was older, I'd let my house be messy and lived in."

I racked my brain thinking back to all the places she and I had lived in after we were married. We didn't have much, but what we did have we kept clean and tidy. I built the furniture we needed or fixed second-hand pieces so we could save a buck here and there.

"Our house and apartment were never messy."

Even in the darkness I could see the sadness on her face. "I didn't want to let you down. I didn't want you to be disappointed in me."

Tears hit my skin as her eyes welled up and spilled over. I pulled her into my arms and cradled her head against my chest.

"The only way I ever earned love was by being good and doing what I was told," she cried. "I tried, Caleb. I really tried."

"Hey," I said in a hushed whisper as her breathing grew ragged. I held her as close as I could. "Love doesn't require obedience." I stroked her cheek and tried to wipe her tears away.

"Love, praise, acceptance, belonging—none of it was freely given to us."

I rolled onto my side and held her as her breathing steadied. "You didn't deserve that. Neither of us did. You deserve to be loved because of who you are, not how compliant you are."

Her hand curled around my bicep. "I love you," she said softly. "Always. Madly."

I smiled against the top of her head. "Baby?"

"Hmm?"

"Next time I come back here, I expect clothes all over this floor."

26

PODCAST TRANSCRIPT

One Small Act of Rebellion
Season Two
Episode 3
"Are you there, God? It's me, Blair."
Aired Two Years Prior

"**E**veryday holiness."

"*On the surface it doesn't sound bad,*" Sophia said.

"*You're right. But it wasn't just about standing on a moral high ground. To my parents and the people teaching us, everyday holiness meant perfection in everything you do. It means kids never talked back to their parents. It means wives never told their husbands they were wrong. It meant that the house was spotless and dinner was on the table and everything was perfect. It meant a world without conflict.*"

Sophia laughed. "*That sounds like the opposite of my home growing up. My parents yelled at each other because that's how they loved.*"

"*You'd think that growing up with a big family the size of a*" soccer team meant our house was loud and chaotic, but it wasn't. You had little girls scurrying around like maids, cooks, and nannies all day long. Sometimes homeschooling got done, but only after we had done our housework."

"How was that legal?" Sophia asked, completely baffled. "That goes beyond kids doing chores. That's child labor."

"Back then there was very little oversight on homeschooling. There's more now, which is great. But it didn't matter. What was the point of a girl getting an education if it went against the Fellowship's teachings for her to go to college or work outside of the home?"

"Do you remember the first time you rebelled against your parents?" Sophia asked.

"I do," I said with a laugh. "When I was fourteen or fifteen, I volunteered at a local library that was run by some people in The Fellowship. It was deemed 'appropriate' for me to do that, even though it was work out of the house. I took any chance I could get to be out of the house. I spent most of my time reshelving books, doing the children's story hour, or just tidying up. But one day they had me go through the donation bin."

"Oooh," Sophia said. "What did you find? A raunchy romance novel with a sexy cover?"

"Nothing quite as tantalizing as a Whitney West novel. But while the librarians used permanent markers to color in the immodestly dressed cover and advertisement models in the magazines, I got to go through boxes and boxes of second-hand books. Most of it was just sorting out books that were in good condition and ones that needed to be thrown out. You have to understand, until then the only books we read were part of the school curriculum the Reverend created."

"So, what did you find?"

"At the bottom of a box was the most well-loved copy of Are You There God? It's Me, Margaret by Judy Blume."

"Ah. Classic."

"I asked the librarians if I could take a book home if it was too tattered to salvage, and they said yes."

"How much did you read before your parents went ballistic?" Sophia asked.

"I got through half of it before I had to go to bed. One of the little ones found it under my pillow and took it to my oldest sister and asked her to read it to them. Anna thumbed through it and caught a whiff of a story about a young girl questioning religion, the way she was raised, her changing body, and what growing up was like. My sister went nuclear."

"What did she do?"

"She took it to my mom who always deferred to my dad when it came to punishment. Anna was rewarded for keeping our house holy."

"And you?"

"I was told to go to the prayer closet and have a 'season of fasting and repentance.'"

"Mind explaining for those of us who did not grow up in Little House on the Prairie meets Jim Jones and his special Kool-Aid?" Sophia quipped.

"It meant I had to fast and pray. I got nothing but water and had to sit in a dark closet and pray until I was sorry for what I had done."

"How long were you in there?"

"About a day and a half, I think. It's incredible to consider the measures that people will take to keep you from having an idea."

"They didn't want you questioning anything," Sophia added.

"The funny thing is, outwardly, the Reverend and all of the Fellowship leaders would tell you it was okay to question them and question your faith."

"But?"

"*They were only okay with you questioning what you believe if you came to the conclusion that everything you thought you believed remained true. The biggest threat to high-control groups of any kind is someone questioning why they have that authority to begin with.*"

"I can't imagine locking a child in a closet," Sophia said with complete disgust. "What did you think about when you were in there?"

"I tried to pray. I tried to repent. I tried to be good. I tried to be all the things I was supposed to be. Meek and quiet and submissive and holy. I tried to be perfect. Maybe some people are made like that. But there's always been this part of me that's skeptical and loud and obstinate and take-charge."

"Let's fast forward to when you finally left and moved away with your husband. What was that like?"

"I really did love him. I tried for so long to be their version of perfect. To be the version of perfect that Caleb was brought up to believe made a good wife." There was a pause. "Until the day I realized that losing their version of perfection was the only way to love who I was made to be."

"When you were done praying in the closet, what did you think about."

"Caleb. I thought about the boy I was going to marry in a few years. I thought about the fact that he was going to be waiting for me under our tree and I wasn't going to be able to meet him. I wondered if he would be angry that I wasn't out there. I wondered if or when he would rat me out for sneaking out to meet him the way Anna had ratted me out about my book."

"I can't imagine living with the stress of always wondering if someone was going to tattletale on you."

"High-control communities don't raise obedient, compliant children. They raise excellent liars. Children who can't trust the people *around them become adults whose poker faces are so unflappable it becomes who they are. Emotionless, calculated, self-reliant humans who isolate themselves out of a sense of self-preservation. No one can protect me like I can."*

"What did Caleb say when you saw him next after missing him at your tree?"

"He already knew what I'd done. We were betrothed as children. Our adolescence was simply waiting out the days until we were both eighteen. Caleb and his parents often got 'reports' on my behavior as a child and teenager so they could be prepared for the kind of wife I would be."

"Like a puppy going from its breeder to their new home," Sophia said.

"Exactly."

"So, what did he do?" she asked.

"Being sent to the prayer closet for punishment meant you were sitting in near darkness for a long time. When your parents thought you were properly repentant, you were allowed to go outside on a walk to appreciate the light. Caleb knew that. It was a staple in The Fellowship. I'm guessing he knew I had been in there for a day and a half, so he left a little box of snacks at our tree, hidden under a pile of leaves."

"Awww!" Sophia cooed.

"He was always good at doing things like that. He was very thoughtful, always filling needs. Doing things that need to be done."

"Do you think not being able to see each other like a normal teenage couple hurt your marriage?"

"Absolutely. I mean, can you imagine not being able to talk to your future spouse without someone else in the room making sure you're not sinning by sitting too close or talking about 'intimate' things that might make you mentally promiscuous? Can you imagine being under a microscope? You can't even go out for ice cream without someone making comments. Fast forward a few

years. We're legal adults, but also still teenagers, and we're married."

"Where did that leave you?"

"Terrified to speak up about my needs. Too intimidated to address conflict. Too nervous or immature to talk about things like finances and the future. Scared and hurt after blasé sex when sex had been the one thing that was built up to be this penultimate moment in our lives."

"But you and Caleb would sneak out to meet up under your tree. That had to count for something," Sophia said.

"It did. Caleb was my best friend. He was the one person I wanted to make happy. I wanted to be good for him. I felt myself light up when I talked to him. But the thing is, you do what you see done. How you behave in a marriage is largely based on how you saw marriage portrayed to you."

"There's my little psychology bookworm," Sophia teased.

"Most of the husbands and wives in the Fellowship were Jekyll and Hyde couples. My dad loved my mom in public and cursed her in private. But she stayed because "love is staying." But what good is a marriage if the people in it are only married on paper?"

"But people in the Fellowship don't believe in divorce," Sophia filled in.

"I remembered wishing for my parents to get divorced. I sent myself to the prayer closet for that. I remember sitting in the dark and wishing that my mom would choose herself. That she would choose us kids. I remember playing through scenarios in my mind and planning what I would do if my parents divorced. It wasn't like I knew what would happen if they did. I didn't know anyone who had done it. But something happened in the years between sixteen-year-old me wishing for her parents to get divorced—to put themselves out of their misery—and twenty-six year old me feeling unseen in a silent marriage."

"What was that?"

"I realized that no matter what, I would never trust my husband as much as I trusted myself. I realized that all my life I had wanted for someone to see me and think I was 'good,' but that I would never feel fulfilled by it because I didn't believe that I, myself, was good. I realized that losing perfection meant choosing myself. And that, for once, loving him meant choosing me."

27

CALEB

"There you are," I snarled as soon as Blair set foot inside my house, shaking off the snow.

Before she could toe off her boots, I had her up against the wall, kissing her breathless. Blair squealed as I kicked the door closed and threw her over my shoulder.

"Caleb James Dalton!" she shrieked as I hauled her ass into the kitchen and laid her out on the heavy wood table.

"Fucking layers," I grumbled as I started peeling her clothes away piece by piece. "I hate the cold."

"Same," she blew out in a breath.

Her boots clobbered as they hit the floor. I grabbed the waistband of her leggings and yanked them down.

"Feet flat on the top."

"That's unsanitary."

"So is fucking you on my table." I unzipped my fly. "But you like being a dirty girl, don't you?"

When she didn't move fast enough, I grabbed the back of her legs, pushing them up and out while pulling her ass to the edge of the wood.

"Already wet for me and everything." I dragged my finger through her sex. "Yes, ma'am."

"Please," she whispered, nearly trembling as I teased her clit.

I groaned in satisfaction. "Please what?"

"I thought about you the whole way here. I—I need you."

Deviously slow, I slid two fingers inside of her. "Tell me something."

"Huh?"

"Did you get yourself turned on?"

Blair swallowed. "Yes."

"Thinking about what?"

Blush painted her cheeks and neck.

I smirked. "Tell me and I'll let you come before I fuck you," I said as I stroked her G-spot.

"I... I was listening to an... audiobook." She gasped, toes curling as I massaged her clit. "Whitney West. Her book. She was a guest on the show last season."

I cupped her jaw and pushed my index finger into her mouth. "Show me what you're going to do to my cock when I put you on your knees."

Eyelids fluttered closed as she bucked her hips in time with the deep pulls from her mouth around my finger. I pulled it out with a *pop* and slid it into the cleft of her fine ass, pressing against her hidden rosette. "I knew I liked you reading those books." Slickened with her saliva, I pushed my finger inside of her, making Blair arch her back and writhe on my table.

"Caleb!"

"That's fine. Scream my name. Make all the noise you want." I pulled out slightly and pushed inside of her again. "Try to break my table. I spent the afternoon reinforcing it with new joists just so I could fuck you harder."

She thrashed, nails scratching the surface of the table as I filled her pussy and ass with my fingers. She was stretched tight around me like a rubber band about to snap.

"Caleb—" she whimpered, eyes screwed shut. "Caleb!"

I pushed my finger deep inside her tight ring of muscle and palmed her ass as I crooked the fingers inside her pussy and stroked her walls.

Blair's fist pounded on the table. Platinum hair sprayed behind her in waves as her chin tipped up. She gasped, knees widening and hips pushing toward me, desperate for me to touch her deeper.

She exploded, letting out a regal roar like a lioness as she came. I pinched her clit, distracting her as I pulled my hand away from her ass.

She jolted, a high-pitched cry catching in her throat.

My cock had pushed its way out of my boxers. I nudged my jeans down low enough to be out of the way before wrapping my arms around her thighs and pistoning into her wet cunt.

"Fuck, Breeze..." My words choked off as I set the pace. "You feel so fucking good. I want to live in this pussy."

Her head lolled across the table, and she gave me a lazy, well-fucked smile.

"Shirt off," I grunted as pleasure built at the base of my spine. "Let me see those pretty breasts."

She obliged, hooking her thumbs under the hem and lifting it over her bra.

I pushed deep inside of her and held there long enough to push the cups of her bra up. Her rosy nipples bounced as I thrust inside of her again. "So fucking pretty."

Her mouth twitched in a subdued smile. Blair turned her head, letting her hair fall across her face.

"What?" I said with a quiet groan as I settled into a steady pace. "You don't want to hear how fucking beautiful your body is?"

She whimpered when I teased her clit. "It makes me uncomfortable," she admitted quietly.

I scoffed. "Hearing that I'm attracted to you makes you uncomfortable?"

Her voice was so small. "Yes."

I slid my hand up her stomach and pressed down in the valley of her breasts, holding her to the table as I softened my thrusts. "You're gorgeous, Blair." I ran my hand up her thigh, stretching her leg up until her ankle rested on my shoulder. I tilted my head and kissed it. "You've got these gorgeous legs that make me hard as a rock the second I see them. Your ass is a work of art. Your pussy is so fucking soft. I love seeing it. It's beautiful like a flower. Delicate and intricate." I let out a wry laugh. "I've been obsessed with your tits since I was a teenager." I caressed one soft swell and squeezed. "Perfect."

She whimpered, biting her lip to stay quiet.

"I love when you're not looking at me because your neck stretches tight and I get to see all these lines and grooves. You're like a statue. Regal and strong, but still so soft. I love that about you. Your eyes take my breath away—whether they're smiling when you're laughing, or sharp and eviscerating when you're mad. And these lips—" I thumbed her pillow-soft pout. "I've thought about them since I learned what kissing was. It's always been you, Blair. Only you for me."

Tears glimmered in her eyes. "Always. Madly."

I came, filling her to the brim and immediately getting hard again when I pulled out and saw my seed spilling out of her.

As much as I wanted to take her again, right then and there, we had plans—unfortunate as they may be.

I helped her off the table and waited as she went to the bathroom.

"Hello to you too," Blair said with a giggle as she stepped out of the bathroom wearing absolutely nothing.

I leaned over and pecked her lips as we traded places. "Hey."

I swatted her ass as she strutted out. Blair plucked a pair of panties out of her weekend bag and wiggled them on.

The doorbell rang, but I really needed to take a piss. "Do you mind getting that?"

She cackled as she grabbed the flannel button-up I'd been wearing. "It might be your family. Do you care if I piss them off?"

I thought back to the showdown at the job site when my brothers had shown up. "Be my guest. Just don't get blood on the couch."

I did my business and was yanking on a clean pair of jeans when I heard a shrieking female voice.

That wasn't Blair.

I stuck my head out just in time to see Blair leaning on the doorframe.

In her underwear and my mostly unbuttoned shirt.

Face-to-face with Priscilla.

And she was holding a fucking loaf of bread. Dammit.

"Oh my God!" Blair squealed in the fakest voice I'd ever heard. "Priscilla! Long time no see!"

Priscilla visibly paled at Blair saying, "oh my God."

"You—" she stammered. "You're ... here."

Blair laughed like she didn't have a care in the world.

And that's when I realized all those times I had listened to her podcast and wallowed in her moving on, I was all wrong.

The laugh she let out just now was the same one she had

used when she would talk about the first dates she went on after our divorce was final.

Meaningless and empty.

A façade.

"Of course I'm here," Blair said as she propped her hand up on her hip, opening up my shirt just a little more. "It's Thanksgiving. Holidays really are better when you get to spend them with the person you love."

Dear fucking heavens. Either Blair was going to claw her eyes out and beat her with a loaf of bread, or she was going to give Priscilla a coronary from flashing most of her cleavage.

I pitied Priscilla, but I also liked watching Blair stake her claim.

"And you made bread!" Blair said in that fake, cheery voice.

It was flurrying outside and I knew she was freezing. But if Blair was anything, it was stubborn.

"That looks great. I bet some lucky guy will be over the moon that you baked him a loaf," she said with a saccharine smile.

I stepped into the doorway, looming behind Blair. *Fuck, it was cold.* The draft bit at my bare chest. When I looked down, I could see Blair's nipples poking at the flannel.

"Priscilla," I said curtly.

Her eyes widened as she drank in my chest. "So it's true?" she said in that cottony voice. "You two are having relations out of holy matrimony and—" She didn't even finish before she blurted out, "You have a *tattoo*?! You marred your holy temple with the devil's ink? But—but I thought—"

"What?" Blair said, feigning concern. "What did you think?"

Priscilla clammed up. "Nothing," she sniped. "It's not my place to judge."

Blair crooked her finger, beckoning Priscilla closer. "Even if you don't say it out loud you're still judging," she whispered. "Pretty is as pretty does, sweetie."

Priscilla humphed, clutching the bread to her chest like a life preserver. "I'll be taking *this* back with me."

"You do that," I grumbled as she trounced down the walk and headed back to the street where her chaperone waited.

"Happy Thanksgiving!" Blair called out, loud enough to be heard across the entire lake.

I slammed the door shut and pinned her against the wall, right back where we started. Her lips were cold as I whispered against them. "Have I mentioned how much I fucking love you, Breezy?"

———

"You look like you're about to throw up," I muttered as I pulled into an open patch of grass in front of my childhood home.

"Yep," she clipped. "That's about right. I'm sitting somewhere between heartburn, indigestion, nausea, and diarrhea."

I popped the dashboard console and handed her a pink medicine bottle. "I have Pepto."

"No thanks," she groaned. "If I throw up then I can leave, right?"

"Yes, but let's try to avoid that, shall we?"

"I should have worn something different," Blair said, looking down at her jeans and boots.

Anywhere else it would have been perfectly acceptable holiday attire. She looked incredible.

But this was not 'anywhere else.'

This was the Dalton family Thanksgiving.

"I didn't go to this even when we were married," she hissed

as I took her hand and helped her down from the truck. "I'm pretty sure there's a rule out there that says you can't bring your ex-wife as a plus-one to Thanksgiving."

"How should I know? You got the rule book in the divorce."

"Caleb." Her tone was annoyed, and when Blair sounded annoyed it usually meant she was scared.

"Hey," I said as I caged her in against the side of the truck. "I'm right here. I'm not sending you in there alone."

"Oh yeah?" She arched an eyebrow. "And what happens when you have to go to the bathroom and it takes you forty-five minutes and I'm stuck sitting there, staring at my fork. What *then*?"

"Pretty sure we sat through a therapy session about not weaponizing past grievances for current frustrations."

"It's not weaponizing. It's predicting the future based on previous patterns of behavior," she groused.

"Fine," I clipped. "If I have to go to the bathroom, we'll go home."

Her jaw ticked. "Do you mean it?"

"I mean it." I pressed a kiss to her forehead. "I'm not abandoning you, baby."

Blair's eyes turned down and she looked at her feet. "They hate me."

I didn't bother denying it. She was smarter than that and would accuse me of being patronizing if I tried to tell her otherwise.

"But I don't." Standing on the ground where we were never allowed to touch, I kissed her. "It means a lot to me that you came. That you're doing this for me. But I'm choosing you. If it's them or you, it's you. Every time."

She rested her head against my chest and closed her eyes.

"I've waited so long to hear that." A tear streaked down her cheek.

"I'm sorry I never said it before." I pressed a kiss to the top of her head. "I'm on your side. We're a team in there."

Blair nodded, wiped her tears away, and put on her game face.

The house was bustling with a flurry of activity. Casserole dish Tetris was played in the oven. A golden turkey was being basted. Heaps of dinner rolls were doled out into baskets and covered with tea towels. Pies of every variety lined the countertop.

As soon as Blair and I stepped inside, everything stopped.

It was like seeing a tornado pause in the middle of a storm. The silence was eerie and—as she always liked to put it—unsettling.

Even the babies stopped crying.

"Happy Thanksgiving," I said to the crowd of onlookers as if it was just any other Thursday.

Blair smiled softly. "Hi."

I stood behind her and took her coat like so many times before. I had told my mother that Blair would be joining me, but I don't think she quite believed me until this very moment.

She stepped out of the kitchen, wiping her hands on her apron as she assessed Blair from head to toe.

"My, my," she said. "It's certainly been a long time."

"It has," Blair said in the most neutral tone possible. "Thank you for having me today so Caleb and I could spend the holiday together."

Mom's silver bun bobbled at the nape of her neck as she gave Blair another slow perusal. "Don't you look … metropolitan. That lipstick is very … red."

A devilish smile crossed Blair's ruby lips. "Thank you, Mrs. Dalton. It's my favorite color."

Luckily, my father called everyone into the joint dining room and den. We stood along the walls, waiting patiently as everyone went around the room and said what they were thankful for.

I barely held in my laugh when Blair said she was thankful for shellfish.

Instead of serving me my plate the way the rest of the Dalton women were doing for their men, Blair stood in line beside me and fixed her own while I filled mine.

I didn't miss the way her eyes kept finding Greta across the room. I had been doing the same with Cade, but we all kept our distance and focused on the food. It was the one good part of the day.

My mom was one hell of a cook. Even Blair agreed.

As we bobbled plates piled high, my mom caught Blair's attention. "The ladies sit on the far side of the tables, Blair. I believe there's an open spot next to Cameron's wife, Margaret.

"Actually," I said as I took Blair's plate. "I'd like Blair to sit with me." I looked down at her. "If that's okay with you, sweetheart."

Her lips quirked in silent amusement. She knew I was playing with fire. "I'd like that."

Eyes darted around the room; no one quite knew what to make of us.

"You're causing trou-ble," Blair whispered as she took the chair beside mine.

I snickered under my breath. "I can't let you be the only rebel, now can I?"

Trying to regain her composure, my mother directed Greta to serve Cade his plate, then take her spot at the very end of the table after she got back in line for her own food.

"Hold on," Cade said as Greta slid his food in front of him.

Blair's eyes widened.

Greta, already turning to head back to the kitchen, stopped in her tracks. "Did I not fix it right?" Fear filled her voice.

Cade's smile was kind. "Will you sit with me?"

Cameron choked on a bite of turkey.

"Actually," Cade said, rising to his feet. "You helped mom prepare the food all day. You must be tired." He pulled out the chair next to him like a gentleman. "Sit and catch up with your sister. Let me fix your plate."

Now it was my father who was pale and my mother who was turning purple. I could already make out the grumbling from my aunts and sisters-in-law.

"*Holy shit*," Blair whispered under her breath.

Carter, my next youngest brother, nearly spat out his water at her hushed expletive.

Greta stood, wide-eyed.

"Sit!" Blair hissed through gritted teeth, both frantic and excited.

Greta looked panicked as Cade disappeared into the kitchen.

"You look nice today, Greta," Blair said as she speared a green bean.

Greta shifted nervously as she sat and tried not to make eye contact with the men on our end of the table. "Thank you."

"Did you make all the rolls?" I asked her as I cracked one open, smothered it in butter, and took a bite.

Her cheeks turned pink the way Blair's did. "Yes," she said, quiet as a church mouse.

"The rolls are the best part." I shot her a wink. "Good job, kiddo."

Embarrassed, Greta looked down at the napkin in front of her, but there was no missing the smile on her face.

Blair beamed at me as she found my hand under the table and squeezed.

I nudged her with my shoulder. "Go team."

28

BLAIR

Dessert was served with a side of hostility. Eyes darted around the room as everyone silently picked at slices of pie.

Caleb had his arm slung around my shoulders in a blatant show of affection.

Cade and Greta didn't dare touch, but I didn't miss their shy smiles and quick glances at each other.

"Anyone got the score on the Red Cocks game?" Caleb asked, breaking the tension.

His father scoffed. "We don't let such filth in this home. Those flagrant advertisements and dancers dressed like..."

I tuned him out, rolled my eyes, and caught Greta pursing her lips to keep from smiling.

Cameron was in the process of decimating a pecan with the prong of his fork until it turned to dust. His jaw was locked, and I could hear his teeth grinding down to nubs from six seats away. "Are we just going to ignore the elephant in the room?" His eyes cut to Caleb and me.

I didn't cower. I didn't even flinch. I'd cry on the inside.

There was no way I was going to let these people see how wounded I still was.

Silence was my armor. They wanted me to give them a reason to throw their spears. They wanted to see me slip, and I wasn't about to give them that satisfaction.

Caleb licked his lips. "Maybe you should be a little more specific. I'm not sure what you're talking about."

Cade choked on his coffee.

Cameron narrowed his eyes. "You're just going to sit there and pretend like this is *normal*? That she—"

Caleb grinned at the table, letting a maniacal laugh slip. "I believe I ended this discussion when you showed up at my work and talked out of turn."

Slowly, Cameron stood. "I would have respected that—we all would have respected that—if you hadn't brought her in here, parading the two of you around like this. Putting ideas in Cade's head that—"

"That what?" Caleb clipped. He hadn't moved a muscle. His arm was still around me. He was still reclining in his seat, full from the meal. Nothing about his posture had changed, but I could feel the fight reverberating off of him in waves of potent energy.

He was a coiled spring.

Cameron clammed up.

"Go ahead," Caleb said, cool as a cucumber. "Finish your sentence. What ideas am I putting in Cade's head?"

Greta looked like she wanted to disappear into the floor. I caught her eye and lifted my chin.

Keep your head up. Don't cower.

She sat just a little taller.

Cameron leaned forward and rested his hands on the table like he was a general mapping out a battle. "We've stood at the sidelines for too long, not saying anything about the way you live your life. We all thought you'd eventually come back to the family, behaving and living up to the standard we were all raised to uphold. But this is too far."

"Dramatic much?" I muttered under my breath.

Caleb raised an eyebrow. "We're blood, but we don't have to be family. That choice is up to you."

Caleb's father spoke up. "Don't forget who chose *her* for you."

It was one step away from the threat of, *I brought you into this world and I can take you out.*

I still remembered the day I was sitting in a freshman psych class, listening to the professor lecture about psychological abuse.

I was always fascinated by the types who would give presents just to take them away. The ones who would provide the bare minimum and then remind you that you would have nothing if it weren't for them.

It takes a special kind of sociopath to do that, yet here we were watching Exhibit A play out in front of us.

It's incredible how that sort of behavior is easily demonized in romantic relationships, but when it's a parent using the same rhetoric it's applauded as firm child rearing.

But these threats weren't meant for Caleb and me.

I could see it in his father's face. He didn't care about bringing his firstborn back into the fold like the prodigal son.

These threats were meant for Cade and *my* baby sister.

Fury raced through my veins. I had never wanted to spill so many secrets so badly.

Every rule we broke.

Sneaking off to talk to each other in private when we were teenagers.

Caleb driving out of the way to take me to a doctor's appointment so I could go on birth control.

Him helping me submit my college application when he was still living under this very roof.

Every time we raised a small, silent middle finger to all of the bullshit they tacked on to religion.

Caleb was outwardly nonplussed by his father looming behind Cade, keeping Cade's shoulders in a tight grip.

"Blair and I are choosing to work on our relationship in our own time, in our own way. After everything we've been through, I would have thought you'd be supportive of that."

"Why would we be supportive of a—a—*Jezebel*?"

Really? That was the best he could come up with?

"I think we're done here," I said, soft enough for just Caleb to hear.

"I'm not," he clipped. Caleb grabbed his napkin and wiped his mouth. "Let's cut to the chase." He turned to Cameron. "You don't actually care who I'm with. You just don't want your wife to see a man treating his partner like just that—a partner. Not a child who needs managing, yet still runs your life, raises your children, and waits on you hand and foot."

Caleb's mother paled. She pushed away from the table. "Girls, come along. Bring the children. Let's leave the men to talk."

The older generation women were just as complicit as the male leadership. They were the ones perpetuating everything to the next generation. *Hello, pyramid scheme.*

The Fellowship had a lot in common with the high society types I occasionally rubbed elbows with.

They could really learn a thing or two from each other.

Like dutiful little robots, all my former sisters-in-law followed with the kids who used to call me Aunt Blair, disappearing deep into the house.

"Greta," his mom snapped when my sister didn't budge.

I raised my eyebrows, a silent communication that I wasn't moving and neither should she.

My heart sank when Greta scooted back and scurried away with a contrite, "Yes, ma'am."

Disappointment turned to anger.

Caleb's fists were balled under the table. "I asked Blair to come with me because I was hoping that we'd be able to put the past behind us and have some sort of relationship with you all."

"That's possible," his dad said, as amicably as a traveling salesman about to pull a fast one. "But the Fellowship is not pleased with your conduct. Nor that of Blair's. Reverend Reinard is aware of the tall tales she tells on that radio show of hers. Your repentance must come before reconciliation. To The Fellowship. To your families. Your words and actions have affected all of our standings in the community."

Caleb laughed as he stood, taking my hand in his. "Well. Thank you for proving my theory."

His dad reared back, letting go of Cade's shoulders. "And what's that, son?"

Caleb smiled, but it was sad. I could see the hurt in his eyes. "That I'm not your son. I'm just a chess piece. Something for you to move around to suit yourself. That's why you and mom kept sending Priscilla to my door, isn't it? Not because you want me to be happy, but because you wanted more leverage in the Fellowship. Your "wayward son" is keeping you from getting the *power* you so desperately want." He pushed our chairs in and led me to the door.

No one else moved except for his dad turning to face us. "It breaks my heart to see you turning your back on us after we worked so hard to raise you right."

"Does it?" Caleb countered with exasperation. "Because love and control aren't the same thing. Love exists outside of control. You don't have to agree with how I live my life or the choices I make. But if you expect a place in my life, then you are going to respect me and the person I love."

We gathered our coats in silence. It wasn't until Caleb fished out his keys and opened the door that his dad spoke up.

"You're a disappointment, Caleb. An arrow that turned its back on the quiver."

Caleb held his head high. "Yeah. That's the point."

———

"How are you doing?" Caleb asked when he found me curled up by the fireplace.

I let the worn paperback close in my lap and traced the lettering on the front. "I should be asking you that."

He unloaded the stack of split wood in his arms and arranged them in a neat pile. "It's been a long time coming."

"Still doesn't make it any easier," I said quietly.

Caleb sighed as he wiped his hands on his sweatpants and sat. "Come here."

I wiggled out of the corner of the couch and curled up to him.

"We never really talked about what it was like when you went no contact with your family."

I stared down at the dog-eared pages. "You know me. Easy breezy."

"I'm sorry I believed you when you said you were fine." Caleb held me closer. "Tell me what it was really like."

I sighed, closing my eyes and playing through the day when I told my parents we were moving to Chicago so I could go to college.

Wives are not to have a higher level of education than their husbands. It would cause her to disrespect him and question his authority.

"I knew it wasn't going to go well. I used to play out different scenarios in my mind, trying to anticipate their reaction to every possible outcome. None of them were exceptionally great. The best I expected was indifference."

He dropped a kiss on top of my head.

"The silence after I broke the news was the worst. I don't know how much you remember. We just got up after a few minutes and went home to pack. When we went by the house the day we moved and they wouldn't let me see the little ones, it hurt worse than anything I had felt until the day you agreed to sign the papers. There were days I wondered what they had told my sisters. If they knew I had gone to college. Did they hate me? Did they secretly admire me? Did they want to go too?"

I picked at the edge of the book. "Birthdays were the worst. No one should have to spend their birthday in silence. You and I always did something small together to celebrate, but I always found myself spending the day waiting by the phone for a call that would never come. And then one day you wake up and the hurt is gone, and you just stop caring."

"Did you forgive them?"

"No," I said simply. "I forgave myself."

"And now?"

"Your dad confirmed it. They know what I do. They know who I am now." I traced the letters of the author's name on the book cover. *Whitney West.* "There's always going to be someone judging you from a distance. There's always going to be someone looking you up on the internet, hoping to see you doing worse than they are. There's always going to be someone waiting for you to fail so they can feel justified for the hate they hold. Knowing that they're watching makes me work harder. I'm not going to give them the satisfaction of me living a life that's palatable for them."

He chuckled.

"Some days I wake up and I have empathy. They didn't know better. They were just raising us the same way their parents raised them. And other days I wake up with the sole purpose of making them uncomfortable with my very existence."

"That's my girl," Caleb murmured, pressing a kiss to my temple.

"How are you feeling?" I asked as I set the book aside and traced the bulging veins on his forearm.

He let out a blustering sigh. "I guess I'll start waiting for the day when I stop caring."

"You don't have to stop caring," I said. "I..." There was a big admission on the tip of my tongue that I had been holding on to. "I always felt like you chose your family over me. You know —when we were married. You're a peacemaker. You see the best in everyone and fight for everyone. You put up with a lot to give *them* the chance to have *you* in their lives."

"I guess sometimes you only get one happy ending," he said as he tipped my chin up and pecked my lips.

I opened my eyes and stared into his soul. "But tonight you chose me. You walked out for me."

"You've got half of it, Breeze." He laced our fingers together. "I chose myself. I chose what I wanted. And I was able to make that choice because I watched you do it a decade ago, and every day ever since. Choosing yourself doesn't mean you're not choosing me, too. It took losing you and growing up to learn that."

A knock at the door startled us both. It was well after dark, and we hadn't seen headlights around the lake in hours.

Caleb's brow furrowed. "I'll see who it is."

I waited, clutching the Whitney West book like a shield.

"Can we come in?"

I popped up like a gopher, recognizing that voice.

Cade and Greta stood under the porch light. She was wrapped up in his coat.

Caleb ushered them in and quickly closed the door.

"What's wrong?" I asked as I jumped off the couch. "Are you okay?"

"I'm fine," Greta said, dropping the childish tone all the women used. Her natural voice was mature and sultry with a beautifully raspy texture.

Cade lingered by the door, looking uncomfortable. "I wanted to come by and apologize," he said to Caleb. "For not … you know … speaking up."

Caleb shook his head. "Don't worry about it."

"But I should have—"

"Don't apologize, Cade," I clipped. "You have to pick your battles. You were looking out for Greta and yourself. It means a lot to me, knowing she has someone to stick up for her."

"I'm sorry things went down the way they did," Cade said.

Caleb shook his head, dismissing it. "You and the rest of the family are always welcome as long as you respect me and you respect Blair. We don't have to agree on everything, but as long as you do those two things, we'll be just fine."

"We can do that," Cade said, and Greta nodded in agreement.

Something inside of me warmed as Caleb invited them to settle on the couch while we took the chairs.

Greta smiled as she glanced between Caleb and me.

"There's something we wanted to talk to you about," Cade said as he reached out and took Greta's hand, lacing their fingers together.

Gone was the terrified girl who nearly cracked under the

pressure of Mrs. Dalton as she tried to live up to being Cade's mom. For once, she looked like a giddy, love-struck teenager. It was a good look on her.

"Greta and I have been talking about it, and we really do like each other."

A smile spread across my face as I watched Greta look up at Cade like he hung the moon and stars.

"He's good to me. He makes me feel seen, and he listens to me when I have something to say."

Caleb looked like he was about to cry. "That—that's great," he croaked.

Cade looked absolutely smitten with Greta. "We have to go through with the courtship. I work for Dad and if I don't do what he says then I don't get a paycheck."

"Come work for Gary," Caleb said immediately.

Cade nodded. "Greta and I will talk about it, but I appreciate it. But for now I have to play by the rules so I can provide for her."

Greta's voice was strong, but nervous. "Until we're independent enough as a couple for me to get a job of my own without serious repercussions."

My heart leaped. I was so proud of her.

"Blair," Cade said. "I've already asked your dad for Greta's hand in marriage because I had to. But if it's okay with you, I'd like to ask for your blessing because I want to. Greta tells me stories all the time about how you raised her, and I want to say thank you for that."

Tears rolled down my cheeks. *She remembered.*

Greta's eyes welled up with tears. "I take full responsibility for the fact that you don't have children because I was a handful."

I laughed.

"But I couldn't have asked for anyone better to look up to," she said.

"Of course," I told Cade as I wiped my eyes with my sleeve. "I want her to be safe and happy and loved and respected."

"I promise." Turning to Caleb, he asked, "I don't know if getting marriage advice from divorcees is a good idea, but if you have the time, I'd appreciate it if we could—you know—talk once in a while." He cracked a smile. "Whatever's going on here—you must not have messed up that bad that you can't fix it." His eyes were soft as he looked at Greta. "I want to do right by her, and I think that means I need to learn from someone who respects his—" Cade racked his brain for a moment "—*partner* as an equal."

29

CALEB

B y nature, I was an early riser. I always had been. But Blair's soft breathing tickling my chest hair nearly lulled me back into a trance.

She had fallen asleep on top of me, legs straddling my hips. I brushed her hair out of the stubble that had grown in on my jaw and pressed a kiss to the top of her head.

I never remembered her being this snuggly. We hadn't been a pillow wall couple, but if there was physical intimacy, we did it, then quickly retreated to our respective sides of the bed.

We didn't have sides of the bed anymore. She slept on top of me or laid smashed against my side with her leg thrown over mine.

If she ended up on the far side of the mattress, I was always quick to find her and pull her back.

It wasn't just that the sex was better than it had ever been. It was that we talked more. We were quick to shoot texts to each other throughout the day. We didn't shy away from talking about things that hurt us in the past, whether it was from our community or from each other.

Most of the time, those conversations started with, "Did I ever tell you..."

And with each one, wounds—old and new—began to heal.

Blair shifted, snoring softly. She wiggled, trying desperately to get a little more body heat.

I probably needed to get up, bump the thermostat up a notch, and throw some more logs on the fire to coax her out from under the sheets.

I smoothed my hands down her ribs to her hips, palming her ass and hitching her up a little higher.

She grumbled in her sleep as she buried her face in the crook of my neck. I held on to her like she was the only thing keeping me afloat.

I loved her with everything in me. Always. Madly.

Losing her nearly broke me. I was drifting aimlessly. Blair was my anchor and my oar—the thing that grounded me and pushed me.

My thoughts were shattered by my phone ringing.

Whoever was calling me on the day after Thanksgiving could wait until Monday.

Still curious, I glanced at the screen.

Allen Walker.

Maybe it couldn't wait.

I tipped onto my side, begrudgingly sliding Blair off my chest. She grumbled with the cutest frown on her lips.

"I'll turn the heat up," I promised with a kiss to her forehead.

She let out a grumpy grunt as she burrowed into my pillow.

I couldn't help but laugh at how much she hated waking up in the morning.

Yanking on a pair of sweatpants, I grabbed my phone and slipped out of the bedroom. "Hello?"

"Caleb. Happy Thanksgiving," Allen Walker said with a quintessential Texas drawl. "You got a minute to talk?"

"Yes, sir."

"Good. Look, I know we talked not too long ago about you coming on board with us in the spring, but we've had some projects shift around."

I held my cards close to the vest, a little unsure if this was good news or bad news. Granted, with Blair eyeing a move to Los Angeles, was any of it good news? "Okay."

"We'd need you down here right after the holidays. One of our timelines got moved up and they want to break ground in the first week of January."

Rather than making a move for the coffee pot, I paused and rested my elbows on the kitchen counter. "That's soon."

"I know it isn't ideal."

Nothing was ideal. Blair was going to be leaving for the exploratory Los Angeles trip tomorrow, and now this?

I thought I had more time.

Those six words toppled me like a wrecking ball.

Three years ago, they were the first words that went through my mind when Blair admitted she wanted a divorce.

I thought I had more time...

To talk things through.

To plan a date.

To get back on track.

To hold her.

To tell her I was still in this.

I always thought I had more fucking time. But something was always more important than having a fight.

God, I wish we'd had those fights...

I guess I always thought fighting meant you didn't love

each other. But maybe that wasn't it at all. We should have fought because we had something worth fighting for.

I let her go the first time because I wanted her to be happy. I wasn't the type to look for signs from the universe, but I wanted to believe that if Blair was meant to be mine that she'd want to stay. That she would choose me. Choose us.

Was I just biding my time with this Texas bullshit?

"Is that doable for you?" Allen asked, snapping me out of the haze.

"I, uh... I'll have to have a talk with Gary and see what we've got going on. Can I give you a call back?"

"Sure thing," he said. "Let me know Monday or Tuesday."

We said our goodbyes and I hung up.

Staring at the countertop wasn't doing me any good. I needed to move my body to think straight.

Before I could pull on my boots to trudge outside to split some wood, there was a knock at the door.

Guessing it was probably Cade—since he was the only relative who still spoke to me—I didn't bother with a shirt.

"Coming," I hollered as I rounded the island.

I yanked the door open and froze.

My mother, bundled up, stood on my front step with Mrs. King.

Blair's mother.

Both sets of eyes immediately dropped to my tattoo.

"Mom."

Had yesterday been a fever dream? Did I hallucinate being exiled from my family? Why was she here?

And why was Blair's mom here? She hadn't talked to her daughter in over a decade.

"Hello, dear," my mother said, sweet as pie as she tried to hide the shock in her voice. "So sorry to drop by unannounced."

Both my family and the Kings lived close enough to drop by, but they never had before. That told me this definitely wasn't a casual pop-in.

Did Mrs. King know Blair was here? In my bed?

I tipped my chin to my former mother-in-law. "Mrs. King."

"Caleb," she said softly.

"It's been a while."

"It has," she acknowledged.

"Could we talk?" my mother asked.

I let the ladies inside, pulling on a hoodie I found by the door while they made their way to the couch.

"Would you like something to drink? Water? Coffee?"

"No, thank you. We won't be long," Mom said.

That wasn't encouraging.

I added a few pieces of wood to the fire and sat. "Okay." I didn't know what else to say, so I opened my hands, gesturing for them to lead whatever confrontation or intervention this was.

"I wanted to come by and chat about what happened at the house yesterday," Mom said.

Mrs. King sat still as a statue.

She and Blair shared strong familial genes. It was like staring at Blair from twenty years in the future.

My heart ached at the thought of not growing old with her. Not having her by my side.

"Why didn't Dad come with you?" I clipped.

Her smile was sad. "Your father believes that until you choose to align yourself with the right values that we cannot be in fellowship with one another. It breaks his heart and mine to see you choosing the path that you have. We truly tried to raise you to—"

"Mom," I said, stopping her right there. "Don't speak for him."

Mrs. King looked taken aback.

"If he has something to say to me, then he can say it."

She swallowed.

I looked at Blair's mom. "You disowned your own daughter when she was barely an adult because she didn't think like you. Frankly, I'm not sure what you're doing here since Blair is right through those doors."

Pain and disdain flashed across her weathered face.

"Caleb," Mom said, in that soothing voice that was grating on my nerves. "Son, your father and I love you."

"Then you will love who I love."

She stammered, and I held my hand up to stop her.

"You don't have to agree with us. You don't even have to like us. You can act in love without either of those things." I pinned her with a stone-cold gaze. "Pretty sure you taught me that. Then again, most of what you and dad and The Fellowship taught was 'do as I say and not as I do.' But actions speak louder than words."

She sniffed, dabbing at her eyes, but there wasn't a single tear anywhere in sight. "I don't understand how you can be so... so hateful. You were such a sweet boy."

"What you don't understand is how I can be so protective of someone I love, because all you've ever known is someone lording over you. Someone dictating your every move, treating you as a subordinate, and enforcing it with straw man arguments and a caste system disguised as faith." I ran my hand over my bedhead. "I wasn't a sweet boy. I was obedient. I followed the rules and kept the peace, but I wasn't naïve. I wanted to make you happy, mom. Because Dad never did. I wanted to make you proud of the man I became because you couldn't be proud of yourself. I wanted you to see me treating the girl I loved with respect, because you never got it from your marriage. You taught me that love is patient and kind.

You taught me that it doesn't keep record of wrongs and doesn't respond in anger. You taught me that love forgives. And now you're punishing me and pushing me out of the family because I'm being the man you taught me to be."

"But Caleb," mom's voice cracked. "That girl chose to live her worldly life. She dragged you down with her. You will always have a place with your family if—"

"Go ahead." I looked her dead in the eye. "Say it. Tell me to leave my wife again."

Mrs. King looked down at her hands. "Caleb, your family has always been close to ours. It's why we trusted our Greta to be courted by Cade in spite of what happened with our..."

She couldn't even say it. She couldn't call Blair her daughter.

"Your daughter," I filled in for her. "Your child. Someone you were supposed to love and protect. But you didn't. So I will."

"Blair..." Mrs. King shook her head. "She... She won't make a good wife. I tried to raise her better, but she's always been too headstrong. I've always been afraid to lose one of my little lambs to the wolves, but I'm afraid she's too far gone. She'll never be good for you."

Stunned didn't even begin to cover it. "Do you hear yourself?"

I didn't bother addressing Mrs. King anymore. She made her choice a decade ago.

"If I've learned anything from being without the woman I love for the last few years, it's that love and service are not the same. I tried to do all the right things, but I missed the mark because I did it out of duty rather than love." I stood. "Pretty sure you taught me that too."

I walked to the door and left it wide open. The harsh wind immediately dropped the temperature in the house. "I didn't go to college like Blair did—though sometimes I wish I had. But I remember helping her study for a philosophy class one night and something really stuck out to me." I waited until they had gathered themselves and made their way to the door. "Aristotle said it. Your identity isn't what your circle says you are. Your identity is what you repeatedly do. I love Blair. And I will repeatedly do whatever it takes to make her feel loved. But all I've ever felt from anyone in this community is the repeated attempt to control others through fear."

I was radiating with anger but I tamped it down as they slowly made their way down the front steps.

"Oh—and Mrs. King?" I called out, waiting until she turned. "Blair's doing great. She's beautiful. And smart. And you'd be proud of her if you knew her. But you don't get that honor. I do."

In an out-of-character moment, my mom raised her voice, dropping the charade of the mousey, mild-mannered submissive housewife. "Play house for now. Live in sin. She will always choose something that isn't you, Caleb. Whether it's that slander she calls a career or herself. It'll never be you. I'm sorry that she's blinded you, and I'm sorry for not doing a better job at raising you to see that. You should have cut your losses with the first divorce. That was shameful enough. But now you're bringing more shame and humiliation on your kin with this—this flagrant farce. Until you make the right decision and repent, you will have no place here."

The window panes rattled as I slammed the door, turning on my heels to find Blair hiding in the hallway.

Tears filled her eyes.

"Baby—"

My shirt hung from her shoulders, drowning her in flannel, making her look ten years younger.

"My—" her lip quivered. "My mom was here?"

I didn't bother denying it. "Come here."

But she didn't.

Blair stayed rooted in her spot as tears streamed down her cheeks.

I went to her, pulling her trembling body into my arms and holding her as she cried.

"I'm—" she sniffed "—trying really hard not to care right now."

I smoothed her hair down and tried to temper the boiling rage in my gut. "It's okay to care."

"She doesn't."

Blair was light as a feather when I picked her up. She wrapped her legs around my waist as I carried her across the room and sat her on the kitchen island so we could be eye to eye.

"I love you," I said as I pressed a kiss to her forehead. "I mean it. I love you."

"I love you too," she said softly.

"How much did you hear?"

"Enough."

"They're wrong, you know." I rested my cheek on top of her head. "About you. Me. Us. All of it."

Slowly, Blair shook her head. "They're not."

I pulled back enough to study her face. "What are you talking about?"

Blair wiped her eyes. "They're not wrong about everything."

"Yes—Blair. They are," I insisted.

She just shook her head again. "I'm going to Los Angeles. I... I have to."

"I know. We already talked—"

"And you're going to Texas, aren't you?" Tears filled her eyes again.

I sighed. "I don't know. There are a lot of moving parts and a lot can happen."

I could see it all written across her face. Pain. Regret. Rejection. Anger. Sadness. "We worked so hard to undo everything they did." She wiped her eyes and let out a steadying breath. "I love you and that means I want you to have everything you want, Caleb."

My throat prickled and constricted. "What are you talking about?"

"You have to go to Texas. Become a partner. You've worked too hard to stay here for what? People who don't want you? You deserve everything you gave me ten years ago."

No.

"What are you saying?" I asked, choking on every word.

More tears rolled down her cheeks, one after the other. "I need you to love yourself the way you let me love myself. There's nothing left for us here, but I know you'll stay and try to tie together frayed strings and fight for a family that doesn't fight for you. For once, I need you to be selfish."

30

BLAIR

Gray clouds loomed in a haze across the tarmac. Rain spit at the lunchbox-sized windows.

I watched the ground crew with tired eyes as they battled the miserable Chicago weather while loading up the last of the luggage into the belly of the plane.

There was a mix of passengers boarding in winter gear, still shivering from their trek to O'Hare, and beach bums dressed for the California sun.

The high-pitched whir of the engines and AC pierced my eardrums. Everything moved in a slow blur.

Passengers bumped and shuffled as they made their way down the center aisle of the plane and found their seats.

I rested my temple against the interior of the plane and closed my eyes. *I didn't need to cry again.*

I had spent the majority of the drive back to Chicago in tears, and had yet to shake the headache that came with it.

Caleb had gone radio silent since I left his house. Not that I blamed him.

I walked away from him once.

I didn't know why I thought we'd actually make it a second

time. Maybe we started at the same point in life, but our arrows were always aiming in different directions.

Going back to Caleb had been the best bad decision I had ever made. California for me and Texas for him would be the fresh start we both deserved.

A life without baggage. A life without childhood trauma and emotional scars.

A life where we weren't defined by our pasts.

"Excuse me, but you're in my seat," a familiar voice said.

I was hallucinating.

"Sorry," I mumbled as I found my boarding pass and realized that I was supposed to be in the middle instead of the window.

"That's alright. You take the window. I know you like it better."

Wait...

I blinked at my lap, then looked up.

Caleb, arms braced between the rows sandwiching us, stared down at me with an incredible softness in his eyes.

"What are you doing here?" I stuttered. "On the plane." Frantically, I looked out the window, then back around the cabin of the plane. "To Los Angeles. You're supposed to be—what? I don't understand. What are you doing?"

He squeezed between the seats and lowered down into the middle. "My wife is running away from home, and I'm not going to let that happen again."

"Caleb..." Tears rolled down my cheeks, but he was nonplussed.

Wide hands, safe and warm, cupped my cheeks.

"I'm not running away from home."

"You're running away from me," he said as he slanted his mouth over mine. "I'm your home. Always will be. You don't get to run unless we're running together."

I hunched forward, cupping my hands over my face to keep the flight attendants from seeing me with mascara streaking down my cheeks.

Caleb's hands found my seatbelt and clicked it into place across my lap before lifting the armrest and pulling me into his side.

He held me, whispering reassurances that he wasn't angry while the flight attendants went over the safety briefing.

"You're supposed to be working out things with Gary so you can make it to Texas by the new year," I said, nervously curling the cover of the Whitney West book that rested on my lap.

"I'm more concerned with working things out with you."

"We can't do that in California!" I choked out. "We barely worked things out on our own turf. Baby..."

But he wasn't frazzled. Caleb was calm, cool, and collected like always. "We didn't work anything out because you tried to shut me out of this decision. If California is what you want, then I'm going to be there, by your side. You can't walk away if I'm holding your hand. I let go the first time, and I'm not doing that again."

"But what about—"

"Texas?" He pressed a kiss to my forehead. "It's still on the table. All of it is. What you want. What I want. We're going to take it one step at a time."

I let out a breath as he squeezed my hand.

The plane began to roll down the runway. Even through the uncertainty of it all, I was finally at peace. Since both of us had been tossing and turning in our respective beds, we curled into each other and caught some shut eye.

———

"MR. DALTON." Genevieve Ewen's eyebrows raised in surprise as we made our way out of the terminal and found the EarTreat vice president waiting for us with a sign that had our last name on it.

A calculated smile grew on her lips as shock made way for satisfaction.

I guess it wouldn't have been surprising for her, considering the only thing she knew about my renewed relationship with Caleb was what I allowed her to know through the carefully curated sound bites I offered on the podcast.

Since Caleb was managing my carry-on suitcase and his duffle bag, I accepted the bright green smoothies Genevieve offered and grimaced through a sip of something bitter and unsettlingly grass-like.

"Just Caleb," he said with an easy smile. "Nice to see you."

We lumbered out to the hired car Genevieve had arranged to take us to the new studio space. Caleb and I squeezed in the backseat, while Genevieve took the front. The ride was filled with chatter about the prospective programming she was courting to fill the roster.

Of course, every name she dropped was paired with how they would support *One Small Act of Rebellion* and complement my listenership.

Genevieve looked like a free spirit, but she was a shark inside.

The studios were nothing more than metal skeletons in a vacant warehouse. Construction paraphernalia was strewn about, and I could see Caleb's mind racing as he assessed the progress in the space.

"And this," Genevieve said with a flourish of her hand. "Would be your new home."

I stopped dead in my tracks. Freshly installed glass walled off what would be the recording studio. Either they had stolen the neon show logo sign from the studio in Chicago, or had it recreated just for this visit.

The studio was at least double the size of my unit in Chicago. My mind raced with the possibilities.

"With the bigger space," Genevieve said. "We'd like to see you move into more social media content. Additional live streams, perhaps an exclusive show for paid subscribers. More guests. Bigger names." Her skirt swished across the dusty floor. "As soon as the space is ready we want to hit the ground running in the new year with a big splash to..."

"What are you thinking?" Caleb murmured when he caught me tuning Genevieve out.

My stomach felt like a rock as I looked around the attached office space that was so big that it made my Chicago lair look like a supply closet.

I bit back my comment as Genevieve pointed out the new bullpen and conference rooms.

With every step, the pit in my gut grew.

She rambled on about all the topics she thought I should cover over the next season.

More of the same. Perpetually rehashing everything that had hurt me.

I was getting to the point where I moved on from all the things I rebelled from, but talking them out every week only served to keep me tethered to the past.

The past that stole my best friend from me. The past where I held on to hope of being truly, honestly loved by my family for who I chose to be.

Caleb threaded his fingers through mine and squeezed as he tugged me into his side and pressed a kiss to my temple.

He knew just how emotionally exhausting the last few days had been. Having his shoulder to lean on was the most comforting support.

Chicago was comfortable.

It was familiar.

I remembered sitting in the backseat of my family's passenger van as a child, soothing the babies as we drove through the city on our way to a homeschool conference.

Over the course of just a few miles, Chicago became my dream. I wanted the city. I wanted the freedom. I wanted the independence.

I didn't want to cower under the umbrella of my father or husband. I wanted to stomp through the storm and arrive soaked, but proud.

I wanted to feel capable.

I wanted to feel unashamed for simply existing in the body I was given.

I wanted to be more than a pretty thing kept silent on a shelf.

Was Los Angeles my new shelf?

"So, what do you think?" Genevieve asked with a chipper clap of her hands. "Eddie has been working to curate existing talent and bring on new names. You would be the biggest name for this studio, but we're shuffling some willing programs to ease the strain on the other studio locations and make space to keep things fresh."

"Other locations?" Caleb chimed in.

"That's right," she said. "We'd be pulling Blair and *One Small Act of Rebellion* from Chicago. We've got a sports commentary program and a parenthood and lifestyle program ready to make the move from our Austin studio to LA. We're hoping to pull at least one of our true crime programs to LA as well. They'd do exceptionally well on the West Coast. It'll kickstart the new location here, and it'll give us the room to bring on more shows to the Chicago and Austin studios."

Caleb's hand on my back was soothing. He talked with

Genevieve about the construction timeline, giving me time to poke around and process blowing up my life again.

————

"WHERE'S YOUR HEAD AT?" Caleb asked when I flopped facedown on the bed in our hotel room.

I closed my eyes, exhausted. "My brain is fried."

"That's because you're basically a cold-blooded reptile who needs the sun to live."

I caught sight of Caleb opening the balcony doors and letting the seventy-degree breeze float into the room. The warmth made my skin dance with goosebumps.

"Tell me something," Caleb said as he stretched out across the bed. "Are you going to be happy here?"

"I like cities," I mumbled into the crisp bedding. "LA is like Chicago, but the weather doesn't suck."

He chuckled, but wasn't distracted. "That's not what I mean." Caleb rolled onto his back and brushed my hair away from my face. "Would you be happy with your life here? Would Sophia come out here too? Would you feel comfortable and safe here?"

"I mean, I live in Chicago. Safe is a relative term."

Caleb chuckled. "You know what I mean."

"I don't know," I said softly. "No matter what I choose, I'm losing something important to me."

He rolled onto his side, his nose bumping mine. "What's important to you?"

"You. The show. You being proud of me. Being good at something other than following rules someone else makes to keep me obedient, not safe."

Caleb pressed his lips to my forehead. "Even if we never

found each other again, I would have always been proud of you."

"I want you to know that all the hours you worked and sacrificed for me to chase my dreams were worth it." A tear trickled down my cheek. "And if Texas is your dream then it's about time you start chasing your own."

"You're my dream," he said without an ounce of hesitation. "Always. Madly."

"Caleb—"

"Save it," he clipped.

"I don't want to lose you to gain this," I admitted.

He pulled me into his arms, cradling me against his chest. His arms had always been my favorite place. I closed my eyes and inhaled his scent. Caleb tucked my head under his chin, shrouding me from all of life's problems.

"We can't always get everything we want," he said. "Passion and purpose demands sacrifice."

"So that's it?" I pushed away from him. "You did this romantic grand gesture only to come out here with me to tell me it's okay for us to walk away from this?"

"No—"

"Well, that's what it sounds like. If it's not door number one, then it's door number two. And if we can't decide between those, then we're at an impasse." My voice changed pitch with frustration.

But he was cool and calm as always, unfazed when I felt like I was on the verge of losing it.

"Tell me something," he said calmly. "Where do you see the show going after this season?" He kissed up my neck. "After you wrap up the saga of us."

"Ex-capades," I corrected.

He chuckled. "We're not exes anymore."

"Oh really?" I mused as I rolled onto my back. "Then what are we?"

Caleb laid on his side, looking down at me. "I don't give a damn what you call us. You've always been mine."

"I don't want to lose you," I said quietly. "I just... I don't know what to do."

"You know," he countered. "You know what you want, you're just scared. I thought that's what the point of the podcast was. You know—back when you were working a day job and recording in the closet in our apartment, using the clothes hanging up to absorb sound. You started it to unpack all the baggage you left Lily Lake with."

A lump started to grow in my throat. "Why does it feel like you're trying to get around to a point without hurting my feelings?"

He sighed.

"Just say it," I clipped, blinking away the tears in my eyes. "If this is going to end with us on different sides of the country, then don't hold back on my account."

"You're still letting them control you," he said.

Anger pulsed through my veins immediately. I started to argue that it wasn't true, but his eyes told a different story.

"You're still putting on that easy-breezy façade—pretending like growing up the way we did didn't hurt you. But it's still controlling you. It's all you talk about. It's what you've built your whole identity around. Until you actually let it go, no matter where you live, you will always be tied to Lily Lake."

"I moved away from Lily Lake. You moved back," I countered.

"And how do you think I managed to live there and maintain contact with my family?"

"I don't feel like being judged for the choices I was forced to make about my family."

Caleb squeezed my hand. "I'm not judging you," he said gently. "But I learned a few things when we separated and I moved back."

I swallowed, hating the guilt churning in my gut. "What's that?"

"That minding someone else's business is much more exhausting than minding my own. I live my life the way I'm going to live it. If they have a problem with it, that doesn't mean I have to make it my problem. It's why I can actually stay unbothered."

"I've moved on," I insisted.

"You haven't. Because moving on means you're not living to spite them. You're living in spite of them. Which one are you?"

31

CALEB

"You two look absolutely smitten," Genevieve said when Blair and I walked into the restaurant, hand-in-hand. "Did you have a good afternoon exploring?"

"We did," Blair said as I pulled her chair out and helped her into her seat before taking mine.

Blair shared a coy smile with me before turning back to Genevieve.

Blair had been given the afternoon to explore the area around the studio to see if she thought it would be a comfortable fit for her. When, in reality, we went back to the hotel and had a heart-to-heart.

We were enticed out of the room with the smells wafting from a taco truck parked on the curb. The green juice Genevieve gave us at the airport tasted like a goat's backwash, and it didn't give me high hopes for the reservations she had made.

Pre-dinner supper was always a good idea.

"Tell me all about your findings," Genevieve said, bracelets clashing together as she clasped her hands. She looked giddy to the bone. "I feel like you have California in your soul. Tell me. Did you feel a connection?" She whispered it as if she was an enchantress casting a spell.

When Blair didn't immediately answer, Genevieve went on.

"One or two more seasons of you and your—" she paused for dramatic effect "—*ex-capade* reconnecting, and you will be cemented into—"

"I'm sorry," Blair said, cutting off the server who had just stepped up to take our orders. She held up a "one more minute" finger and he backed away slowly. "One or two more seasons of what?"

Genevieve smiled. "Of you two falling in love or breaking up or working things out. Moving to a new city together. Detailing the move—all of it!"

Absolutely the fuck not.

I cleared my throat and caught Blair's attention.

I could see it written all over her face. She was done trading one leash for another.

"I think I'm ready to leave Chicago," Blair said calmly.

I reached under the table and squeezed her jittery leg.

Genevieve sat back in her seat with a pleased smile on her face. "Well, that's excellent news."

"To take one of the spots opening up in the Austin studio," Blair said confidently.

Genevieve took pause, sipping something unnervingly purple and chalky from her glass. She folded her hands together neatly. "You seem to have something on your mind. Why don't you share it, and then we'll discuss your options?"

"Actually," Blair said. "I think we should discuss *your* options." Her tone was sharp and decisive. "I called Sophia this afternoon and had her pull the contract I signed with EarTreat so I could discuss some of the finer points of the language in it with legal."

Genevieve dropped her peace, love, and good vibes persona and donned the look of corporate authority.

Blair didn't cower. "The non-compete and exclusivity agreement ended last year. I was happy, so it never crossed my mind. But the last few weeks have made me reevaluate where I should be." She reached under the table, finding my hand and squeezing. "And that's with my husband. We're moving to Texas for his job." She turned her cheek slightly, looking at me with adoration glimmering in her eyes. "He put me first so I could chase my dream, and I'm going to do the same for him."

Genevieve's eye twitched. "How nice," she said flatly.

"The Ex-Capades series will end after this season's run," Blair said. "And I'll be shifting the focus of the show in the following season. We might even rebrand." Before Genevieve cut in, Blair folded her hands on top of the table, mimicking Genevieve's posture. It was a power move. "The question is if EarTreat will be the production company that gets to be a part of the new brand that will deepen my existing listenership and widen my reach to new demographics."

"Is this an ultimatum?"

The server appeared again, looking nervous to approach. I caught his attention and handed him my debit card. "For Ms. Ewen's drink. We'll be out of here in a minute."

"It's not an ultimatum," Blair said with that easy-breezy smile. Except, this time, it was real. "I think an ultimatum comes with multiple conditions. All I want is a spot in the Texas studio."

Genevieve straightened. "I'll see what can be done..." Her lips quirked. "*If* we can get two more seasons of the Ex-Capades. You'll need the familiarity to survive a rebrand."

"No," Blair clipped. "Texas studio, rebrand, and complete creative control." She waffled for a moment. "Fine, it's an ultimatum."

The waiter shuffled back with my card and a receipt. My eyes nearly bugged out of my skull. *That much for one drink? Yeah, screw California.*

Whatever.

"One more season of the Ex-Capades," Genevieve countered. "Texas studio, and we'll discuss creative control with the program director down there."

"Let me be clear," Blair said. "Caleb and I reuniting was a happy accident, but I'm not about to question it." She pushed away from the table and took my hand. "And I'm more than prepared to walk away from anything that will threaten it."

We walked out of the restaurant, hand-in-hand, leaving Genevieve gaping at the table.

Thank goodness for pre-dinner.

"You didn't have to do that, you know," I said as we meandered down the bustling sidewalk, enjoying being able to fade into the crowd.

"I did," she said, squeezing my hand. "I did it for you. For us. But I did it for myself too." She rested her temple on my arm as we waited to cross the street. "You were right. I wasn't moving on. I was looking ahead, but I was still standing in the past."

I kissed her head. "And now?"

Blair took my hand and led me to a park bench. The sun shone through the trees, making her hair light up in brilliant filaments of pearl and gold. She reached into her purse and pulled out a familiar pink envelope.

Opening it up, she pulled out an anniversary card from last year and scanned it for a moment.

Her eyes were hopeful as she lifted them from the paper and recited some of the words I had penned just for her. "I hope you have empathy for the person you were, faith in the person you are, and optimism for the person you have yet to become."

———

"DID I JUST MAKE A HORRIBLE DECISION?" Blair blurted out as soon as we got back to the hotel room after grabbing an actual dinner. She started to pace in front of the bed, raking her fingers through her hair. "Why the heck did I do that? We're about to move and uproot everything, and I basically just quit my job. I don't know anyone in Texas. What are we thinking?"

I caught her around the waist when she pivoted, holding her tight against me. "Deep breath. Where's the badass from two hours ago who told the company VP where she could shove her two seasons of drivel?"

Blair squeezed her eyes shut and groaned. "I wasn't a badass. I was stupid and hangry. I shouldn't be allowed to make decisions on an empty stomach. Nothing good ever happens."

"Hey," I tipped her chin up, forcing her to look at me. "Are you second-guessing moving?"

Blair's decision still weighed heavily on me. I didn't want to rip her away from the comfort of her life, but there was a certain appeal to starting over together.

She sighed. "No. Winter in Texas sounds way better than winter in Chicago."

"That's true." I held her close as I swayed from foot to foot. "I'm proud of you for speaking up for what you want."

"What if this is a colossal mistake?"

I smiled into her hair. "What if it's the best thing that ever happened to us?"

"How are you not freaking out right now? I'm about to be unemployed."

"Do you trust me?" I asked.

"Well, yeah. But—"

"But nothing. If you trust me, then trust that we'll figure out each next step as partners."

"I thought I was done turning my life upside down," she murmured into my chest.

I kissed her head once more, then peeled her hands away from my waist. "Then let me turn it upside down one more time."

Reaching into the back pocket of my jeans, I pulled out a pink envelope.

It was crinkled from walking around the city with it, but Blair didn't know what was in this one.

I watched as her brows knitted together as she tried to work out what I was holding.

It wasn't flat like the rest of the cards in the box I had given her. There was a small lump in the center that I was certain would give it away in a matter of seconds.

Before she could dissect it in her mind, I dropped down to one knee.

I'd never done this part before.

Blair looked startled. "What are you doing?"

Nerves boiled up in my throat, and my heart pounded violently inside of my chest. "Something I never got to do the first time."

She clasped her hands over her mouth, hiding a gasp as her knees buckled and she fell back to sit on the bed. "Is that..." Her eyes widened. "Is that my ring?"

I dropped the ring into my palm. The diamond was minuscule. Maybe one day I could afford to upgrade it for her but, at least for now, it was the ring that meant the most.

Maybe some people would think our original wedding rings were cursed or something, but I saw the fight.

I saw the scratches and dents on the metal. I saw the age. I saw the memories. The hard nights. The sadness. The leaving.

But I also saw hope. Resilience. Second chances.

I saw something lasting that couldn't be tarnished.

"I'd rather have ten bad years with you and seventy good, than a lifetime without your soul being a part of mine."

"They weren't all bad," Blair sniffed as tears welled up in her eyes.

"Here's what I need from you," I said calmly as I took her hands in mine. "I need you to trust me with your bad days. I don't need you to hide your goals so you can show me your success in the end. I want you to let me fight for them beside you. You're my partner, Blair. The one I'll keep secrets for. The one I'll choose above all else. Every time."

"Yes," she said through rolling tears.

I shook my head. "Not yet."

She laughed. "What?"

"If we do this again, we do it for ourselves. Because you're who I want most in this life and the same of me for you. We don't do it because of any expectation or pressure. No external expectations, commentary, or opinions."

"You and me," she said with a splitting smile. "Always. Madly."

"That's my girl," I said as I eased up and kissed her, sliding my tongue across the seam of her lips.

Blair opened for me, immediately turning pliant as I drew her into my arms. Finding my place on the edge of the bed, I pecked her lips once more as I set her on my lap.

"I don't want to wait," I said as I took her hand in mine and slid the thin gold band onto her ring finger. "I don't need a wedding unless you want one." The ring slid into place like it had never left that spot. "If you want a wedding, we'll have a wedding."

Blair shook her head as she admired the diamond. "I was ready for the wedding the first time. I wasn't ready for the marriage."

I felt that.

"This time—" she wiped her tears away "—I'm going into it with my eyes open. I know how much work it'll take to get back to us, but I want to work for it."

I dropped my wedding band into Blair's waiting palm and splayed my fingers so she could slide it on.

"Eighteen years with you as my best friend. Nine years with you as my wife. Three years parted, separated, and severed—" the ring stopped when it hit the base of my finger, fitting like a glove "—but I still want eternity with you as my soulmate."

Blair wrapped her arms around my neck and brushed her lips against mine. "'Til death do us part."

32

BLAIR

I stared down at the diamond, speechless.

If I was being honest, I didn't remember what had happened to the rings in the midst of splitting everything down the middle.

I took mine off when we started the legal process, but Caleb had worn his wedding band until the day everything was finalized. I remembered watching him from across the parking lot as he sat in his truck and took it off.

I cried harder watching him do that than I had over any of the preceding days.

"You left it on the kitchen table next to a box of my stuff that you set out for me to come pick up," he said as he kissed up my neck. "I knew you hadn't been wearing it for a while. I don't know why I picked it up." He trailed his thumb over the diamond. "We can change the stone or get a different ring if you want. But I don't want to wait anymore. I don't want to hold out and follow some arbitrary set of rules. I want you. Today. Tomorrow. I don't want to live another minute without you as my wife."

"Then let's not wait," I said, turning in his lap.

Caleb blinked. "What?"

I pressed my hands to his cheeks. "Marry me—again—right now."

"Where exactly do you think we can have an insta-wedding?" He chuckled. "Besides. Don't you want Sophia or your attack grandma to be present?"

I touched the little scar from Sabina's broom that marred his ruggedly handsome face. "I just want you." A slow smile curled up my lips. "One *big* act of rebellion."

———

A KNOCK at the bathroom door made my heart leap. I put on one last swipe of lipstick and studied my reflection in the mirror.

Gone was the naïve, fresh-faced teenager who had married her childhood crush because it was the "righteous" thing to do.

In her place was a recovering people pleaser, a more confident woman, and a heart that was at peace with who she was becoming.

"Just a second," I called out. Smoothing my hands down my outfit, I stole one more peek, then slipped out of the bathroom.

Caleb was waiting on the bed. His hair was neatly combed, and he had thrown on a button-up shirt. The sleeves were cuffed at his elbows, blatantly tempting me with those forearms. A bouquet of roses was in his hand.

As soon as he looked up, a wide smile started to stretch across his face. "Damn." Caleb pressed his thumb to his lower lip, slowly dragging it back and forth as his eyes crinkled at the corners. "You look..."

"Better than a hospital gown?"

His laugh was loud and bright. "You're breathtaking."

I looked down at the red romper I had wiggled into. The off-the-shoulder straps gave it a flirty feel, while the sweetheart neckline that dipped between my breasts, showing off my cleavage, was all sex. I took advantage of the West Coast weather and left my legs on full display.

There were some things that I had been conditioned to believe about my body that would take just as long to shake as it had to convince me to believe them in the first place. I was not responsible for what other people believed about me, only what I believed about myself.

Caleb smoothed his palm up the back of my thigh and groaned. "On second thought, we can get married tomorrow."

"No!" I laughed as I threw my arms around his neck. "Today."

"Fine," he grumbled to my breasts before tugging on the bow between them. "This makes me want to unwrap you like a present."

"I like the sound of that."

"Speaking of presents—" Caleb handed me the cellophane-wrapped bouquet. "Didn't seem right to have a wedding without a bouquet."

I brought the blooms to my nose and smiled. "Thank you."

"I got us a cake too."

I lifted my eyebrows. "You did?"

He grinned like a mischievous little kid and produced two white-frosted snack cakes. "Vending machine on the third floor."

It was a good day to marry my ex-husband.

We left the hotel hand-in-hand, jumping into the hired car Genevieve had—probably begrudgingly—left for us to use.

Nervous butterflies filled my stomach, and I couldn't help my bouncing knees. Caleb grinned as he gave my thigh a squeeze.

My heart thumped like a kick drum. "Yeah," I choked out. "I think I'm finally ready for us." My breath hitched and tears filled my eyes as the driver pulled up to the courthouse. "I'm sorry I wasn't ready before."

His lips were warm and comforting against my forehead. "Don't blame yourself. We lived. We messed up. We learned. And we're gonna fight every day to keep growing in the same direction."

Caleb held the door as I slid out. The white-pillared court-house loomed before us.

This felt *big*.

I squeezed his hand. "Remember what I said just a minute ago? About not being ready?"

Caleb tugged me into his side. "Don't tell me you're getting cold feet."

"No, it's just..." I looked down at our feet. "Back then... I married you because I trusted you, but I felt like I had to. It was survival."

"And now?"

In broad daylight, I eased up on my tiptoes and planted a kiss square on his mouth. "I'm marrying you because I love you, and I want to. Because I've seen what days without you are like and I never want to repeat them again."

As we walked inside, fingers laced together and nerves bouncing around like fireflies, words that had been drilled into me all my life started playing in my head.

Only ever enter into a relationship if you're prepared for marriage. Courting follows the righteous laws. Dating is like playing Russian roulette. It's a crash course in divorce. If you treat a relationship like it's a game you can quit at any time, you'll quit. Human beings are inherently fallible, but if you follow the holy plan your marriage will be blessed.

We were living proof that it wasn't true.

Caleb and I followed the rules. We did all the right things.

There's no recipe for a happy marriage. You can't follow a list and come out with a perfect product at the end.

There's always a variable. *The people in the marriage.*

Call it fate. Call it magic. Call it serendipity. We were lucky enough to find each other again and fix those mistakes.

Because the end is worth the struggle.

Sometimes finding yourself means finding who you're not. It means making mistakes. It means admitting when you made those mistakes and making them right.

It means forgiving yourself for things that you couldn't control.

And that's exactly what we said to each other in our totally unrehearsed, unscripted, impromptu vows.

With the magistrate officiating, and some random people who worked there as our witnesses, we publicly forgave each other for our shortcomings, we declared our intent for rebuilding our relationship, and we made promises for love and partnership for the future.

There was no pomp and circumstance. There was no solemn ceremony. There was no 'giving me away.' No leering men snickering about what I'd be like on our wedding night.

There was no fear.

There was just us.

"By the power vested in me by the great state of California, I now pronounce you husband and wife." The magistrate gave us a sly smile. "Again." He closed the small book that held the rehearsed speech he gave, and stepped back to give us some breathing room. "Mr. Dalton, you may kiss your bride."

Caleb didn't need to be told twice. With one arm behind my back and the other hand cradling my head, he planted an obscene kiss square on my lips.

His heart beat rapidly against mine as our chests pressed

together. "Mine. For better or for worse." Caleb kissed me again. "For richer or poorer. In sickness and health. Till death do us part."

I dropped the bouquet of roses he had given me and threw my arms around his neck. "Thank you for always loving me where I'm at. Even when I made it hard."

Caleb cupped my cheeks and kissed me hard and fast. "I loved the girl I met under the oak tree. I loved the teenager who trusted me with her dreams and secrets. I loved the young lady who broke free and held her head high as she paved her own path. I even loved the wife who broke my heart. And I love the woman who came back and chose me, not out of obligation, but out of love. And whoever you become from this day forward, I'll love her too." He smiled against my lips. "Marriage isn't about sealing the deal with the person you fall in love with. It's knowing that you'll love every version of them that they become."

The magistrate dabbed the corners of his eyes. "Get out of my courtroom before I cry."

Laughing, Caleb scooped up the flowers and pulled me out behind him. Bright sunlight blinded us as we landed on the courthouse steps.

And just like the moment had been choreographed for a movie, Caleb dipped me backwards at the top of the steps and kissed me for the world to see.

"How's that for one *big* act of rebellion?" he whispered.

I raked my hand through his hair, kissing him again and again. "Feels pretty good, doesn't it?"

He grinned. "Gotta say. Sometimes a public middle finger feels really fucking good."

"That's the spirit," I said with a laugh.

We barely sat still on the drive back to the hotel. By the time we made it up to the room, my hand was trembling as I inserted the key card. Caleb's hands were already searching for the zipper on my romper.

I pushed the door open and stumbled in. Caleb caught me around the waist. "Not so fast, Mrs. Dalton."

Pulling out every move in his arsenal, Caleb scooped me up and carried me over the threshold. "Now," he said gently. "I believe I owe you a redo."

I raised an eyebrow. "A redo?"

He lowered me to the bed, laying me down and setting the flowers aside.

My mind flashed back to the scared eighteen-year-old who had never been given any kind of sex education, or even seen the male anatomy, panicking in the bathroom before she was expected to lose her virginity.

"Let me treasure you," Caleb said. "Let me make you feel the way I wanted to make you feel for ten years. Let me love you."

My eyelids lowered, and I nodded as he wiggled off my stilettos.

"I don't want you wearing anything but that ring on your finger."

Instead of undressing myself, I slipped my arms out of the loose sleeves and raised them behind me.

Caleb worked the zipper down, then shimmied it off, leaving me in lace lingerie.

The corner of his mouth drew up in a smirk as he trailed his finger across the edge of my pale blue panties. "Something blue?"

I bit my lip. "I like a little tradition sometimes."

Caleb stripped down in the blink of an eye before joining me on the bed. He gripped the inside of my thighs with both hands and slowly separated them. "You look beautiful, baby," he said as he pressed his thumb to the wet spot dampening the fabric between my legs. "And already so turned on." He groaned in satisfaction as he lowered down and growled like a predator against my sex. "I want to devour you."

"Yes," I whispered.

He chuckled. "But not yet."

He found my clit through my panties, then grazed his teeth over it. The vibrations from the fabric heightened my arousal.

"Does that feel good?" Caleb murmured. His mouth was hot against my sex.

"Yes," I whimpered. "Please just fuck me."

He clicked his tongue. "You're in too much of a rush." Caleb slid his hands behind my back and unhooked my bra, pulling it away and throwing it across the room. "Relax. Let me see you. Let me pleasure you." He cupped my breasts, squeezing and massaging the stress away.

I groaned in delight, melting into the mattress as he soothed me into a trance.

Caleb rolled his thumbs over my nipples, then squeezed them in tandem. I whimpered, attempting to press my thighs together for relief, but he trapped them open with his shoulders. "Be a good girl and relax for me. Because when I fuck you, it's not going to be sweet."

"Skip to the end."

"No," he said as he laid gentle kisses to my skin. "It's the getting there that means the most."

Slowly, he peeled my panties down and kissed across my pelvis, teasing the place where I craved him.

Sparks bloomed across my hips and stomach as he kissed my clit and flicked it with his tongue.

I whimpered, fingers and toes curling into the sheets.

"As soon as you feel yourself about to come, I want you to take it."

Fingers slid inside my soaked pussy, curling and teasing me with each steady pump. I whined as he pushed them deep inside of me and stroked my G-Spot.

Desperation blazed in my core.

"You're almost there, pretty girl." He latched onto my clit and sucked hard.

Each pull and stroke was unrelenting until I was careening off the edge.

Before I could recover, Caleb pulled away.

Darkness fell over his eyes as he flipped me onto my stomach, then grabbed my hips and yanked me up to my hands and knees.

"On your knees," he clipped as he gently smoothed his hand up and down my spine, going higher and higher into my hair each time.

A moan escaped as he curled his fingers into the hair at the back of my scalp. Pinpricks of heat danced across my shoulders.

"You like that?"

I nodded.

"Good." Caleb rubbed the head of his hard cock against my soaked pussy and notched it inside. "Relax for me."

"I think that orgasm you gave me did the trick."

His laugh was dirty and devious. "We'll see."

I choked on my words as he thrust into me. His dick filled me to the brim in the first stroke. I bit down on the pillow to keep from screaming.

"Not so sassy are we now, huh?"

I coughed out a breath. "Warn a girl."

"The last few months have been warning enough," he clipped. "Hands behind your back."

"But if my hands are—"

My words were cut off by another harsh thrust jolting me into the mattress.

Fingers found my clit, teasing it until my thighs were trembling.

"Caleb," I whispered.

"Are you close?"

"Yes."

His lips grazed my spine as he hunched over me. "Do you want to come?"

"Yes."

"Then put your fucking hands behind your back."

I fell onto my chest and reached backward. Caleb caught my wrists, shackling them in his hand. With the other hand, he fisted the back of my hair at the root and yanked me upright.

His chest pressed against my back.

We were as connected as two people could be. I felt all of him. I wanted all of him. I wanted to be his.

Wholly and completely.

"Make me come," I said with determination.

Caleb tightened his grip. "Yes, love."

Slaps of skin on skin and our mingling moans filled the room as he drew me closer and closer to the edge, whispering deliciously filthy fantasies into my ear.

We had so much time to make up for, but I'd rather play catch-up than regret losing him completely.

"Caleb—babe—"

"Right here," he soothed. "I've got you."

My body tightened. Nerves fired and hormones soared as I shattered.

Caleb jerked and grunted as he grabbed my hips and pressed into me as his orgasm crashed into him.

He filled me. Consumed me. Loved me. Carried me.

He was everything.

This was everything.

We were everything.

Our bodies buckled, but Caleb never let go as he took me down to the bed. Hands wandered; soothing and stroking exposed skin.

I looked up at him and caught a tear sliding out of the corner of his eye. "Babe..."

"You're so fucking beautiful," he whispered as he brushed my hair back and tangled his fingers in the tresses. Caleb pressed a kiss to my forehead, breathing out a sigh of relief. "So beautiful. So precious."

I cupped his cheek, his stubble abrading my palm. "What's the matter?" I ran my fingers across his hairline, teasing the gray strands that I loved. "Today should be a good day."

He let out a blustering laugh. "I've never been happier."

"Then why are you crying?" I asked softly.

"I thought I'd lost you. Not being the man you needed will always be my biggest regret."

I curled into him, resting my hand on his stomach and lazily teasing his happy trail. "You were always the man I needed." I sighed. "I guess I thought relying on you meant I wasn't enough on my own. I wanted to prove myself to people I don't care about so badly that I lost the one person who I've always cared about."

His touch was comforting as he twined his fingers with mine and drew them up to kiss the back of my hand. "What matters most is where we go from this day forward."

33

CALEB

I was watching the clock like it was going to attack me as I slapped the end of the packing tape dispenser to one side of the box and yanked it down, sealing up the cardboard flaps.

Flames crackled in the fireplace, warming the house that was slowly emptying. I was jolted out of my thoughts when my wedding band caught on the corner of the box.

Smiling to myself, I hefted the box of linens and walked outside to shove it into the trailer. It was nearly full.

December had been full of changes. Blair and I came back from California as man and wife.

The impromptu restart to our marriage and impending life changes meant we were scrambling to figure out some pretty big logistics.

But we were figuring them out together, and that's what was most important.

Blair split her time between Chicago and Lily Lake. She rearranged her schedule to be in the studio Monday through Wednesday. I slept in her bed on those nights since I had to be in the city working on the retail space renovation.

She'd leave work on Wednesday evening and make the drive to my place. I turned one of the spare bedrooms into a temporary office so she could work remotely on Thursdays and Fridays while I oversaw the local crew finishing up the residential builds. Though, I usually found her curled up by the fireplace with her laptop when I came home.

Weekends were strictly off-limits for anything work-related.

It was a rule we had imposed to set aside time just for us. Nothing ever came up that couldn't wait until Monday.

Gary always gave the crew time off for the week between Christmas and New Years, so we spent the holidays in the city, watching Christmas movies, eating takeout, and doing a whole lot of nothing together.

Both of us were content to leave the looming cloud of moving to the other half of the country for the new year.

We spent a whirlwind thirty-six hours in Texas, escaping an Illinois blizzard. I met with the partners at Allen Walker Development while Blair explored Austin and oversaw house hunting.

I came away with a job, and she came away with a long list of potential housing options.

My dream was to build us a forever home. Something for the two of us, crafted by hand.

But she didn't know that yet, which was why I was glad we had settled for a rental for the time being.

I shuffled back inside, looking anxiously at the clock again.

Headlights flashed in the driveway.

Finally.

Blair had called me almost three hours ago, saying that she was about to leave the studio. It was only an hour away, which gave me two hours of panic that felt like twenty.

The texts I had sent to see if she was okay had gone unanswered.

I yanked open the door as Blair slid out of the car, blonde hair blowing from under her hat.

"There you are," I said, exhaling a sigh of relief that clouded around us.

Blair pressed her lips to mine. "I'm sorry I'm late."

"Everything okay?" I asked as I grabbed her bags out of the back and slung them onto my shoulder.

"Yeah." She locked the car and pocketed her keys before beginning the trudge up the driveway with me.

Warmth from the house was a welcomed hug. I dropped her bags in the entryway and had her pinned against the wall as soon as the door closed.

"I was worried about you."

Blair nodded, licking her lips. "Genevieve showed up at the studio when I was walking out."

My eyebrows lifted.

Genevieve Ewen had been artfully evasive ever since the showdown in Los Angeles.

Blair and Sophia had finished recording the season in a batch as if it was their last. They went out with a bang—or rather, Blair and I went out with a bang—but the higher-ups at EarTreat had remained silent.

One Small Act of Rebellion had been on a mid-season hiatus but, in a few weeks, the final episodes would air.

It was the end of an era.

I cupped her cheeks and pressed a reassuring kiss to her lips. "I've got pizza. Sit and tell me about it and I'll get you a slice."

Considering the table, chairs, couch, and arm chairs were loaded into the trailer and the floor was covered in boxes,

Blair hopped up onto the kitchen island. Her feet dangled off the edge.

"Genevieve wanted to talk when I was walking out, so we went into one of the conference rooms. She had someone from HR and someone from legal already in there."

Shit, I thought to myself as I put a slice of room temperature pizza on a paper towel and popped it into the microwave.

I wanted us, but I didn't want Blair to lose herself.

Blair nervously picked at her nail beds. "They ended my contract."

I swore under my breath as I ripped the microwave open and pulled out the slice. "I'm…" I rubbed the back of my neck and sighed. "Shit. I'm sorry."

A wicked smile curled at the corner of her mouth as she took the piece from me. "And they offered me a new contract at the Austin studio."

My heart stopped. "Say that again?"

"Full creative control, no more pimping out our love story, and I get to rebrand the show or just start from scratch with a new name and concept."

"That's—" I ran down the list in my head.

"Everything I wanted," she finished for me. Blair set the pizza aside and wrapped her arms around my neck. "Everything I wanted *and* you."

I laughed as I wrapped her up in my arms. "I'm so fucking proud of you."

"I was terrified," she admitted.

It struck me as odd because Blair had never said that to me before.

"Why?"

She sniffed, wiping her eyes. "I laid my cards on the table in Los Angeles and I knew you were on board with me, but I didn't know what I was going to do if I lost my job and we moved."

"We would have figured it out."

"I know. But..." She sighed. "It's important to me that I equally contribute to our household. It scares me to not do that." Before I could jump in, Blair kept rambling. "And I know you wouldn't hold it over my head or abuse that power, but I just think of my mom and Anna and the rest of my sisters, and that they have to blindly trust—"

"Having a safety net doesn't make walking a tightrope any easier," I said, cupping her cheeks. "Taking steps to feel safe doesn't mean you're going to put less effort into our marriage."

"Thank you," she whispered.

"What about Sophia?" I asked, hopping up onto the counter and sitting beside her.

"I called her on the way here to talk it out," she said as she took a bite of pizza. "Sorry I didn't see your texts."

"That's alright."

"She's comfortable in Chicago. If she doesn't get attached to another show in the studio there, she might stay on with me and record virtually."

"How are you feeling about that?"

She laughed and peeled a slice of pepperoni off the pizza, then popped it in her mouth. "Alright, I guess. I feel like there's a million new unknowns now that I know I'll have a job. A few hours ago it was just if I had a job or didn't."

"You'll have time to figure it out. The end of the season is coming soon. You can spend the break getting comfortable in Austin and sharing a bed full-time again."

She smiled. "Now that—I'm excited about."

I squeezed her thigh and slid off the counter. "Good. Keep that hope because we've got more boxes to pack."

Blair finished eating while I carted out the boxes that were stacked up by the door.

Tomorrow we'd be handing over my house keys to our realtor and starting the two-day drive to Austin.

Blair's apartment was mostly packed—something we had been working on over the last few weeks—but she planned on keeping it through the rest of her lease, just in case either of us had to travel back to Illinois.

I shook off the heavy snowflakes that pelted me on my way back inside. "Snow's picking up."

Blair set down the tape dispenser and swiped into her phone, sighing happily. "It's sixty-five and sunny in Austin."

I chuckled. "Two days."

"These two are ready," Blair said, pointing to the boxes labeled *KITCHEN UTENSILS* that she had finished packing.

I stacked them one on top of the other, and picked them up. I froze in place as soon as I turned to head back out the door.

My parents stood on the threshold. My father loomed, grim-faced and arms crossed.

Blair's phone dropped out of her hand, clattering as it hit the kitchen floor.

"What's the meaning of all this?" my father snapped, eyes scanning the mass of boxes, packing material, and not much else. The rest of the house was already loaded up for the drive. "Why is there a 'for sale' sign in your front yard?"

I set the boxes back on the kitchen island and squatted to pick up Blair's phone. Handing it back to her, I said, "I don't remember inviting you into our home."

A more self-aware person would have taken the hint that their presence was unwelcome, but my father was completely undeterred. "You're moving?"

"Not that it's any of your business, but yes."

He was aghast. "And you were—what—just not going to tell us?"

Years of judgment were etched into the lines on his face.

"Considering you didn't know and we've been packing for a month, you could make that logical assumption."

"Caleb," Blair chided quietly.

This coldness killed me inside, but there was no going back. They had stolen love from me in the name of what was right in their eyes once. I wouldn't let them do it a second time.

I gave Blair a subtle shake of my head. This wasn't the battle I was going to fight with them. It was the fight I was going to walk away from.

My dad huffed. "Don't tell me you two are—are back together and living in sin."

A laugh slipped. "According to you, we're actually not." I held up my hand and flashed my wedding band. "You'll be unhappy to know that we've reconciled and are working through the things that got between us in the first place. And you're one of them. So, if you don't mind, shut the door on the way out. It's cold."

"You're... married?" Words full of hurt and betrayal slipped from my mother's lips.

"Yes," Blair said calmly. "Have been for almost a month and a half."

"Throwing your life away again," he hissed with more vitriol than I thought possible. "When will you learn? You're a disgrace."

"Where are you moving to? Back to Chicago?" Mom asked.

My dad gave her the terse shake of his head the way he always did when he was silently telling her to be quiet.

Blair looked at me, unsure if she should tell them where we were going or not.

I lifted my eyebrows. *Up to you.*

"I believe you have Caleb's phone number should you need to get in touch," Blair said. It was a reasonable boundary.

I slid my hand onto the small of her back to reassure her.

"Unbelievable," my father muttered. "Absolutely unbelievable. Does her father know about this? I don't want to have to be the one to break this wretched news to him when we meet tomorrow about the progress Cade has made in courting his daughter."

"Greta," Blair clipped. "*His daughter* has a name. *Her name* is Greta. And no, he doesn't know. *He* chose to cut me—*his daughter*—out of his life. What kind of loving father does that?" The question she left him with was so simple, but it spoke volumes.

I wasn't a criminal. I hadn't done anything but fall in love with a woman. A beautiful, wise, quick-witted, kind-hearted, loving woman. All I had done was stand up for the woman I had vowed to love, honor, and cherish.

Ironically, they were the same canned vows my father had probably said to my mother.

Maybe fulfilling those vows made me more of a rebel than I thought I was.

I fell in love with Blair, sneaking around to try and know her heart. And I kept loving her with all of mine when I wasn't supposed to.

If there was anything I had learned in the interlude between promising forever and fighting for it, it was that there was no sitting on the fence in marriage.

I was either in or out.

When Blair and I were being counseled for marriage by Reverend Reinard, he would often say things about marriage being two people becoming one.

I truly believed that, but not the way we had been taught.

My dad would often joke that he was the head of the household and my mom was the backbone. He dictated what she did, while she held everything together.

But that wasn't being one. That was being a king in a crumbling castle; self absorbed enough to believe he still reigned supreme while his kingdom was covered in rubble.

Being one meant looking out for her best interest the way I wanted her to look out for mine; not seeking her deference for my gain. Being one meant that we chose each other before anyone else and above anyone else.

For once, my dad actually talked back to Blair instead of pretending like she was a mute statue. "The father who prunes a dead branch from his tree is a father who cares for the rest of the fruit."

"As long as they're up to his standards," she countered. "Or they get cut off too."

"An empty shelf is better than one full of garbage. Those who obey and follow the righteous way have nothing to worry about."

"Enough," I snapped.

My parents looked taken aback at me raising my voice. It was probably a first for all of us.

"We have things to do. You can see yourselves out."

Blair's expression was cold as she looked on.

"That's it?" he sneered. "After everything we did for you?"

"No," I laughed. "Because of everything you did."

"I'll be telling Mr. King about this," he jeered as he led my mother outside.

A gust of frigid wind hit us as the door slammed, and I pulled Blair into my chest. "Are you okay?"

"Are you?" she countered.

"He got something wrong," I murmured, kissing the top of her head.

"He got a lot wrong, but what are you thinking about?"

I chuckled. "It's not always the branch that needs to be cut off before it kills the tree. Sometimes the tree is dead at the roots and the branch is the only thing that can be saved."

"We'll put down our roots elsewhere." Blair wrapped her arms around me. "We won't just be good. We'll get to create a good life. One on our terms."

Tears filled her eyes to the brim as I tilted my head and kissed her. I could still taste the pizza sauce on her lips. "Do you want to tell your parents we're moving? You know— before my parents spin their version of the story?"

Blair shook her head.

"You sure?"

"Yeah," she said with an unsteady exhale. "Loose ends either get tied up or they fray and need to be cut off. Mine are already frayed." She choked on her words. "I just wish I was as over it as I want to think that I am."

"Hey," I said as I cupped her cheeks, wiping her tears away with my thumbs. "It's okay to still be hurt. You can be hurt and move on. Both can happen simultaneously."

She nodded and looked around and the slowly emptying house. "I hope they're haunted by the dust void left behind by their pretty things."

34

BLAIR

I stared at the text message that lit up my screen while I was taking a break from searching for the box that held all of our forks and spoons.

Even though it was January in Texas, I had every window in the apartment open to let in the cool breeze.

CADE

Just married. Now we're both Mrs. Dalton. Miss you. Love, Greta

My heart ached as I read the text and stared at the attached picture. Greta made a beautiful bride, and Cade was handsome as ever.

Throughout the move, Cade and Caleb had been in constant contact. Occasionally, Cade and Greta would sneak off together and she would use his phone to call me.

Cade had promised that, as soon as they were married and moved in together, he would help her get a phone.

I was holding on to that promise like a lifeline.

I remembered how scared I felt on my wedding day. I hated to think about what Greta was feeling.

The lace edge of her veil caught my eye and lifted my spirits.

She wore it.

My smile grew, thinking about the pride she must have felt as she pinned it into her blonde hair this morning. Wearing *my* veil was her one small act of rebellion.

Cade had asked if I had anything "old or borrowed" that Greta could have on their wedding day since Caleb and I were *personae non gratae*. I found my veil as I was packing up my apartment and hid it by the oak tree.

Not sure how much alone time Cade and Greta had before they headed to their reception, I texted back quickly.

BLAIR

You look absolutely beautiful. Talk soon?

As soon as the text was sent, a call came through. I swiped across the screen instantly. "Hey, sweetie. Happy wedding day."

"Thanks," Greta said in a hushed voice.

I settled on the floor and rested my elbows on my knees. "How are you feeling? Are you okay?"

"I'm good. The ceremony is over and we just finished taking some pictures. I get a few minutes to myself while Cade has *the talk* with his dad before we're announced at the reception. Cade slipped me his phone before he went into the other room. Thank goodness for wedding dresses with pockets."

I groaned, remembering what Caleb had recounted from his post-ceremony talk with his dad.

It was a crude overview of 'tab A goes into slot B' that completely negated consent and the woman's pleasure or comfort.

"Anything you want to talk about? This is a judgment-free zone. I'll tell you anything you want to know."

Greta was quiet for a moment. "I don't think we're going to do... *it* tonight."

"That is absolutely okay," I said quickly. "Even if you're married, it's still your choice to give your husband access to your body. You can say no anytime."

"Thanks," she whispered. "Everyone's been watching me like a hawk since you guys moved. But I met Cade by the tree a week ago and we talked about it. He's excited to have..."

"Sex," I said, supplying the sinful word she was taught to never say.

"Yeah. But I told him I wasn't ready, so we talked about taking it slow and you know ... just getting used to being together and being allowed to touch each other first."

A tear streaked down my cheek. "I'm so proud of you. You're miles ahead of where I was on my wedding day."

"I had you to look up to, even when you didn't know I was watching." She sniffed on her end of the line. "Thank you."

"Enjoy today, okay?" I laughed as I wiped my tears. "Eat some cake. Give Cade a full hug."

"Can I ask you one thing?"

"Anything."

"Will kissing get better? Because that was *so* weird."

I laughed. "It will. It gets way better after having your first kiss in front of the entire Fellowship is over with."

She giggled. "I hope so."

"Call me when you can."

"I will," she said.

"I love you, Greta."

Greta sniffed again. "I love you too. Thanks for... Everything. For being my mom and my sister."

The waterworks exploded as soon as I hung up. I clutched my phone to my chest as I heard the footfalls of heavy boots coming up the stairwell.

The door creaked open, and Caleb strolled in. "Hey—*shit*." He knelt before me and cupped my cheek. "What's the matter, Breezy? You hurt?"

I shook my head and simply lifted my phone.

"You got to talk to Greta?"

I nodded. "Yeah."

"How'd the wedding go?"

"Good," I said as I wiped my cheeks. "She sounded a little scared, but I think she's holding it together pretty well. She hated kissing him. Thought it was weird."

Caleb laughed. "I remember ours. It was awful."

I nodded, a smile breaking out across my face. "I guess that's the way it is when you don't get to ease into the physical stuff. You just get thrown into the deep end."

"I called Cade yesterday. We had a long talk."

"Please tell me you gave him a better version of the talk so he's not relying on whatever awful, archaic information your dad is telling him right now."

"It was a good talk," he promised. "And he told me that once they get to the apartment, he's going to surprise Greta with a movie night tonight so she can take her time getting comfortable around him."

Cade and Greta were saving up to move out of Lily Lake, though Caleb and I were the only ones who knew that. They were going to spend a long weekend at my apartment in Chicago, and hopefully go on a proper honeymoon in a few years.

I took a deep breath and closed my eyes. "That makes me feel better."

Caleb kissed my forehead.

"Did you warn them about Sabina?"

"Yeah, I told Cade you have an attack grandma armed with an assault broom."

"She's not that bad."

"She gave me head trauma."

I glanced over at the kitchen table that was way too big for our one-bedroom apartment.

Two porcelain cat figurines sat on top of it.

I grimaced. "They really are awful."

"As soon as you give me the go-ahead, I'll drop them down the garbage disposal."

I smiled sadly. "Yeah."

"What's on your mind?" Caleb asked as he sat beside me and draped his arm around my shoulders.

I tucked myself into his side. "I worry about the rest of my sisters. I moved. Greta's moving. Who's left to show them the way out?"

He kissed the top of my head. "They watched you both walk through the door. Even if they can't see it, they know it's there."

We sat in silence for a little while, soaking in the comfort of a new city and a fresh start.

"What's in that little box?" I asked. "A milk jug?"

Caleb brushed it off. "Just something I wanted to make sure came with us. Hey—did you see that the last episode went live today?" he asked, pulling out his phone to show me the podcast's streaming page.

"The end of an era," I said wistfully.

"Eras have to end so a new one can begin," he said. "I'm proud of you."

This morning I had made a quick trip to studio in downtown Austin that I would call home when the next season began. Even though I had creative control of whatever I wanted to do next, I met with their program director to grease some wheels and start things off on the right foot. I still had no idea what the new program concept was going to be. All I knew was that I needed a change.

Doing one small act of rebellion at a time had a snowball effect.

The idea of changing my life was terrifying. Where did I even start? But just over fifteen years ago, I made one small choice that led to another.

And another.

And another.

"What room do you want me to start unpacking?" Caleb asked.

I looked around. "Honestly, if we could tag team the kitchen, that would be great. I can't find the utensils."

Caleb pecked my lips. "Wanna do your ceremonial episode listen while we work?"

I laughed. "You were very much present when we recorded it. There aren't any surprises this time."

"Unlike hearing you talk about our drunken hookup."

I laughed and scrolled through my phone. "Fine," I said as I turned the volume all the way up and hit play.

Caleb brushed behind me, smoothing his hand across my ass as he made a move for another pile of boxes while the intro music played.

I listened to myself go through the announcement that not only was it the last episode of the season, but the final episode of *One Small Act of Rebellion*.

Sophia and I bantered back and forth as we went through a highlight reel of our favorite moments. Hers was our second season guest roster, an episode of truth or dare, and meeting MMA fighter Miles Zhou.

My favorite throwback moment was meeting famed romance author, Whitney West.

Shortly after the episode I recorded with her aired, she

was kidnapped and her real identity was revealed to the world.

I had sent a get well card and flowers after the incident, but she stayed on my mind often.

There were some people who imprinted on you for life.

"*We've had a good run,*" Sophia said wistfully. "*Most shows don't last as long as we have.*"

"*And we're going out on our terms,*" I said. It was important that I threw that in there.

This change wasn't an end. It was a fork in the road.

Sure, I was choosing the path with an uphill climb, but I'd rather feel the burn than become apathetic.

"*So,*" Sophia said. "*We've been teasing a very special guest for our final episode.*"

"*That we have,*" I chimed in.

Caleb shared a sheepish smile from across the kitchen as he unloaded the utensils.

"*I think it would be fitting if you introduced our guest, B,*" Sophia said with the handoff.

"*I started* One Small Act of Rebellion *as a way to detail growing up, getting married, and then leaving a high-control group. I wanted to show the process of breaking free and creating an identity that was mine.*"

Caleb passed by and pressed a kiss to my temple, whispering, "I'm proud of you."

I caught his hand and squeezed it. "I'm proud of us."

"*But in the process of finding myself, I lost someone who had always been the most important person to me. But I guess fate saw fit to bring my ex-husband back into my life this season when I was —ironically—trying to throw myself back into the dating pool.*"

Caleb and I shared sheepish smiles.

Sophia chimed in. "*If you've been keeping up with the season, you know all about Blair and Caleb's hospital meet cute, their sala-*

cious bar hookup, and you probably even caught the Q-and-A episode we did where the man himself came and answered all of your burning questions."

"And now he's back," I said. *"But not as my ex-husband."*

"Ladies, gents, furry friends, and whoever else is listening," Sophia said. *"It's my greatest honor, to introduce to you, for the very last time on this show, Mr. and Mrs. Dalton."*

"Thank you," Caleb said as he situated himself in front of the mic.

He was blushing as he carefully unpacked plates and stacked them in the cabinets while listening.

"Well," I said. *"Caleb and I have some news."*

"Some big news," he agreed.

"We've been keeping it quiet for our sake, but we're ready to let the cat out of the bag."

"Drum roll please," Sophia said as a snare drum sound effect faded in.

"We're married!" I squealed.

"Again," Caleb said with a good-natured chuckle.

"Blair, what's the biggest takeaway from spending the last few years unpacking your upbringing?" Sophia asked

I knew the question was coming, but it had still taken me a moment to come up with a good answer. *"Speak your mind even if your voice shakes. Don't drink poison just because you're thirsty. And if you stumble, make it part of a dance."*

"What about you, Caleb?" Sophia asked, turning the question on him. *"Obviously, you've been around the show, but not unpacking week by week like Blair has. What's your takeaway from the last few years? Your separation, divorce, and reconciliation."*

"Thank you for immediately throwing me in the deep end, Soph," Caleb joked. *"I think I learned that setting an example is two-fold. Sometimes it means tolerating a little discomfort to stay in someone's life so they can see the change in you and want it for*

themselves. But sometimes setting an example means not tolerating disrespect for the sake of keeping the peace."

There was a little sadness with his words, especially as we prepared to start our new life together.

"Did you two ever imagine getting back together?" Sophia asked.

"No," I said. *"If it hadn't been for an impromptu trip to the hospital, I don't think I would have ever had the bravery to reach back out."* There was a moment of silence as I contemplated what could have been. *"I don't think I would have ever come to terms with the role I played in the downfall of our marriage."*

Caleb came up behind me and wrapped his arms around my waist. "What *we* did to end our marriage," he said softly. "Both of us."

"And what we did to fix it," I said, turning to look up in his eyes.

"You can be a rebel even if you're scared," I said on the episode. *"No where in the definition does it say anything about confidence or bravery. It's about rising in spite of and against opposition. Sometimes that opposition is someone else. Sometimes it's rising against yourself."*

Caleb's voice was strong as he spoke to the listeners. *"There will be people in your life waiting for you to fail. They'll be happy when you do. Because you will fail in life. But what makes failure worth it is doing it on your terms. Because it also means that getting up and trying again is on your terms. And it means you're going to fight harder the next time."*

"Caleb wrote me birthday and anniversary cards while we were divorced," I said. *"I've read these words and claimed them for myself every day since he gave me the card."*

With a deep breath, I offered the last piece of us I was ever willing to give for my personal gain. I did it because somewhere, someone needed to let go of their past the way he had taught me to.

"*I hope you have empathy for the person you were, faith in the person you are, and optimism for the person you have yet to become. You inspire others to show up for themselves every time you show up for yourself. And no matter what happens from this day forward, I believe that you will do good in the world because you are no longer living as the person you were conditioned to be. Rather, I see you becoming the person you were created to be. I'm proud of you. And I will love you. Always, madly.*"

EPILOGUE
CALEB

My heart thumped in my chest as I held both of Blair's hands and led her up the driveway. She stumbled, hindered by the blindfold I had covering her eyes.

She was still dressed from a long day at the studio.

The upside of starting a new show was that she had complete creative control. The downside was that she had to do all the work.

Eventually she wanted to find a "new Sophia" but, for now, she was content.

My girl liked a challenge.

"Oh my god. Can I just take it off already?"

"Not yet," I said with a chuckle.

"Caleb!"

"Patience, Breezy."

I looked over my shoulder at the brand-new house that had sprung up in a matter of months.

Perks of doing a lot of the work myself.

The days were long, but the end result was worth it.

"If you wanted it to be a big reveal, you could have let me

walk backwards or something. I know what the street looks like."

"What fun would that be?" I joked. I had picked her up from work, thrown her in my truck, and blindfolded her like a kidnapper.

Maybe I'd put that blindfold to good use later...

After we got settled in Austin, I started looking for land to build on.

And then I asked Blair for one big act of trust.

Let me surprise you with the house.

She was hesitant at first. I knew just how Type-A she was, but we compromised.

Blair and I hashed out what was most important to her in a floor plan, and I even let her look at some renderings to see which one brought the most excitement to her face.

She and I found the land together. We wanted something that was equidistant for our commutes, but a place far enough outside of Austin where we could have space to breathe.

Just when I thought we had exhausted our options, Blair found a lot on a small lake just outside of Austin.

The first time we set food on the overgrown land, I knew it was perfect.

Blair agreed to trust me with the build and only pestered me with questions twenty times a day.

After the land was cleared and the foundation was laid, I banned her from driving out here.

Six months later, the house was finally—*mostly*—done. Some of the rooms I'd get around to finishing after we moved out of our tiny apartment.

But we were home.

Blair was trembling as I positioned her in the middle of the driveway so she could see the entire house. "I'm so nervous," she whispered.

I surprised her with a kiss. "Don't be nervous. It's just a half of a year of work and a nauseating mortgage."

"I trust you," she whispered.

I stood behind her and pulled the blindfold off. "Welcome home."

Blair blinked, taking in the two-story white-sided Cape Cod. "Babe..." She cupped her hands over her mouth. "It's..." Swallowing, she said, "It's everything."

I was on top of the fucking world. "Just wait until you see the inside." I wrapped my arms around her waist and pulled her back against my chest. "That big bathroom with the claw-foot tub... The kitchen with that fancy range... The home studio."

The house was arguably too big for just two people who didn't plan on having kids, so we turned the rest of the bedrooms into—well—whatever the hell we wanted.

We both had home offices—hers outfitted for recording. There was a library ready to be filled with her books. An excessive den for lounging and entertaining, and the biggest bedroom for the two of us.

And absolutely no rain showers. She hated those.

But that wasn't what I was most excited about.

Blair lurched out of my arms, ready to run inside, but I caught her around the waist. "Not so fast, Mrs. Dalton."

"But—"

I took her hand in mine and kissed it. "There's something out back I want to show you first."

"But I want to see the—"

"It'll just take a second."

Grass that needed to be cut two weeks ago swished under-foot as we rounded the garage and walked to the backyard.

Blair rubbernecked at the house, a little gasp slipping from her lips. "You built me a screened-in porch *and* a deck?!"

I chuckled. "I know how much you wanted one after living in apartments." I had to tug on her hand when she stalled to stare at the back of the house. "Baby, I promise. Just a minute and then we'll go inside."

She relented and let me lead her to the lakefront.

"This," I said, kneeling down by a ring of soil pushed up around a sapling. Stakes and string would hold it up until the roots deepened.

"The view's amazing," Blair said dreamily, looking across the water. "I can't tell you how many times I was tempted to drive out here just to sit."

"Not the lake. This."

Blair looked down at where I was pointing.

"Nice," she said nonchalantly. "It'll be good to have some shade down here."

"It's from our tree."

"Cool. Can we—" Blair froze. "What... What did you say?"

I chuckled as I studied one of the leaves. It felt strong and healthy. "It's from our tree in Lily Lake. I cut a slip from it before we moved and propagated it so I could plant it here."

Blair knelt beside me and touched a slender branch that was no more than a twig.

"I figured I'd give us a spot to talk if we ever needed it. A fresh start."

"Caleb," she whispered, blinking away tears. "I... I can't believe you did this."

"And it'll give us a place to hang out with our neighbors."

"Neighbors?" Blair said, rearing back and wrinkling her nose. "I thought the whole point of living here was that we *didn't* have neighbors."

Standing and offering her my hand, I pointed to the acreage to the left. "I got an offer today. Someone wants to buy that piece from us."

"But then I can't sunbathe naked on the deck," she said, poking a finger into my gut.

"I'll build a fence and plant a hedge."

Her face fell. "You really want to sell half of the land we just bought?"

I pressed a kiss to her forehead. "Cade and Greta want to move down here."

Blair froze. "You mean..."

"Yeah," I said, smiling from ear to ear. "He's gonna come work with me. And if you're okay with having someone living next door..."

"Yes!" she squealed with tears in her eyes. "Oh my gosh, yes. Why didn't Greta tell me? I talked to her this morning."

Taking her hand, I led her back to the front of the house. "She was dying to tell you."

She skipped and hopped back to the driveway. "This is the best day ever."

I smirked. "Just wait until we get inside."

Blair was in tears by the time we made it to the second floor. At every turn she was gasping and squeezing my hand and gushing. Watching her eyes flash with delight was the highlight of my life.

I wanted to give her everything.

I wanted to be her joy. To be her peace. I wanted to be her home, and building ours had been a pinnacle moment for me.

It was the moment where I realized we had done it.

We were forging our own path. Building something that was distinctly ours.

The house was nearly empty except for the construction mess. We'd have to do a deep clean to get rid of the drywall dust and random screws strewn about.

But that was a problem for another day.

The only room that had any sort of functionality was the bedroom.

I took Blair's hand and pushed open the door.

A king-sized bed with a swirling iron frame was situated between two floor to ceiling windows. The mattress was freshly made with clean sheets and a new comforter. I had spent the morning at a box store looking for bedding that Blair would like.

She walked over to the windows that overlooked the lake and let out a heavy breath.

"Are you happy?" I asked as I stood behind her and slid my hands onto her hips.

A soft smile painted her lips. "The happiest I've ever been. I've never felt like this."

"Like what?"

She turned and pressed her lips to mine. "At peace."

BONUS EPILOGUE
BLAIR

"Caleb," I panted, bucking up against his mouth as he dug his fingers into my hips.

He slid his tongue up my slit in a slow lick before sucking on my clit. I cried out, throwing my head back and pleading for him to make me finish.

"Let me," I gasped, "Please. Let me come."

"Then come," he growled against my pussy.

Caleb floored it and brought me to the precipice again, then eased off the gas.

"Please!" I shrieked.

What I thought was going to be a quickie before a busy Saturday had turned into him edging me for the better part of an hour.

With heavy eyes, I looked over my shoulder and studied his hard cock. It jutted straight in the air as he held out on his own pleasure to *fucking torture me.*

Caleb let out a despicable chuckle. "Come on, Breezy."

"I'm gonna smother you," I groused.

I went airborne. Caleb threw me off him. My back

slammed into the mattress, and he scrambled to get on top of me.

"Legs around my waist."

I hooked my ankles together and pulled him close. Caleb smoothed his hands up my ribs, cupping both breasts.

I whimpered as he teased my nipples into hard peaks. "We need to hurry."

"Why's that, baby?" he murmured as he slowly slid his cock into my soaked pussy. "Why are you in such a rush?"

"They're—" I squeezed my eyes shut and breathed through the pressure. "Gonna be here soon."

"The doors are locked," Caleb countered. He held deep, grinding against my clit.

I turned to putty beneath him.

"Caleb, please!"

"I like hearing you scream for me," he said in a rumbling baritone. "Go ahead. *Beg.*"

An animalistic grunt that wasn't at all ladylike escaped my mouth when he levered up and grabbed the iron bed frame. He slammed his hips into mine, drilling his dick into me at an unrelenting pace.

A heavy hand shackled my throat. Fingers pressed into my jaw as he held my head in place and slid his tongue against mine.

I could taste myself on his lips and, heaven help me, it turned me on even more.

"Now," I demanded, feeling the creeping sensation of an impending orgasm. "Make me come now."

Caleb laughed.

He fucking laughed.

"Ask *nicely.*"

I grabbed his hips and slammed them into mine.

I didn't even have time to catch my breath. Caleb pulled

out and rolled, flipping me onto my hands and knees with surprising ease.

"Ahh!" I cried out as he spanked my ass and left a searing handprint.

Caleb grabbed a fistful of hair at the base of my neck and pulled, sending prickles of delight dancing down my spine. "I said to *use your fucking manners*, Mrs. Dalton."

I whipped my head around, making him tug on my hair again as I looked over my shoulder. "Make me."

His cock slammed inside of me again, driving my shoulders into a pillow. I let out a muffled grunt as he landed another smack to my ass and fucked me with abandon.

I managed to turn my head and rest my cheek on the pillow between thrusts. My eyes closed as I let out a steady breath, sinking into the rhythm and rocking with him.

"That's my good girl," Caleb growled in approval. The praise made me arch my back a little more, pushing my ass up toward him.

He slid his hand over my hip and pressed the pads of his fingers against my clit.

"Please," I whispered again. "I need to come."

He pressed harder against my clit. "Who makes you come, beautiful?"

"You do," I said in short staccato gasps. "You."

Caleb pushed his cock inside of me and held deep as he massaged my clit with smooth, steady strokes. "Come for me."

I detonated, crashing into the bed as my chest heaved.

Caleb rolled me onto my back, straddling my hips as he furiously pumped his cock in his hand.

I watched through weary eyes as he tipped his head back. Strong lips parted with a sigh as his brow furrowed.

It was incredibly erotic to watch him pleasure himself.

To watch the cords in his wrists and forearms flex as he fucked his hand.

The desperate groan that reverberated from his chest.

The hitch in his breath as he came.

His release marked my breasts in thick lines as he painted my skin.

Caleb paused to catch his breath before dropping down to his forearms and pressing a kiss to my lips. "You're incredible. You know that?"

I smiled lazily against his mouth. "That was fun."

Caleb pecked my nose. "Good."

He carried me into the shower and proceeded to wash me clean. When he had soaped up and rinsed off my chest, he knelt in front of me and pressed a kiss to my hip.

"What's the matter?" I asked as I ran my fingers through his hair.

He looked up at me with an incredible softness in his eyes. "Are you happy?"

"Happy?" I laughed. "Baby, of course I am." I tugged on his arm until he stood. Snaking my arms around his waist, I reveled in the feel of his skin against mine. The warmth and comfort never got old. "I love our life."

"Promise?"

I studied his eyes with concern. "I promise. Where's this coming from?"

He shrugged sheepishly. "I guess with Cade and Greta moving in today, it has me thinking about how things used to be."

I cupped his cheeks. "I love you. I love us. Always. Madly."

Caleb turned me away from him and massaged an inordinate amount of shampoo into my hair.

I didn't care that it was too much. I melted into his touch

and closed my eyes, relaxing into the feeling of him massaging my scalp.

"Speaking of Cade and Greta," I said when he pulled the hand-held shower head down and rinsed my hair. "They're probably here."

Caleb put the shower head back and repeated the whole process with my conditioner.

"They had a long drive. They'll probably want a few minutes to get settled and look around before we go over to unload the truck."

Caleb and his crew had finished Cade and Greta's house a few weeks ago. We had tag-teamed a deep clean so that it was move-in ready on the day they finally packed up their life in Lily Lake and moved away.

As excited as Greta was, she was nervous.

I knew how it felt.

Starting over was never easy.

After years without family, I couldn't put into words what it was like to have a sister again.

"Are you excited?" he asked as we rinsed off together.

"Yeah." I couldn't hide my smile. "And it'll be fun having a little one around."

"How's Greta doing?" he asked as we stepped out of the shower and dried off.

I wrapped a towel around my body and tucked it between my breasts. "The first half of the drive was hard on her yesterday, and sleeping in a hotel bed made her back hurt. Hopefully, Cade can convince her to take it easy today and let us do the heavy lifting."

Caleb laughed, his muscles shaking as he ran a towel over his torso. "You know she's not going to sit on the sidelines. Are you forgetting who raised her?"

We shared coy smiles.

Caleb had always known I didn't want to have kids, and not once had he pressed the issue.

But two months after Greta and Cade had gotten married, she called to break the news that they were expecting.

I didn't want to be a mother, but I was *thrilled* to be an aunt.

"I bought some baby stuff to distract her while we get the furniture and boxes in."

He grinned. "You sneaky woman."

We pulled on shorts and t-shirts, and laced up our sneakers.

I peered out the window at the massive moving truck that had backed in next door.

"How'd your family take it when Cade broke the news?" I asked as I watched an adorably pregnant Greta ease out of the passenger side with her hand on a baby bump that was covered by a tight tank top.

"A little better than when we left," he hedged. "Apparently, my parents asked if they would spend the holidays in Illinois."

"That's good for them," I said softly as I came up behind him and wrapped my arms around his waist. "Our path doesn't have to be theirs."

"I know." He turned and pulled me into his arms. "I'm happy for them."

We headed outside to the fence that had a door for easy access to both yards. A gentle breeze blew through the leaves of our tree. The trunk was barely thicker than my arm, but Caleb had managed to carve our initials into the bark.

C & B

"Hey, Daltons!" I called as I poked my head through the fence.

A smile popped up on Greta's tired face and she waved.

The four of us congregated on the freshly paved driveway and hugged. The boys laughed as they cracked some inside joke. Greta's eyes widened and she grabbed my hand, pressing it to the side of her belly. "Feel her kicking?"

I froze. "*Her*?"

Greta's eyes welled up with tears. "Yeah. We found out at my appointment right before we left Lily Lake. We're having a girl."

"Oh my gosh," I whispered with excitement. "Have you picked out a name yet?"

She beamed and looked at Cade. "Yeah." Her hand laid daintily on top of her belly. "We really like the name Nyssa."

"Why that one?" Caleb asked.

Cade pressed a kiss to Greta's temple. "It means 'new beginnings.'"

AUTHOR'S NOTE TO THE READER

It all started with a text message about a year and a half ago. I (Maggie) had been adding ideas to a story about a divorced couple who married young in a high-control environment. But the thing about writing arguments with yourself is that you can easily win all of them.

Enter the text that changed everything.

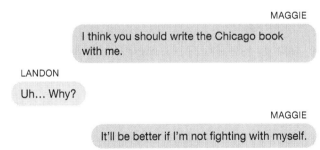

Over the next eighteen months, we slowly determined what parts of ourselves we would give to these characters. We unpacked things that we had never really talked about with each other. We had many "did I ever tell you that" moments.

And we grew closer because of it.

Sometimes, we fought over our characters arguing (because obviously, I thought the POV I was supposed to be writing was right, and so did Landon). Sometimes, we called each other during the workday to share an "ah-hah moment" or a good line we wrote. Some nights, we sat side-by-side on the couch and wrote dialogue together, snarky comment by snarky comment.

Ultimately, we created a story that means so much to both of us. We hope it meets you where you are and becomes something special to you, too.

Burn the bridges. Blow up your life. Stand by the crater and build anew from the ground up.

XO,

Mags & Landon

PS. Because you're super cool, let's be friends!

Want to spread the love? Tell others what you thought of this book by leaving a review on Amazon and GoodReads (I'll do a literal happy dance if you do)!

MAGGIE HAS A NEW SERIES COMING SOON!

While you're waiting for what's next, check out *100 Lifetimes of Us* and get to know Blair's favorite special guest, Whitney West.

Or read *Cry About It* to meet Jo and Vaughan—the couple Blair is seated with at the charity dinner!

Click the link to read *100 Lifetimes of Us or Cry About It!*

ACKNOWLEDGMENTS

To Mikayla and Mandy: for the sweet, spicy, and salty days and 3 AM meme hauls.

To Kayla C: Thank you for being the most quietly dependable presence! I'm so freaking thankful for you!

To: Sam Young, Hayley Kring, Sam Warren, Paula Sundby, Carissa LaForge, Emily Kaye, Lindsey Kelch, and Morgan Halladay, just to name a few.

To My Street Team: Thank you for your enthusiasm and encouragement! You all are an imperative part of my book team and I'm so grateful for every recommendation, video, and post!

To My ARC Team: You guys are the greatest! Your excitement and support astounds me on a daily basis. You make me feel like the coolest human being alive. I'm so grateful for each and every one of you. Thank you for volunteering your time and platforms to boost my books!

To My Readers: Because naming all of you one by one would double the length of this book: You all are the reason I keep writing books. I'm thoroughly convinced that there's no greater group of people in the world than my real life poker club. Y'all are amazing human beings! Thank you for loving these characters and getting as excited as I do about their stories! Thank you for your hype, encouragement, and excitement!

ALSO BY MAGGIE GATES

Standalone Novels

The Stars Above Us: A Steamy Military Romance

Nothing Less Than Everything: A Sports Romance

Cry About It: An Enemies to Lovers Romance

100 Lifetimes of Us: A Hot Bodyguard Romance

Pretty Things on Shelves: A Second Chance Romance

The Beaufort Poker Club Series

Poker Face: A Small Town Romance

Wild Card: A Second Chance Romance

Square Deal: A Playboy Romance

In Spades: A Small Town Billionaire Romance

Not in the Cards: A Best Friend's Brother Romance

Betting Man: A Friends to Lovers Romance

The Falls Creek Series

What Hurts Us: A Small Town Fake Engagement Romance

What Heals Us: An Age Gap Romance

What Saves Us: A Small Town Single Mom Romance

ABOUT THE AUTHOR
MAGGIE GATES

Maggie Gates writes raw, relatable romance novels full of heat and humor. She calls North Carolina home. In her spare time, she enjoys daydreaming about her characters, jamming to country music, and eating all the BBQ and tacos she can find! Her Kindle is always within reach due to a love of small-town romances that borders on obsession.

For future book updates, follow Maggie on social media.

facebook.com/AuthorMaggieGates

instagram.com/authormaggiegates

tiktok.com/@authormaggiegates

ABOUT THE AUTHOR
LANDON GATES

Landon Gates is an author, cover designer, and editor. He has called North Carolina home his entire life. In his spare time, he enjoys reading fantasy novels, football, and doing internet deep-dives on pretty much anything.

For future book updates, follow Landon on social media.

instagram.com/authorlandongates

tiktok.com/@landongatesbooks

Printed in Great Britain
by Amazon